# Two Tears in a Bucket

## By Traci Bee

### Contributions from Darnell King

*Two Tears in a Bucket*
A soulful novel
Copyright © 2009 by Traci Bee

King George Publishing, LLC books may be ordered through booksellers or by contacting:

King George Publishing, LLC
145 Fleet Street, Suite 330
National Harbor, Maryland 20745
www.kinggeorgepublishingllc.com

Because of the dynamic nature of the Internet, any Web addresses or links contained in this book may have changed since publication and may no longer be valid.

This is a work of fiction. All of the characters, names, incidents, organizations, and dialogue in this novel are either the products of the author's imagination or are used fictitiously.

ISBN:   13-digit 978-0-9791795-0-1
        10-digit 0-9791795-0-5

Printed in the United States of America

### *To George Thomas Brewington, Sr.*

You encouraged me to reach for the stars.
I caught a few and I'm still reaching. Can you see me, Daddy?
This star, my book, and every other star I catch will forever be
dedicated to you and your memory.
I love you.
Love, Traci

\*     \*     \*

### *To Dumas Brewington*

Greatness has many definitions. One of which is "a person who
has achieved importance or distinction in a field." Married 71
years to the love of his life, with 15 children, 48 grandchildren,
and oodles of greats and great-greats. A true man of God,
Granddaddy, you ARE the definition of GREATNESS in the
field of life. It's no wonder my dad was so amazing.

\*     \*     \*

**In Memory of:**
George Thomas Brewington, Sr.
Dumas Brewington, Sr.
Ronald LeCount King
Texanna Roberta Ferguson
Clifton H. Ferguson, Sr.
Michelle Evans
Jermaine Denard Davis

**Special Dedications to:**
Michael, Tania, Donnell, Brandon, Monet, Kennedy,
and the Brewington Family
*And the innocent victims of senseless violence*

# *Acknowledgments*

Thank you, Father God, for not only blessing me with the gift of story-telling, but giving me the strength to persevere through so many obstacles. Without you, this would not have been possible.

Natasha Small, Creative Writing Department of Prince George's Community College; Michelle Chester of EMB Professional Edits; Monique D. Mensah of Make Your Mark Editing; Carla M. Dean of U Can Mark My Word Editing; Leona Romich of APOOO Book Reviews; and Tamika Newhouse of Delphine Publications and African Americans on the Move Book Club - all of you not only graced me with your various services, but you exceeded the call of duty by sharing your suggestions for the betterment of the novel. Unselfishly, you offered guidance in this unfamiliar territory, and for that, I sincerely thank you.

Rally Point Studios, thank you for your awesome technical support and creations.

Tracy Robinson and all the ladies at Salon Contour in Forestville, Maryland (winners of the 2009 Golden Scissors Award and Steve Harvey 2010 Hoodie Award for Nails), words can't describe my gratitude. You ladies are the straight up all-of-it and I love you. Thanks so much for spreading the word.

Michael Ashe, you uncovered talents that I never realized I possessed. Thanks for constantly challenging me to be better.

To my Pocahontas mother, thank you so much for the

breaks! There's no way I would have gotten any of this done without the special services of "grandma."

Lachelle Brewington, Sabrina Sims, Geraldine and Nate Ford, Sr. - As I buried myself into this project, I sometimes lost track of the world around me. From the depths of my soul, I thank you for stepping in to make sure the important events weren't neglected but exploded in celebration as they should have been.

Alicia Byrd, Bettye Brown, Robin Erwin and Lachelle Brewington, you were with me from day one and still remain by my side, always down for whatever. You crave the success of the novel just as much as I do, and for that, I sincerely thank you.

Starleta Sprately and Tina Benjamin - if it weren't for the two of you, there probably wouldn't be a *Two Tears in a Bucket*.

To my beautiful kids, I love you. Thank you for granting me peace and solitude as I sat glued to the corner of the bed not wanting to do anything but write. You're the reason why I write. Someday soon I hope and pray I can show you the meaning to that statement.

To my husband Darnell King, I can still hear you walking around the house hushing everybody as I tried to write and rewrite. Thank you for your unconditional love, support and contribution to the novel.

And finally to you, the reader. In a world saturated with wonderful works of fictions, you decided to read *Two Tears in a Bucket,* and for that, I thank you. I hope you enjoy...

# Part One

"If you love something..."

# Chapter One
## 1987

$\mathcal{B}$ lood dripped from the gash in Ricardo's head as he stood like a bull, in the middle of his living room. His chest heaved up and down as he fought to regain his composure.

"You see what he did to me!" Simone cried from the floor, her face a swollen mass of blood and tears. "You gon' just stand there and not do nothing?"

Angela ignored her daughter's cries and darted to the kitchen. She snatched open the freezer and filled the towel dangling from the refrigerator door with a tray of ice to address her husband's wound. But Ricardo didn't want her help, and he knocked the towel out of her hand.

"Ricardo, you might need stitches," Angela whined as she kneeled down to collect the ice cubes that had scattered across the floor.

"I don't need no gotdamn stitches. But I tell you one thing; her ass better be gone by the time I get back." As his command settled on those around him, Ricardo turned on his heels and stormed from the house.

"Ricardo!" Angela called after him, but her words fell on deaf ears as Ricardo jumped inside his pickup. Tire rubber screeched from the driveway as he zoomed from the concrete to the asphalt. Pounding the floor with her fist, Angela bolted past her daughter to her bedroom and slammed the door.

Hurt by her mother's abandonment and lack of concern, Simone pulled herself up from the floor and threw the ashtray she'd used to bust open Ricardo's head across the room, disappointed at the dull thud it made as it landed on a cushy armchair instead of crashing to the floor in a riot of noise. Slumped on the sofa, Simone threw her head back, and cried.

● ● ●

That cool Saturday in September of 1987 had started so perfectly. Climbing from her bed, Simone cracked her bedroom window and allowed the brisk morning air into the room. She nestled back under the warmth of her covers, where she planned to relax until her mother beckoned her with the never-ending list of Saturday chores.

*I know one thing; I won't be cleaning this place after today. I'm outta here tomorrow.* Just the thought put a smile on Simone's beautiful, mocha-colored face. She couldn't wait to see her mother's expression when she told her she was moving. Only three people knew about Simone's apartment—Lavon and Melanie, her two best friends from junior high, and Thomas, her dear old dad, who wasn't a fan of the idea.

"Simone, you're too young to be livin' on your own. Hell, you just graduated high school three months ago," he'd said. "The ink on your diploma is not even dry."

But there was nothing her father or anyone else could say to change Simone's mind. The sooner she got out, the faster she could rid herself of her stepfather's house and his stupid-ass rules.

Simone heard the faint sound of Angela's voice outside her bedroom door and buried herself deeper under the covers. *Ah, hell... here she comes.*

"Simone, get up!" Angela yelled, barging into the room. "What, you gonna sleep all day?" She leaned inside, pressing her body against the open door. "I'm running around the corner to the store real quick. I'm taking Alicia with me."

*Good,* Simone thought, thankful she didn't have to watch her stepsister, Alicia, Ricardo's ten-year-old daughter from his previous marriage.

"Is your husband going, too?" Simone asked from under her comforter.

"No, he went to run an errand, but he's coming right back. Now get up, Simone, and clean the kitchen while I'm gone." Angela closed the door, but reiterated sharply, "Now, Simone. I'm not playing with you!"

Simone sucked her teeth and glanced at the alarm clock on her dresser. *Damn. Why is she buggin'? It's not even eight o'clock.* Hearing the front door close, she kicked off her covers, sat up in bed, and looked around her room. She needed to do a ton of things by tomorrow. Not a single item had been packed and the wicker laundry hamper in the corner of her room overflowed with dirty clothes.

*I may as well wash for free while I still can.*

With a frustrated sigh, she peeled herself from the warmth of her bed, stretched the kinks from her body, and popped Janet's *Control* cassette into her boom box. Home alone, she turned the volume up as loud as it would go.

"Now this is how I'll be playing my music in my place

come tomorrow," she said as she danced over to her hamper, singing with Ms. Jackson. A gifted songstress, Simone loved to sing. In fact, it was her voice that made her popular in school. If there was a talent show, school assembly, or any other function, Simone was often asked to serenade the attendees.

*Man, I shoulda been a Jackson,* she thought. *Or, Daddy, you shoulda been like Joe Jackson,* she continued in thought as she scattered her dirty laundry out on the floor. She tossed her first load back into the hamper and headed to the unfinished basement to wash them.

With the clothes in the machine, Simone pulled the cord dangling from the ceiling to turn off the light. She grabbed the hamper and headed back up the steps to clean Angela's kitchen for the last time. Engulfed in her thoughts, she never noticed the shadow lurking in the stairwell.

"Oh my God," she gasped as she stared up at Ricardo. "You scared me," she said, standing at the bottom of the steps in the midst of his large shadow. Ricardo loomed near the top of the steps, glaring down at her.

"You can come down 'cause I'm coming up," she said, her eyes on the concrete floor. She knew Ricardo sensed her uneasiness as she clung to her empty hamper, using it to camouflage the parts of her that her oversized nightshirt left exposed.

"Then come on up. And turn that mess down when you get up here." Simone didn't budge. "Did you hear what I said? I said come up," Ricardo commanded again.

*Aww, he's so fuckin' stupid!* Simone screamed inside as she marched up the steps one by one. *How I'm 'pose to come up when you standing in the way?*

The stench of marijuana and Jack Daniel's exploded from

Ricardo's pores. It wasn't the first time Simone had smelled this foul stench on him or seen his bloodshot eyes. The funky smell of weed flowed from the basement vents and roamed through the rest of the house nearly every day.

Three steps away from her stepfather, Simone stopped and waited for him to move.

"Umm... excuse me," she said. It killed her to be polite to him. She hated Ricardo just as much as he hated her.

With a cynical smirk, Ricardo turned his body toward the stairwell wall. "Go 'head."

"Why couldn't you just go down the steps?" Simone mumbled through tight lips as she squeezed past him. Before her foot could grace the next step, she felt the roughness from Ricardo's dry hand reaching under her nightshirt. Shocked by his touch, Simone missed the step and stumbled. She caught her balance and threw the empty hamper at Ricardo as he marched down the steps, chuckling.

*He touched me!* Simone screamed inside as she slammed the door and secured the lock. Her heart thumped as she rushed into her room across the hall from the basement door.

"He touched me. He fucking touched me," Simone repeated out loud as she threw on a pair of jeans from the remaining pile of dirty clothes on the floor.

The basement stairs creaked. She froze as footsteps echoed from the stairwell. Ricardo was on his way up. All hell would break loose when he realized Simone had locked the door. She ran a trembling hand through her hair, pacing back and forth. The door knob turned.

"Simone!" Ricardo screamed. The house began to shake as Ricardo threw his 280-pound frame violently against the door. "Simone!" he roared.

Petrified, Simone bolted from her room. She had to leave. *I'll go to the neighbor's house.*

The sound of splitting wood echoed through the tiny rambler as Ricardo burst through the basement door, ripping it from the frame. Inches away from the front door, Ricardo snatched Simone's 125-pound body back like a rag doll.

"Don't you *ever* lock another fucking door in my house! You hear me!" he yelled as he threw Simone into the wall.

She tried to flee his wrath but he yanked her up by the collar of her nightshirt, choking her. Unable to scream, she clawed at Ricardo's hands, trying to pry them from her neck, but he tightened his grip.

On top of the entertainment center, next to Simone's senior class picture, sat Ricardo's crystal ashtray, loaded with ashes and cigarette butts. Scared of his drunken rage, Simone reached for the heavy glass and busted open the back of Ricardo's head.

"What the fuck?" he mumbled, releasing his grip as blood oozed down the back of his neck. He reached behind his head and dabbed at the fresh wound. His face turned red as the devil, shocked by the blood on his fingertips. His chest inflated as he inhaled strength. With the back of his hand, he slapped Simone across her face and knocked her to the floor.

Angela and Alicia entered the house. Their grocery bags crashed to the floor.

"Oh my God, Ricardo!" Angela cried.

Ricardo pointed his stubby finger at his stepdaughter and snarled at his wife through gritted teeth, "I want this piece of shit outta my gotdamn house tonight!"

## Chapter Two

"It don't make no sense for one person to be that damn fine," Gwen shared with her girlfriend, Tammy, as they stood in front of the apartment building watching Kevin, the handsome lova-lova thug, pimp down the sidewalk.

"Girl, stop drooling over that damn boy and ask him to come help. I'm not standing out here with you all night," Tammy said. The three-inch pumps she'd worn all day had her feet throbbing. "It's damn near nine o'clock, and my feet hurt," she said, stepping from her patent leather heels.

Gwen cleared her throat. "Excuse me," she hollered out, waving her hand to get Kevin's attention. He glanced Gwen's way. "I'm sorry." She twisted her shoulder-length hair around her finger like a bashful schoolgirl. "Can you come here for a second, please?"

Agitated, Kevin turned and headed in Gwen's direction.

"Mmm, mmm, mmm. That boy is fine. Look at them hazel eyes," Gwen mumbled under her breath, not caring that Kevin was young enough to be her son.

"How you doing, sweetheart? I'm Tuffy's mother, Gwen, and this is my girlfriend Tammy," she introduced.

"Okay," Kevin said with a shrug.

"You know my son, right?"

"We know of each other. Why, what's up?"

"I'm sorry. I don't mean to bother you. I'm locked out of my apartment. I know Tuffy's in there. I've been banging on the door for I don't know how long, and I can't get him to answer it."

Kevin stood silent, having no idea why any of that pertained to him.

"Umm... I was wondering if I could get you to climb through my window and maybe open the door for me."

Kevin thought he saw Gwen pass him a seductive glance. He hoped not. She was old... too bold... the mother of a fellow thug... and not at all his type.

"Naw," Kevin said, irritated. Although he'd never had an altercation with Tuffy, Kevin didn't know him or his mother well enough to climb through their window, especially at night. "What you tryna do, set me up for your son or something?" he asked, suspicious of anything out of the norm.

"No, Kevin!" Gwen frowned, insulted. "I don't play games like that, baby. I'm a grown-ass woman."

"She's telling the truth," Tammy spoke. "Her dumb butt really is locked out." But her words meant nothing to Kevin. Neither woman had any credibility with him.

Kevin studied them both. They appeared clean-cut, dressed in their casual work attire. *Shit,* he thought, as his mind screamed *hell no.* But his heart took him back to the days when he was barely five, watching his father beat the mess out of his mother, Beatrice, while she lay helpless on the floor. From that day forth, every damsel in distress tugged on his heartstrings and transformed into his mother.

"Please," Gwen pleaded. "I would do it myself, but I ain't never climbed through a window a day in my life."

Kevin sighed. "Look," he threatened as he cut through the grass and headed toward Gwen's window, both ladies following behind him, "don't make me regret this."

Kevin surveyed the distance to the window. He knew he could do it. He'd climbed through his second-floor window many days.

In one leap, Kevin grabbed the ledge of the open window with his lengthy arms. Using his upper body strength, he snatched the window screen out and pulled himself into the darkness of the unfamiliar room. His leg bumped a lamp and sent it crashing to the floor. *Shit!* Kevin thought as he stepped on the sharp pieces, hoping they wouldn't puncture the soles of his shoes.

*CLICK, CLICK, CLICK.*

*What the fuck is that?* Kevin thought, although deep inside, he recognized the sound of the gun. He stood frozen in the dark room.

The bedroom light came on. Tuffy appeared shaken and caught off guard, with his gun drawn and pointed at Kevin. Sean, Tuffy's occasional sidekick, stood at his side armed with a wooden baseball bat, his eyes darting from Tuffy to Kevin.

*What the fuck is this shit?* Kevin said to himself as his heart raced.

"What's up, Kevin, man!" Tuffy yelled, bouncing around nervously. "Why you tryna rob me, man? Ain't never had no drama with you!"

"Hold up, Tuffy," Kevin said easily. "It ain't even like that, man. Your moms was locked out, and she asked me to climb through y'all window and open the door."

*I knew I shouldna did this shit,* Kevin said to himself as he stood in the middle of the floor, staring down Tuffy's pistol.

Knocks rang out from the front door. Tuffy and Sean didn't budge. The knocks rang out again.

"Look, Tuffy," Kevin said. "You can come check me. I ain't even packin'. How I'ma rob you if I ain't gotta gun? Go answer your door, man. That's your moms. Just ask her. She asked me to climb through your window."

"Go check the door, Sean!" Tuffy ordered.

Sean backed out of the room, heading down the hall to the front door. Kevin stood there, regretting his decision to help. He kept his eyes off of Tuffy, knowing his angered expression would probably piss him off and tempt him to pull the trigger. Seconds later, Gwen and Tammy's heels click-clacked along the parquet wood floor.

"Oh my God, Tuffy! What the hell are you doing?" Gwen screamed hysterically, shaken at the sight of Tuffy standing with his gun pointed at Kevin. "I asked Kevin to climb through the window."

"Yeah, man." Sean stood off to the side, nodding his head in approval. "She was knockin', like Kevin said. I told her he was tryna break in this muthafucka and they ran right past me."

Sean and Tuffy both spoke at a snail's pace, obviously high, which explained why neither had opened the door when Gwen knocked originally.

"Damn." Tuffy lowered his gun and stuck it in the waistband of his jeans.

"I want that gun outta my house," Gwen cried. She stormed over to her son and showered him with a windmill of smacks.

Tuffy threw his arms up to block his mother's blows. "Ma, I thought he was tryna break in."

"Just imagine had you shot him," she cried, delivering the final smack to the back of Tuffy's head.

The same thought ran rapid through Kevin's mind as he headed out the room, leaving Tuffy to his beating.

"Yo! Hold up, Kevin," Tuffy hollered. "I thought you was tryna break in," he said as he and Sean chased after him. "Listen, man," Tuffy said as they entered the hallway, where their voices bounced off the concrete walls. "We cool, right?"

"Yeah, man, we cool," Kevin replied as he trotted down the steps. In his eyes, Tuffy's actions were justified. He'd seen another thug he barely knew crashing through his apartment. Tuffy had followed the gangster's code of conduct by pulling his gun.

"But hold up, Kevin. Hold up," Tuffy said once they were outside. Kevin stopped in his tracks. "I bought this piece of shit gun from a dude on the strip yesterday. Man," he chuckled nervously, "I shot at you like nine times... nine times, Kevin, and this bitch didn't do nothin'."

"Let me see it."

Tuffy handed Kevin the gun. Walking around to the side of the building, Kevin examined the gun and pointed it in the air. He pulled the trigger. A bullet exploded in the sky without hesitation. Kevin handed the gun back and walked off, leaving Tuffy and Sean in awe.

Something inside Kevin's gut told him his evening would be better spent on the couch in front of the television. He contemplated listening to his instincts, but as he approached the little section of the drug strip that had become his corner, he spotted a few of his regulars, scratching and twitching.

Guaranteed money.

"Ah!" James, Kevin's best friend, yelled out as he jogged across the parking lot. "I just ran into Tuffy. He told me what happened, man."

Kevin passed the last addict a tiny plastic baggie that contained the blessing to his hell and shoved the money in his pocket.

"Now get the fuck outta here, man," James threatened through tight lips. He stomped his foot, lunging at the addict. Kevin shook his head while James held his stomach in laughter as the addict tumbled over his feet and sprinted toward the darkness of the strip.

"Hey, look, man. I'ma run up here to the liquor store and get us somethin' nice. We need to celebrate. You 'pose to be in a body bag."

"Yeah, that ain't a bad idea. I could use a drink," Kevin agreed as another loyal junkie approached.

James took off through the dirt trail that connected the drug strip to the liquor store and the greasy spoon that Kevin and his friends nibbled from nearly every day as the addicts continued to come, searching for their Friday-night high, one behind the other.

*Damn, where the hell James go?* Kevin thought. He glanced at this watch. James had been gone for over an hour. *Let me go put this shit up,* Kevin thought, tapping the wad of bills in his front pocket. The stickup boys worked overtime on the weekends. *Then I can go to the store my damn self.*

As he turned to head down the walkway that led to the apartment he shared with his mother and older brother, LeCount, Kevin felt the barrel of a shotgun poke him in the back.

*Get the fuck outta here. This cannot be happening,* he screamed to himself. He couldn't believe his luck.

"Yeah." The gunman chuckled. "What's up, muthafucka! Where your boy at?"

"Don't know who you talking 'bout," Kevin responded carefully.

"You know who the fuck I'm talking about! That bitch-ass James! Where that muthafucka at?" the gunman yelled.

"I don't know," Kevin responded.

The gunman pumped the chamber and punched the barrel of the shotgun into Kevin's jaw. Kevin's heart thumped as his mouth filled with the salty taste of blood. Lady Luck had already saved him once by defecting Tuffy's gun. The possibility of her showing up again was slim to none.

"Oh you don't know, huh? Well tell'em that Lil' Bits looking for his ass," the gunman shouted. "You heard me, muthafucka?"

"Yeah." Kevin spoke nice and slow. "I heard you, Lil' Bits."

"I know he robbed me," Lil' Bits replied through clenched teeth as he forced the barrel deeper into Kevin's jaw. "And I'ma get my money back one way or another."

Removing the shotgun, Lil' Bits marched off like a solider at battle. But the streets were a different type of war, and Lil' Bits had forgotten the most important rule—never pull a gun on a gangster and not use it. Kevin's nerves erupted into anger as he spat a wad of blood on the ground.

"I'm gon' get your ass."

"Damn, Kevin!" Tuffy's friend, Sean, stepped from Kevin's building. "I saw that shit, man! You a'ight?"

"Watch out!" Kevin ordered. "I'm get that muthafucka."

"Naw, here, man. Take mine before his ass runs off somewhere." Sean reached in his pants and offered Kevin his gun. "This ain't that raggedy shit Tuffy had earlier. My shit works."

Kevin preferred his 9-mm, but snatched the .25 automatic from Sean, determined to get Lil' Bits before he disappeared. But as long as he remained in the vicinity, he couldn't hide. Kevin knew every inch of the strip like the back of his hand. Ducking between parked cars, he went on the prowl, searching the complex for Lil' Bits. Finally, he spotted him puffing away on a cigarette, still armed with his shotgun.

*Yeah, you bitch muthafucka,* Kevin thought as he crept up behind Lil' Bits. *I got your ass now.*

"Ah, Lil' Bits!"

Lil' Bits dropped his cigarette and spun around on his heels. Kevin met his eyes. He remembered the bullet in the chamber of the shotgun and fired before Lil' Bits had a chance to pull the trigger. The bullet connected, ripping open the side of Lil' Bits' face.

"Aaaggh!" he cried. Blood oozed down his face. Lil' Bits fired back but missed. He tried to run, but Kevin shot again. The bullet snatched open Lil' Bits' back and sent him to the ground in a pool of blood.

Police cars flooded the scene within minutes, illuminating the dark drug strip with their flashing lights. In the midst of the crowd, Kevin spotted his mother. As the police car zoomed from the scene, Kevin threw his head against the backseat of the car and mumbled, "I'm sorry, Ma." The image of her tear-drenched face rode with him all the way to the station.

● ● ●

September, 1987 - six months later, Fat Ed sat outside the

prison, waiting for his god-brother in his milk-white S500 Mercedes, with two bottles of Moet chilling in a Styrofoam cooler in the trunk. It was time to celebrate. Lil' Bits survived the ordeal but failed to appear in court as the state's key witness, forcing the judge to throw the case out due to lack of evidence. Kevin was a free man.

Fat Ed exploded on the drug scene while Kevin was incarcerated. He'd stumbled across a Floridian with a Columbian connection and invested the money he'd earned as a corner pusher in large quantities of cocaine and marijuana. Now, not only was he one of the area suppliers, but the corner pushers on the strip were employed by him. With money pouring in from all ends, Fat Ed purchased a fleet of automobiles—a white S-Class Mercedes, a black Porsche, and a money-green Range Rover, all of which he parked in the driveway of his new house.

"Welcome home, man! I got you a little something," Fat Ed beamed, dangling the keys to the Benz as Kevin made his way through the prison gates.

"You got who a lil' something?" Kevin asked, staring at the car in awe.

"You! This is your car. Your Benz. C'mon and drive," he said as Kevin took inventory of the flashy automobile. "I'm serious." He chuckled. "It's yours, Kevin."

"What I do to deserve this?"

"Nothing, yet."

"That's what I thought," Kevin said and detoured to the passenger seat. "I don't like that yet shit, so I think I'll ride over here."

Fat Ed's brows drew together. "What, you don't like it?" he asked as he climbed in the driver's seat.

Kevin ran his hand along the polished wood grain while his body sank into the soft, cream-colored leather seats. "Shit, what's not to like?"

"Well, it's yours," Fat Ed repeated. The jolliness in his voice had subsided.

The shooting was the buzz on the strip. Just like Fat Ed's drug game, Kevin's reputation had stepped up, making him just what Fat Ed needed—a notorious, no-nonsense gangster that the knuckleheads on the strip feared, one they knew would pull the trigger.

"I want us to be partners. This here is like a lil' signing bonus."

"Partners?"

"Yeah. I need a no-nonsense type of partner to collect that paper and deal wit' them knuckleheads when they don't pay."

"Deal wit'em how?"

"However you see fit. That's your department. If they owe a few dollars, hell, just beat their asses. But if it's major paper," Fat Ed said, looking over at Kevin, "flatline 'em."

"Boy, you must be crazy!" Fresh out of the penitentiary, the last thing Kevin wanted to discuss was an illegal activity that would send him right back. "You want me to kill a chump 'cause he owes you a few dollars? What's a few dollars to you anyway? Hell, if they mess up one time, cut 'em off. Just don't fuck wit' 'em no more."

"Man, you know it don't work like that! Then all them lil' youngins will be tryin' to get over at least one muthafuckin' time. That ain't no way to run the business, and plus, you the only person I'd trust collecting for me."

"Well, then, you got a problem, 'cause I ain't no hit man," Kevin said. "I ain't a killer."

Fat Ed sucked his teeth. "Why you cold fakin' on me, man? You damn near killed Lil' Bits!"

"That shit was different. You know the laws on the street. You don't pull a gun on nobody unless you plan on using it."

"But..."

"Ain't no buts, man," Kevin interrupted, tired of the meaningless chatter that was going nowhere. "Hey, look. What's up? What we getting ready to get in-to? I'm fresh out the pen. We 'pose to be celebrating."

"Hell, I know your ass gotta be horny, so I got some strippers waiting for you up in a hotel."

"Word?"

"Yeah, man. They some stripper bitches, too. And I got some Mo on ice in the trunk."

Kevin smiled his approval. "Now, that's what I want to hear."

"I figured you'd like that shit. Maybe after you bust a nut or two, you'll stop lunchin' and we can talk business. I want us to be partners for real."

● ● ●

Kevin's mother stretched her depleting budget and said farewell to her three-bedroom apartment in the drug-stricken community in exchange for a two-bedroom in a better neighborhood. She knew LeCount and Kevin would scream bloody murder about having to share a bedroom, but she didn't care. She had to get control over her sons before the streets swallowed them whole.

A registered nurse at an area nursing home, Beatrice had pulled a few strings and got Kevin a job caring for the elderly men. To make it even better, she was his supervisor and therefore made sure their schedules coincided.

After three weeks, Kevin finally had his first day off and had no plans on spending it cooped up in the house under the watchful eye of his mother. He hadn't had a moment to himself since Fat Ed brought him home.

*I gotta get out of this house,* he thought, just as Beatrice strolled from her room dressed in her nurse's uniform.

"Where you going?" Kevin asked, unable to hide the excitement in his voice.

"Where it look like I'm going?" Beatrice huffed.

Kevin could tell from her sigh that a lecture was a syllable away.

"I almost told them no, I couldn't work overtime because part of me feels the need to stay here and watch your behind. But," Beatrice said, heading to the front door, "you're twenty years old, Kevin. I've taught you right from wrong. I can't sit here and babysit you every day."

"Ma, I'm not gonna get in no more…"

Beatrice threw up her hand, silencing him. "I've heard it all before. This time, I just hope you mean it. One day your luck is gonna run out."

Kevin didn't waste a second. The minute the deadbolt turned, he jumped from the couch and headed to the room he shared with LeCount.

*I wonder if it's still in here.*

He yanked the covers and sheets from his unmade bed and squeezed his large hand inside the secret compartment he'd cut in his mattress a long time ago.

*Yes,* he rejoiced as he pulled out the plastic baggie filled with tiny rocks of cocaine. *I gotta get me a car, Ma. Then I'll be done with this shit for real.*

● ● ●

Kevin ignored the October chill and placed the tiny baggie into the addict's hand.

"Thank you, Mr. Kevin," the addict said with a bow. "We missed you, man."

Kevin filled the hours slinging the few rocks he had and catching up with the fellas he hadn't seen in months. Glancing at his watch, he knew his mother was home, smoldering on the couch in disappointment.

*Shit, it's damn near eleven o'clock,* Kevin thought as a sparkling black Lincoln slowly crept down the street. He eyeballed the car as he reached underneath his sweatshirt and wrapped his fingers around his 9-mm. He gripped it tighter as the driver's window eased down.

"Hey!" Puffing on a joint, James blew a cloud of smoke out the window and grinned. "What's up, man? Fat Ed told me you were home. Why it take you so long to come see a brotha?"

Kevin released his gun and breathed a sigh of relief. He stepped into the parking lot to slap hands with James. "Man, I was gettin' ready to blast your ass."

"You still shooting muthafuckas? Your ass must like the pen."

"Yeah," Kevin said as he looked over the shiny Lincoln. "You must like it, too. Whose car your hot ass don' stole now?" A screwdriver was jammed inside the ignition, clear as day.

James chuckled. From the front passenger seat, Nic leaned his head forward. "What's up, Kevin, man?"

"What's up, Nic?" Kevin greeted the one and only friend he had who sought education over dealing drugs. "What, you slingin' drugs to pay for college?"

"Naw, man." Nic chuckled. "I'm tryna catch a ride, but James is sightseeing and shit."

"Well, hell," Kevin opened the door and climbed inside the back. "I'm tryna catch a ride, too. Take me home, James, and I mean straight home. I ain't tryna get caught in no stolen car fuckin' 'round with you."

# Chapter Three

At the top of her lungs, Simone sang along to her Jody Watley cassette as she ran the vacuum across the living room floor. Every morsel of Simone's being wanted to celebrate. Finally, she was in her own place after spending the last ten days on her grandmother's couch nursing her fractured nose, thanks to Ricardo's backhand slap. A smile eased across Simone's face when all of a sudden she realized she could blast her music as loud as she wanted, just as she'd envisioned. She danced over to her boom box to turn the music up even louder.

*Shoot. That's as loud as it'll go.*

Melanie snatched the boom box's plug from the wall.

"Girl!" Simone protested as she turned off the vacuum. "What you doing? I was listening to that."

"The whole neighborhood was listening to it. C'mon," Melanie said. "Me and Lavon are done in the kitchen. Let's take these boxes out."

"Yeah, I left my bag in your trunk, too, Melanie," Lavon added as she eased into her shoes. "What's up? We going out tonight or we staying in?"

"I'm tired," Simone said as she gathered up a few boxes and led the way out the door. "I say we stay in."

• • •

James pulled the stolen Lincoln into the parking lot. "That'll be fifty dollars," he said over his shoulder to Kevin.

"Yeah, I got your fifty dollars," Kevin said, tugging at the crotch of his pants as he climbed from the backseat. Nic opened the front door and hopped out, too. "Where you going, Nic, man?" Kevin asked as he slammed the door.

"What?" Puzzled, Nic looked around. "You getting out here, too?"

"Yeah, I live in that building right there."

"Man, get outta here. My girl's best friend just moved in that building. They having some lil' girly sleepover. I came over here to crash that mug."

"Girls? Now that's what I'm talkin' 'bout," James said from inside the car. "Close the door, Nic, so I can park this muthafucka."

"What he parking for? Don't nobody want his dirty ass," Kevin joked.

Before Nic could close the door, James punched the gas and whipped the stolen Lincoln into a parking space.

"Damn, man," Kevin said. "Look at them bammas over there? The one holding the bag looks familiar."

Nic turned his focus toward the handful of scruffy roughnecks seated on a rusty, abandoned car parked next to the trash dumpsters. While sipping on bottles concealed by brown paper bags, they took turns puffing on a joint.

"Ah, Kevin, you know them. That's whatchaface and 'em," Nic said as he snapped his fingers to recall their names. "Shit, I can't think of slim's name, but all them hang with your brother."

"Why LeCount got them out here smoking that shit?" Kevin was pissed. "This ain't that kinda neighborhood. They need to keep that shit up on the strip. My mother would have a fit if she knew they was out here like that. She moved over here to get away from that whack-ass shit."

The building door flew open. Laughing loudly, Simone, Melanie, and Lavon walked out, toting boxes.

"Damn," Nic said. "There go my girl and her friends right there."

"Gotdamn, y'all bitches lookin' good!" One of the scruffy dudes yelled out as the girls approached the abandoned car parked next to the dumpster. He passed the joint to his buddy. "Can I go?"

"Yeah, to hell," Lavon responded bluntly.

"Ah girl, fuck you. I wasn't talking to your big ass no way."

"Fuck your dirty ass," Lavon retaliated as she dropped her boxes in the middle of the street.

Melanie grabbed her arm. "Girl, come on. Let's just go back in the house."

"Come on nothing," Lavon spat, snatching her arm away. "How he gon' just up and call us bitches? Who this dirty muthafucka think he talking to?"

The ringleader eased off the car. "What!" He chuckled. "Bitch, you better listen to your girlfriend and take your fat ass back in the house 'fore I bust you in the head wit' this bottle."

"Ah!" Kevin approached the crowd with Nic and James in tow. "What the fuck wrong wit' you, man? I wish you would hit her."

"Aww! What's up, Kevin, man." LeCount's friend smiled,

displaying a mouth full of gold teeth. "Count told us your ass was home. Do me a favor and go tell your slow-ass brother to hurry the fuck up." Leaning back on the car, the ringleader took a swig from his bottle.

"I ain't your muthafuckin' gofer, nigga."

The ringleader ignored Kevin and turned his attention toward Simone. A sly smirk cracked his frown as he watched Simone swing the boxes Lavon had dropped into the dumpster.

"Damn, girl. You phat to death. Can I go?"

"Man, what the fuck is wrong wit' you?" Kevin asked. "I got this, baby," he mumbled to Simone as he gathered the few remaining boxes.

"What? That's you, Kevin, man?"

"Yeah, that's me," Kevin lied, tossing the boxes in the trash. "And the one you talkin' 'bout hitting with your bottle is her sister."

"Man, I ain't trippin' off that damn girl. I wasn't gon' hit her ass."

"I know you wasn't," Kevin said, ending the conversation.

Melanie headed to her car and popped open the trunk.

"You a'ight?" Nic asked as he tucked his arm around her waist.

"Yeah, I'm just glad y'all were here. Him and Lavon woulda been scrapin' in the middle of the street, then Simone woulda jumped in," Melanie said.

"And what would you have done?" Nic said, joking with Melanie.

"Nic, you know what she woulda done," Lavon answered as she grabbed her overnight bag from the trunk of Melanie's car and tossed it over her shoulder. "Her ass woulda got the hell out

34

of dodge."

"Naw, I'da ran for help," Melanie said, chuckling a bit. "Here, Simone. I think this box is yours."

"I got it," Kevin volunteered.

"Thanks." Simone smiled.

*Damn*, Kevin thought as he got a real good look at Simone. *A hot-ass mocha number.* "So you the one out here starting all the trouble?"

"How you figure that?"

"'Cause," Kevin said as Melanie slammed her trunk close, "dumbass over there was tryin' to holla at you."

Brushing Kevin's comment off with a wave of her hand, Simone led the way inside the building to her apartment. "I heard him say something about your brother. You live around here?"

"Yeah. Right downstairs in this building actually."

"Really? So are them bammas always out there like that, smoking and drinking?"

"Naw, those dummies waiting for my brother. First time I've seen them around here."

"So what's up?" James said, looking at Lavon as they waited for Simone to unlock her door. "Me and you 'pose to be together since everybody else all paired up?"

Lavon took one look at James and said, "Fuck, no."

"Damn," James huffed. "Why the hell I have to get the evil one?"

"Man, shut up," Nic instructed. "Ain't nobody paired up but me and Melanie," he said as they all headed inside Simone's apartment. "Dag." Nic looked around, nodding his approval. "This is hittin', Simone."

The freshly vacuumed, light-colored carpeting made the

living room-dining room combination seem huge; swallowing the colorful pillows Simone had tossed in each corner. The pillows, along with the cart that housed the television and VCR, were all the furniture the room had to offer.

"Thanks. I don't have anything for y'all to sit on," Simone said with a shrug of her shoulders, "but y'all welcome to the floor. It's plenty of that."

"Most def," Nic replied, still in awe. "Hey, what were y'all gettin' ready to do up in here anyway?" he asked.

"I don't know," Melanie answered, "but I got a bag full of movies."

"What you got?" Nic asked.

"Jason, Freddie, Chuckie. I got all of 'em."

"Oh, yeah? Cough 'em up!" Nic said as he helped himself to the television.

"Hold up, Nic. What you doing?" Simone asked.

"Y'all watchin' movies, right?"

"Yeah, movies are fine, but we ain't watching Freddie, Jason, or Chuckie," Simone protested from the middle of the floor.

Kevin smiled. "What's wrong, you scared?"

"No, I ain't scared. I just don't like horror movies."

"Sure, ya' right," Melanie added, passing Nic a movie from her bag. "Kevin, she scared. You should stay and watch it with her."

"Yeah, Kevin. You ain't 'bout to go nowhere, are you?" Nic asked while he slid the tape inside the VCR.

"I know I'm not," James said as he made himself comfortable on the floor.

"Naw, I don't have nothing to do," Kevin answered. "But hold up. Let me run downstairs real quick. Then," he said, turning his attention to Simone, "if it's okay with you, I'll come back and protect you from Freddie, baby."

"Look at y'all asses," Lavon said, somewhat irritated. "Don't you get no whack ideas," she said to James as she made herself comfortable on the other side of the room.

James sucked his teeth and stood back up. "Hold up, Kevin. I'ma go downstairs with you and holla at your mother."

"Oh, your mom's home, Kevin?" Nic asked.

"Yeah," Kevin said, heading to the door. "She should be."

"Well, hold up. I'ma run downstairs and say what's up, too. Melanie, get us some snacks and blankets 'cause it looks like this sleepover just turned co-ed." Nic grinned as he followed Kevin and James out the door.

The apartment door had barely closed before Melanie said, "Gotdamn, Kevin fine as hell, and he jive digging you, Simone! He had sparkles in them pretty-ass hazel eyes from looking at you!"

"Yeah, he's fine as a mutha with his pretty-ass teeth," Lavon agreed. "Nic's a cutie, too. But that lil' dusty thing they got wit' them ain't hittin' on shit. He needs to take his musky ass home. His gotdamn breath smell like baby shit."

Melanie chuckled as she stretched out on the floor next to Lavon. "Yeah, he's a rotten mess. But, Simone, what you think about Kevin?"

"Oh, like y'all said, he's fine as hell. But he probably dodging panties left and right."

● ● ●

"Damn, Nic," Kevin said as they headed down the steps to his apartment. "What's up with your girl's friend?"

"Hell, ain't shit up wit' the evil-ass fat one," James spat, his voice riddled with disappointment. "Her big ass must need a snack. Kevin, y'all got some Twinkies or somethin' downstairs that I can feed that big bitch? Maybe if I toss her ass a treat—"

"Shut the fuck up, James," Nic interrupted. "Lavon got a thing for niggas that smell better then onions."

"Fuck you, man. What the hell you tryna say?" James said as he sniffed under his arms.

"Hey, c'mon, y'all," Kevin yelled, terminating the feud before it went any further. "Seriously, Nic, what's up with Simone, man?"

"Simone?" Nic chuckled to himself. "Naw, Kevin. Don't even think about it. She ain't your type, man."

"What the hell is my type?"

"I mean, she ain't one of them fast-ass, wham-bams like all your other lil' honeys. Simone's a keeper. She wifey material."

"Ah, man, that's just what I need, Nic. To hell with them fast-ass broads. I'm trying to change."

"You tryna change, huh? Where that little crazy red chick that you was so in love with?" Nic asked.

"Oh, you talkin' 'bout Rhonda," James informed.

"Yeah, Rhonda—that's her name! If you gon' change, Kevin, why not change and just be about her. You were crazy about her."

"Man, I ain't messin' with Rhonda's hoeing ass no more. You know how many penicillin shots I had to get 'cause of her?" Kevin said. "Naw, I'm done with her. I want a real relationship, somebody I can trust." Kevin placed his key in the lock. "So what's up, Nic? You gon' hook me up or what?"

Nic smiled. "Man, please. Since when does Kevin Kennard need to get hooked up?"

● ● ●

The movie credits scrolled the screen. Kevin looked around

the room and noticed sleep had captured everybody but him. James left midway through the movie when he realized Lavon really wasn't interested. After turning off the VCR and television, Kevin crawled across the floor to the boom box. He switched on the power but nothing happened.

"Oh, it's not plugged in," he mumbled as he eased the cord into the outlet. Al Green's "For the Good Times" blasted through the speakers.

"Aww, shit," Kevin said as he quickly turned the volume down, thankful he hadn't disturbed anyone.

Kevin glanced over at Simone, admiring her creamy mocha skin and her long, wavy black hair as she lay on a pillow, knocked out. He took one of the extra blankets lying on the floor and draped it over her. She opened her eyes and smiled.

"Ah," Kevin blushed, slightly embarrassed. "I'm sorry. I didn't mean to wake you."

"You didn't. It was the radio," she whispered.

"Oh, that was my fault, too. I'm sorry."

"Don't be sorry." Simone propped herself up on her elbows.

"You want me to turn it off?"

"Naw!" Nic yelled. "We want y'all to shut the hell up and go to sleep! You, Al Green, and that bear over there snoring are waking everybody up." Kevin and Simone couldn't help but chuckle. "Y'all go back in Simone's room wit' that noise. And take Lavon with you."

Kevin looked at Simone. "So what's up? You got some cards or something?"

"Umm ... I don't think so, but I got a Monopoly game."

Kevin smiled, eager to play anything with the mocha goddess. "Okay, that's cool, but I'm the car."

# Chapter Four

There was nothing Kevin could do to prevent the smirk he'd worn on his face all day. He couldn't believe how close he'd come to making love to Simone. It never took him any time to get inside a woman's panties, but Simone was different. Wifey material, like Nic said. The last thing Kevin wanted to do was rush her.

*But shit, it's been two weeks,* he thought. However, deep down, he didn't care. He was falling for her, which was out of the norm for him. Since Rhonda, Kevin Kennard liked and refused to love. Yet, Simone's innocent smile, her laugh, her physical persona, all coupled with the last two weeks he'd spent with her constantly invaded his thoughts and chipped away the ice around his once cold heart.

*Shit, I'm fallin' for her and I ain't even got none yet.* He smiled to himself.

"Kevin," Fat Ed hollered as he walked down the strip in his long black leather trench and black leather gloves. "What's up, man? What the hell you grinning at?"

"Nothin', man. Hey, run me home real quick."

"What the hell's going on wit' you, Kevin? Why you keep rolling out early?"

"Naw, I got this lil' shorty that I'm jive digging."

Fat Ed shook his head and chuckled. "Yeah, until Rhonda's ass pops up."

"Man, why everybody keep talking that madness. You of all people should know I'm done wit' Rhonda."

"Yeah, but it ain't like I haven't heard that shit before."

"C'mon," Kevin said, ignoring the comment. "You takin' me home or what?"

"We partner up like I said, and you won't need no ride home."

"There you go wit' that crazy shit again. I wish you stop trippin'. I told you I ain't no hit man."

"Here." Fat Ed sucked his teeth and tossed Kevin a set of keys. "Take yourself home. The Rover's 'round the corner. I met another little stripper chick up at our ole spot. She hittin', too. I let her hold the Benz. She'll be up here in a minute. So, take the truck. Shit, keep that muthafucka. Maybe it'll help you change your mind."

"I doubt that."

"Shit, for real you outta stick around," Fat Ed said. "Shorty probably got one of her phat-ass friends wit' her. We can get a room and do like we did when you got out."

"Naw," Kevin said. "I'ma pass this time."

• • •

The next day, Kevin took the first few hours off just so he could drive Simone to work. Driving down the road, he glanced at her. "Damn, you look good in this truck."

"That don't mean you gotta get one."

"That's the farthest thing from my mind. Matter of fact," Kevin said as he pulled in front of Simone's workplace, "I'm giving it back to my man today."

He took Simone's hand, brought it to his lips, and kissed it lightly.

"I'll see you tonight," he said as he leaned over the center console and allowed his lips to greet hers where they surrendered to their passion, kissing nice and slow.

Simone peeled from Kevin's lips and opened the door. "Whew! I better leave while I can."

● ● ●

Beatrice didn't like the idea of Kevin driving around in Fat Ed's flashy truck— not one bit. Even though he had been two hours late to work, she let him leave two hours early just so he could find Fat Ed and give the vehicle back.

All over town, Kevin drove around searching for Fat Ed. He went past his house and checked all the usual spots, but couldn't find Fat Ed anywhere. Just when he was getting ready to give up, a light bulb went off in his head.

*I know where you at.*

Whipping a U-turn, Kevin headed to their old secret hideout, a run-down strip club in a warehouse next to a deserted department store. After parking in a nearby alley, Kevin strolled inside the club and surveyed the thin crowd.

*Damn, where everybody at?* he thought. He headed to the bar, ordered a bottle of Remy Martin, and strolled to the tables in front of the stage, where he and Fat Ed used to sit on a daily basis.

Kevin took a seat, poured himself a shot, and skimmed through the handful of men scattered around the stage. There was no sign of Fat Ed. *Hell, he'll show up*, Kevin thought as he made himself comfortable.

Music popped through the cheap speakers as the dancers seductively made their way to the stage, one behind the other. By the time the fourth dancer sashayed across the stage, Kevin was good and tipsy.

Pulling a ten-dollar bill from his pocket, he made eye contact with the dancer and flashed the money. With her eyes locked to Kevin's, she swiveled her body to the beat of the music and strutted over to him. She stood before him, peeling off the sheer pink bra that accented her chocolate skin. She licked her glossy red lips and held his gaze while slithering down to the ground like a python.

She crawled to the edge of the stage, leaned over, and jiggled her bare, voluptuous breasts in front of Kevin. With a raised brow, she slid her finger inside her pink G-string and toyed with the material. Kevin stood and inserted the ten-dollar bill into her G-string, knowing she wouldn't remove the garment until he did.

With the grace of a trained ballerina, the dancer stretched her legs into an open split and snatched off the rigged G-string, giving Kevin a full view of her Brazilian wax.

*Damn,* he thought as she tumbled over backward, allowing him to see her most intimate parts.

Hours later, Kevin had consumed more than half the bottle of Remy. He glanced at his watch and realized it was after eight. *Damn! Where'd the day go?* he thought as he stood to leave. But the alcohol took control, spinning the room around and around.

Kevin stumbled from the club and wobbled to the truck parked in an alley a few blocks away. He climbed inside.

"Damn," he mumbled as he rested his head on the steering

wheel in a final attempt to gain control of the spinning. But everything seemed to spin more. "Shit, Ed, I'ma have to find your ass tomorrow."

He took a deep breath, started the truck, placed it in gear, and drifted from the alley onto the main street.

*BOOM!*

● ● ●

Bright lights burned through Kevin's eyelids as he struggled to pull from his unconscious state. *Damn, this is a helluva hangover*, he thought. Blinking rapidly, he forced his eyes open. Bit by bit, the unfamiliar surroundings of the hospital room came into view.

"What the fuck is this shit?" Kevin panicked at the sight of the IV protruding from the back of his hand.

"Calm down, Mr. Kennard. You're okay." The doctor stood at Kevin's bedside, making his morning rounds. "I'm Dr. Scott, and as you can see, you're in the hospital."

"Doc, what's wrong with me? Why am I in here? What happened?"

"You were in a car accident three days ago."

"A car accident?"

"Yes, sir," the doctor confirmed. "Mr. Kennard, can you see the clock on the wall?"

*Three days? Oh my God! I know Ma is buggin' out. I gotta—*

"Mr. Kennard," the doctor interrupted him from his thoughts. "Can you tell me what time it is?"

"Yeah," Kevin said as he turned his attention to the wall clock. "It's eight-forty-five."

"That's correct." Dr. Scott rested his clipboard on the bed and applied light pressure to Kevin's limbs. "Are you experiencing any pain?"

"No, none. Doc, you said I've been here for three days?"

"Yes, since Wednesday evening. We've been monitoring you, and you don't appear to have any internal injuries. Seems you got off very lucky."

"Well, since I'm a'ight, can I go home?"

"Can you go home?" The doctor chuckled as if to soften his answer. "Mr. Kennard, you just woke up after being out for three days."

"Yeah, but you said I was fine, right?"

"Well, how about we get some food in you first before we make any plans. Okay?"

"A'ight."

*Damn...when the hell did I have an accident? The last thing I remember is being in the club.*

"Oh, and one last thing before I forget," the doctor said as he made notes in Kevin's file. "Your blood alcohol level was extremely high. Although the police said the accident didn't appear to be your fault, you weren't mentally fit to drive. You, sir, have a lot to be thankful for."

# Chapter Five

*God is truly trying to tell me something,* Kevin thought as he showered. He knew his life had to change, and he wanted that change to include Simone. She was all he could think of and talk about as his mother drove him home from the hospital.

"Kevin, I've heard all this before!" Beatrice said over her car radio. "You ain't telling me nothing new."

"Ma, this time is different. Wait until I introduce you to her."

"Boy, I don't need to be meeting no whole bunch of grown-butt little girls!"

"Ma, she's not like that," Kevin said. "She actually reminds me of you."

"Oh gosh, now that's a new one! What the chile look like? I hope it ain't that funny-looking thing that lives up on the third floor. I told you I don't want any ugly-ass grandkids. I'm not bouncing no lil' monkeys on my knee."

"C'mon now, Ma. Since when have you known me to mess

with monkeys? Simone's pretty. She got nice, pretty black hair, dimples, and," Kevin added, looking at his mother, "she's like your complexion."

Beatrice was stunned. "What? You mean to tell me she's not high yellow? I was beginning to think you were color struck for a minute."

"If I am, I got it from you. Look how light your husband was."

"Yeah, your father was bright as hell, but I've dated all shades. You," she added as she glanced at her son, "seemed to be stuck there for a minute."

"Naw, I date all shades, too, Ma. You've only seen one or two of them, and they just so happened to be light. I'm really liking Simone, though. She's different. She's not like anybody I've ever messed with. And believe me, Ma. If we ever had a baby, it wouldn't be no monkey."

"Well, let that be the farthest thing from your mind. The last thing you need is a damn baby."

"Yeah, plus I gotta get some first. I've been hanging out at her place for like two weeks, and we still ain't done nothing."

"Wait a minute," Beatrice said, ignoring his comment. "You said she's my complexion, with pretty hair and dimples? Does she live on the second floor in the first apartment on the right?"

"Yeah." Kevin was puzzled. "How you know?"

"Ah, boy, I met her at the mailbox a few days ago when you were missing in action! She came in singing 'Mr. Postman' to the mailman. I started snapping my fingers and singing, too. The mailman was dropping the mail in the boxes, dancing with us." Beatrice chuckled. "I like her."

"See and I'm telling you, Ma, she's not a fast butt."

"Hmm," Beatrice mumbled, nodding approvingly. "That's

all right. So what you gon' do about Ms. Rhonda? She's called a few times looking for you."

"I ain't thinking 'bout her."

"Well, you better. You and Rhonda have been going back and forth for years. Every time she pops up, you drop everything and everybody for her fast tail. You better call and get her straight."

"I'ma talk to her and let her know," Kevin said nonchalantly. He could feel his mother's gaze from the corner of his eye. "I'm serious, Ma. I'ma call her eventually and let her know it's over this time for real."

• • •

*Only ten minutes to go,* Simone thought, glancing at the clock as she hung up the phone. Just when she was getting ready to write Kevin off as another sorry ass, he called with a legitimate excuse for his absence. And now in a matter of minutes, Simone could head home and tend to his aches and pains from the accident.

*Shoot,* she thought as the phone rang again.

"Thank you for calling the law offices of Brown, Byrd, and Henson," Simone greeted, answering the phone. "How can I assist you?"

"Simone? Hey, you busy?"

"Hey, Nana," Simone greeted, happy to hear her grandmother's voice. "No, I'm just waiting for five o'clock, and then I'm out the door."

"Well, I just wanted to call and give you a heads-up. I think your mother's getting ready to call you."

"For what? She hasn't called me since I moved."

"I know," Nana said. "But she calls me nearly every day to see if I've talked to you."

Simone didn't respond.

"Now listen, Simone. You know how I am," Nana added. "I *do not* like all this not-speaking mess. It's been going on too long."

"But, Nana," Simone interrupted, "I didn't do anything but defend myself."

"I know that, Simone, and deep down, your mother knows that, too, which is why she's trying to move past it. She has finally mustered up the strength to call you. I know it's been killing her. She even told me Ricardo's seeking treatment for his substance abuse."

"Nana, you didn't tell her what he did, did you?"

"No, as much as I want, to, I didn't because I told you I wouldn't. You swear he's only touched you once?"

"Yeah, Nana."

"Simone," one of the secretaries buzzed through the intercom.

"Yes," Simone answered. "Hold on, Nana."

"You have a call on line three."

"Thanks," Simone said. "That's probably her, Nana."

"You gonna be nice, right? It's been almost two months, and despite everything she is still your mother."

"Alright, Nana." Simone huffed. "Since I'm in a good mood, I'll be nice just for you."

"Good. Now go talk to her before she chickens out and hangs up. I love ya."

Simone glanced up at the clock. She only had five more minutes to go. *She's funny*, Simone thought. Angela knew what time she got off. *I guess she figured if she called me at five o'clock, we wouldn't have to talk long.*

Simone picked up the call on hold. "Hello."

"Sounds like you rushing," Angela said.

"I am. I was just getting ready to put the answering machine on and run out to the bus stop. I get off at five, remember?"

"Oh, that's right. Well, don't let me hold you up. I just wanted to call and check on you."

"No, I can talk. I can catch the next bus. They run every couple of minutes when it's rush hour."

"Oh," Angela said, awkwardly. "Umm, well, how's the apartment coming? You have everything you need?"

"For the most part."

"Well, maybe I'll swing by over the weekend. I can pick up Nana, and maybe we can take you to the grocery store or something."

"Umm, that's fine."

"Well, you go ahead and catch the bus. I just wanted to call and check on you. I'll talk to you later."

Simone hung up the phone, surprised by the conversation. It actually felt good to hear Angela's voice. *Like Nana said, you are my mother.*

• • •

Kevin stretched the kinks from his sore limbs. *Damn, it's freezing in here*, he thought as he got up to close the bedroom window. As he turned to climb back in bed, he noticed Simone's nightshirt had crept up, revealing her plump ass in a pair of bikini underwear.

*Mmm, mmm, mmm,* he thought, instantly aroused as he crawled back in bed and snuggled up next to her. Gently, he nibbled on her ear and allowed his hand to travel under her nightshirt, where he began to massage her perky breasts. She woke with a smile on her face and rolled from her side to her back.

"Good morning, beautiful," Kevin whispered. He inched Simone's shirt up until her chocolate nipples stared at him, making his mouth water. One by one, he took them in his mouth, savoring their flavor as he teased them with his tongue.

Simone moaned tenderly, rubbing the back of his head. "Good morning to you, too. You not sore? You don't need to take anything?"

"Naw, you all the medicine I need," he said. "Tylenol couldn't fix this, anyway." Kevin slid the covers back to show Simone the bulge in his shorts.

"I know how to cure that," she replied seductively.

"Oh yeah?" Kevin asked with a raised brow.

"Mmm, hmm. Just take the socks out." She smiled.

Matching her smile, Kevin replied, "Yeah, maybe I should."

Propped up on her elbow, Simone watched as Kevin peeled from his boxers.

"Damn," he said as he tossed his shorts to the side of the bed. "No socks."

He reached for Simone's hand and guided her to his hardness. Together, they stroked him until his excitement began to leak.

*Shit,* Kevin screamed to himself, fighting the urge to explode. "Okay, okay. That's enough."

"What's wrong?"

"Naw," Kevin said, forcing Simone down on her back. "I don't wanna embarrass myself."

"You were getting ready to…"

Kevin silenced Simone with his lips, kissing her over and over again in slow, sensuous pecks. The passion in the room heightened as he nursed her lips apart. Faint moans escaped them as their tongues became reacquainted. Kevin's hand

51

skated down her curves and rested between the warmth of her legs. He rubbed the center of her panties until he simply couldn't take it anymore. Maneuvering past the crotch of her underwear, he eased his fingers inside her. He peeled his lips from hers and watched her close her eyes in pleasure.

"I wanna make love to you so bad, baby," Kevin moaned, nibbling lightly on her neck as he played in her wetness.

Simone opened her eyes. Without words, she arched her back and gave Kevin the go-ahead to remove her panties. He peeled them off and positioned himself on top of her. With their eyes glued on each other, he worked his erection inside her, teasing her with just a portion, then satisfying her with it all. Their bodies rocked in a deep, slow motion to the whines of pleasure filling the room as they made love for the first time. Soon, their hunger for each other amplified; their rhythm quickened as they found their ultimate pleasure together.

"Damn, Simone," Kevin panted as he filled her with the remaining drops of his orgasm.

"Damn, Simone what?" she whispered, wiping the beads of sweat from his forehead.

"I'm falling in love with you."

"That's good." She smiled. "Because I'm falling in love with you, too."

• • •

Simone woke to the irritating sound of the phone. Tangled in the sheets, she pulled herself from Kevin's arms to answer it.

"You sleep?" Nana asked.

"I was." Simone yawned and smiled down at Kevin as he stroked her arm.

"Well, get up. Your momma's here and we're on our way over. See you in a bit."

Simone hung up the phone and looked around her room. Kevin's boxers and clothes were tossed on one side of the bed, and her nightshirt and underwear were on the other. The nightstand overflowed with the dishes from the late breakfast they had cooked together.

"What's wrong?" Kevin asked as Simone slung back the covers.

"Get your drawers. My mother and grandmother are on their way over."

• • •

The sunroom overlooking the manicured lawns of the nursing home was Mr. Johnson's favorite place to sit while he recovered from his chemotherapy. There, Mr. Johnson could sit and watch the leaves change colors and descend to the ground. Of the eight elderly men Kevin tended to, Mr. Curtis Johnson was undeniably his favorite. He was the closest thing to a father Kevin had in his life.

"Your momma told me you out there slinging them drugs again," Mr. Johnson said as Kevin helped him into a rocking chair. "I guess you like sitting behind bars, huh?"

"No, sir. Not at all. I'm not in the streets the way I used to be."

"The way you used to be? Boy, you shouldn't be out there at all. I know that area where you hang out. I got a sister over there. I been trying to get her from around there for I don't know how long. Every now and then, I spend the weekends with her. That place is like the wild, wild west. Bullets be flying all night long. You better get your tail from over there."

"I'm tryin', Mr. Johnson."

"Aww, that's hogwash. You ain't tryin' hard enough. Ain't nothing in them streets but trouble and fast-ass women. When

53

your little ding-a-ling get to dripping, you'd wish you hada listened to me." Kevin couldn't help but laugh. "You can think it's funny if you want. You know what I'd do if I were your age?"

"What's that, Mr. Johnson?"

"I'd find me a nice lil' gal and start making plans for tomorrow," he said, looking at Kevin firmly.

"I already found a nice lil' gal."

"Yeah, well, if she means anything to you, you'd get yourself together and leave them streets alone. 'Cause if you don't, you gon' end up bringing both of y'all down. Watch what I tell you. Get married and start a family. Hell, do it 'fore this cancer take me away from here. I'm sure I can muscle up enough energy to cut a rug at your wedding."

"Ah, Mr. Johnson, don't talk like that. You ain't going nowhere no time soon. You got a lot of life left in you."

"I don't know 'bout that. Some mornings I feel like I'm a hundred-sixty-two instead of sixty-two. But don't you worry 'bout me. When I'm dead and gon', I'ma still be watching you from up above to make sure you do right, you hear me? You remind me of the son I never had."

"I hear you, Mr. Johnson."

● ● ●

April, 1988 - Spring hit and Kevin began spending more and more time on the strip. The fast money he earned slinging drugs put the chump change he earned at the nursing home to shame. He tried reliving his conversations with Mr. Johnson over and over, but the old man's words weren't powerful enough to quiet the cries from the street.

Kevin reached a fork in the road. Drifting home late at night, he dreaded getting up early in the morning to work at the nursing home. He couldn't take it and finally found the courage to quit.

"Have you lost your damn mind?" Beatrice yelled.

"Ma, I'm wiping ol' men butts for five dollars an hour."

"Kevin, it's more than that. It's a real job, and it's keeping your behind out of trouble. You haven't even been home a year yet! Didn't those six months behind bars teach you anything?"

"Ma, I know you worried 'bout me, but I'ma get outta those streets eventually. I promise. Besides, I ain't doing nothin' compared to what I used to do, and I'm not gon' be out there every day."

"Kevin," Beatrice sighed in defeat, "you've been getting off lucky. One day, your luck is going to run out, and when it does, don't come calling me."

● ● ●

Simone gave Kevin the keys to her apartment and her heart. His toothbrush dangled from the toothbrush holder next to hers, and his clothes hung in her closet. Simone's apartment had become their home, and their relationship was unbelievable. They talked into the wee hours of the morning, laughing and joking like best friends. Every time they unleashed their passion, their lovemaking felt like the first time. Their chemistry was perfect.

Often during the week, Simone would reach inside her purse and find a wad of money or Kevin's fully endorsed paycheck from the nursing home, which she simply deposited into her account. Though the money was great and paid the bulk of the bills, the thing that impressed Simone the most was the sentimental little notes Kevin left for her.

*'You are my light and hope for tomorrow. My heart has never known a greater love.'* Kevin left the notes everywhere—

under her pillow, in her dresser drawer, or taped to the bathroom mirror. Few knew his depth went deeper than his handsome, thuggish exterior.

Kevin's drug game picked up as Spring gave way to Summer, making the weekends he spent cuddled up in bed with Simone—watching movies or making love—history. Two Fridays in a row, Simone rushed home from work hoping to spend time with him, only to find Kevin rushing off to the strip, where he spent the entire weekend.

"I hope you not spending the weekend up there again. That shit is whack," Simone said with an attitude. "Why can't you come home like you do during the week?"

"'Cause, Simone. I told you the crackheads be out on the weekends until the wee hours of the morning, and the cabs don't come up there that late."

"So where you sleep, Kevin? On the strip?"

"Naw," Kevin said as he threw on his black hoodie. "A bunch of us crash up James's girl's house."

"Yeah, and I bet her girlfriends be up there with y'all, too."

Stepping into his steel-toe boots, Kevin watched Simone plop on the bed.

"Naw, it's just a bunch of James's friends."

"Well, what the hell kinda boyfriend is James any-way? I mean, I can't see you saying all your friends can come over here and spend the night every freakin' weekend."

"Hell naw. They can't come over here at all. But James is used to that shit. It's always a bunch of niggas at her house. She let us do our business while she does her business."

"Y'all business?"

"Yeah, Simone. Drug stuff. And you know I don't like talkin' to you about that."

"Damn. So all y'all hanging up there and cooking cook, and that don't bother James?"

"What you know about cooking cook?"

"Kevin, James don't care that all y'all be up there?" she asked again. She wasn't as naïve as Kevin thought.

"Naw, Simone, he don't care. He's used to, it."

"He's used to having a million dudes in his house around his girl?"

Kevin took a deep breath, preparing himself for the argument that was sure to come. Finally, he was in a real relationship. One filled with love, trust, and communication. He'd never lied to Simone, and he hadn't planned to start.

"Simone, his girl operates a little escort-like service."

Absent of a response, Simone sat numb on the bed.

"Did you hear me, baby?" Kevin asked.

"Oh, I heard you. I just figured you were lunchin', so I was giving you a chance to tell the truth. But you're serious. Kevin, don't nobody operate no escort service in the hood. That tramp be tricking."

"Naw, tricking is when you exchange sex for drugs. She ain't like that."

"Oh, so because she actually charges money, it makes it better?" she questioned sarcastically. "Have you bought anything from her?"

"Hell no! Simone, c'mon now. It ain't that type of party," Kevin said, turning toward her. "Plus, she gotta weigh over three hundred pounds."

"Whatever, Kevin. Booty is booty, and I can't believe you just told me this dumbness. So she's never tried to book you or James's friends?"

"Simone, I mean, damn. She comes on to every-gotdamn-body, but I'm not thinking 'bout her. I got what I want right here. Plus, I told you that's James's girl. They just had a baby, too. At least we think it's James's," he said more so to himself.

"Okay, I don't even wanna hear any more of this crazy talk, Kevin. Matter of fact, why don't you just stay home this weekend? We good on money. Let's call Melanie and Nic and hang out with them."

"Simone, I can't. It's the first of the month, and them crackheads splurging and paying off their tabs."

"They can pay their tabs off one day next week."

"Yeah, right," Kevin said. He grabbed his cap from the nightstand and tossed it on his head. "They'll be don' smoked their whole check up by then."

"Come on, Kevin," she pleaded. "We've never even gone out on a date. Stay home and let's go out to dinner or something."

"Look," Kevin pulled Simone up from the bed, "I'll try to come back tonight. Then we can do something here."

"Something like what?" she asked, pulling away from him. "Watch a movie, fix something to eat, or fuck?"

"I've never fucked you."

"You fucking me now," Simone said as she headed into the bathroom. "I'm tired of staying inside and doing nothing. But that's okay. Go collect your money and spend the weekend up the trick's house."

"Come on, Simone. Don't start trippin'."

"I'm not trippin', Kevin. Go do your thing. But I'm going out." She turned on the shower. "And I'm not going out by myself."

"So what you saying?"

"You know what I'm saying," Simone yelled over the

running water.

"Simone, don't play like that. You gon' fuck around and get somebody hurt."

Unfazed by his words, she ignored Kevin. His decision to head to the strip opposed to spending quality time with her hurt.

"You heard what I said, right?" Kevin yelled as Simone slammed the bathroom door.

• • •

Kevin strolled into the apartment a little after ten. The flickering light from the bedroom television illuminated the hallway.

*Damn, I know she ain't sleep*, he thought as he headed to the bedroom, only to discover Simone wasn't home.

He flipped on the light, and there scattered amidst the bed linens were her expensive jeans and the sexy, skimpy tops she wore when she went out.

*Who the hell she getting cute for?*

Kevin's mind started playing tricks on him, rehashing Simone's threats. Reaching behind his back, he retrieved the gun he kept snuggled in the waistband of his pants, and flopped onto the bed. Simone was right. They'd never gone on one solitary date, and he was hoping to change that tonight.

*Damn...did she go out with another nigga?* Kevin thought. *I know one muthafuckin' thing, she better not walk in here with his ass.* Kevin knew he wouldn't kill the guy, but he would put a fear in him that the guy wouldn't experience again until he met the Grim Reaper.

*Shit, I need to calm down.* He headed to the bathroom, turned on the shower, and planted himself on top of the toilet seat. As steam began to fog the bathroom, Kevin's mind replayed the countless other women who had all been unfaithful

59

to him, just as he'd been to them. Yet, for the first time in his life, his appetite for love was satisfied. Simone wasn't as sexually advanced as Rhonda or some of his other quickies, but Kevin loved that, knowing he could teach her sexual tricks.

*Simone's not like them,* he told himself as he disrobed. He climbed into the shower and allowed the hot water to massage away the building tension. After sulking in the shower, Kevin felt better. The hot water had melted away his doubt.

*Simone ain't like none of them. That's why I love her so much,* he convinced himself as he headed into the bedroom with a towel wrapped around his waist. He cleared off the bed to stretch out and waited for Simone.

Hours ticked away. By two in the morning, there was still no sign of Simone. Kevin's anger resurfaced as he tossed on his clothes. He opened the chamber of his gun and placed a bullet on the dresser next to a hand-scribbled note.

*'This is for that fake-ass nigga you went out with.'*

He placed the bullet in the center of the note and left.

● ● ●

Melanie danced around in the hallway, fighting the urge to use the bathroom.

"Simone, you better hurry up 'fore I piss right here on the floor!"

"Why didn't you go before we left?" Lavon asked as Simone placed her key in the lock.

"The line was too long," Melanie answered. "Man, that party was fresh. We gotta go out again before I leave."

"I can't believe you're really going away," Lavon said.

"Girl, you know my mother be lunchin'. She's not feeling the community college thing. So, Labor Day weekend I'll be gone."

Simone caught a whiff of her cigarette-smelling clothes as she opened the door. "Man, I can't wait to hop in the shower."

"Me, too," Lavon agreed. "Simone, wait till you tell Kevin that you won the butt contest!"

"Yeah, y'all heifers were cold fakin'. Y'all set me up."

"Girl, please. You the only one with a butt," Lavon said. "Mine is too damn wide, and Melanie's, skinny, red ass ain't got one."

"Well, it don't matter any way. I probably won't see Kevin 'til Monday. I'd be done forgot about the contest by then."

As she crossed the threshold, Simone walked into the faint scent of Kevin's cologne lingering in the room.

"Whew, girl. Watch out," Melanie said, ready to rush off to the bathroom. "I gotta pee like crazy."

"Hold up." Simone grabbed her by the arm. "I think Kevin's back there. I can smell his cologne. Let me make sure he ain't naked."

"Girl, please," Melanie said, dancing around. "A ding-a-ling is a ding-a-ling."

Excited, Simone rushed to the bedroom, only to greet disappointment. The bedroom was empty. With a suck of her teeth, she turned on the light.

*What the hell,* she thought as her eyes spotted the bullet and piece of paper on the dresser. She couldn't help the smile that crept across her face as she read the scribble.

*He really thought I was going out with somebody,* she thought as she shoveled the note and bullet into her drawer. *Dang, I hope he didn't run back to the strip.* She picked up the phone and paged him.

• • •

The chirping sound from his pager woke him. Kevin looked

around the room, almost forgetting that he'd crashed on his mother's couch. Although there was still money to be made on the strip, he didn't feel like heading back.

Reaching for his pager, he saw Simone had paged him two hours ago. He turned off the television, secured his mother's apartment, and headed upstairs.

After tiptoeing into the bedroom, Kevin pulled back the covers and smiled at the sight of Simone in one of his T-shirts. The smell of her pear-scented lotion rose from the bed and waltzed in the air. Eagerly, he disrobed down to nothing and snuggled up next to the warmth seeping from her body.

"I love you so much," he whispered in her ear. Tenderly, he applied light kisses to her face until her eyes opened.

"Aww, Kevin, baby. I'm sorry. I read your—"

"Shh." Kevin kissed her lips. "I thought about everything you said earlier and it was true, so I came home."

*I wonder if she's ready for this,* he thought as he nibbled lightly on Simone's neck. Bit by bit, Kevin planted a trail of kisses down her body until he reached the center of Simone's silk panties.

"Kevin... boy, what...what are you doing?"

"Just relax," he whispered. He positioned himself between her legs and teased the outskirts of his target with his tongue. Simone began to fidget. He glanced up at her like a wild animal sneaking up on his prey.

"Simone," he whispered. He kissed her inner thighs and slid off her underwear. "Just relax, baby."

With the experience of his tongue, he went after his target, melting through her initial resistance.

"Oh my God, Kevin," she cried as he entertained her for several minutes. Her legs began to tremble. "Shit, Kevin!" she screamed out in pleasure as she grabbed his head and rotated her hips.

"Cum for me, baby," Kevin requested as Simone's entire body began to shake. "Don't fight it, Simone. Cum for me."

Simone's body jerked, releasing an orgasm that Kevin didn't shy away from. He continued to work his magic while catering to each drop that trickled from her.

"Ah, I love you." She was panting as if she'd just run a marathon.

Kevin smiled. His mission was accomplished. "I wanted to do that a while ago," he said as he rested his body on top of Simone's, "but I didn't know if you were ready."

"So now what? I'm supposed to do you, right?"

"Huh?" Kevin was stunned. "You've done that before?"

"No, but I mean..." she said with a simple shrug of her shoulders.

"Naw, baby," he said as he steered his hardness inside of her. "Don't ever think that. This is all I need right here."

Kevin throbbed deeper and deeper inside Simone as the warmth of his pre-ejaculation began to seep from him.

"Mmm, Simone," he whispered, his rhythm quickening. "I love you, baby."

"I love you, too," she panted, matching his pace.

"Ah, here it come, baby. Here it comes," he gasped, breathing heavily. "Ah, Simone. I love you, baby. I love you so much," he cried. Before Kevin realized it, tears had crept from his eyes. Collapsing on top of Simone, he buried his face in her pillow.

Simone rubbed the back of Kevin's head. "You okay?"

"Yeah, I just gotta get myself together, baby. I love you so much."

# Chapter Six

Spending the weekends on the drug strip had become a thing of the past. After their argument two months before, Kevin made his way home to Simone each and every night without exception. Melanie and Nic became their weekend roommates. The foursome watched movie after movie, played games into the wee hours of the morning, and even broke out into a pillow fight, which Kevin brought to an end after Nic swung the pillow at Simone a little too hard for his comfort.

"Here, baby," Kevin said as he placed a ceramic plate filled with Simone's favorites on the nightstand. "Me and Nic fixed breakfast for y'all."

"I don't want it," Simone answered, pulling the covers over her head.

"Why not? That's everything you like."

"Yeah, but I don't feel good. I had to puke while you were in the kitchen."

"You threw up?"

Before Simone could part her lips to respond, she felt the queasiness return. She flung back the covers, sprang from the bed, and rushed to the bathroom just in time to flip up the toilet seat. She kicked the door shut and leaned over the commode as her insides exploded into the bowl.

*What in the world is wrong with me?* she thought, but she knew she didn't need a doctor's diagnosis. Simone hadn't had a period in two months.

After flushing the commode, Simone turned on the faucet and splashed cold water all over her face. The she brushed her teeth and the insides of her mouth with a vengeance, trying to rid the awful taste the vomit had left behind. With a deep-hearted sigh, she opened the bathroom door, ready to greet her audience.

"Damn, baby," Kevin said as he followed Simone to the bed. "You think—"

"Don't even say it. Don't none of y'all say it," she ordered.

"So then you know you pregnant?" Nic asked playfully.

Simone sucked her teeth and crawled back into the bed.

"I'm gonna be a godmother!" Melanie cooed.

"Whatever," Simone said, throwing the covers over her head. "Me and Kevin use protection."

Kevin planted himself on the edge of the bed next to her. "Simone, when was the last time we used protection?"

"Okay." Nic pushed Melanie toward the door. "We don't need to know the details, so we gon' give y'all some privacy," he said as he closed the door.

"Kevin, when we don't use protection, you get up."

"C'mon Simone," he said as he tugged on the covers. "When was the last time I got up?"

Simone peeked from underneath the covers. "Kevin, I've *seen* you get up. Hell, you make sure I see you. You squirt it on me, remember?"

Kevin smiled, aroused by the memory. "Yeah, but you've felt me not get up, too. Matter of fact, remember the first time I went down on you? That was like two months ago. I didn't get up then, and we didn't use nothing. I bet that's when it happened."

"You bet that's when what happened? You know what? Don't even answer that. Let's just change the subject, 'cause the last thing we need is a baby. You don't even have a job! You gave it up to sell drugs, remember?"

"Yeah, but it ain't like I can't get another one." Kevin was getting excited. "This is probably the motivation that I need."

"Look, don't get your hopes up, Kevin, because I'm not having no baby. If my period don't come soon, we'll just have to take care of it."

"Take care of it?" Kevin frowned at the mere thought. "I know you ain't talking 'bout having an abortion!"

Simone sighed and pulled the covers back over her head.

"You right," her muffled voice said from under the comforter. "I'm not having an abortion, 'cause I'm not pregnant."

● ● ●

Another month drifted by, and Simone still hadn't had a cycle. The frequent bouts with morning sickness caused her to miss work. Kevin stayed by her side each and every day, hoping that in a few months she would bestow on him the greatest blessing… the greatest joy of his life… a baby… a baby girl.

Realizing that she couldn't take off work forever, Simone mustered up enough energy to go back after a two-week absence. Not ready to return to the chaos of the street, Kevin took a detour from the drug strip, and spent his day in the mall with Beatrice.

"Hold up, Ma." The red-and-white sale sign dangling in the window of the jewelry store caught his eye. "I wanna go in here real quick," he said, heading into the store.

Beatrice grinned suspiciously and elbowed Kevin in his side. "Oh, do you now…"

Kevin browsed through the store, studying each case one by one, until one particular sparkling gem caught his eye.

"Can I help you, sir?" the saleswoman asked from behind the glass counter.

"Yes." Kevin pointed inside the case to an engagement ring. "Can I take a look at this one?"

"Oh, you have magnificent taste. This is one of my favorites." The clerk unlocked the case and reached inside. "It's twenty-four-carat solid gold, and the diamond, I believe…" She checked the fine print on the tag. "Yes, it's a carat. Is the occasion what I think it is?" she asked, passing the ring to Kevin.

"Yeah," Beatrice chimed in. "Is the occasion what we think it is?"

Kevin shrugged his shoulders as he studied the ring. "Well, I guess. I'm thinking about proposing."

The clerk smiled. "Well, congratulations. Is this your son?" she asked Beatrice.

"Yeah, he's my baby. I have two."

"Well, he has excellent taste. A trait I assume he inherited from you."

"But of course, he did," Beatrice said, proudly.

"How much is it?" Kevin asked.

"Well, we're running a sale this week. Normally, this ring is twelve hundred dollars, but today, I believe it's on sale for nine hundred ninety-nine. Would you like me to wrap it up for you?"

Out of the blue, déjà vu flooded Kevin's thoughts. The image of the engagement ring he'd purchased for Rhonda nearly two years ago danced in his mind.

*Damn*, Kevin thought. He could still picture the day Rhonda's exquisiteness had sashayed into the arcade where he worked. It was as if she'd walked out of a Prince music video. Every head turned, watching the hot number in her gray wool mini, tight black sweater, and thigh-high leather boots. Her sexy attire and the strands of gray in her shoulder-length hair told Kevin she was definitely older. But what the hell was she doing in the arcade?

"How you doing?" Kevin had greeted her, feeling a little intimidated. "You need help with anything?"

"Yeah, actually, I do," Rhonda said, leisurely surveying the games. "Can you teach me how to play this game?" she asked, pointing at the 'Galaxy' machine.

"Yeah, I can do that."

Kevin opened the door to the game, programmed ten credits of play, and proceeded to teach Rhonda the basics.

"Shouldn't you be behind me?" she asked, batting her lashes as she sat on a stool. Happy to oblige, Kevin smiled and slid behind her to assist with the control.

"I got it now, handsome." She smiled up at him, glancing over her shoulder. "But you don't have to let my hand go."

Kevin introduced Rhonda to every game in the arcade. A few days later, she introduced Kevin to her sexual willingness and know-how. To his astonishment, she was a year younger than him. Dress-Up was a game she used to get the attention of men—even if they were Kevin's friends.

Kevin had never loved anyone the way he'd loved Rhonda. However, over and over again, he caught her in compromising situations. So, he proposed, hoping the ring and the commitment it symbolized would solve all their problems. But it didn't. Frustrated with the unbalanced relationship, Kevin flushed the ring down the toilet and joined Rhonda in her games of deceit.

For every man Rhonda entertained, Kevin entertained three women. His harem grew, yet he never officially terminated his relationship with Rhonda. After she went away to school, she would ease back in town during the holidays and numerous breaks to reclaim her throne—Kevin's heart. But he hadn't talked to her since he'd come home from prison almost a year ago.

*So why the fuck am I thinkin' bout Rhonda now?*

Rhonda's and Simone's images danced around in Kevin's thoughts. Just when he believed it was impossible to have a serious relationship, Simone had proved him wrong and showed him how love really felt. So why couldn't he buy the ring? And more importantly, was he really over Rhonda?

Kevin needed to talk to someone, someone other than his mother. He needed some fatherly advice. *Shit, maybe I should go to the nursing home and talk to Mr. Johnson.*

"Sir?" the saleswoman said. "Should I wrap this up for you?"

Kevin handed her the ring, suddenly feeling as if he'd been unfaithful to Simone.

*Damn!* he screamed inside. *I gotta call Rhonda and let her know this shit is over.*

Beatrice suspiciously watched the son she knew inside and

out. She could tell he was battling demons, and it didn't take a rocket scientist to know the devil's name.

"Hey," she said, rubbing his back for support. "If you not ready, you not ready."

"Naw, it's not that, Ma," Kevin said.

"Well, sir," the saleswoman interjected in one final attempt to close the sale, "we do have a wonderful layaway plan."

● ● ●

Simone sensed something was wrong when she walked through the doors of the law firm that morning. The place was a ghost town. *Dang. Everybody called out sick?*

"Hi, Simone. I need to speak with you. You mind joining me in the conference room?" Joan, Simone's supervisor, said.

*Uh-oh*, Simone thought as she followed her.

"Is this about me being out sick?" Simone asked, noticing the file folder tucked underneath Joan's arm as she sat at the cherry wood conference table.

"I wish it was that simple, Simone. Does the place look a little deserted to you?"

"Yeah, I noticed that when I walked in," Simone replied. "The phones haven't even rung. I thought it was a holiday that I didn't know about."

"No, Simone. It's no holiday." Joan sighed. "Unfortunately, the partners have decided to dissolve the company and go their separate ways."

Joan placed Simone's file on the conference table and peered down at the papers to avoid looking at her.

"Each partner has written you a letter of recommendation. Although you've exhausted your leave, you'll still receive a full paycheck next Friday, and..." Joan rambled on, babbling words of no interest to Simone.

*Oh... my... God,* Simone screamed to herself. *I don't have a job.*

• • •

Kevin wasn't there when Simone arrived home in the early afternoon. With the weight of the world hovering over her, Simone undressed and climbed back in bed. When her cycle skipped another month, she'd accepted fate and realized that a baby was growing inside of her. Now, since she was unemployed, Kevin needed a job more than ever.

*My last paycheck will cover the rent for August, but then what?* Simone thought. *Shit... I know Kevin's really gonna be on the strip now.* Simone heard the apartment door close.

"Hey," Kevin said halfheartedly as he walked into the bedroom. "What you doing here so early?" Simone noticed his somber expression and figured his day had been as bad as hers. "You got sick at work?" he asked.

"No. I lost my job. Why you look so sad?" Simone asked, quickly changing the subject.

"You lost your job? Why, 'cause you were out sick?"

"No, the company dissolved. I get my last check next Friday, so that'll cover the rent for August. But after that, I don't know what we gon' do."

"Simone, don't worry 'bout that, baby. I'll take care of it." Kevin plopped on the bed and dropped his head into his hands.

Simone crawled to the end of the bed where Kevin sat. Slowly, she rubbed her hands up his back, across his broad shoulders, and worked them down his muscular chest.

"So," she whispered, nibbling softly on his ear, "why you look like you lost your best friend?"

He squeezed her hands and kissed them, thankful that the jewelry store had layaway.

"How's that possible when my best friend's right here?"

• • •

Kevin stood on the street corner peddling drugs, feeling burdened from all ends. This wasn't how he wanted to provide for his family, but since Simone was unemployed, the fast money was a need —not a want.

*I better call a cab 'fore it gets too late,* Kevin thought as he headed into the building where James stayed with his girl so he could use their phone. The local cab companies refused to acknowledge requests from pay phones.

The building was dark and reeked of urine from the thugs and addicts pissing in the hallways. Vague sounds of life escaped from behind a few of the apartment doors as Kevin headed up the steps. Turning to embark on the last flight that led to Felicia's apartment, Kevin ran into two Jamaicans sitting on the steps, filling Top paper with marijuana. The larger of the two glared at Kevin through fiendish eyes and stood, his six-four frame towering over Kevin.

"You just the muthafucka I been wanting to see. You need to pick another spot to sell your shit, pretty boy. I'm taking that corner over."

"Look, man," Kevin said, "I ain't lookin' for no trouble. Ain't nobody stop-pin' you from doin' your thing, man."

"What, muthafucka?" The huge Jamaican took a few steps forward, backing Kevin into a corner.

After lighting the freshly-rolled joint, his pint-sized partner stood, tossing the match to the floor. That's when Kevin reached under his sweatshirt and pulled out his gun.

"I tell you what. I'm not gon' be too many more of your muthafuckas," Kevin said, backing the two Jamaicans up.

"Hold up, man," the shorter one finally said, easing his

hands in the air. The fiery-red tip of the joint shone in the darkness.

A door slammed. A figure lurked at the top of the steps where Kevin had been trying to go.

"Steve! Toby!"

Kevin recognized Mike's voice; an older Jamaican who'd lived on the strip for years.

"What the hell is going on?" Concern overpowered his voice as he hurried down the steps.

"Mike, man, these your muthafuckin' peoples?" Kevin asked with his gun still drawn.

"Yeah, Kevin! They my nephews." Mike trotted down the steps, his eyes bouncing from Kevin to Steve and Toby. "What the fuck is goin' on?"

"Man, you better talk to your fuckin' nephews 'bout who they approach in these dark-ass hallways."

"What!" Mike screamed as he directed his attention to his nephews. "You was 'pose to be smokin' your joint and coming upstairs wit' me to get some head from Felicia! What the fuck happened? Do you not know who this man is? Huh?" Mike said, upset. "This," he continued, pointing his finger at Kevin, "is Kevin Kennard!"

Steve and Toby looked Kevin up and down as he stood ready to terminate their tomorrows with a simple pull of the trigger.

"Man, he's one you want on your side," Mike further informed his nephews. "Kevin, this was a misunderstanding. Toby and Steve just came here two weeks ago. They don't know the ways of these streets."

"Hey, man." Steve, the smaller one, offered his hand to Kevin. "My apologies."

Kevin tucked the gun back in his waistband and shook Steve's hand. Toby hesitantly followed suit.

"Yeah, man," Toby said. "If my uncle say you cool, then you cool."

• • •

For two weeks, Kevin worked the strip like never before. Finally, he'd made enough money to cover the rent and the utility bills for the next two months.

*This should hold us over till we find jobs,* he thought as his burdens slowly began to lift. He couldn't wait to get home and tell Simone everything was going to be all right.

"Freeze, nigga!"

Kevin recognized the familiar sound of a Tec-9 semiautomatic machine gun locking forward, chambering a bullet.

"Yeah, muthafucka," the assailant said as he reached around and snatched Kevin's gun from his waistband. "We've been watching your ass make that money! Now give that shit up!" The assailant stuck the semiautomatic into Kevin's spine. "And, nigga, if you so much as flinch, I'ma blow your brains out and still take your fuckin' money."

A million different forms of retaliation ran through Kevin's head as he eased his hands into his pocket and handed over the rent money. *We've been watching you,* kept replaying in his head, but he didn't recognize the voice.

"Count to a hundred, nigga, 'fore you turn around. You turn around 'fore then, and you gon' catch one of these bullets."

• • •

September's rent was due in a week, and Simone had no idea where it was coming from. She tried calling her father, but his solution wasn't the remedy she had in mind.

"Daddy, I need a favor. Now, before you say anything, keep in mind that I haven't asked you for a thing in a long time."

"Uh-oh." Thomas chuckled. "I guess you 'bout to make up for it now."

"No, not really. I just need a few dollars."

"A few dollars for what?"

Simone sighed. "I lost my job a month ago, and I'm a little short on the rent."

"Simone, why you just now calling me? How much you short by?"

"Six-fifty."

"How much is your rent?"

"Six-fifty," she replied shyly.

Thomas snickered. "I don't know what to tell you, baby girl. Why you wait 'til the last minute to call me? Is the rent behind? How'd you lose your job anyway? You were doing so good. I was proud of you," he ranted.

"See, Daddy, that's why I didn't call you when it first happened. I wasn't fired. The company dissolved. I paid the rent for August. I just don't have September's."

"Have you called your momma?"

"See, now you tryna be funny." She could hear her father laughing. "She wouldn't give it to me if she had it."

"Yes, she would. You just have to ask her."

"Daddy, she won't have it. I told you she took an early retirement, so now it's all *Ricardo's* money, and I'd live on the streets before I ask him for anything."

"Why you hate him so much?" Thomas asked.

"I don't know," she lied. She'd never shared the Ricardo incident with her dad. She made the mistake of sharing it with Kevin and had to work overtime to keep him from retaliating.

She knew her father would act no differently. Simone simply wanted to forget the incident even happened.

"Well, Simone, if I don't have it and you can't get it, I guess you gotta pack it up and move in with me. I thought you were too young to be moving on your own anyway."

Simone gasped her disapproval. After being on her own for a year, there was no way she wanted to move in with her father, Nana, or anyone else for that matter.

"Even if I came up with the money, what you gon' do about October's rent?"

"Daddy, I'ma find another job."

"Well, it's already been a month and you haven't found one. Where's your little boyfriend at? Hell, why can't he pay it? He laying up there with you, ain't he?"

"He was gonna pay it, but he got robbed."

"Robbed?"

"Yep, robbed."

"Baby girl, I know you hate to hear it, but I think you know what you need to do," Thomas advised. "It won't be forever, just until you get back on your feet. You not over there starving, are you?"

"No," she moped. "I have some money, just not enough for the rent."

"Well, if you find the money, let me know. That'll give you another month in your place. Otherwise, I'll be there next Saturday. That's Labor Day weekend, ain't it?"

"Yeah," she said, forcing the words out, "I think so."

"I'm off that weekend," Thomas mumbled more so to himself. "Don't sound so down. Hell, its two tears in a bucket. You know what comes after that, right?" He chuckled.

"Yeah, I know."

"I'm still proud of you. You did good out there for a year. Hell, look at your so-called big brother. Stan's twenty-three and still leeching off me. Talkin' 'bout he wanna open up a damn recording studio. His ass needs to go and get his own place. I'm tired of sitting on the nest. You ain't but nineteen, but at least you tried," Thomas said.

Simone didn't respond.

"Well, unless something changes, I guess I'll see you next weekend."

Hanging up the phone, Simone looked around her room, taking it all in. In a matter of days, her apartment would be nothing more than a memory.

# Chapter Seven
## Labor Day, 1988

Simone jumped from her bed and rushed to the bathroom, thankful she was home alone. There was no way she could tell her father she was pregnant. Not after losing her job and her apartment. There was no doubt in her mind that he would want her to have an abortion, which was no longer an option. She was having her baby.

Flushing the commode, Simone heard the phone ringing and rushed to answer it. *This has to be Kevin,* she thought as she snatched up the cordless.

"Hello."

"You okay?" Kevin asked, recognizing her hurried tone.

"Yeah, I was in the bathroom doing what I do best. I figured it was you. It's after two," she said, glancing at the clock. "You just getting up?"

"Yeah, I didn't get to sleep till 'bout six this morning. You just moved yesterday, and I hate this already. I'm so used to waking up next to you."

"Well, since you miss me so much, maybe now I can get you to go to a movie or something. We still haven't gone on a single date."

"Well, let's go today."

"Today?"

"Yeah. I need to see you."

"Wow, just like that? I should've moved a long time ago. I'll call Melanie. I know her and Nic are doing something. She's leaving tomorrow."

"Dang, I forgot she was going away to school," Kevin said. "Call Lavon, too. See if she wanna go. If she need somebody to go wit' her, I can call James."

"Yeah, right." Simone chuckled. "I don't have to call her, though. I'm right down the street from her and her mom now."

"Oh, y'all met around there?"

"Yeah, I met her and Melanie around here. Melanie moved a few years ago." Simone heard a faint tapping sound. "Somebody's knocking on your door?"

"Yeah," Kevin said as the taps turned into anxious banging, echoing throughout the apartment as he headed to the door. "You can hear it?"

"Yeah, real good now."

"BOY, I BEEN OUTSIDE KNOCKING ON THIS DAMN DOOR…" an angry female yelled.

Simone's natural antennas shot up. "Kevin, who's that?"

"I'MA CALL YOU BACK!" The phone went dead.

*What the hell?* Simone thought.

She called Kevin back, but his phone rang several times with no answer. *Okay, I know I ain't stupid,* Simone said to herself, knowing damn well she'd heard an irate female. Something wasn't right.

She snatched off her nightie and threw on the sweatpants and T-shirt she'd worn to move in. She stepped into her tennis shoes and pulled her silky tresses into a ponytail. Unable to sit still, she paced the floor and tried calling Kevin again. *You better answer this phone.*

"Hello!" a female answered.

"May I speak to Kevin?" Simone asked, a slight edge in her voice.

"For what?" came the response.

"Excuse me?"

"I said, for what?"

"Is your name Kevin?"

"Ah, no, but he's my boyfriend. So whatever you have to say to him, you can say to me."

"He's your boyfriend?"

"Yeah, bitch! What, you deaf?"

Simone chuckled sarcastically. "You know what? Let Kevin know his *pregnant* girlfriend is on the phone."

"What?"

"Yeah, bitch," Simone replied. "Now who's deaf?"

Sucking her teeth in pure ghetto fashion, the female said, "Bitch, I will fuck you up!"

"Please, you'll get fucked up. Give the fucking phone to Kevin. I didn't call to play with you."

"Here, take the phone, you sorry-ass muthafucka." Simone knew she was yelling at Kevin. She could hear their conversation.

"What the fuck you doing?" Kevin asked.

"Take the fuckin' phone!" she yelled. "You got some bitch pregnant?"

"Girl, hang up the gotdamn phone!"

"No, muthafucka, talk to your pregnant bitch."

"HANG UP THE MUTHAFUCKIN' PHONE!" Kevin ordered, and then the phone went dead.

Simone's entire body shook in a heated fury. She denied the tears pooling in her eyes permission to splash down her cheeks. There was no time for a pity party. She was too pissed to cry. She needed to get to Kevin's house. She picked up the phone and called Melanie.

● ● ●

"Who the fuck told you to answer the phone?" Kevin yelled, grabbing Rhonda's arms as she flipped out, swinging crazy punches. He'd been so engulfed in his conversation with Simone that he'd forgotten about Rhonda's surprise call earlier that morning. Worse yet, Kevin knew his outlandish reaction on the phone just now would probably make Simone think he was cheating on her.

"You got some bitch pregnant?" Rhonda screamed, snatching her arms from Kevin as tears flooded her face. "I don't fucking believe this shit! What the fuck did you want me to come over here for, huh?" she said, pushing him in his chest.

"I told you. I needed to talk to you."

"About what?" Rhonda asked through her sniffs. "The bitch you got pregnant!"

*Shit*, Kevin thought as Rhonda stood there crying. He let out a deep sigh.

"Look, just calm down," he said, embracing Rhonda and her madness. She accepted his embrace and bawled into his chest.

*Oh my God, Simone*, Kevin thought, knowing she was probably going crazy and there was no one to comfort her. His mother's warning danced in his head. He should've called Rhonda months ago and let her know that this time he was really done with her. Now she stood before him in a cloud of havoc. Such was life with Rhonda.

Rhonda had called that morning at the crack of dawn, announcing she was in town for Labor Day. "You know I gotta come see my baby," she'd purred into the phone.

"Good," Kevin mumbled, half asleep, "'cause we need to talk." This was his opportunity to sweep up the remaining crumbs of their so-called relationship and toss them into the trash where they belonged.

"Talk?" Rhonda had snickered. "Yeah, we can talk afterwards. I'll be over later."

*Whatever,* Kevin had thought as he hung up the phone and drifted back off to the slumber he'd just captured. When he awoke, the only thing on his mind was Simone.

"You want something to drink?" Kevin had asked Rhonda when she walked in.

"Who was that on the phone?" Rhonda asked as he sat the phone on the coffee table.

"Damn, how you walk in the door jockin' me? Do you want something to drink? Yes or no?"

"No," Rhonda said seductively. She strutted over to Kevin and eased her arms around his neck. "I want a kiss."

He moved her arms.

"Ugh, why you acting all whack? What… you mad 'cause I ain't been calling? Shit, you ain't been calling, either. So, stop buggin' and give me a kiss," she said, replacing her arms around his neck. Kevin pecked her quickly on the lips, leaving Rhonda dumbfounded. "What the fuck was that?"

The phone started ringing. Kevin moved her arms again. Rhonda's eyes bounced back and forth between the phone and Kevin's uneasiness.

"Answer it," she said.

"For what?" Kevin asked. He knew it was Simone, but there was no way he could talk to her now. *I'll explain it to her later,* he thought, as the phone finally stopped ringing. "You want a soda or what?"

"Or what," Rhonda said as she plopped on the couch, looking at Kevin suspiciously. "I wanna know why you acting so funny. Normally, by now you'd be pounding me in your mother's bed."

Kevin ignored her and headed down the hall to the secret stash of sodas his mother kept in her walk-in closet.

*Shit,* Kevin thought. Rhonda was right. Normally, they'd be on their second wind. Rhonda took it however, wherever. Just the mere thought was getting him aroused.

*Where the hell the sodas at?* Kevin dug farther and farther through the closet. He moved a shoebox out the way and couldn't help but laugh at the weight of it. A few sodas were hidden inside. He grabbed two cans and put everything back where he'd found it.

*I'll buy you some more sodas, Ma.* He knew why she hid them. LeCount guzzled them one behind the other, as if he'd bought them himself. As he closed the closet door, he heard Rhonda yelling.

*Who the fuck she talking to?* Then it dawned on him as he hurried down the hallway. *Oh my God! Simone musta called back.*

"Here!" Rhonda yelled. "Take the phone, you sorry-ass muthafucka!"

• • •

"I can't believe this! See? Men ain't shit!" In her sweatpants and tennis shoes, Lavon paced back and forth as they waited for

Melanie. "And you fucking pregnant."

"Yeah, but I'ma take care of that as soon as I get another job."

"Girl, you need to go with me on Tuesday to take the civil service test. I'm trying to get a job in the government."

"Say no more. I'm there," Simone replied as she sat on the concrete stoop in front of Lavon's building, tapping her feet.

"Look, Simone," Lavon said as a white Jeep Cherokee pulled into a parking space. "There go Big Bob. He been asking 'bout you, too! Look at him smiling."

Big Bob stepped his huge, six-three, 260 pounds of solid muscle from his truck.

"Welcome back, beautiful! Your brother told me you were moving back over here," Big Bob said, smiling from ear to ear. His crush on Simone had been no secret. "What y'all getting ready to get into?"

"Simone's 'bout to go whip this bitch!"

"Girl," Big Bob frowned, "don't you know you too pretty for all that nonsense?"

"Too late," Lavon said, bouncing around like a professional boxer, when Melanie pulled up in her broken-down blue Buick. "Melanie's here."

"Damn, y'all serious!" he said as Simone and Lavon headed to the car.

"Yeah," Lavon said. "You thought it was a joke?"

"Ah, shit. Hold the fuck up. I'm goin' wit' y'all," Big Bob said, heading back to his truck. "Hey," he hollered to a group of guys standing on the corner. "Git that and c'mon." He climbed into his truck and rolled down the window. "What's up, Melanie? What you going for? You ain't gon' fight no damn body."

"Whatever," Melanie yelled through the passenger window. "You going?"

"Yeah, I'm going. All us going," Big Bob responded as his herd of friends crowded the Cherokee.

"Simone!" Melanie warned. "Kevin is gonna trip for real when he sees a truck full of niggas."

"I don't give a fuck," Simone said, more irritably than she meant to. She wasn't mad at Melanie.

"Okay, so what the hell you gonna do when you get over there anyway?" Melanie asked. "I thought you were going to talk. You can't be fighting—not with my godchild."

"Whatever!" Lavon added from the backseat. "Just drive, Melanie. I ain't got on sweats for nothing. Let that bitch step. I'll stomp her ass into the ground, Simone, even if you are having an abortion."

"What?" Melanie was shocked. "You having an abortion?"

"Why would I keep it now?" Simone looked out the window, struggling with the array of emotions stirring inside her. In less than twenty-four hours, her life had turned upside down.

Bob started his truck and yelled out the window, "C'mon! What the hell y'all waiting for?"

Melanie backed from the parking space and led the way. Within a matter of minutes, the convoy arrived at North Hill Apartments. As she drove through the gates, Melanie noticed three individuals walking up the hill.

"Simone, ain't that Kevin right there?"

Simone looked out the window and spotted Kevin, James, and the infamous female. *Ugh, that's her*, she thought.

Rhonda was attractive, but for some reason, Simone was expecting more competition. To her surprise, though, there was nothing spectacular about Rhonda. Her complexion mirrored Kevin's and her hair was pulled into a simple ponytail that brushed against the back of her neck. Beyond those few supposed selling points, she was homely, dressed in pinkish skintight jeans and a gray and green striped sweatshirt. She wasn't at all what Simone had imagined.

"Pull over!" Simone yelled, coming to life as Melanie swiveled into a parking space. Simone and Lavon jumped out before the car was parked.

"Kevin!" Simone yelled. The threesome stopped and looked her way.

"Is that that bitch?" Rhonda yelled. "That's your pregnant bitch!"

"Girl, shut the fuck up!" Kevin grabbed her by the arm. "What the fuck is wrong with you?"

"Ugh, Simone," Lavon said, kneeling down to tie a double knot in her shoes. "She a bamma-ass bitch, too. Look at her fuckin' outfit and her outdated-ass tennis shoes. We wore that shit two years ago."

"Kevin!" Simone called out again, attempting to gain Kevin's attention as he and Rhonda fussed. "What's up? Who the fuck is that?"

"Come see who I am, bitch!" Rhonda yelled, trying to free herself from Kevin.

Big Bob and his fellas got out of the truck. "Don't even think about it," Big Bob said, grabbing Simone by her arm. "She got all that mouth, let that broke-down bitch come over here. Then you pound her ass into the ground."

"Here, Simone." One of Big Bob's friends handed Simone a wooden bat. "Go bust that bitch in her head."

"Boy, I don't need no damn bat!" Simone yelled back.

James tapped Kevin on the shoulder and pointed to the little mob that had formed. "Look at this shit! Who the fuck is all these niggas, man?"

"What the fuck," Kevin mumbled, shocked by the crowd. "Who all these niggas?" he hollered to Simone.

"Man, come see who the fuck we are!" Big Bob yelled, letting Simone go as he stepped out into the street, raising his arms, sending Kevin an invitation.

"What?" Kevin frowned.

"Yea," Big Bob said. "Nigga better check himself 'fore he wreck himself."

A car turned into the apartment complex and screeched to a halt. LeCount jumped from the driver's seat. "Hey, man," he said to Kevin. "What's going on?"

Ignoring LeCount, Kevin opened the back door, grabbed Rhonda by the arm, and shoved her into the backseat. "Get the fuck in the car!" he demanded. James ran around to the other side and jumped in the backseat.

"Stay your big ass right there. I'ma show you some wreck," Kevin said before jumping in the car. After surveying the crowd, LeCount jumped back in the car and sped off toward their building.

"Ain't that some shit," Simone said as the car disappeared down the hill. "He's probably going to get his gun. Then what he gon' do with it? Shoot all of us?"

"Let his ass go get it. We'll turn this muthafuckin' parking lot into the wild, wild west," Big Bob said, pulling his shirt up to reveal his own pistol. "This is my American Express card, and my credit is damn good 'cause I got more than one of these muthafuckas! A real gangsta's always strapped. And if his punk ass had any heart, we coulda went toe-to-toe right here in the street. Bitch niggas always run for their pistol."

"Big Bob, who the hell wanna fight your big ass?" Lavon joked. "And you got a damn gun."

"Come on, Simone," Melanie said from the car. Everyone had gotten out but her. "Let's go. It's not even worth it. Kevin comes back shooting, then what?"

"What he do, Simone, cheat on you with that raggedy-ass red chick?" Big Bob asked as they headed back to their vehicles. "Niggas kill me chasing these broke-down red chicks. That muthafucka crazy. I'd take your pretty chocolate ass over her any day."

"Yeah, whatever," Simone mumbled half-heartedly. "She can have him."

"Well, all this excitement don' made me hungry. Let's go get somethin' to eat," Big Bob said as he climbed back in his truck.

"I'm down!" Lavon yelled.

"I can't. Me and Nic going out," Melanie said. "Remember, I'm leaving in the morning."

"Y'all, let Scared Britches go," Big Bob said, referring to Melanie. "I'm just playing, baby. But you are the only muthafucka who didn't get outta the car. Come on, Simone and Lavon. Y'all can ride with me, but Simone sittin' up front!"

"Naw, Bob," Simone said. "I don't feel like going."

"Simone, c'mon. Don't let that shit get to you. Fuck that soft-ass punk."

"Naw, I'm cool." Simone climbed back into Melanie's car.

"A'ight," Big Bob yelled, backing up. "We'll see y'all 'round the way."

"Thanks, Melanie, for coming to get me," Simone said as she fought the urge to cry. She wanted to scream and fall to the ground in a pool of tears, but she couldn't. Not in front of Melanie and Lavon.

"That's alright, Simone. I'm just glad you weren't out here fighting. I can't believe Kevin, though. Dang, I wish I wasn't leaving tomorrow. Wait 'til I tell Nic."

"Simone, I gotta give it to you. You the most def-est bitch I know. You took that bullshit to the chin like a soldier," Lavon voiced from the backseat. "I'da been a mess, but you haven't shed a single tear. That's my muthafuckin' girl."

● ● ●

"Stan? Simone?" Thomas hollered from the back bedroom as the front door closed. "Who is that?"

"It's me, Daddy," Simone yelled, locking the door.

"Some Kennard lady called here looking for you. She said to call her."

"A'ight," Simone yelled back, but she had no plans to call Beatrice back.

Simone felt the queasiness resurfacing. *I thought this shit was called morning sickness.* There was no time to spit up. All she wanted to do was bury her face in her pillow and cry. Heading to her bedroom, that's what she did.

# Chapter Eight

The ringing phone woke Simone from the sleep she'd captured merely hours ago. Her eyes burned from the tears she'd shed all night long.

"Hello?" she answered, hoping it was Kevin with an apology or some type of logical explanation for yesterday. Something that would straighten things out and bring back some form of normalcy.

"Hey, Simone. I wanted to call before I left. Have you heard from Kevin yet?" Melanie asked.

"No." She sighed in disappointment. "Not one word. You getting ready to go?"

"Yeah, we leaving at ten. It's what, nine-thirty now?"

"Something like that," Simone mumbled.

"So are you going to call him?"

"And say what? My father said Ms. Kennard called last night, but I'm not calling her either."

"Simone, maybe you should. I mean, Kevin spent too much time at your house to have had another girlfriend."

"But he spent just as much time on the strip."

"I think you should call Ms. Kennard and talk to her."

"Yeah, whatever. *You* can call and talk to her."

"Actually, that's not a bad idea." Melanie said. "Maybe I will call her. You can just stay on the phone and listen."

"No, I don't have to be on the phone."

"Yeah, Simone. I'll pretend like I'm worried about you and I haven't spoken to you since yesterday." Simone didn't respond. "I mean, what harm could it do? All you gotta do is listen."

"A'ight. Whatever."

Melanie dialed Beatrice on the three-way. The phone rang three times before someone answered.

"Hello," a groggy male's voice said.

"Kevin?"

"Who this?"

"It's me, Melanie. Is your mother there?" Kevin didn't respond. Melanie's faint chuckle filled the awkward silence. "Kevin," she said, "can I speak to your mother?"

"Hold on," he said before screaming, "Ma! Pick up the phone."

"Who is it?" Beatrice hollered back, somewhat agitated.

"It's Melanie, Simone's girlfriend."

"Hang up, boy. I got it," she yelled. "Yes. Good morning, Melanie."

"Hey, Ms. Kennard. How you doing this morning?"

"I'm fine, baby, but you didn't call to see how I was doing. So, what's up?"

*Damn*, Simone thought. She knew how direct Ms. Kennard could be, but today she appeared rude.

"I'm just calling to see if you've heard from Simone. I

didn't wanna ask Kevin. I guess you heard about yesterday."

"Yeah, I heard. I called Simone last night, but she hasn't returned my call. She'll call me when she gets ready, I guess. Either way is fine."

"Well, I called her, too. She hasn't called me back, either."

"She's probably hurt. I told Kevin months ago to tell that girl about Rhonda."

"Rhonda?"

"Yeah, Rhonda. She's the love of Kevin's life. She moved away a few years ago to go to school. I don't know what's up, but whenever she pops up, Kevin drops everything and everybody for that chile. He proposed to the girl a few years ago and everything."

"So that is his girlfriend?"

"Like I said, I don't know what's up, and I'm not gon' sit here and give her a title, but I know she ain't going nowhere. They go through their little breakups, and before you know it, she's ringing my phone again like a stalker."

"Wow. If they're like that, he definitely should've told Simone. I mean, now she's pregnant and everything."

"Yeah, well, I'm not taking anything away from Simone. I thought she was a beautiful girl up until yesterday. Don't no lady come looking for no other lady, swinging a bat over a man! Naw, that's not how you do things. I thought Simone was better than that. The part that I really don't like is that she's supposed to be pregnant with my grandchild."

*Supposed to be?* Simone said to herself. *What the fuck is that supposed to mean?*

"Yeah, but she didn't start it," Melanie responded in defense of her friend. "And the bat wasn't hers. One of them guys gave it to her."

"And what was the purpose of all that?" Beatrice asked. "Why she bring a million and one niggas over my house? Were they supposed to do something to Kevin?"

"They weren't supposed to even come. It was only me and Simone, and before we knew it, they were following us."

"Yeah, well, like I said. Simone can call me when she gets ready, or we can leave it alone. I just thought she was better than that, and I don't appreciate a trillion guys coming to my house looking for my son."

"That's not how it was, but okay, Ms. Kennard," Melanie said. She knew Simone had heard more than enough. "I just wanted to see if you've heard from her."

"No, I haven't, and I hope she's okay. I really mean that."

"Well, if I talk to her, I'll let her know."

"Okay, baby. You take care and tell Nic I said hello."

"Simone?" Melanie called after making sure Beatrice was gone. "Simone?" The line went dead.

*I hope I'm not too far along to have an abortion,* Simone thought. Kevin had crossed the thin line that divided love and hate. She despised him and the last twelve months she'd wasted with him. The last thing she wanted was his child.

Tears drizzled down her face as she pulled the Yellow Pages from the coat closet. She blew the layer of dust from the cover and took the book into her room to search for an abortion clinic. Eager to learn the price, she called the first one she stumbled across.

"Yes, I'm pregnant, and I need to know the cost for an abortion," Simone said.

"I'm sorry. We're closed. I don't know what possessed me to even answer this phone. I guess it's just second nature. We're open tomorrow from…"

"Please," Simone begged, her voice barely above a whisper as she struggled to speak over her tears. "All I need is a price."

"Oh, honey. It's going to be okay," she cooed in response to Simone's tears. "How far are you?"

"I'm not sure. I'm guessing four months."

"Umm…you're really pushing it. The further along you are, the more complications there are and the more expensive it is."

"But can it be done?"

"Oh yeah, it can be done."

"How much do you think it would cost?"

"Well, based on what you've told me, it could cost you up to eight hundred dollars."

"Okay. Thank you."

"Sweetheart, if you want, I can go ahead and schedule the appointment since I have you on the phone."

"No, I'll call back." Simone hung up the phone and jotted down the number.

*I have to pass this test tomorrow. Then I can find a job and pay for an abortion.*

● ● ●

Kevin lay in bed, listening to his mother's muffled voice as she chatted on the phone with Melanie. When her mumbling stopped, he headed out to the living room.

"So what she say?"

"Nothing, really. She was wondering if I'd heard from Simone. She's not calling anybody," Beatrice shared.

Kevin sighed at the mess he'd made. "So what all did you tell her?"

"I just explained who Rhonda was, which is what you should've done a long time ago. You know how you and Rhonda are. She pops up and you two pick up where you left off."

"That's not what you said, is it?"

"Yeah, boy! That's the truth!"

"That's not the truth, Ma. I love Rhonda, but not enough to be in no relationship with her! I told her all about Simone."

"Well, you need to call and explain that to Simone, if that's who you claim you really love. I just told Melanie that Rhonda was the love of your life."

*Damn*, Kevin screamed to himself. *What the fuck gon' happen next?*

# Chapter Nine
## Five Days Later

Kevin was devastated by everything that had happened. The mere thought that he'd lost Simone was crushing him. She was his everything, and being without her was pushing him over the edge. He loved Simone more than he thought was humanly possible, and now growing inside of her was a child made from such an intoxicating love. Kevin wanted to right his wrong, but how? Apologizing was new to him. Rhonda had taught him that all was fair in love and war. However, this time, things were different. He wanted and needed to make amends. He contemplated going to get some fatherly advice from Mr. Johnson, but after everything that had happened, Kevin knew there was no way Simone would forgive him.

Seated on a chair in a corner of Felicia's house, Kevin dangled a cocaine-laced joint between his fingers, preparing to break the number-one rule of hustling. The streets had taught him not to dabble in his supply. He'd seen firsthand what the product would do, as a few of his friends, like James, had fallen prey to the drugs. Kevin's world had crumbled around him, though, and he needed an escape. A doctor couldn't prescribe a better remedy than the one he carried in his pockets.

Ready to mimic the habits of his clients, Kevin fired up the joint. Taking a long drag, he gave the joint permission to take him far away from his troubles. He wasn't new to the drug. He'd gotten high a time or two in the past, but since his breakup with Simone a few days ago, he'd become his number-one client, smoking every day.

*Oh yeah,* Kevin thought, as his problems began to fade into the puffy white clouds of smoke he blew into the room.

The cries of the squeaking bed echoed throughout the apartment as Felicia worked one of her clients from the bedroom in the back. Kevin heard her client scream, "Ah, shit." He chuckled to himself.

Taking one last puff from his joint, he stumped the butt out in the ashtray. The squeaks stopped. Minutes later, Felicia's client strolled from the room, adjusting his belt. Kevin didn't recognize the guy, which wasn't surprising. Men came from hoods far and near to sample Felicia.

"Man, that bitch might be ugly as hell, but she worth every fuckin' penny. You gon' get your money's worth," he said to Kevin as he headed out the front door.

A hint of light from the streetlamp outside peeked through the dusty blinds. As the apartment door slammed, Felicia strolled into the room, shoveling her hard-earned money inside her bra.

"You know," she said while walking over to Kevin, seductively swaying her oversized hips, "you would never have to pay me. I'd do your fine ass for free."

Kevin stood from the chair.

"C'mon," Felicia said. "Just let me suck that muthafucka."

"Go 'head with that shit, girl. Go suck James." Kevin stood face-to-face with Felicia. He grabbed her hands as she reached for his belt. "Go 'head, Felicia."

"Naw," she whispered. She tilted her head to the side, staring seriously into Kevin's hazel eyes. "Come on, Kevin. Shit, James knows. This is my hustle. This is what I do."

Felicia wiggled her hands from Kevin's grip with little effort and stroked the bulge in his pants.

"I feel him gettin' hard, too." Slowly, she undid Kevin's pants and unzipped his zipper. "Just let me taste him," she whispered.

She shivered as she eased her hands inside his pants. With her fingers wrapped around his hardness, she freed him from his boxers.

"Damn," she expressed in awe more so to herself. "I didn't know you were packin' like this."

With Kevin's erection in the palm of her hands, Felicia lowered herself to the floor, stroking him nice and slow as his body swayed from the influence of the narcotic. Teasing the tip of his erection with her tongue, she licked away the excitement oozing from him.

"Mmm," she moaned. She kissed every inch of his shaft before welcoming him inside her warm, juicy jaws. "Mmm, mmm, mmm," she continued to moan, working her magic as she deep-throated him.

Kevin's eyes rolled to the back of his head. It wouldn't take him any time to coat her tonsils. He grabbed the back of Felicia's head and met her bobs with deep-planted thrusts. She gagged once, but kept with his rhythm.

"Ah, Simone, baby," Kevin moaned. His high had complete control over him. Mission accomplished. "I told you, you never had to do this shit, baby, but damn... Hmm..."

Felicia released him from her mouth and frowned. "That shit got you straight lunchin'," she said while stroking him with her hand. "I told you I want to."

Kevin's eyes shot open and fell on Felicia. He staggered backward, confused. Where was Simone?

"Hold up, Kevin. What you doing?" Felicia crawled forward, attempting to regain her position. Kevin shot her a threatening look and shoved his saliva-coated hardness back inside his pants.

"What you doing?" Felicia stood. "Let me finish."

*What the fuck was I doing?* Kevin thought.

Reaching inside his pants pocket, he pulled out another cocaine-laced joint and left the apartment. He stood in the hallway, fired up the joint, and puffed away. High was where he wanted to be, and the episode with Felicia had tainted his original groove. The apartment door opened. Felicia leaned against the doorframe.

"That's a'ight." She winked at Kevin. "I'ma get it one day. I promise you that."

High as hell, Kevin staggered out to the strip. Fat Ed, James, and Tuffy were outside, talking shit as usual.

"Damn, man!" Fat Ed hollered. "You look high as a muthafucka!"

"That's a'ight," Kevin mumbled at a snail's pace. "I feel good, though."

"Well, since you feeling all good, let's roll up to the club later. What's up, y'all?" Fat Ed turned to James and Tuffy. "C'mon, Tuffy, you ain't never been out wit' us. James, go wash your dirty ass, man, so we can roll."

"Man, I remember a time when we couldn't pay your fat ass

to set foot in a club," James retaliated. "Now that you got some flashy-ass wheels and them thick-ass chains, you always ready to fly up to the club. The chicks don't want your fat ass, for real."

"Shut up, nigga. I bet five hundred dollars that your dumb ass can't even spell club," Fat Ed said, knowing James hadn't gone past the fourth grade. "What's up, Tuffy?" Fat Ed asked, ignoring James. "You trying to roll or what?"

"Man, I'd love to hang out wit' y'all, but my girl's on her way over here. She'd have a heart attack if she knew I was in the club chasing ass."

"I ain't fooling wit' y'all, either. I got some business to take care of," James said.

"I hope it's with soap and a toothbrush," Fat Ed replied.

"Fuck you, man. You ain't the only muthafucka tryna get that paper."

Fat Ed turned his attention to Kevin. "What's up? You tryna roll after you sleep some of that shit off?"

"Shit, man, I don't need to sleep. Just let me run home and shower, and I'll be good."

● ● ●

All night long, Kevin chased his high with shots of cognac, one behind the other. He danced, flirted, and filled girls' heads with bullshit. His pockets overflowed with phone numbers from girls he wouldn't even remember in the morning.

Close to four a.m., Kevin stumbled into his mother's apartment. He kicked off his shoes and tossed his smoke-filled clothes in a pile on the floor. A scrap of paper fell from his pocket. He didn't have to pick it up to know what it was.

"Man, to hell with all y'all gold-diggin' tramps," Kevin said. He didn't want any of the girls from the club. He wanted his Simone.

*Shit, I'ma call her,* Kevin thought. He staggered into the kitchen and snatched the phone from the wall. He dialed the number. After a few rings, a sluggish male voice answered.

"Hello."

Kevin froze. His eyes darted to the time on the microwave. It was a little after four.

"Hello?" the voice repeated.

Kevin hung up. Waiting a few more minutes, he called again, hoping this time Simone would answer. However, the male voice answered again.

*Shit,* Kevin thought, riddled with disappointment. "I love you, baby," he mumbled as he hung up the phone.

# Chapter Ten

"Kevin! Kevin!" Beatrice yelled. She barged into the room, turning on the light. "Get this gotdamn phone!"

"Ma, what?" Kevin sprang up in bed, rubbing his eyes as he adjusted to the bright light. "What's wrong?"

"Felicia been ringing this gotdamn phone off the hook! Tell her don't call my house at five o'clock in the morning no more! Here!" Beatrice threw the cordless phone on Kevin's bed.

Kevin picked up the phone and fell back on his pillow.

"What the fuck is wrong wit' you? Why you callin' here?" he growled.

"Kevin! Oh my God," Felicia screamed. "That Jamaican Toby is looking for James! He's been up here banging on my door with a shotgun, saying he gon' kill all us, and James not even here!" Felicia's hysterical cries agitated Kevin's throbbing head.

"And what the fuck you callin' me for?"

"Kevin! He got a muthafuckin' shotgun and my baby in

here! He tryna tear my door down! He illin' for real."

"If you don't stop screamin' in my ear. Shit! Where the fuck is your piece? Shit, shoot that muthafucka!"

"Kevin, I'm scared," she cried.

"Shit, man," Kevin said more so to himself. "Who there with you?"

"It's just me, the baby, and Tuffy. Tuffy's the one who told me to call you," Felicia cried. "He said you was cool wit' Mike and them Jamaicans."

*Scared-ass muthafucka,* Kevin thought. "Look, Felicia, Toby ain't gon' do nothing. If he was, he'da already done it. I'll come up there later and talk to him. Just don't open the door if he comes back."

"Kevin, no." Felicia sobbed into the phone. "This muthafucka crazy. He got me and Tuffy in this bitch scared for real!"

"Shit," Kevin moaned into the phone. "Page James's ass."

"I did, but he ain't calling me back. Please, Kevin," Felicia begged. "Please come talk to him and get him away from my door."

"Damn, girl!" The infamous tears of a damsel in distress did it every time. "I'll be up there in a minute."

Kevin kicked back the covers and forced himself from the bed he'd settled into less than an hour ago. Beatrice walked out of the bathroom just as he pulled his gray sweatshirt over his head.

"Where the hell you 'bout to go?"

"To Felicia's," he said as he stepped into his shoes. "This nigga Toby's banging on her door looking for James, and she scared."

"Kevin, keep your ass right here in this house. That mess

103

ain't got nothing to do with you."

"Ma, I know the dude. I'm just gonna talk to him to calm his butt down."

"Kevin, listen to me for once in your life. Let James handle his own mess," Beatrice ordered.

The front door closed. Kevin knew it was his brother coming in.

"Hey, Count," Kevin called as he brushed past his mother. "You driving, man?" LeCount always had some female's car.

"Yeah, why?"

"Run me up to the strip right quick."

"Why? What's up the strip at five o'clock in the morning?"

"Nothing but trouble," Beatrice said. "So don't take his ass nowhere."

"Ma…" Kevin called out as he headed to the door. "Stop trippin'. It's not gon' be no mess. I'll be back later."

"Lord have mercy," Beatrice mumbled as she watched her sons walk out the door.

● ● ●

Kevin rested his throbbing head against the window of the car.

"Kevin." LeCount slapped him on the arm as they pulled up in front of Felicia's building.

"I ain't sleep, man," Kevin mumbled. "My head just banging like a muthafucka."

"You need me to go wit' you?"

"Naw, everything's cool," Kevin said, hopping out of the car. "Don't pay Ma no mind." Closing the door, he headed into Felicia's building and took the steps two at a time until he stood before her badly beaten door.

*Damn, he lunchin' for real*, Kevin thought as he knocked.

*What the fuck is wrong with Toby's ass?*

"Yes?" Felicia asked.

"Bitch, open the door! It's me, Toby!" Kevin joked. "I'm playing, girl. Open the door. It's me." The dead-bolts turned. Felicia swung the door open with her baby resting on her hip.

"He been back?" Kevin asked, walking into the apartment to see Tuffy sitting in the living room on the edge of the couch.

"Naw, not yet," Felicia said as she quickly closed the door and secured the locks.

"Kevin, man, you need to talk to your peeps," Tuffy said. "I couldn't even leave this bitch! Me and my girl got into it, I came up here to get Felicia to do her thing on my shit, and this nigga fucked it up, banging on the door like a fuckin' loony!"

"What the fuck you tell her to call me for? Where your raggedy-ass pistol at? Better yet, have y'all heard from James's ass yet? Why the hell Toby lookin' for him anyway?"

"'Cause James robbed him," Tuffy said.

"'Cause he what?"

"Kevin, don't listen to Tuffy," Felicia said. "He don't know what the hell he talkin' 'bout."

"Man, c'mon. That's why he ain't go to the club wit' you and Ed. Remember he said he had some business to tend to? Some paper to collect? That's what that shit was," Tuffy informed. "You see his ass ain't around, and he ain't calling Felicia back. He somewhere hiding."

*Damn, Ma. Why didn't I listen to you?* Kevin screamed to himself as he plopped down on the couch. *Shit, I can't even call a fuckin' cab to take me home.* Not only was Kevin pissed, he was stuck. *That's a'right. I'ma call a cab in a few hours and take my ass back home,* Kevin thought as he laid his head on the arm of the couch and dozed off.

A few hours later, Kevin awoke and headed into the kitchen to call a cab just as he'd planned. As he switched on the light, he saw what seemed like a million roaches scatter, trampling over the sink full of dirty dishes and baby bottles.

*Damn, these muthafuckas trifling*, he thought as he reached for the rotary phone on the wall.

"Your cab should be there within twenty minutes," the operator informed him.

As he hung up the phone, the thought of the baby sipping on a nipple that had been trampled over by a squad of roaches made Kevin's stomach weak. He rolled up his sleeves, placed the stopper in the sink, and turned the hot water on full blast. While the sink filled with water, he squeezed nearly half the bottle of dish detergent into the scalding-hot water and swished it around with his finger.

*Damn, let me look out for my cab*, Kevin thought as he shook the excess bubbles from his hand and opened the kitchen blinds.

*BOOM! BOOM! BOOM!* The apartment shook.

Kevin jumped, caught off guard by the sudden outburst.

"Open this muthafuckin' door!" Toby yelled, hammering the door with his shotgun.

"Shit," Kevin said, heading out into the living room.

"See, that muthafucka back," Tuffy said, sitting up on the floor. "Listen at his crazy ass. That's how he was doing last night."

"Damn. He making the whole building shake."

"You'da thought one of the neighbors woulda called the police or something," Tuffy said.

"Yeah, right. They just as scared as y'all are. Let me go talk to Toby's crazy ass," Kevin replied.

106

"No, Kevin." Felicia ran out from her back bedroom, her baby on her hip. "Don't open the door."

"What, you think I'm stupid?" Kevin asked, heading to the sliding glass door. "I'ma climb down the balcony and run around to the front."

*BOOM! BOOM! BOOM!*

Kevin eased the glass door open and stepped out onto the second-floor balcony.

"Hold up, Kevin," Felicia yelled. "Tuffy, gimme your piece."

Tuffy jumped from the floor, pulling his gun from his waistband.

"I don't need no gun." Kevin threw his legs over the railing.

"No, Kevin. Take it, please," Felicia pleaded, handing him the gun, a Luger 9mm.

"Yeah, man. Take somethin' wit' you," Tuffy said, standing in the doorway next to Felicia.

*BOOM! BOOM! BOOM!*

"Let me get down here 'fore he breaks the door down."

Kevin shoved the gun in the waist of his pants and lowered himself onto the patio underneath Felicia's balcony. As he ran around to the entrance of the building, Kevin spotted James ducking in between the cars in the parking lot.

"Man, where the fuck you been?" Kevin asked, full of rage. "Felicia was paging you all fucking night."

"I was out wit' this girl last night, man. I thought she was paging me to see where I was."

"Go somewhere wit' that bullshit, man. Toby been lookin' for you all night. What the fuck you rob him for?"

"Kevin, man, I ain't rob no muthafuckin' body. I'm just getting home. I heard that nigga tryna bust my door in, so I

107

went and got my shit."

"He should be pounding on your door looking for your bitch ass!"

"Man, I'm telling you. I ain't rob him." James's voice shot up two octaves, the way it always did when he was lying.

*This shit ain't good*, Kevin thought. *If Toby sees me with James's ass, he gon' think we in cahoots.*

Toby's lunges at the door echoed throughout the building.

"Look, just stay the fuck out here," Kevin ordered as he entered the building alone. He crept up the steps until he stood on the landing that separated him from Toby. He called his name. "Hey, Toby!"

But Toby was in a daze, pounding the door over and over again as if he was possessed.

James crept up the steps behind Kevin and yelled, "GET THE FUCK AWAY FROM MY DOOR!"

"What the fuck you doing?" Rage turned Kevin's face upside down.

James had done some cold-blooded shit, and now Kevin stood knee-deep in the pile of crap right along with him.

Toby spun around, his face full of hatred as he pumped a bullet in the chamber of the shotgun. James shot his pistol and missed.

"Ah, shit," Kevin growled as Toby shot toward the stairwell, lodging the bullet inside the mortar of the brick wall inches away from Kevin's head. Kevin pulled Tuffy's gun from his pants. He tried to shoot, but the gun jammed. James fired again, casting a bullet in Toby's shoulder.

"Argh!" Toby screamed, leaving a trail of blood down Felicia's door as he slid to the floor. Kevin pulled the gun's slide to the rear, clearing the jam while Toby struggled to his feet and scrambled to the top level, pumping another bullet into the shotgun.

Chaos broke out. Bullets ricocheted all over the building.

"Open the door! Open the door!" Toby yelled frantically, banging on every apartment door.

"What the hell is going…"

"Let me in! Let me in!" Toby screamed to the neighbor as he forced his way inside the apartment. Kevin and James fired as Toby disappeared behind the door.

Sirens echoed off in the distance. Blood spilled from underneath the apartment door.

"Shit! C'mon!" Kevin said. He and James took off down the steps and out the building. "Man, we gotta split up. Hop in the car and get the fuck outta here 'fore they get here," Kevin ordered.

"Man, that shit stolen! How the fuck I'ma leave in a stolen car?"

"I don't know, man, but go some fuckin' where!"

Scrambling around to the back of the building, Kevin grabbed the metal rails and pulled himself back up to Felicia's balcony.

"What happened, man? What happened?" Tuffy hopped around nervously.

"Man, that piece-of-shit gun jammed. Where the fuck is Felicia?"

As if on cue, Felicia pounced from the back, a sea of tears flowing down her face as she screamed into the phone.

"Shit," Kevin said, noticing the gunpowder burns on his hands. He rushed to the kitchen and dunked his hands in the sudsy hot water he'd prepared for the bottles. "Felicia, who the fuck you talkin' to?"

"It's the police!"

Water flew all over the kitchen as Kevin yanked his hands from the sink and snatched the phone from Felicia.

"What the fuck is wrong wit' you?" he screamed in her face. He slammed the cordless phone to the ground, shattering it to pieces. "Why you ain't call those muthafuckas last night?"

"I heard the gunshots. I didn't know what else to do. I ain't know if you got shot."

*Shit!* Kevin thought. The situation was getting out of control.

"Here. One of y'all do something with this," Kevin ordered, passing Tuffy's gun to her.

She scanned the room and hid the gun inside the baby's diaper bag. Just then, mayhem broke out in the hallway.

"Shit, man," Tuffy said, nervously pacing back and forth. "What we 'pose to do?"

"Man, just calm the fuck down," Kevin ordered.

There was a tap at the door.

"Oh my God," Felicia cried.

"What the fuck I tell you," Kevin mumbled through gritted teeth. Heading to the door, he roared like a lion, "Who is it?"

"It's the police. There's been a homicide, and we need to ask you some questions."

*Ah, shit. Toby died,* Kevin thought as a horn blew outside. *And there go my fuckin' cab.*

# Chapter Eleven

*I*solated in a room with Sergeant Young, Kevin's eyes darted back and forth between both two-way mirrors, watching Felicia's and Tuffy's interrogations.

An hour into the questioning, Sergeant Young and his detectives called the local greasy spoon and placed an order for carryout. Kevin was starving; his mouth watered as he watched Sergeant Young chop away at a steak-and-cheese sandwich loaded with everything. He tried to make a meal from the aromas floating in the air, but it wasn't working. The smell of onions surged into his nostrils, but all Kevin could taste was the remnants of the alcohol he'd poured into his system at the club.

"Hey!" Kevin squirmed restlessly in his chair. "Ain't I entitled to a phone call or something?" he asked, just as an officer dressed in a crisp white shirt decorated with what seemed like a gazillion ribbons strolled into the room.

"Hey, Lieutenant Goldstein," Sergeant Young said, chewing on the plastic straw from his fountain soda. "You're just in time. Mr. Kennard here is asking for a phone call." He pulled the straw from his mouth and let out a loud, foul-smelling belch.

*This stinky-ass muthafucka,* Kevin thought.

Lieutenant Goldstein plunked his chubby butt on the table, causing it to squeak from his heaviness. "Did Mr. Kennard write his statement?"

"He says he doesn't have anything to write because he doesn't know anything. He went to the club last night, and now the poor baby has a hangover."

Lieutenant Goldstein looked at Kevin. "Did you have fun at the club last night, Mr. Kennard?"

Slumped in the metal folding chair, Kevin dropped his head in his hands.

"Where'd you go after the club?" he continued to question.

"Look," Kevin sprang up, "y'all have had me in here for hours. I'm starving, I'm tired, and my head is banging. All I wanna do is use the phone."

"Mr. Kennard, you can do whatever you want," the lieutenant informed. "You aren't under arrest yet." He glanced toward the two-way mirrors. "Sergeant Young, turn the mic on so I can hear what's going on. Looks like Mr. Kennard's girlfriend is getting a little antsy."

Through the two-way mirror, Kevin heard Felicia cry, "Fuck dis shit! Where's Kevin?"

Lieutenant Goldstein turned to Kevin with a raised brow and said, "Seems like you might want to write a statement before she breaks."

"How I'ma write a statement if I don't know nothing?" Kevin stood from his chair and headed toward the door. "And since you just said I wasn't under arrest, I guess that means I can go."

Sergeant Young tossed his straw to the floor, leaped from his chair, and hurried to block Kevin's exit.

"Lieutenant, we can't let him go!" he said. "Have you seen this clown's criminal record? And he was in the apartment where the shit started!"

"Then charge him with something," Lieutenant Goldstein demanded.

Sergeant Young sighed. He didn't have enough evidence to charge Kevin with anything.

"We can't hold him on your suspicions," Lieutenant Goldstein added.

Kevin stood face-to-face with Sergeant Young, unable to conceal his victory smirk. "Excuse me, sir."

"Shit! I'm telling you, Lieutenant," Sergeant Young said as he stepped out of Kevin's way. "He had something to do with it."

● ● ●

*Damn, where the fuck is a payphone?* Kevin thought, rushing out of the precinct. He had to call his mother. *Shit, where the fuck is a phone?*

Kevin was ready to break as he turned the corner of the old brick building. He needed to put some distance between him and the police station as soon as possible. As he released a sigh of relief, a convoy of police cars approached, their sirens screaming as they screeched to a halt.

"Freeze, muthafucka!" The policemen jumped from their cruisers with their guns drawn. "Put your hands above your head."

Kevin obeyed and inched his hands in the air. Two officers rushed up and threw him against the building.

"Damn, man," Kevin said. His lips scraped the bricks as

they nearly pulled his arms from their sockets to smack on the cuffs. "What the fuck y'all doing?" he yelled as they ushered him back inside the station. "Man, I'm telling you. The lieutenant just told me I could go."

"Only place you're going is jail."

The officer opened the door to a smaller interrogation room and shoved Kevin inside.

"Take a seat," he ordered

Kevin squirmed nervously in the folding chair, trying to figure out what the hell had gone wrong in a matter of minutes. He'd just been released.

*Felicia's ass musta fuckin' broke,* he thought as he glanced in the two-way mirror, but his assumption was wrong.

"Get the fuck outta here," Kevin gasped.

James sat on the other side of the mirror, handcuffed to the table. Blood oozed from his busted lip, and the swollen knot above his brow weighed down his eyelid. Positioned in the middle of the table like a freshly bloomed bouquet was the diaper bag where Felicia had hidden Tuffy's gun.

"Mr. Kennard," the lieutenant beamed, greeting Kevin as if they were long-lost friends. "No sooner than I let you go, my guys walked in with Mr. Harris," he said, patting Kevin lightly on the shoulder.

Sergeant Young strutted in behind the lieutenant, grinning the way Kevin had when he'd left.

"So? What does you finding him have to do with me?" Kevin asked.

"Nothing yet." Lieutenant Goldstein straddled a chair and turned to face the mirror. "But we're running prints on the gun that somebody shoved in the diaper bag. We believe that may be the murder weapon." Turning his attention back to Kevin, he said, "And you were in the apartment where the potential murder weapon was found."

Lieutenant Goldstein's pager started chirping. He snatched the pager from his belt and dismounted the chair. "Great. It's the fucking captain. This shit is all over the gotdamn news," he said, storming from the room.

Sergeant Young sat at the table with his face buried inside a file, studying documents. A few moments later, Lieutenant Goldstein reentered the room, slamming the door.

"This is fucking nonsense. The captain's screaming down my ass. Sergeant Young, you or one of your detectives better beat a confession out of that piece of shit," he screamed, pointing at James through the two-way mirror. "Hell, come up with some trumped-up charges if you have to. I don't care how you do it, but I want a confession!"

"Hold up," Kevin protested. "Y'all can't do that shit. That's against his constitutional rights."

"Constitutional rights?" Lieutenant Goldstein frowned, as if Kevin's words gave him heartburn. "What about the victim's rights? I have a grieving family to deal with, thanks to your little game of Cowboys and Indians."

"Sergeant Young," Lieutenant Goldstein yelled, shifting his attention from Kevin. "Go in there and get a confession outta that son of a bitch, or your entire detective team will be writing parking tickets tomorrow."

"Hold up, Lieutenant. I may have something." Sergeant Young closed the file. "I pulled up some information on our men, Mr. Kennard and Mr. James Harris, our guest of honor in the other room. Seems like we should refer to James as Jesse James. According to his file, he gets a kick outta robbing people at gunpoint. The bastard damn sure didn't finish school."

Sergeant Young chuckled. "You should read some of the statements his dumb ass tried to write. My German Shepherd can spell better than him."

"Hey." A plainclothes detective walked into the room and handed the lieutenant a piece of paper. "I think you guys can use this."

"What's this?"

"It's Toby Lucille's written statement. I just left the hospital. He admits that he was looking for Mr. Harris. He claims Harris robbed him last night for five thousand dollars."

"Excellent work, Detective. Now we're getting somewhere." Lieutenant Goldstein passed the statement to Sergeant Young.

*Toby?* Kevin thought. *I thought Toby was dead.*

"Seems like Jesse James was up to his favorite pastime," Sergeant Young said, scanning the statement. "But how are you involved in all this?" he said, eyeing Kevin.

"I'm not. That's what I've been trying to tell you."

"Oh, no," Sergeant Young chuckled wickedly, "you're involved."

"Well, why don't you figure out how so we can arrest one of these bastards for killing the old man!" Lieutenant Goldstein said.

"Old man?" Kevin questioned with a dumbfounded look. "What old man?"

Lieutenant Goldstein pulled a small tablet from his back pocket. "As if you care," he said more so to himself as he flipped through the pages in the tablet. "Curtis Johnson."

Kevin gasped as if God himself had sucked the wind out of him.

"The old man was visiting his sister for the weekend. He

heard a ruckus in the hallway, opened the door, and one of you fools shot him."

*Oh my God,* Kevin trembled, horrified. *Oh my God,* he repeated in his head, ready to fall to pieces.

"Hold on, Lieutenant. Mr. Kennard just gave me an idea." Sergeant Young shoved Toby's statement inside James's file and walked to the door. "Jesse James probably thinks Mr. Lucille died, too. This case is as good as solved." Sergeant Young winked at Kevin as he headed out the door.

"Bases are loaded, Sergeant Young. The victim's family and I are counting on you to bring 'em all home."

"Lieutenant," Kevin uttered softly, "what was the victim's name again?"

"Kennard, if I didn't know any better, I would think that you actually gave a shit," the lieutenant said, shaking his head as he glared down at his pad. "Mr. Curtis Johnson. Poor old man didn't even live there. He was visiting from a nursing home."

● ● ●

Sergeant Young entered the interrogation room where James sat bloodied and bruised. "Okay, guys. That's enough. What you trying to do, kill the man? Shit," he said, looking at James with phony compassion.

Digging deep inside his pants pockets, Sergeant Young passed one of the detectives a dollar bill.

"Leave us alone and get the man a soda and something to clean his face with," he said as he made himself comfortable in one of the metal folding chairs.

Sergeant Young pulled a pack of cigarettes from inside his suit jacket as his detectives left the room. Tapping the pack against his fingers, he offered one to James.

"Naw, man," James said, declining the smoke.

"You don't mind if I indulge, do you?"

James offered Sergeant Young an empty-headed gaze.

"Umm…you don't mind if I smoke, do you?" he rephrased.

"That's all you had to say," James mumbled. "Smoke your fuckin' smokes, man. You don't need my permission."

"You're right. I don't." Sergeant Young flicked his lighter and brought the tobacco stick to life. Taking a long drag, he filled the small room with smoke and tossed the pack on the table.

"Hey, I'm sorry 'bout your face. I woulda rescued you sooner, but I was over there listening to your boy. He's singing like Luther Vandross. I was getting ready to offer him a recording contract."

James sucked his teeth. "Who the hell you talkin' 'bout?"

"Kevin Kennard. Ain't that your boy?"

"Ah, here we go with this shit." James threw his head back in frustration.

One of the detectives entered the room, placed a soda and a wet paper towel on the table, and left.

"Look, I know you guys have some kinda gangster code of conduct that you're supposed to abide by, but your boy, Kennard, ain't following the rules today. He's singing like a bird."

"Yeah, man, whatever. Pop that soda for me."

Sergeant Young opened the can and passed the soda to James's free hand.

"Listen, Kennard knows that first-degree murder carries a life sentence, so he wrote his statement. He's been to the big house once, and believe me, he's not trying to go again." Sergeant Young opened the file and pulled out Toby's statement.

"And it actually makes perfect sense," he said, pretending to read the statement. "Let's see. Kennard went to the club; while he was gone, you robbed the deceased for five thousand dollars."

James coughed, choking on the soda.

"Mmm," Sergeant Young sighed for effect. "Mr. Lucille came to your apartment to retaliate, shots were fired, and wah-lah! We have a murder."

"Man," James struggled, trying to clear his throat, "that's some bullshit."

"Here, read the statement for yourself." Sergeant Young extended the statement out to James, knowing damn well he wouldn't be able to decipher a single word.

"Naw, I ain't gotta read that shit."

Sergeant Young placed Toby's statement back in the file. "I don't believe this snitchin'ass muthafucka," James mumbled. "I'm sittin' in this bitch getting fucked up, and he squealing like a pig."

"Yep. We believe we already have the murder weapon, too. We found it in the diaper bag."

"Well, dust that muthafucka for prints, 'cause everythin' that bitch nigga said is some bullshit, and that gun damn sure ain't mine."

Sergeant Young leaned back in his chair and crossed his legs. "Well, whose gun is it then? Kennard's?"

"Yeah, that muthafucka's his! He wanna be a fuckin' snitch, do he?"

"So Mr. Kennard was involved?"

"Fuck yeah, his ass was involved. I ain't even gon' sit here and act like I ain't do shit. Yeah, that nigga was looking for me. Shit, he was fuckin' beatin' down my door. I had to defend my household," James ranted. "We exchanged some ammo, but that bitch nigga Kevin was in the shit, too. That's his muthafuckin' gun in the diaper bag. You don't believe me? Then dust that bitch for prints like I said."

Sergeant Young slid a blank statement sheet toward James. "Will you put it in writing?"

James frowned at the piece of paper. "Man, I ain't no fuckin' writer. You write that shit, and I'll sign the muthafucka!"

"No problem, Mr. Harris." Sergeant Young winked toward the two-way mirror. "No problem at all."

• • •

During the three-month trial proceedings, ballistic testing proved that the bullet from Kevin's gun did in fact kill Mr. Curtis Johnson. Every night during the court proceedings, Kevin begged God for a heart attack, a stroke, or any other element that could take him out. He wanted to trade places with Mr. Johnson. He couldn't eat, and the nights when slumber finally caught up with him, his dreams were all of Mr. Johnson drowning in a pool of blood.

The day of sentencing came. Kevin hoped the judge would leave him behind bars forever or award him the death penalty. But Fat Ed got Kevin one of the best attorneys around. First-degree murder was tossed out the window, along with the death penalty and life behind bars.

"Mr. Kennard," the judge began, "for count one, second-degree murder, I hereby sentence you to thirty years. For counts two and three, possession of a handgun and reckless endangerment, I sentence you to the mandatory sentence of five years each. According to the criminal file I have before me, Mr. Kennard, you've been headed down the road of destruction for some time now. I hope you realize you're getting off better than your victim. Good luck through your incarceration, Mr. Kennard. This court stands adjourned."

● ● ●

Simone stumbled through the door exhausted. Three months ago, she'd not only passed the civil service test, but she'd secured a full-time position in the government.

"Hey," Thomas greeted from the living room couch. "You look tired as hell. How was work?"

"It was work," Simone said as the phone rang.

"Hello," he answered. Frowning, he placed the phone back in its cradle.

"Who was that?" Simone asked.

"I don't know. You know somebody in jail?" he asked, his voice pierced with concern.

"Huh?"

"That's the second time today somebody has called here from prison."

"Naw," Simone said as she headed back to her room. "Check with Stan. It may be one of his friends."

## Chapter Twelve
## Beginning of January, 1989

Simone caught a glimpse of her reflection in the mirror of the ladies' room. *Man, I look a mess*, she thought. Her raccoon eyes screamed sleep deprivation, while the puffy bags told a tale of many tearful nights, thanks to Kevin's deceit and her predicament. The clock was ticking. However, once the baby had started moving, Simone couldn't follow through with the abortion.

*At least no one can tell yet*, she thought as she turned to check her reflection sideways. *I got a lil' stomach, but not enough for anybody to think I'm pregnant.*

Pulling up the oversized sweater she'd borrowed from Lavon, Simone retied the makeshift shoestring belt around her corduroys. She hadn't bought any maternity clothes and hadn't planned on it. The one thing she desperately needed to do was schedule a prenatal visit.

Simone pulled the sweater down as the bathroom door squealed open. A slender white woman dressed in a crisp Army uniform walked over to the dated peach-colored sink next to Simone.

"Hi." She smiled, turning on the faucet.

"Hi," Simone responded, smiling back as she checked herself in the mirror one last time, making sure the oversized sweater covered the opening in her bogus maternity pants. As she turned to head toward the door, a slight gush of liquid escaped her, soaking the lining of her underwear.

*What the hell was that?* she wondered as she stood frozen in the middle of the floor.

The woman looked at Simone cockeyed and asked, "You okay?"

"Yeah...I'm fine." Simone forced a smiled, but to herself she screamed, *Ugh! I need to line my underwear with some tissue.* She took a step toward the bathroom stall, and it happened again. Another gush, larger than before, drenched her down to her shoes.

"Oh my God," Simone said, looking down at her two-toned pants.

"Honey, what's..." The woman noticed Simone's wet clothing and the small puddle of fluid on the floor.

"I'm pregnant," Simone mumbled, "and I think my water broke."

• • •

The next day, tears dropped down Simone's face as she sat in a wheelchair staring helplessly into the incubator, watching her daughter cling to life. Barely two pounds, her tiny body rested, engulfed in the midst of a preemie-sized diaper.

"You think she'll live?" she asked the neonatal pediatrician.

"Well, twenty-seven weeks is really early. We'll just have to wait and see. All I can say is keep praying." The doctor placed his hand on Simone's shoulder. "Have you thought about a name?"

"Yeah," Simone said somberly. "Jordan."

"Jordan…hmm," the doctor said, as if he were allowing the name to marinate. "That's nice. It sounds rich. Any special reason?"

"Yeah," Simone mumbled, staring at her daughter like a zombie. "When my water broke, the sudden gush kinda reminded me of a river. And the Jordan River is biblical. It's where Jesus was baptized. So…" she shrugged her shoulders and stared up at the doctor to see if he thought her logic made sense. "I don't know. I guess I'm hoping that since so many others got saved at the Jordan River, maybe God will save my baby, too."

"I'm sure he will, Ms. Woodard." The doctor squeezed Simone's shoulder. "I'm sure he will."

● ● ●

As hard as she tried, Simone couldn't keep her eyes off of the empty chair in the corner of her hospital room. *I guess that's supposed to be for Kevin.* The mere thought of his absence sent the tears that she'd been fighting to maintain back down her face. She missed him. His voice, his touch, his kiss, and most importantly, his love—however fake it may have been. Her heart wanted to believe the love they had shared was authentic, but her mind muzzled her heart. They'd been apart for months, and Kevin hadn't made a single attempt to call her.

Laughter and baby wails filled the maternity ward. Looking down at the phone, Simone wondered if she should even call him to share the news, but a male voice disrupted her thoughts.

"Hey."

"Uh-oh," Simone mumbled, wiping away her tears with the

back of her hands.

"Uh-oh, nothing," Thomas said, approaching the side of Simone's bed and shaking his head. "My nineteen-year-old daughter in the gotdamn hospital having a baby. Why didn't you tell me you were pregnant, Simone?"

"I don't know. I knew you'd be disappointed."

"Simone, you're supposed to be able to tell me anything. I thought I knew you better than that. How in the world you end up pregnant anyway? I thought you were smarter than that. Why didn't you use protection?"

Stan walked in. "Where's the little monkey at?" he asked.

Thankful for the distraction, Simone said, "I'll take you to the nursery."

"Naw, keep your butt in bed," Thomas ordered. "I'll get a nurse to show us where she is."

Thomas and Stan were gone barely ten minutes before they strolled back into Simone's room. Worry lines were etched across Thomas's forehead.

"Granddaddy over here couldn't even look at her. Simone, tell him she gon' be okay," Stan said.

"They don't know yet. They won't know for a couple of days."

"I ain't never in my life seen a baby that small," Thomas said, barely above a whisper. "I mean, damn. That little pamper is twice her size."

"How'd you find out I was here?"

"You ain't come home last night, so I called you at work to make sure you were okay and your supervisor told me."

"Surprise," Simone whispered.

"Surprise, my ass," Thomas said, with more bark than bite. "So where the hell is the father?" He looked around the room as if Kevin were hiding. "Is it that red guy I met at your apartment? What's his name?"

"Kevin...Kevin Kennard."

"KEVIN KENNARD!" Stan was stunned. "Kevin Kennard is your baby's father?"

"Why you say it like that?" Thomas asked, looking at Stan.

"Simone knows why I'm saying it like that!"

"What, Big Bob told you about the incident?" Simone asked.

"Naw. What incident?" Stan asked.

"I know one damn thing," Thomas said. "His ass got my daughter pregnant, so he better be 'round here some damn where."

"He don't know I had her, Daddy. I was getting ready to call him when y'all walked in."

Stan sucked his teeth and rolled his eyes. "How you gon' call him?"

"Duh, stupid! How you think? I'ma pick up the phone and dial his number. How else would I call?"

"Oh, and what, the prison guards gon' take him the phone? He got it like that?"

"Prison guards!" Thomas and Simone both replied in shock.

"Stan, what you talking about?" Simone asked.

"You don't know?"

"Know what?" Simone's anger at Kevin turned to worry.

"Girl, Kevin locked up. He's been locked up a few months now."

"What?"

"A friend of mine introduced me to his god-brother, Ed. You know him?"

"Yeah, I met him once or twice when he brought Kevin

home."

"Well, me and him tryna open up a recording studio. We had to hold off for a second 'cause Ed was going back and forth to the trial. He paid all the attorney fees and everything."

"Ain't this some prime-time bullshit. So he's the one who been calling the house from jail," Thomas mumbled, shaking his head. "What the hell he locked up for?" His look of disappointment was back.

"Murder. He got like forty years, too. So you," Stan said to Simone, "won't be getting no child support."

• • •

"Simone!" Thomas rushed down the hallway two weeks later. "Here," he said, nearly throwing her the cordless phone. "It's the hospital!"

"Hello."

"Hi, Ms. Woodard, this is Dr. Mason of the neonatal intensive care unit. Umm…I'm going to need you to come to the hospital right away. Unfortunately," he sighed, "we need to operate on your daughter's heart."

"Oh my God," Simone gasped, slapping her hand over her mouth. "What's wrong with her heart?"

"Oh, Lord." Thomas stood listening outside Simone's bedroom door. For the last two weeks, the house had frozen every time the phone rang, for fear of the worse from the hospital. Jordan was nowhere near out of the woods.

"Well, to sum it up in layman's terms, blood is flowing into your daughter's lungs from an opened vessel that hasn't closed, which isn't uncommon with premature babies. We've been administering medicine to help the vessel mature, but it isn't working the way we'd like. And unfortunately, if we allow the blood to continue to flow into her lungs… Well, let's just say we don't want that to happen. So, we need your consent to perform the surgery. Ms. Woodard? Are you there?"

"I'm sorry," Thomas said to the doctor, taking the phone from Simone as she sat on the bed and cried helplessly. There was nothing she could do for her tiny baby. She figured God was trying to punish her for wanting to abort his gift. "We'll be there shortly."

Simone and Thomas rushed into NICU. The hospital cardiologist was standing over Jordan's incubator, documenting her file.

"Ms. Woodard, after examining your daughter, it appears the medicine is working, just not as fast as we'd like. For now, I've simply instructed the staff to increase the medication. Its unhurried velocity is a lot safer than the surgery. So, let's all pray the medicine does the trick."

Over the weeks, the frantic phone calls died down and Jordan finally began to progress the way the doctors wanted. Three months from the date of her premature birth, she finally weighed enough to come home.

*Is this going to be too big?* Simone held up the designer jumper she'd purchased for Jordan to wear home from the hospital. *I better take a sleeper just in case,* she thought as the phone rang.

"You haven't left yet?" Angela asked.

"I'm packing her bag. I'll be leaving in a few minutes."

"I know you went out and bought her a whole bunch of unnecessary stuff. All she needs now are sleepers."

"Sleepers are pajamas, and she's not wearing pajamas every day."

"Why not? She ain't going anywhere. She can't run the streets with you. She's a premature baby, remember?"

*Oh, goodness. Here we go,* Simone thought. "First of all, I don't run the streets," she said, irritated. "The only place I go is to Lavon's house, and I won't be doing a whole lot of that during the week. I've talked to Ms. Kennard a few times. She said since Kevin's not around, she has to play a double role. So, she wants Jordan on the weekends."

"Mmm, hmm. You ready to dump the poor child off already."

*Lord have mercy,* Simone thought. "Ms. Kennard is Jordan's grandmother. What's wrong with her going over there?"

"And just where do you think Ms. Kennard's going to take her? To the germ-infested prison."

Simone sighed. "Look, I have to go. I gotta take a CPR class before I can bring her home."

"I hope you took some more time off."

"Just the next three days. I don't have any more leave. I'm already taking the rest of the week off without pay."

"Well, who's going to watch her when you go back to work?"

"This lady named Ms. Alice. She's Big Bob's mother."

"A stranger?"

"She's not a stranger. Besides, it's not like I had any other option."

"Why can't you bring her to me? I'm sitting here retired, doing nothing. After all, I'm her grandmother, too."

"How am I supposed to get her to you? I don't have a car, and Ms. Alice is only a few buildings away."

"Just ask your daddy if you can use his van," Angela suggested. "You know he'll let you, especially if it's for his granddaughter."

"He might, but what about your husband?"

"I assumed I was going to be watching her, so I already told him. He didn't say anything," Angela said. "Besides, it's not like you have to come in. All you have to do is pull up outside, and me or Alicia will come out and get her."

"Huh!" Simone chuckled sarcastically. *For that reason alone, I shouldn't bring her.* Simone hadn't stepped a foot in their house since she'd whacked Ricardo upside his head with the ashtray. "If I'm not welcomed, how's my child welcomed? She's part of me."

"Jordan's an innocent little baby. Plus, Ricardo won't be watching her; I will."

Simone zipped up Jordan's diaper bag and tossed it on her shoulder. "We'll see. Meanwhile, I have to go. I'll call you when we get back."

● ● ●

Thomas smiled as he watched Simone sit on the bed, cradling her baby in her arms. "Make sure you call Ms. Alice and let her know Jordan's home."

"Oh, I'm glad you brought that up. My mother said she'll watch her."

"How you gon' get her there?"

"I was hoping you'd let me use your van."

"I don't mind you using the van, but you gotta drop her off early in the morning. I gotta be at work by seven-thirty."

Ugh," Simone said, immediately having second thoughts. "That means I gotta leave here by six o'clock, which means I gotta get up at five. Hmm." Simone looked down at Jordan. "I wouldn't have to drop her off to Ms. Alice until seven-thirty."

"Just let me know what you wanna do."

## Chapter Thirteen
## Early Spring 1989

Kevin sat behind the colorless cinder blocks, ducking and dodging life. The news of Jordan had fluttered his heart, but the rhythm subsided that night when sleep finally tackled him, sending him on another horrific journey.

Night after night, Kevin dreamt he was running through a dark wooded area filled with bloody bodies. Some were dead, and the others used the little life left in them to squirm along the ground, reaching out to Kevin for help. Men screamed, babies cried, women hovered over the bodies of their loved ones in a state of desperation, and the leaves of the huge oak trees were all drenched in blood. Petrified, Kevin ran, leaping over bodies. He saw Lil' Bits missing half his face. James was there, too, lying on the ground. Kevin couldn't tell if he was asleep or dead, and he didn't care. Something was after him, and he didn't know what it was. A faint light glistened off in the distance through the thickness of the trees. Night after night, Kevin sprinted toward it. Inches away from the light, he'd wake, panting profusely, soaked in sweat.

The first few months of Kevin's incarceration, Felicia wrote letters that Kevin mailed back to her unopened. Every chance she got, she made her way to the jail on visiting day in hopes of seeing him. However, each and every time, Kevin turned her away. The only visit he welcomed was his mother's and Simone's, but he knew the chances of Simone coming were slim to none.

• • •

"Look, Officer, how does this work?" Felicia asked, determined to see Kevin. "You call upstairs to another guard and that guard tells the inmate he has a visit?"

"Yes, ma'am."

"Okay, well, I've been coming up here for months now, and the person I'm tryin' to see won't come down." Felicia glanced over her shoulder. There was no one else in line. Surveying the guard's station, she didn't see any video cameras, but she knew to be discreet nonetheless. "Here's my license," she said with a raised brow. Two crisp hundred-dollar bills were taped to the back. "You need that in order for the inmate to come down, right?"

"I sure do, ma'am." A smile cracked the officer's solemn expression. "Have a seat. He'll be down," he assured.

Ten minutes later, Felicia walked through the metal detector on the verge of tears. Finally, she was going to lay eyes on the person her mind labeled her hero and her heart labeled her love.

With emotions running wild, Felicia spotted Kevin sitting in a booth behind the glass. He was fuming as he glared at her, but his angered look didn't faze her in the least. She was happy just to see his handsome face. She squeezed inside the booth.

"You can't take a hint?" Kevin asked the minute she picked

up the phone. He'd realized months ago that he couldn't blame Felicia or anybody else for what had transpired. It had been his choice to respond to her frantic phone call and his bullet that had killed Mr. Johnson. But still…

"I know," she whispered softly into the phone, "but I had to see you. I feel like it's all my fault that…"

"Hey, hold up," Kevin cut her off. "If you came down here to clear your conscience, then consider it cleared. We done now?" He slid his chair back, ready to leave.

"No, Kevin, that's not why I came." Felicia's eyes pleaded with him. "You didn't have to come, but you did. You saved me and my baby's life, and I love you for that. I owe you my life."

"You don't owe me nothing."

"Yes, I do. You know," she said, avoiding Kevin's eye contact, "all those times when I tried to pull up on you…I mean, I acted like I was playing, but deep down inside I've always had this thing for you. Shit, what bitch 'round the way didn't?" Felicia chuckled as she wiped away her tears. "I never said anything, 'cause, you know…you and James was boys…but since that day, I haven't been able to shake you. You on my mind all day. You my hero, man. That's why I'ma try and come every visiting day. That's why I write you three, four times a week. I love you, Kevin."

"Felicia, I don't wanna be your hero. A good man died over some bullshit."

"I know, Kevin. But I just want you to know that whatever you need, I got it, and if I don't got it, then I'll get it. I'm here for you. I'm down for the long haul. I'ma ride that forty with you, and when your forty is up, I'm here. You won't even have to go out and look for nobody. No matter where I am or who I'm with, you'll always come first."

After Felicia's visit, Kevin followed a handful of inmates from the visiting room to the recreation hall. He stopped at his locker to grab the letter he'd been trying to write to Simone. Since the birth of their daughter, he tried hard to take dictation from his heart in hopes of composing a letter that would not only express his deepest apology for the incident with Rhonda, but a letter that would also testify on behalf of his unwavering love. Yet, the more he scribbled pages of nothing, the more his mind screamed *why bother?* Months had already passed. Today, however, Kevin was determined to get beyond 'Dear Simone.' Slamming his locker shut, he planted himself at an isolated table in the recreation hall, hoping his mind wouldn't intimidate his heart once again.

Dale sat at a neighboring table, shuffling a deck of cards with his personal bodyguard, Brown, nicknamed Kong by the guards because of his massive physique and slate complexion. Sentenced to five years for armed robbery, Dale, a fragile little white boy who probably didn't weigh more than one hundred pounds soaking wet, had spent the first three days of his incarceration fighting off the booty bandits who preyed on petite men like him. He ducked and dodged, bobbed and weaved, until finally his fight was gone. Seconds away from penetration, Kong stepped in and beat the shit out of everybody with an erection.

Dale hid in the midst of Kong's shadow, and before the week was out, he'd moved into Kong's cell. Just when he'd thought all was kosher, Kong shared that his protection wasn't without cost. In exchange for security, Dale spit-shined Kong's knob on a regular basis. Dale didn't have to worry about Kong wanting the ass. Kong loved women and had no desire to plunge inside anything unauthentic. A blow job was all he needed, and since it kept the booty bandits out of Dale's britches, he was happy to oblige.

"Hey, man," Dale called out to Kevin. "The ladies be lovin' your ass. My girl had her girlfriend with her, and good Lord! That chick had a fuckin' fit when she saw you. Was that your girl up on the visit?"

"Naw, man, that wasn't my girl," Kevin said without looking up from his letter.

Dealing the cards, Dale chuckled. "I didn't think she was your type. The chick my girl had wit' her is mixed. Man, she had a big ol' phat ass, too. If you want, I can hook you up."

"Just tell her to write me," Kevin said. He wasn't in the mood for socializing.

"Damn, man," Dale continued, oblivious to Kevin's subtle hint. "You really into reading and writing, huh? Every time I see you, your face is buried in some paper. You pretty good with letters?"

"I'm a'ight," Kevin huffed. "I mean, shit, I can spell."

Dale laid his cards on the table and slid his chair closer to Kevin. "Then you one up on half the muthafuckas in here. You know," he whispered, nearly in Kevin's face. "Me and half the dudes in here can't read or write worth a damn. You think you can hook my letters up to my girl? Hell, Kong," Dale said, inviting Kong into the conversation. "He could write your letters to Momma Bear. Shit, Kevin. Writing letters could be your lil' hustle."

Kevin finally looked up. Dale was onto something. The money was pouring into his prison account from Fat Ed, Felicia, and everybody else who felt sorry for him at the moment. But as time ticked on, the donations would fade, and the last thing Kevin wanted to do was be a financial burden to his mother.

Not on top of everything else.

"What about poems, man? Can you write some 'roses are red, violets are blue' type of shit?" Dale asked.

The extent of Kevin's poetic talents had been the little notes he'd left around the apartment for Simone. Motivated by love, the words had flowed so effortlessly.

"I can probably hook somethin' up. We can work somethin' out," Kevin said with a shrug of his shoulder. "Just give me your girl's—" Kevin caught Kong glaring at him and shot him a fierce look. "What's up, man?"

"Ah," Kong said to Dale with a voice as deep as Barry White's. "Don't he look like that nigga Dirty James be talkin' 'bout?"

Dale gave Kevin an once-over. "Yeah, he do. You know some dirty, beady-headed dude named James? He use to work in the kitchen wit' us. What the fuck is dude's last name?"

"Harris," Kong belted.

"Yeah, Harris. You know that dude, man?"

Kevin knew he and James were housed in the same prison. They'd run into each other a few times without incident or love. The Department of Corrections had made a mistake. Codefendants in a trial weren't supposed to be housed in the same penitentiary.

"Why, what's up?" Kevin asked, avoiding the question.

"Naw, I don't know if dude tryna build a rep or what, but he runnin' 'round telling people he set up his codefendant, some hazel-eyed dude."

"What?"

"Yeah. You know him?" Kong asked.

"Yeah, I know him. What the fuck y'all mean he set me up?"

"Damn, man. Dude braggin' he had you robbed for two grand, and on top of that shit, you got forty years helping him with his shit and he ain't get but ten."

Kevin remembered the assailants' words the night he was robbed of the rent money. *We been watching your ass.* The robbery was when Kevin's life had gone to hell. Had the rent been paid, there wouldn't have been an incident with Rhonda or a shootout at Felicia's. No one knew where Simone lived, and no one had her number. Beatrice didn't even have it. When she needed Kevin, she simply knocked on Simone's door. And now as Kevin recalled the ordeal, he remembered Tuffy saying that James had been robbing people. But never did he think James would rob him or set him up to be robbed. They'd been best friends since elementary school. It all made sense, though. At that very second, Kevin realized he could be holding Simone and his daughter. More importantly, Mr. Johnson would still be alive.

"That bitch-ass muthafucka!" Kevin was furious.

"Man, look…" Kong surveyed the room. "You hook our letters up, and I'll take care of that bitch. I don't like that little nigga anyway. He talks too fuckin' much."

Kevin was steaming. "Naw, I got that shit myself."

"SHOWER!" the guard yelled into the recreation hall.

"Good." Kong looked over at Dale. "Look." He pointed down to the hardness in his sweatpants. "Let's hit the cell first."

"Shit," Dale mumbled, shaking his head.

*These gay-ass muthafuckas*, Kevin thought, thankful he'd showered that morning.

"Hey, man," Dale whispered, shrugging his shoulders as if he'd read Kevin's thoughts. "It could be worse."

# Chapter Fourteen

Thomas's van wasn't parked in its normal parking space. *Good,* Simone thought. Exhausted, all she wanted to do was lie across her bed and steal a few winks. No matter how hard she tried, she couldn't get Jordan to sleep all night. At seven months, Jordan still woke up all hours of the night. She wasn't wet or hungry, just fussy. By the time Simone got her back to sleep, the sun's rays were creeping over the horizon and it was time for Simone to get up. Hitting the snooze button on her alarm clock wasn't an option. Thomas needed his van to get to work, and Simone still had to catch a bus.

Inside the apartment, Simone headed straight to her room. Fully dressed in her work clothes, she lay across the bed and was asleep in no time.

A few hours later, the ringing phone disrupted Simone's sleep. Stretching the kinks from her weary limbs, she switched on the light to illuminate her dark room.

*Damn, what time is it?* she thought. It was after eight. She'd been asleep for hours, and to her surprise, she was still home alone, which was rare. As the phone rang for a third time, Simone snatched it up.

"Where have you been?" Angela questioned, without a hint of a salutation. "I've been calling you all night. Do you know what time it is?"

"I fell asleep," Simone mumbled through her yawn. "And my father's—"

"Simone, it's after eight! How come you haven't picked up your daughter?"

"My goodness. I was trying to tell you that my father's not here, and I don't have a car, remember?"

"So what am I supposed to do?" Angela asked. "Wait all night?"

Simone sucked her teeth. "You act like I didn't come to get her on purpose. I told you my father's not here, but the minute he walks through the door, I'll be sure to run every traffic light so I can get there."

"And just suppose I had something to do, then what?"

"I don't know. I guess you'd have to bring her to me."

"Huh!" Angela chuckled sarcastically. "I may as well keep her overnight."

"You don't have to."

"Simone, there's no telling what time you'll get here. She may as well stay."

"Well," Simone laughed silently, "since tomorrow is Friday, can you take her to Ms. Kennard's? It wouldn't make sense for me to pick her up from you just to take her over there. Especially when Ms. Kennard's only five minutes away from you."

"She just went over there last weekend. Why she gotta go

every weekend?"

"That's her grandmother. What's wrong with her going over there? Plus, I think she's taking Jordan to see Kevin this weekend. He still hasn't seen her yet."

"Mmm, mmm, mmm, she's going to see her jailbird daddy, the murderer. Lord have mercy, Simone. I don't know what in the world possessed you to have a baby. You know how many…"

The front door closed. The soles of Thomas's hard-bottom shoes click-clacked down the hallway. He poked his head inside Simone's room.

"Is that your momma?" he whispered.

Annoyed, Simone nodded her head while Angela continued to rant and rave.

Thomas tossed the keys to his van on Simone's bed. "Tell her you on your way. The van's acting funny, though. You gotta put it in neutral when you stop. If you don't, it'll cut off on you. It may not start without a jump, so come get me before you leave."

"Who's that?" Angela asked.

"My father," Simone said. "He just walked in. Something's wrong with the van. He said he may have to find me a jump."

"Yeah, Jordan may as well stay here, especially if the van's acting up. I'll take her to Ms. Kennard's house tomorrow since she just has to go. Give me her number so I can call her."

● ● ●

"Ma!" Alicia walked into Angela's room. "Some man wants you at the door."

"Who is it?" Angela barked as she grabbed Ms. Kennard's number and scooped Jordan up in her arms.

"I don't know," Alicia said, heading back into her room

while Angela walked towards the front door.

"Wow! How old is your baby?" the man cooed.

"Seven months," Angela shared, speaking through the screen door.

"Oh, I didn't even know you were pregnant. I live around the corner on the next street. My wife and I use this street a lot to avoid the traffic light. We see you and your husband out here working in the yard. She's a good combination of both of you."

"Thank you." Angela smiled, never bothering to correct him.

"Sorry for stopping by so late. The light was on, so I figured I'd bring you this," he said, handing Angela a few pieces of mail. "We have the same house number. I guess the mailman put it in our box by mistake. Congratulations on the baby," he said as he trotted down the steps towards his car.

"Thank you," Angela said, closing the door. "Everybody thinks you're my baby," she said as she kissed Jordan on top of her head.

Tossing the mail on the end table, she placed Jordan in her seat and starred at her granddaughter as her mind drifted back to five years ago. Five years ago when the doctor told her and Ricardo that the little girl that they were expecting had stopped developing in Angela's womb. Due to Angela's age, the pregnancy had been deemed high risk. That being the case, Angela and Ricardo decided to keep the pregnancy hush, hush until she reached her third trimester. But the third trimester never came.

"She probably would've looked just like you," Angela said to her granddaughter, Jordan.

Ricardo hated Simone, but he cherished Jordan nearly as much as Angela did. It was hard for anyone not to. With eyes as bright as the moon, silky jet-black curls, and dimples engraved in her golden-colored cheeks, one glance in Jordan's direction and she stole your heart.

Picking up the phone, Angela dialed Beatrice's number.

"Hi, Ms. Kennard? How you doing? This is Angela, Simone's mom."

"Ms. Kennard?" Beatrice gasped playfully. "Why we so formal? Girl, we kinfolks now, thanks to little Miss Jordan. Is that her I hear cooing in the background?"

"Yeah, that's her. We sitting here waiting on her momma. No telling where that girl is. I'm so sick of Simone's mess."

"Oh my goodness. Is everything okay?"

"Oh yeah, everything's fine. It's going on nine o'clock, and like I said, we're sitting here waiting. It's nothing new. I won't be surprised if she doesn't even show up. Her famous excuse is her father's van is broke. I bet she gets her to you on the weekends with no problem, and she never has a problem dropping her off. It's just picking her up."

"What!"

"Chile, please. I can tell you some stories about missy. I don't know what she's doing, but whatever it is, she needs to stop. You would think having the baby prematurely would make her change her lil' habits."

"What you mean by that?" Beatrice asked, taking Angela's bait.

"Just think about it. She didn't lose her job, her apartment, and birth this little baby two months early for nothing. All that should tell you and everybody else something. Not to mention it's late and I'm still sitting here waiting for her."

"Oh my God, Angela." Beatrice was stunned.

"Yeah, I've been trying to talk some sense into her, trying to convince her to get herself together."

"Lord, what in the world is going on with Simone?"

"Chile, who knows? But whatever you do, don't mention this conversation to her. I don't want her going off on the deep end 'cause I'm telling her business. Anyway, I was calling to let you know that more than likely I'll be dropping Jordan off to you tomorrow. It's looking like she'll be here all night again."

"Angela, this don't make any sense. I thought Simone was doing good. I mean, she looks good."

"Yeah, everybody thinks that. Just pay closer attention."

"Man, this is crazy," Beatrice mumbled, more to herself. "Listen, Angela. You've had Baby Girl all day. You want me to come get her from you tonight?"

"Oh, no, she's fine. I'll just drop her off to you tomorrow. Have you taken her to see her daddy yet?"

"No, and I know it's killing him. I thought she was a little too fragile for the ride at first, but now that she's put on a little weight, I can take her. Plus, my oldest son is off this weekend, so he's going to tag along so Kevin can see his baby. Hopefully, seeing her will cheer him up some. He's been down in the dumps for so long. You know he knew the man he accidentally killed."

"He knew the man?"

"Yeah, he tended to him at the nursing home where we used to work. I had to leave that place after that." Beatrice sighed. "Now I'm up here at this doggon' hospital working like a slave. Every time you turn around, they calling me in to work a double shift. I told them don't call me this weekend."

"Well, I bought Baby Girl some cute little outfits. I'll put a few in her bag so she can look extra cute for her daddy."

"Okay, thanks, Angela. And listen, you make sure you call

me if you need me. I don't have a problem coming to get her."

"Yeah, but she's fine. Like I said, I'm use to it. Listen," Angela added, "I have some pictures of Jordan that I could send to Kevin if you want."

"Oh, good idea. Here, take down his address."

Hanging up the phone, Angela sat on the couch with a conniving smile plastered on her face, amazed by her performance. The web of lies rolled off her tongue so effortlessly.

"Something smells good," Ricardo said, startling Angela from her thoughts as he walked in from work. He smiled at Jordan as she sat in her infant seat, kicking her little legs. "What she still doing here?"

"That's a good question," Angela responded. "I haven't heard from Simone, and look how late it is. That girl wasn't bit more ready for no baby."

"I could've told you that." Ricardo sat on the couch and lifted Jordan from her seat. "So what's the story?"

"Your guess is as good as mine."

"Well, stop babysitting," he said with Jordan cooing in his arms. "That'll fix her."

"Yeah, that may fix Simone, but it'll do more harm to Jordan. No telling who Simone will get to watch her. Plus, it's a lot of things you don't know."

"Like what?" Ricardo stepped right into the sticky web.

Angela repeated the lies she'd just shared with Beatrice.

"Damn, we need to do something," Ricardo said, looking at little Jordan.

"Well," Angela said, "if she keeps it up, we may have to go to the courthouse and see about getting custody."

• • •

Beatrice picked up the phone that connected her with her son. "Surprise, Big Daddy!"

*Damn,* Kevin thought as he marveled over the little life he and Simone had created.

"I already checked her out, too. She's definitely yours."

Kevin frowned. "Hell, I know she mine, but damn, why she so small?"

"She was premature, remember? She's gotten a lot bigger, though. Ain't she gorgeous? A good combination of you and Simone."

Kevin fought back tears as he marveled at his daughter. "She's my complexion, but to me, she looks just like Simone. How's Simone doing anyway?"

"Well, I thought she was doing good. I mean, she looks good. You can't even tell the girl had a baby. But her mother's been complaining that she's not picking Jordan up."

"What, she working late or something?"

"I don't know what's going on. She'll get it together. Hey, Jordan," Beatrice cooed as she held Jordan in her lap. "You see that funny-looking man. That's your da-da."

For the duration of the visit, Kevin did his best to maintain, but every tick of the clock stabbed at his heart as reality set in. Jordan's first words, her first steps, her first day of school, her first everything—all of that he would miss.

## Chapter Fifteen
## End of Summer, 1989

The neighborhood playground was decorated with police cars early in the afternoon. Simone surveyed the crowd and spotted Big Bob with his hands spread across the back of a cruiser. A few of his boys sat along the curb with their hands cupped behind their heads.

"Simone!" Lavon growled, appearing from out of nowhere.

"Damn, girl. You scared me. Where the hell you come from?" Simone asked. "I was on my way to your house."

"Girl," Lavon whispered in excitement as she nearly dragged Simone down the sidewalk, "one of them Jamaicans threw their bag of shit on the ground when the police rolled up."

"And?"

"And I found it!"

Simone stopped dead in her tracks.

"Yeah, c'mon," Lavon said, tugging on Simone's arm as she led the way to her apartment.

Inside, Lavon closed her bedroom door and dumped the contents of the brown paper bag on her bed.

"Look at this shit!" Lavon tossed the tiny crack-filled baggies in the air. "I know this gotta be more than three thousand dollars' worth of crack! Here," she said, tossing half of the baggies to Simone.

"What the hell I'm supposed to do with this?"

"Girl, we fuckin' partners, you know that. This is fifteen hundred dollars apiece!"

"Yeah, but who the hell gon' sell it?" Simone picked up the tiny baggie and examined the hard white substance. She'd never seen the infamous drug before. "It looks like pieces of soap."

"We can get Big Bob to sell it. Matter fact," Lavon said, picking up her phone, "I'ma page him."

"I hope he calls back," Simone said. "The police were searching him a minute ago."

"That ain't nothing new. He don't walk around wit' his stuff on him. Watch, he'll be knocking on my door in a few minutes."

Lavon and Simone sat outside on Lavon's patio in the plastic lawn chairs, fantasizing about their big plans for the fast money.

"What's up, ladies?" Big Bob stepped onto the patio. "Which one of y'all paged me?"

"I did," Lavon whispered, anxiously waving her hand for Big Bob to come closer.

"What?" He frowned as he squatted down next to her chair.

"You know the police was looking for them Jamaicans," she whispered.

"Yeah, them hot-ass muthafuckas. One of them threw their shit down. I hope somebody find that shit."

"Somebody did." Lavon smiled a toothy grin.

"Who? You? Y'all found that shit?"

"Yeah! It's like three thousand dollars' worth of halves, too."

"Hey, hold up," Big Bob said seriously. "Don't y'all tell nobody else that shit."

"Come on now. We look stupid to you?" Simone asked. "The only reason we telling you is 'cause we need you to sell it."

"Oh yeah?" Big Bob chuckled. "And what I get?" He winked at Simone.

"What, you want us to pay you?" Simone asked, ignoring the suggestion in his wink.

"Naw, I tell you what, Simone. Go to the movies with me, and you ain't gotta pay me nothing," Big Bob offered. "It might take me a minute to get rid of it, since the strip is blazing. I'd have to nickel-and-dime it to you, but I'll get rid of it."

"Okay, but if I go to the movies with you, you gotta sell mine and Lavon's."

"A'ight, but we going today."

"Okay, and Lavon's going, too."

"Ah, see," Big Bob stood. "You messin' it up."

"Come on, Bob, please," Simone begged. "And if we going today, we need to go soon, 'cause I gotta pick Jordan up from her grandmother's."

"Okay, let me see if my man Donté wanna roll so Lavon don't feel like the third wheel. I'll be back in 'bout five minutes."

After the movie, rain poured from the skies, drenching Simone, Lavon, Big Bob, and Donté as they ran from the theater to Donte's black Audi.

"Hey, Simone, I know you gotta pick up your lil' shorty. You want Donté to swing you past there?" Big Bob asked as he

148

climbed in the front seat.

"Yeah, if he don't mind. It's not that far from here," Simone said from the back seat.

"Naw, I got you." Backing from the parking space, Donté cracked his window and pulled a joint from his sun visor. He heated up his car lighter and asked, "Y'all want a hit?"

"Fool, what the hell you doing?" Irritation flooded Big Bob's voice. "Ain't you taking Simone to pick up her daughter?"

"Yeah, man. I said I was." Donté fired up the joint and took a long drag. He blew the smoke toward his open window, but the bulk of the cloud floated to the back.

"Donté, you blowin' that funky shit all over the place, and her baby gotta get up in here!"

"Ah, nigga, stop fuckin' trippin'. This that good shit. It don't smell like that bullshit y'all pushin' on the corner. Y'all don't wanna hit this muthafucka?"

"Simone," Big Bob called out, rolling down his window, "we can swing past the way and jump in my truck. I'll take you to pick up your lil' shorty."

"Stop cryin' like an ol' bitch...damn." Donté took another drag and tapped the joint out in the ashtray. "Y'all fuckin' happy now?"

"Who the hell told you that shit don't stink?" Lavon asked. She couldn't roll down her window because the rain was coming down in buckets.

"Ah, now there you go." Donté shot Lavon a look of annoyance in the rearview mirror. "Gimme the five dollars I spent on your damn movie ticket!"

"You ain't said shit." Lavon crumpled up a ten-dollar bill from her purse and bounced it off of Donté's head. "Buy some air freshener with the change."

A bolt of lightning cracked the sky as Donté pulled in front of Ms. Kennard's building. Simone and Lavon leaped from the car and sprinted to her apartment.

"Dang, is she home?" Lavon asked as Simone knocked on the door over and over.

"I guess not," Simone said, stomping down the steps. "Miss Kennard knew I was coming to get her."

"Hey, Simone!" One of her old neighbors stood at the top of the steps.

"Hey," Simone said. She recognized her old neighbor, but for the life of her she couldn't recall her name.

"I seen your little girl. You and Kevin made a pretty little baby."

"Thank you." Simone smiled. *Damn, what the hell is her name?* "Have you seen Ms. Kennard by chance?"

"No, not today. Why, something wrong?"

"No, I'm just here to get Jordan, and she's not home. Can I use your phone?"

"Sure," she said, leading the way to her apartment. "C'mon up."

Inside the apartment, Simone picked up the phone and called Angela, while Lavon waited by the door.

"Hey," Simone said, "have you spoken with Ms. Kennard? I'm here to pick up Jordan, but nobody's home," Simone smiled as her old neighbor headed into the kitchen.

"Yeah, Jordan's here with me. Ms. Kennard said she'd been calling you since five o'clock. They called her in to work. Where were you?"

"I went to the movies."

"Why would you go to the movies knowing you had to pick

Jordan up?"

"I'm here to get her now."

"It's thundering and lighting outside and you shoulda—"

"Ma," Simone said, cutting her off. She didn't have time to go back and forth with her. "I'm on somebody else's phone, so I can't fuss with you. I'm on my way."

"Simone, you may as well wait until tomorrow. It's raining and—"

"All right, bye," Simone said, hanging up the phone. "Thank you," she hollered toward the kitchen.

Her old neighbor came out of the kitchen with a can of air freshener. "No problem," she said, filling the air with aerosol. "Take care, Simone."

● ● ●

Beatrice pulled herself from her car, exhausted after working all night. She could barely keep her eyes open. Her body craved the warmth of her bed, and in a matter of minutes, she'd satisfy the yearning.

"Hey, Ms. Kennard!" her neighbor chanted as she headed over to her car. "You coming from work and I'm going."

"Girl, I'm so tired I could fall out in the middle of this parking lot. How you doing this morning?"

"I'm fine. I saw Simone last night," she said, approaching Beatrice's car. "She was looking for you. I let her use my phone. Her and her girlfriend lit my apartment up." She chuckled. "I don't know what the hell they were smoking, but whoa. I was spraying my apartment all night."

"Huh?"

*Damn, her mother said she was doing something she ain't had no business doing,* Beatrice thought.

"Hey, now don't get me wrong. I take a little hit on

151

occasion, too," she whispered. "But it don't smell like that. See you later," the neighbor said as she climbed inside her car.

● ● ●

Kevin sat on the edge of his bed, staring at the pictures of Jordan that Angela had sent him.

*Dang, look at you,* Kevin said to himself. Lining the pictures across his mattress, he read the few lines Angela had scribbled.

*Hi Kevin,*

*Hope all is well. I figured you might enjoy these pictures. Give me a call when you can. There are some things that I really need to discuss with you.*

*Take care,*

*Angela.*

*What she gotta discuss with me?* Kevin wondered. He'd only seen Angela a few times, and their exchanges had been polite but minimal.

One of the five wall phones was free. Kevin made his way to it and called Beatrice.

"Hey, Ma," he greeted after the operator announced his call. "I got a letter from Angela today. She wants me to call her. You know why?"

"I don't know, but I gave her your address. Did she send you some pictures?"

"Yeah, I got 'em. Jordan and Simone okay?"

"Well, Jordan's okay, but like I told you already, something's not right with Simone."

"What you mean? She okay, right?"

"I don't know. You ever known her to get high?"

"Who, Simone?" Kevin asked, somewhat appalled. "Naw. What in the world made you ask that?"

"Well, the gal upstairs ran into Simone, and she said Simone was high."

"Naw, don't believe that."

"I don't know. I'm starting to wonder. Angela's been hinting around, saying the same thing."

"I'm telling you, Ma, that's not Simone. She wouldn't mess around."

"Yeah, well, I don't have any reason to make it up, and why would her mother?"

"I don't know," Kevin said, confused. "Just talk to Simone and make sure she's okay."

"Why don't you call her?" Beatrice suggested.

"I've tried calling. They never accept the calls."

"Then write her a letter or something."

"Naw, I tried and I can't get my words together. Besides, you out there, Ma. You can do more than I can. Just make sure she okay. I know she ain't doing drugs, so if that's what Angela wants to talk about, there's no need for me to call her."

# Chapter Sixteen
## Late October, 1989

The light up ahead turned yellow. Simone slowed down and prepared to shift the van into neutral the way Thomas had instructed. However, before she could brake to a complete stop, the van trembled like a small quake.

"No, no, no," Simone pleaded, but the van ignored her cry and rattled off.

"Aww, come the hell on!" she moaned, slapping the steering wheel with her hand.

All week the van had given her problems, stalling before starting and cutting off when she least expected it. Thomas had finally tracked down his back-alley mechanic and made arrangements for him to work his magic. While the lack of a shop made the repair less expensive, the wait time was longer. Simone thought Angela was going to go into convulsions when she told her Jordan wouldn't be there for a week.

The light changed. Horns tooted and cars whipped around Simone as drivers tossed up the "fuck you" finger. Simone ignored them all.

"Please, please, start up," she mumbled.

Jordan was strapped in her car seat, sucking loudly on her pacifier. The last thing Simone needed was to be stranded with her baby.

She tapped the gas pedal a few times and turned the key in the ignition. The van hesitated a bit, but roared to a smoky start, sending a white cloud of funky fumes from the exhaust. Simone threw the van in drive and shot through the fresh red light. Silently, she prayed the entire drive home. She didn't breathe a sigh of relief until she was settled in a parking space.

"Hey, Simone!" Big Bob called, jogging in her direction. "Hey, Cutie Pie," he panted, grinning at Jordan. "Damn, you and that punk did something right." He chuckled.

"Here," he said, passing Simone a wad of bills and a handful of crack-filled baggies. "That's some more money for you and Lavon. Five-O and the fuckin' feds just pulled up on the other side of the complex. Hold that for me. You know they ain't gon' check you."

Without a second thought, Simone shoveled the money and the baggies in her jacket pocket. It wasn't the first time she'd held the drugs for Big Bob.

"I'll come back and get 'em from you later," he said as he jogged off.

"Hey," she yelled out to him. "Is your mother home? I need her to babysit for me next week."

"Yeah," he hollered back. "She in the house."

Just as he'd promised, Big Bob paid Simone and Lavon their money in bits and pieces...two hundred here, four hundred the next time. It didn't matter to the girls, especially when all he'd requested was a simple date to the movies.

One by one, the police cars flooded the parking lot.

155

Instantly, Simone felt a little awkward. No, the police had never checked her, but there was a first time for everything.

*Should we be going to Ms. Alice's house right now?* Then it dawned on her. Her burgundy short skirt and suit jacket were nice and professional, and she figured with Jordan on her hip, she didn't look like a drug dealer or a drug dealer's girlfriend.

"Naw, they not gonna mess with your momma, are they?" she cooed to Jordan as they continued down the walkway leading to Ms. Alice's.

"Hey!" a forceful voice yelled. "Hey, you!"

Simone glanced over her shoulder, wondering who the hell he was referring to.

"Yeah, you," he said, pointing at her.

*Oh my God.* Her heart started pounding as the officer marched in her direction.

"Hey, hold up, Officer Bristol." A professionally suited black man trotted down the walkway. "She's straight."

"She's straight?" Bristol frowned. "Y'all already checked her?"

"Yeah, I checked her," he said with authority, as if daring the officer to challenge him. "And she's straight like I said. Go catch one of the drug boys."

Officer Bristol stared at the federal officer as if he wanted to challenge his decision. Simone stood there, silently wishing Bristol would tuck his tail between his legs and do as he was told.

"Yeah, whatever, Perkins," he said, shaking his head.

A slight smirk eased across the federal officer's face.

Simone changed her mind about going to see Ms. Alice. Fighting her rattling insides, she casually headed toward her own building.

"You know you owe me, right?" the federal officer said, trotting behind Simone.

"For what?" Simone asked nonchalantly.

"Come on, now." He laughed as he quickened his pace to catch up to Simone. "I bet you got something on you right now. The drug boys always get the pretty ones to hold their stash, thinking we ain't hip to that, but we are. That's why the county officer wanted to check you."

Simone didn't know what to say.

"Is that your baby?" he asked, letting her off the hook.

"Yeah."

"She's pretty, just like her mother. I bet her father's out here hiding from us."

"No," Simone said, "he's not." *Y'all already locked him up,* she thought to herself.

"Good. Don't let these fake ass roughnecks get you in trouble. What's your name?" he asked.

"Simone."

"Well, Simone…" He stopped, causing Simone to stop, too. "If any of these lil' officers ever harass you again, give them my card and have them call me." He passed Simone his linen-textured business card. "I'm Agent Perkins, but you can call me Andre."

"Thanks," Simone said. She accepted his card and headed home where it was safe.

The savory aroma of meatloaf, mashed potatoes, and mixed vegetables, also known as Thomas's Tuesday night special, greeted Simone as she and Jordan walked through the door. Thomas was in the kitchen wiping down the stove and whistling along with the O'Jays.

"There go my little boo-boo," he said. Jordan's face lit up.

She kicked her legs and grinned with excitement at the sight of her grandfather. "Dinner's done," he said as he tossed the sponge in the sink and reached for his granddaughter.

"Did you tell your momma she won't be there tomorrow and next week?"

"Yeah, I thought she was going to have a fit. I still have to talk to Ms. Alice, though. I'll probably just call in sick tomorrow and talk to her then."

"Go talk to her now. You don't need to be missing no unnecessary days from work," Thomas said.

However, going back outside was too risky and the farthest thing from Simone's mind.

"I'll go later on," she said as the phone rang.

Thomas glanced at the caller ID box. "That's your crazy momma."

"Hello?" Simone greeted into the cordless phone.

"I got a solution," Angela said excitedly.

"A solution to what?" Simone asked, heading back to her room. She tossed her suit jacket across her bed.

"Jordan can stay with me until the van is fixed."

"Ma, it might be two weeks before the van is fixed. I'm just gonna ask Ms. Alice."

"Simone, Jordan's not used to her."

"Sorry, but Jordan doesn't have any options. Besides, it's not like she won't get use to her."

"Well, why can't she just stay over here with me?"

"Because it might take two weeks. The guy's fixing the van on the side, not at a shop."

"And again, why can't she stay here? She's only spent the night with me twice, but she's at Ms. Kennard's every weekend. I'm her grandmother, too."

Simone mulled it over. "Actually, I never thought about it because I never knew it was an option. Since when you start wanting to keep her overnight, anyway?"

"I rather keep her than have her go over some stranger's house."

"She's not a stranger," Simone chanted, slightly irritated.

"Listen, Simone," Angela said. "Ricardo's vacation starts next week. We're thinking about driving down to North Carolina for a few days. Jordan can go with us. She can have her first vacation with her grandma. And just think," she added. "It'll give you time to sleep, since she's still waking up all hours of the night. I'll probably have her trained by the time she comes home."

"Come get her!" Simone said. She didn't need any more convincing.

"No, I'm serious."

"I know. I'm serious, too. She can stay. Hopefully, it won't take two weeks for him to fix the van, though."

"Yeah, well, just in case it does, she'll be here. Ricardo's getting ready to go to his mother's house. I can get him and Alicia to swing past and pick her up. So, get her ready. Oh, and send her swing, too."

Thomas walked in the room, cradling Jordan in his arms. "She fell asleep," he said, laying her across the bed. "What you doing?"

"My mother's gonna keep her while the van's getting fixed. They coming to pick her up."

"Umm, I don't know if I like that idea."

Simone noticed the unsettled look on her father's face. "What's wrong with her keeping her for a week or so?"

"Simone, you think I'm playing when I say your momma's

crazy." Simone chuckled. "You laughing, but I'm serious. Remember, I was married to the woman."

"So what you saying? You don't think I should let her go?"

"A few days is a'ight, but not for no two weeks."

Simone chuckled. "Well, hopefully, it won't take that long for the van to get fixed."

An hour or so later, Alicia tapped on the door. Simone carried Jordan's swing out to the living room and opened the door.

"Here," she said to Alicia. "Carry this out to the truck. Then you can come back and get Jordan. I don't want to see your father."

Alicia chuckled and toted Jordan's swing to Ricardo's pickup. Minutes later, she returned and followed Simone back to her room.

"You can grab her bag while I put on her jacket," Simone instructed.

Alicia grabbed the bag from the bed, knocking Simone's suit jacket to the floor. Two crack-filled baggies fell from the pocket.

"Aw, Simone!"

"Aw, Simone what?"

"I know what that is!" Alicia said. Wide-eyed, she pointed at the baggies on the floor. "This boy in my class brought some to school and got suspended."

Simone saw the baggies lying on the floor. Brushing Alicia off with a simple wave of her hand, she kicked the baggies under her bed, just in case Thomas walked by.

"I love you, baby," she said, kissing Jordan on the cheek. "See you in a few days."

● ● ●

A gentle breeze flowed through the sheer panels draped at Simone's bedroom window. Lying across the bed, she starred into space as she absentmindedly toyed with one of Jordan's rattles. Thomas stood at the bedroom door. The entire weekend had slipped by, and she hadn't even left the house.

"Call your momma and tell her you coming to get your baby." Thomas startled Simone, waking her from her daydream.

"They not home. I think they still in North Carolina."

"Jordan's been gone almost two weeks. Didn't you tell her the van was fixed?"

"I've been calling over there. I guess they're not back yet."

"Well call 'em again," Thomas suggested.

Simone grabbed the phone from her nightstand and hit redial. To her surprise, someone answered.

"Hello," Alicia greeted.

Simone's face lit up. "Hey," she sang into the phone as she sprang up from the bed. "How come nobody called and told me y'all were back?"

"Huh?"

"Did you have fun? How was North Carolina?" Simone could hear Jordan cooing in the background. The mere sound nourished her spirit.

"North Carolina?" Alicia questioned.

"Who is that?" Angela yelled in the background.

"It's Simone," Alicia responded.

"What did I tell you about answering the phone?" Angela screamed.

"Dang, Alicia, who pissed her off?" Simone laughed to herself. "Just let her know that I'm on my way to get Jordan."

"You're coming to get her?" Alicia seemed surprised.

"Yeah. Y'all back, so I'll be leaving here in a few minutes."

"Mommy, Simone said she's on her way to pick up Jordan," Alicia repeated, sounding almost in a panic.

"What do you want, Simone?" Angela asked coldly, taking the phone from Alicia.

"Dang, hello to you, too. I'm on my way to pick her up."

"Oh yeah?" Angela barked.

"Oh yeah?" Simone repeated. "What's that supposed to mean?"

"Simone, you can come if you want, but Jordan's not going with you. You left her here for damn near two weeks, and now you want to come get her? Please!"

The phone went dead. The annoying tone echoed in Simone's ear as she sat there dumbfounded.

"What the fuck?" she mumbled.

Thomas poked his head back inside her room. "I heard you talking to somebody. They back?"

"Yeah, but she just told me I wasn't getting Jordan back and hung up."

"What the hell she mean you ain't getting her back? Call her ass again."

Simone hit redial. This time the bass from Ricardo's voice bellowed through the receiver. Any other time, Simone would've hung up the minute he said hello. But this time, she refused to be intimidated.

"I'm on my way to pick up my daughter."

Before Ricardo could utter a response, she slammed down the phone.

"See what the hell I mean. I told you your gotdamn mommy crazy. Her and that gotdamn Ricardo over there playing house with your baby. They ain't bit more took their ass to North Carolina than we did." Thomas stormed down the hallway to his room, yelling, "Call the police and tell them your mother's trying to keep your baby!"

Dazed, Simone followed her father's instructions.

"Operator. What's your emergency?"

"Yes. My mother has my baby and she's refusing to give her back."

"Does she have custody?"

"No."

"Why is she refusing to give her back?"

"I don't know." Simone was baffled.

"Do you have documents supporting that you're the child's mother, like the birth certificate, her insurance card, or anything of that nature?"

"Yes, I have all of those things."

"Okay. Take those items with you, and we'll arrange for an officer to meet you there in about thirty minutes."

Simone gathered everything she could find—Jordan's birth certificate, her insurance card, and the tiny bracelet she had worn around her wrist in the hospital.

"They gon' meet us?" Thomas asked, standing in the doorway with his jacket on and his keys in hand.

"No, Daddy. They are going to meet *me*."

"You better bring your ass on here," Thomas said, heading to the front door.

"No, Daddy!" Simone chased behind him. "You can't go. You and Ricardo mess around and get into it, and then I'll be bailing you out of jail."

Thomas ignored her.

"Daddy, I'm serious! The police will be there and I'll get Lavon to ride with me, but you can't go. It's just gonna make it worse."

Thomas sighed. His stiff shoulders softened. "You pick up Lavon and don't knock on your momma's door until the police come, you hear me?" he yelled, extending his keys to Simone.

• • •

Simone sat outside her mother's house, eyeing the door as she waited for the police.

"You okay?" Lavon asked.

"Yeah, I'm fine, but you best believe, Ms. Alice will be watching Jordan from now on out."

"I don't blame you," Lavon said as a bright set of headlights came down the street. "This is fuckin' crazy. You had to call the police to get your baby from your mother. Wait 'til Melanie calls and we tell her about this shit."

Simone and Lavon climbed from the van as the officer parked along the curb.

"How you doing, Officer?" Simone asked politely as he stepped from his car.

"Fine, ma'am. Are you the mother?" he asked, lowering the volume to the radio on his hip.

"Yes, and here is my daughter's birth certificate, insurance card, and hospital bracelet."

"Can I see your driver's license?"

Simone pulled her license from her back pocket and passed it to the officer. He illuminated the birth certificate with his flashlight, comparing the name with the driver's license.

"Okay, let's go," he instructed as they headed up the driveway to the porch.

The front door swung open before the officer could knock.

"Come on in," Ricardo said to the officer. Simone knew the invitation wasn't extended to her.

"Girl, why you ain't go in?" Lavon asked from the bottom

of the front steps as the officer disappeared.

"I don't go in when he's home. They come out and get Jordan in the morning and bring her back out in the evening."

"Get the fuck outta here!" Lavon said in disbelief.

"Yeah, and I should tell the police to search the basement."

"Search the basement for what?"

"Girl, please. Ricardo is the biggest weed-head around."

The officer opened the screen door. "Ma'am," he said to Simone, "I need you to come in."

Simone shot Lavon a look of disgust as she crossed the threshold she had vowed never to cross.

"Officer, can you come back here, please?" Angela's tone was tender and delicate, unlike her vicious bark over the phone. Dressed in a pale blue flannel robe and matching slippers, she stood in the hallway that led to the back rooms. "Simone, you wait out there."

"I wanna see my baby."

"You heard what she said," Ricardo ordered as they headed to the back.

Simone plopped on the couch, confused. What the fuck was going on? What had she done? Tapping her foot, she looked down at the floor as her anger liquefied into tears.

"Hello! Hello!" a voice called out.

*What she doing here?* Simone asked herself as Beatrice strolled through the door.

"Hey, Simone," she greeted casually. "Haven't talked to you in a few weeks."

"Yeah." Simone looked up from the floor, wiping her eyes with the back of her hand. "Jordan's been over here."

Ricardo heard the front door close and peered around the hallway.

"You can come on back," he said to Beatrice.

Simone sucked her teeth. *This is some fuckin' bullshit,* she screamed to herself. She hadn't seen Jordan in two weeks, and just like that, Ms. Kennard was allowed in the back room. Why was she there anyway?

Minutes later, Ricardo and the officer strolled out to the living room. The officer caught Simone's attention and beckoned her outside with a wave of his hand.

Simone stood from the couch and followed the officer outside. "What about my baby?"

"I'll explain out here. It's okay, though."

"Have a nice evening, Officer," Ricardo said.

The door closed and the deadbolt latched. Lavon stood outside at a complete loss as Simone and the officer proceeded down the steps.

"Where's Jordan?"

"She's inside," the officer informed as he led the girls back to Thomas's van.

"Okay, Ms. Woodard, here's the deal. Because she's a preemie and it's late," he said with a glance at his wristwatch, "your mom suggested you come back tomorrow and get her. Your daughter was asleep, and your mom needs time to get her stuff together."

"That's some bullshit!" Simone screamed, bursting into tears. "I want my baby tonight!" she demanded. "She can keep her stuff, but I want my fuckin' baby."

"Miss," the officer touched Simone lightly on the shoulder. "Calm down."

"Don't tell me to calm down," Simone said, snatching away from him. She hadn't called the police for their sympathy. She wanted her baby like she said. What the fuck was going on?

Why was Beatrice there and still inside? Why didn't she make Angela give Jordan back?

"Calm down, Simone," Lavon said.

"Ms. Woodard, like I said, your daughter was already asleep, and your mom wants time to get her things together."

"But I didn't even get to see her," she cried. "Y'all got to see her, and I couldn't even fuckin' look at her."

"Come on, Simone," Lavon said, taking Simone by the arm. "Let's just come back tomorrow like he said."

"Yeah," the officer confirmed. "Tomorrow is more than enough time for your mother to have her ready. If you want an officer to meet you here tomorrow, just give us a call."

● ● ●

"Thanks for calling me, Angela," Beatrice said as she cradled Jordan in her arms, rocking wearily in the glider. "This nursery is beautiful."

Angela spent the last two weeks transforming Simone's old room into the very nursery that she'd planned for her and Ricardo's little girl. Tucked away in a hope chest buried in the back of her closet were the paint swatches for the walls and the trim and the dancing white and pink teddy bear border with its coordinating comforter set.

Poor little helpless Jordan, abandoned by her drug-addicted mother, Simone—at least that was the lie Angela spread like butter. When Alicia told Angela about the crack falling from Simone's pocket, Angela began to think there was some truth to her story after all. Jordan was now her baby. The baby Simone had dropped off two weeks ago and simply forgot about. Angela had Ricardo convinced, and now, as Beatrice sat mesmerized by the nursery and the fact that Angela had to call the police on Simone, yep, she had her convinced, too. Still, she needed to convince Kevin so she could get his signature on the custody papers.

With Simone supposedly on drugs and missing somewhere out in the streets, the family court shared that Angela had to obtain the father's signature, or Jordan would become a ward of the courts. A ward of Angela's lies. But Angela knew she could convince Kevin, just like she'd convinced everybody else. If only he would call.

"I haven't seen Baby Girl in a few weeks. I was wondering why Simone hadn't called."

"Yeah, Jordan's been here with us. Simone hadn't called us either. Then, all of a sudden, she pops up today," Ricardo said.

"She can't go back to Simone tomorrow," Angela said. "We gotta do something."

"Did you tell her about the crack that fell out her pocket?" Ricardo asked Angela.

"Damn, is that what she's smoking?" Beatrice asked as she laid Jordan back in her crib.

"Who knows? So what are we gonna do? The police said we have to give her back tomorrow. I have the custody papers, but there's no way I can get Kevin's signature by tomorrow. I've written him a few times asking him to call, but he hasn't."

"Where the papers?" Beatrice asked. "Shit, that's my son, and this is my granddaughter. I'll sign his doggone name. Won't nobody know it's not his signature but the three of us."

"Angela, you have them?" Ricardo asked.

"Yeah," Angela said, fighting to contain her victory. "Of course, I have them."

● ● ●

Eight o'clock the next morning, Simone and Lavon pulled up in front of Angela's house, but both cars were gone. After waiting for over an hour, Simone headed back home, pissed off.

Hour after hour, Simone called. Morning transformed into afternoon, and still no one answered. Something was up. Picking up the phone, Simone called Ms. Kennard to see if she knew anything.

"Hey, Ms. Kennard, have you talked to my mother by chance?"

"Naw, not today."

"Hmm," Simone said into the phone. "The police told her she had to give Jordan back today. I've been over there and everything but they weren't there and nobody's answering."

"Well, she couldn't have gone far. Just keep calling."

Simone was sick of calling. Instead, she called the police and made arrangements for them to meet her again. Within twenty minutes, she pulled up in front of her mother's house. An officer was already waiting for her. Without being asked, Simone greeted the officer with Jordan's birth certificate and her driver's license, and then she shared what had taken place the night prior.

The officer walked to the door and rang the bell. Unlike the night before, Angela appeared jovial, standing with a bright-eyed and bushy-tailed Jordan on her hip, sucking away on her pacifier.

"I guess you need to see this?" Angela passed the officer a piece of paper.

The officer skimmed the document and passed it back to Angela.

"Thank you, ma'am."

Simone stood in uttered awe as Angela closed the door and latched the deadbolt.

"What happened? Where's my baby?"

"I'm sorry, ma'am." The officer shrugged his shoulders and headed down the steps. "There's nothing I can do. Your mother has custody."

● ● ●

Simone was an emotional disaster. She rang her mother's phone like a stalker, but her calls went unanswered. Yet, the more they ignored her calls, the more annoying the calls became.

"Simone," Angela finally answered close to four in the morning, "if you keep playing on my phone, I'm going to press charges. That's my first and last warning. Now what is it that you want?"

"I want my baby!" Simone screamed. "Why would you do this to me? What did I ever do to you to make you hate me so much?"

"Simone, don't play innocent with me," Angela said. Her calmness fueled Simone's fury. "You know good and well you weren't ready for no baby. What about the drugs that fell out of your pocket, hmm? And one of Ms. Kennard's neighbors said you were high when you came to pick Jordan up."

"That's a lie. I've never gotten—"

"Simone, save it! I don't want to hear it! And let me tell you something. I have witnesses ready to testify. So you remember that if you even think about fighting it. Now stop playing on my phone."

"I HATE YOU! I FUCKIN' HATE YOU!" Simone screamed to the dial tone for Angela had hung up.

Despite Angela's threats, Simone pulled out the phonebook and called a few attorneys. However, it seemed as if they, too, were on Angela's side.

"Getting custody isn't easy. You have to be able to prove

that the parent is unfit. Obviously, your mother was able to do that," one attorney advised over the phone. "What could she have possibly used against you?"

"I'm not sure," Simone lied. Naïve to the law, she was too afraid to mention the drugs that had been in her possession.

"Well, in order to get your daughter back, you're going to have to convince the judge that the accusations your mother made aren't true. I must admit I'm baffled," he added. "Why would your mother do something like this? I mean, it's your mother. And I'm sure a judge is going to wonder the same thing."

"Thank you," Simone muttered as the tears she'd grown accustomed to shedding resurfaced. She just didn't understand how *her own mother* could do something like this. It was the ultimate act of betrayal, and for what?

No matter how many attorneys Simone called, the advice was all the same. Nothing in life mattered now. She disassociated herself from friends and stopped showing for work without as much as a phone call to excuse her absence. After being a no-show for two weeks, she received a letter from her job, terminating her employment within the government. Mentally, she'd already quit her job and life.

Thomas couldn't sit back and watch his daughter sink deeper into her depression. "Listen to me, Simone. You're letting your momma win."

Simone broke down and told Thomas everything. The drugs they had found outside, the scent in her clothes from Donté's joint, and the little crack-filled baggies that Alicia had seen fall from her jacket.

"Simone, you gotta get yourself together. Laying in the bed crying is not gonna get Jordan back. I know you not on no damn

171

drugs, just like your momma know. Get yourself together and get your baby back. Find you another job, something you would want to stick with. Become successful, baby girl, and get your gotdamn baby back from your crazy-ass momma. You bigger and better than any rumor she can start. Show your momma and everybody else. Don't let her win!"

"But all the attorneys…"

"I don't give a gotdamn about them attorneys. Listen to what I'm telling you. You get yourself together. Get another job, get you a place and become successful. A judge will give you back your daughter."

# Chapter Seventeen
# November 1989

Kevin took a detour through the courtyard on his way back to his cell. Dale rushed over to him, nearly knocking him down.

"Hey, Kevin, man," Dale panted, fighting to catch his breath. "He over there. You want Kong to handle his ass?"

Kevin knew just who he was referring to—his fake-ass buddy, James. He scanned the crowded courtyard searching for him.

"Naw," Kevin said. "I got that. Where the fuck he at?"

Dale pointed toward the basketball court. "Over there."

With fire in his eyes and revenge in his heart, Kevin headed to the basketball court, ready to add to his prison sentence.

"Ah! What's up, Kevin, man!" James hollered out as Kevin stormed in his direction. "Come on over here and help me whip these bammas!"

James knelt down to ties his shoes, dropping the basketball at his feet. Kevin slowed his pace as a shadow larger than his own fell over James.

James stood just in time to connect with the twenty-five pound dumbbell being swung at his head. The forceful impact split his skull. Blood splattered on Kevin's socks and shoes as he watched James fall to the asphalt, dead, with his eyes wide open. A wad of spit landed on James's face, mixing with the blood.

"That's for Toby, nigga," the unknown man said in his Jamaican accent.

As the alarm rang out, Kevin locked eyes with the strange Jamaican standing before him.

"We ain't got no beef with you," the Jamaican said.

*Yeah, whatever,* Kevin said to himself. *I'm watching your muthafuckin' ass anyway.*

Kevin sat in his cell with James's blood all over his legs.

"SHOWER!" the guard yelled.

When the iron gates popped open, Kevin and a handful of the other inmates headed for the shower.

"Damn, man," Dale said, catching up with Kevin. "Can you believe that shit? Your boy got clocked right in his fuckin' head. Man, that shit was something."

Kevin had no words. A part of him wished he'd swung the weights. The person he'd once considered his closest confidant next to Fat Ed had destroyed his whole life. Just the thought pissed Kevin off all over again.

*My muthafuckin' friend.* Deep in thought, Kevin closed his eyes and allowed the shower water to run down his head.

Dale tapped Kevin on the arm.

"What!" Kevin snapped.

"Shit, man," Dale whispered. "One of the booty bandits looking at you and jerkin' his shit, Kevin. Look."

Kevin looked toward the end of the shower. A huge white

guy covered in tattoos stared back at him. Licking his pale pink lips, he stroked his penis and blew Kevin a kiss.

The devil himself took over Kevin as he rushed to the other end of the shower. Blood splashed all over the dingy white tiles as Kevin took his frustrations out on the booty bandit. The inmates' cheers echoed throughout the shower, alarming the guards and setting off the sirens for the second time in an hour.

A few of the inmates pulled Kevin off the guy, who lay drenched in his own blood on the floor of the shower. Ending the confrontation saved Kevin from an old-fashioned prison guard beat-down, but it didn't save him from the sixty days he'd have to serve in the black hole, isolated from the rest of the prison population.

● ● ●

Kevin's nightmares tracked him down yet again. The screams and cries were louder than usual as he ran through the dark forest. The trees had come to life, dripping with blood. Kevin ran, ducking and dodging the branches as they reached out to grab him. Something was chasing him, and today it was faster than ever. Kevin ran toward the light. The closer he got, the thicker the woods became.

"Run, Kevin," he heard a male's voice encourage. A hand appeared through the light, reaching out to him. Whatever was chasing him was on his heels. Without a second thought, Kevin reached for the hand and was yanked into an area so bright that it nearly blinded him. He threw up his arms, covering his eyes. Slowly, the light began to soften. Kevin lowered his arms and gasped as he came face-to-face with Mr. Johnson.

"No, Kevin." Mr. Johnson smiled, reading the panic on his face.

"Am I dead?" Kevin asked anyway.

Mr. Johnson raised an eyebrow. "Kevin, you know good and well that if you died today, you and I probably wouldn't be in the same place."

A train of tears poured from Kevin's eyes as he stared at Mr. Johnson and his heavenly glow. "Mr. Johnson, I'm sorry," he cried, dropping to his knees. "You know I didn't mean to kill you. I would never, ever do anything to harm you. I loved you like a father."

"I know that, son. I know that," Mr. Johnson said. "But, Kevin...would you have killed Toby? What about James or the guy you nearly beat to death in the shower?"

Kevin was so caught up in his emotions that he couldn't respond. He sat on the ground and bawled. Mr. Johnson lowered himself to the ground and patted Kevin on the back in an attempt at comfort.

"I'm sorry, Mr. Johnson," Kevin cried. "I'm sorry. I didn't go to—"

"Kevin, Kevin...It was an accident, son. I know," Mr. Johnson interrupted. "Do you remember our talks at the nursing home?"

Engulfed in his emotions, Kevin could only answer with a nod of his head.

"I told you I was gonna be watching you, and God has allowed me to do so. That's why you didn't get to James. I wish I could've prevented his death altogether, but I could only help you. The only reason I didn't stop the fight in the shower was because you needed this time to be alone, to think about what it is you're going to do with your life."

Mr. Johnson helped Kevin stand to his feet. "I don't know any pain now, son. But don't let my death be in vain. I've seen your future." He lifted Kevin's head with his fingers and smiled with a raised brow. "But the only way you can have it is if you get yourself together. If you're really, really sorry, you'll do it for me."

"I'm sorry, Mr. Johnson. I am," Kevin cried.

"Then get it together, my son. And remember," Mr. Johnson said as his image faded, "I'm watching you."

The sun's rays beamed through the window of his small cell in solitary confinement. Kevin sprang up in bed and sighed. It had all been a dream. *I'm going to get myself together, Mr. Johnson.*

A few weeks into his confinement, Kevin got a letter from his mother. The first sentence stole his breath. Beatrice had signed over custody on his behalf to Angela.

"Ah, Ma," Kevin said. "You *didn't* sign for me!"

• • •

Sixty days to the date he was put in the hole, Kevin was released back into the prison population with the promises he'd made to Mr. Johnson tattooed on the brain. However, before he executed anything, he had to call Angela. He hunted through her letters until he found her number, and went to the phone. He dialed Angela's number, but the call, for some odd reason, didn't go through.

*Damn, what's going on?* Kevin wondered. He called his mother.

"Hey, boy!" Beatrice greeted. "You outta the hole?"

"Yeah, I got out today."

"You got my letter, right?"

"Yeah, I got it. Did you ever talk to Simone?"

"There was no need to. I saw her for myself. Don't worry, though. Your baby's in good hands now, and I'm still planning on getting her on the weekends as soon as they hire some more

177

nurses."

"Yeah, I just wish I was home. I'm telling you, the stuff y'all saying don't sound like Simone at all."

"Kevin," Beatrice said, "I saw her for myself."

"Listen, though," Kevin said, ready to change the subject. "I just called over to Angela's, and the call didn't go through. It was like her number was disconnected or something. Have you talked to her?"

"Boy, I've been working like crazy. I haven't had a chance to do anything in the last three weeks." Beatrice yawned into the phone. "I'll call over there later on and check on things for you. I love you, boy, and behave yourself."

Kevin called Fat Ed. Later wasn't going to work for him. Something wasn't right, and he knew it.

"What's up, nigga!" Fat Ed screamed into the phone. "You straight, man?"

"Yeah, man, I'm good. Thanks for looking out for me, too."

"Yeah, man. I got your letter. Who the hell you in there paying to write for you?" Fat Ed chuckled through the phone.

"Nobody. Shit, why everybody think I'm some dummy?"

"Naw, man, I ain't say you was no dummy, but ain't no way in hell you wrote that gotdamn letter! Man, I couldn't believe that shit about James. Damn, and that shit happened right in front of you?"

"Yeah, man." Kevin didn't want to talk about James. "Hey, listen. I need you to do me a huge favor."

"What's up? You short on dough already?"

"Oh, naw, I'm straight on money. I need you to ride by Simone's mother's to check on Jordan. She got custody of my daughter."

"Yeah, man. I met Simone's brother, Stan, a while back. Me

178

and him partnered up, tryna do some things. That nigga into music like shit. We 'bout to open a recording studio."

"Yeah," Kevin said, uninterested, "but listen. I been trying to call and check on Jordan, but the phone is disconnected or something. Do me a favor. Ride past there and check that out for me. Or call Simone's brother and make sure everything's okay."

"I'll ride past, man, and check it out. But I don't wanna be asking Stan no whole bunch of questions."

"That's cool. When can you do that for me?"

"Shit, man. They don't live but a few minutes away. Call me back in an hour. I'll swing past there now."

*Shit, why the hell did I give up smoking?* Kevin thought as he paced back and forth in the recreation hall. He couldn't wait a whole hour. He called his mother again.

"I'm sorry, Ma. I had to call you. Did you call over there?"

"Yeah, and the number's disconnected."

"Shit! Something ain't right. I called Fat Ed and he's gon' ride past there for me."

"Why you so nervous? Everything's cool. If Angela changed her number, I'm sure she'll call and give it to me. Then I'll give it to you. Stop stressing over nothing. Now go make some license plates or something," Beatrice joked before hanging up.

"Kennard!" the guard yelled out. "You had some mail returned. I put it on your cot."

Kevin headed to his cell. Two letters he'd written to Angela while he was in confinement lay on his cot marked 'Unable to Forward.'

*Unable to forward?* Kevin knew the address was right.

An hour hadn't passed, but he called Fat Ed back anyway.

179

"Hey, man," Kevin said. "So what happened?"

"The house looked empty, man. And there was a 'For Sale' sign in the yard. They must've moved."

"Get the fuck outta here," Kevin said.

"Yeah, man. What's wrong wit' that, though? She got your baby, so I'm sure she'll send you something in the mail. She got *your* address, right? Stop trippin'."

# Chapter Eighteen
## January 1990

Simone couldn't bring herself to call Angela no matter how many times Thomas suggested it. Hearing Jordan in the background would only dig the dagger further into her heart. She hated her life, but she had to find the strength to fight back. Thomas bought her a used car, and she found employment through a temporary agency. Still, neither revived the part of her that she felt had died.

"Simone!" Thomas yelled. "Your grandmother's on the phone!"

*Nana?* She hadn't talked to Nana in months. *How'd she get this number?*

"You know, I should come over there and beat your tail!" Nana said. "Why haven't you called me? Thank the Lord, Stan dropped by yesterday."

"I'm sorry, Nana."

"Don't be sorry, Simone," Nana said softly. "I've been praying for you. Every single night. I can't tell you how many conversations I've had with your momma, telling her to give you back your baby."

"She got people thinking I'm on drugs, Nana, and I swear I've never, ever—"

"Simone, honey," Nana cut her off, "you know I know that. The only person on drugs is your momma. Now, you listen to me. Your momma is planning a birthday party for Jordan, and I'm calling to let you know. Her and Ricardo don' up and sold their old house and bought a new one a few weeks ago. They're having the party at the new house and you should come."

"Nana, you know if Ricardo's there, I can't come."

"Who cares if he's there? He don't like me either, and I ain't studying his foolish behind. The party is this weekend, so write down this address."

• • •

Simone drove up and down the street a few times, unsure if she really wanted to go inside. The pit of her being needed to see Jordan, to inhale her sweet baby scent while she cradled her in her arms. And for that reason alone, she squeezed her car into a parking space a few houses down from her mother's.

Looking around, she recognized a few of the cars. *Stan got an invitation,* Simone said to herself, recognizing her brother's Pathfinder. *How can she call Jordan's uncle and not her mother?*

Simone rested her head on the steering wheel, trying to ward off the tears and muster up the strength to go inside. *It's Jordan's birthday. I gotta go,* she tried convincing herself over and over just as someone tapped on the passenger window. Simone looked up.

"Oh my God," she said, releasing the locks. Alicia stood at the passenger door with Jordan on her hip.

"Say, hi, Simone," Alicia said to Jordan as she opened the car door and climbed inside.

Simone was so stunned by the sight of her baby that she didn't even bother to correct Alicia. To Jordan, she wasn't just Simone; she was her mother.

"Stan told us you were outside," Alicia said. "Wow, Simone. You look so pretty."

Simone had made sure to look better than her best, for everyone in the house probably assumed she was on drugs. Just for the occasion, she'd gotten her hair done the day before and bought a new pair of jeans and an expensive wool sweater that was itching the hell out of her.

"Oh my God. Look at my little baby," Simone said, her eyes tearing up. Jordan's hair had grown and was neatly brushed into two curly ponytails. "Come here, baby."

Simone took Jordan from Alicia and squeezed her. "Wow, you look just like your daddy, too," she said. The resemblance between Jordan and Kevin was unreal. Jordan smiled, displaying two bottom teeth. "Look at your little teeth. Who told you to bring her out?" she asked Alicia.

"Nana did. Stan saw you parking."

"Your mother didn't say anything?"

"No, she put Jordan's jacket on and told me to bring her out." Jordan turned to look at Alicia. "Hey, Jordan," she cooed.

Jordan let out a little whimper and reached for Alicia, killing Simone softly. She refused to hand her over, though. Part of her contemplated driving off with Alicia in the car, but she knew she wouldn't get far before the police were called. Knowing her mother, she'd press charges and have Simone thrown in jail for kidnapping the baby her mother had stolen.

"Dang, she don't even know who I am," Simone whispered.

"You coming inside, Simone?" Alicia asked, opening the passenger-side door.

"Yeah."

"I'll get the stuff out the backseat," Alicia volunteered.

Simone climbed from the car with Jordan in her arms. Her heart quickened with each step up the walkway as she followed Alicia inside the house. The living room grew quiet when they walked in. All eyes fell upon Simone. She took a deep breath and forced her fakest smile ever.

"Hello," Simone greeted happily to the entire room.

"Hey, Simone!" Nana greeted, cracking the silence. "Don't you look beautiful."

"Hi, Simone," Angela said without a pinch of guilt. Jordan squirmed in Simone's arms, reaching for Angela. "I need to change her anyway," Angela said as Simone passed her baby over to the thief without speaking.

"Here, Simone. Come sit with me." Nana made room for her granddaughter on the couch.

Squeezing next to her, Simone scanned the room. The bulk of the people present were either Angela's friends or Ricardo's family.

*Me and Kevin supposed to be giving this party,* Simone thought.

"You okay?" Nana noticed the look on Simone's face.

"No. I can't stay here, Nana. Jordan doesn't even know who I am," she mumbled on the verge of tears.

"I know." Nana patted Simone's leg. "I thought it would be a good idea, but I guess I was wrong. I've been trying to talk some sense into her, Simone," Nana mumbled underneath her breath.

Angela walked back in the room, the happy host with Jordan

on her hip.

"I gotta go, Nana," Simone mumbled. She stood from the couch as her tears began to fall.

• • •

A message was taped to Simone's bedroom door when she got home. Her placement specialist from the temporary agency wanted Simone to call her at home. Simone headed toward the phone to place the call.

"Great news, Simone. You've been asking for an office assignment without the typical office environment, right?" she said in her chipper valley-girl accent.

"Yes."

"Something that wouldn't have you confined to a desk, right?"

"Yes."

"Well, I have something for you. I got an emergency page today from a large property management firm that's in desperate need of someone. One of their consultants had to take a sudden leave of absence. So, here's the job you've been requesting, and it's long-term. There's an awesome chance that you'll be placed permanently. They're expecting you Monday morning."

# Part Two

### "Let it go..."

# *Chapter Nineteen*
## *June 1992*

Two and a half years after walking into the leasing center as a temporary consultant, Simone had not only been welcomed on board permanently, but she'd been offered the sales manager position. Finally, she'd found a job that held her interest, one she looked forward to going to every morning. The passion she developed for her managerial position in sales was the perfect distraction from the rest of her life.

Ten o'clock in the morning. The clock was ticking. The Monday morning reports were due to the corporate office in less than an hour. The door to the leasing center chimed, indicating a visitor. The four consultants Simone now managed were all out showing apartments.

*I hope they don't wanna see no apartment,* Simone thought as she mentally transformed into the happy-go-lucky sales manager.

"Hey there. How you doing?" She flashed her dimpled smile to the suited gentleman. "How can I help you this morning?"

"Yeah." He stared at Simone. "Umm…" he moaned, squinting his eyes, deep in thought. "I came to turn in this application. I understand y'all are looking for law enforcement people to work surveillance around here part-time."

"Yes, the residents are complaining about the kids loitering and selling weed. We don't want it to escalate so…" She allowed her simple shrug to complete her sentence. "You're a police officer?"

"Kinda. I work for the DEA, and my particular unit works closely with the county police. We oversee a lot of drug operations, and we've cleaned up quite a few apartment complexes."

"Okay, cool. Maybe you could actually be in charge of the operation here. Like I said, it's not bad, but we don't want it to get bad."

"I understand."

"Since you have the experience and know the cops already, maybe you can run the schedule, hire your own team, everything. I won't have to do anything but hire you." Simone smiled.

"I'm sorry," he said, staring at Simone, "but this is killing me. It seems like I know you from somewhere."

"You think so?"

"Yeah. I never forget a pretty face, and yours has to be one of the prettiest I've seen in a long time. It'll come to me when I leave," he said as he handed her the application. "So what do I do now?"

"When did you want to start?"

"I can start tonight, for real."

"Then tonight it is…" Simone glanced at the application for a name. "Perkins?" Her memory kicked in. "Agent Perkins! Oh

190

my goodness, I remember you."

"So we have met?"

"Yeah." Simone lowered her voice. "You stopped this other officer from checking me a few years ago over in Stanford Woods. I'll never ever forget that. I was scared to death."

"Yeah! That's where I know you from! You have that pretty little baby."

"Shh," Simone said, looking around the office, making sure they were the only two present. "Nobody knows I have a baby."

"Why? Something happened to your daughter?"

"No, but it's a long story. Never mention her in here."

"Okay, but you gotta explain that some day. Maybe over dinner." His pager vibrated. "Ah, man. They would call me when I was getting ready to ask you out. I'll be back," he said, heading out of the office.

Later that week, Simone sat behind her desk, finalizing the leases for the ten families that were scheduled to move in Saturday morning. Eight of the apartments were ready to go, and two were still being worked on by the maintenance staff. Simone wasn't leaving until she'd inspected each and every one. She didn't have far to travel. Home was now a two-bedroom apartment within the community. She walked to and from work every day.

"Hey!" Agent Perkins walked into the leasing center. "What you doing working late on a Friday night? Somebody as pretty as you should be out on a date."

"Sounds good, but I have people moving in tomorrow. I still have to inspect two more apartments, but that may have to wait until the morning. I'm starving and I'm tired."

"Well, I'm going to pick up something to eat. I can bring you back something."

"Good," Simone said, reaching for her purse.

"You don't need your purse. I got it," Agent Perkins said. "Just tell me what you want."

"No, that's okay, Perkins. I can get it."

"Simone, I'm not taking your money, and stop calling me Perkins. I told you before to call me Andre."

She glanced up from her purse. "Okay, Andre. Bring me whatever. I'm so hungry that it won't even matter."

Simone's workday rarely ended on time, and night after night, Andre kept her company, filling the time with chatter and Styrofoam containers stuffed with their dinner. He surprised her one Saturday night, strolling into the leasing center in a crisp white linen outfit.

"Wow, don't you look nice," Simone complimented. "I guess you're not working here tonight, huh? You look like you have a hot date."

"I do," he said confidently. "With you."

After much persuasion, he convinced Simone to say goodnight to her desk and join him for dinner at an exquisite restaurant.

"You belong in places like this," Andre whispered softly, caressing Simone at the small of her back as the maître d' escorted them to an intimate booth.

The relationship progressed, and each weekend, Andre surprised Simone with something different. He wined and dined her as if she were a queen and impressed her with his gentlemanly mannerisms. He opened her car door, pulled out her chair, and allowed her to order first with a graceful wave of his hand. It was those simple things and more that carried a lot of weight with Simone. No other man had ever treated her like Andre.

Two hundred and thirty pounds of solid muscle, Andre walked with the confidence of a soldier. Chiseled to perfection, with a clean, bald head and dark features that rested handsomely along his milk-chocolate skin, he was the epitome of sexy. He was rough, but not thuggish like Kevin. And while Andre often conversed with the higher-ups in corporate America, he could break it down and keep it real with the niggas in the hood. He was sexy, diverse, and a perfect gentleman.

● ● ●

Andre pulled the dark federal cruiser into a dimly lit park that overlooked a manmade lake.

"What are we doing here?" Simone questioned.

Andre had told her two days ago to wear her infamous black wrap dress on Friday. He adored the dress and had gone ballistic the first time he saw her in it, admiring the way the wind flirted with the flimsy material, allowing him a little glimpse of her shapely thighs.

"Hold on a second," Andre said as he hopped from the car and walked around to his trunk. Seconds later, clutching a wicker picnic basket, he opened Simone's door and reached for her manicured hand.

"We going on a picnic?" she asked, stepping from the undercover vehicle.

"Yeah, I saw this little basket in the store a few weeks ago, and I've been planning this day ever since."

Strolling across the park, Andre pulled a small blanket from the basket and draped it on the grass for Simone.

"Have a seat, Maybelline."

"Maybelline?" She knelt down and sat on the blanket. "Why you call me that country-ass name?"

"Maybelline, the cosmetics. You look like you should be a

CoverGirl model or something."

"Ah." She blushed, flattered by the compliment.

Andre pulled a bottle of white wine, two plastic cups, and a deck of cards from the basket. "Let's toast," he said.

"To…"

"To us. Three months ago today, our paths crossed."

"You mean they crossed again."

"True. But we've been going out strong for about a month, and I've enjoyed every second of it."

"So have I," Simone agreed.

He popped the cork and filled their glasses. "I want to play a game. You ever played dirty hearts?"

"No," Simone said as she sipped her first glass of wine. "How you play?"

Andre opened the fresh box of cards and shuffled through their stiffness. "It's easy. We just keep picking from the deck until someone draws a heart. If you pluck a heart, you get to ask the other person a dirty question."

"Okay, that's simple enough."

Andre placed the cards in the center of the blanket. "Ladies first. Pluck a card."

Andre and Simone sipped the white wine and plucked card after card. Finally, Simone plucked a heart. She chuckled nervously.

*What in the world do I ask him?* she thought. How dirty was dirty?

"Ask me something."

"Something like what?"

"Anything. It has to be dirty, though. And just so you know, mine are gonna be real dirty, so don't be acting all shy."

"Okay…umm…shit," she said. "Damn, I don't know what

to ask you! You can have my heart."

Andre smiled, but he wasn't letting her off the hook. "No, just ask me something dirty."

Simone sighed. "Okay, umm...did you wash your ass?"

The twosome laughed.

"Yes," Andre chuckled. "Here, drink some more wine so you can loosen up. The questions have to be about sex—sexual dirty," he said as he topped off her cup. She gulped the entire thing down. "Damn," he said, filling her cup again.

"You gotta drink yours, too," Simone urged.

Andre drank his and replenished his cup, as well.

Two more cards were plucked and Simone got another heart.

"Hold up, hold up," she said, gulping down her third cup. "Okay," she huffed, bracing herself. "What's your favorite sexual position?"

"That's not that dirty, but you're getting better. My favorite position..." Andre looked toward the sky, contemplating his answer. "All of them are my favorite."

"See, you talkin' 'bout me needing to loosen up. How you gon' just say all of them? That's too generic." Simone unfolded her legs and stretched them out on the blanket. "Come on, you need to drink some more, too."

Nearly thirty minutes later, Andre and Simone were working their way through the second bottle.

Andre plucked a heart and asked Simone, "Have you ever had oral sex?"

"Yes," she said without hesitation.

"You have?" He seemed surprised.

"Yes."

"You did it or someone did it to you?"

"How do you know it wasn't both?"

"Was it?"

"You already asked your one dirty question," Simone said. Moving the game along, she plucked. Andre plucked another heart.

"Okay, explain the oral sex thing."

"I never did it, but it was done to me."

"Oh, I was getting ready to say. You don't seem like the type to do it."

"What does that mean?"

"Naw, you just seem so innocent."

"It's not that I wouldn't. He just didn't want me to."

"So you've never done it?"

"No, I haven't, and you have to stop cheating. You be trying to ask too many questions on one heart." Simone plucked. She came up with a heart and passed Andre a seductive glance. "Do you eat booty?"

He smiled his biggest smile of the night. "The wine really loosened you up. To answer your question, yes. It's one of my favorite desserts."

Five plucks later, Andre plucked a heart. "Would you mind if I eat you?"

"Ah, that's why you wanted me to wear this dress and drink all this gotdamn wine."

"Yep, that's exactly why." Andre eased from the blanket and crawled over to Simone. "So can I?" he asked, whispering in her ear as he nibbled gently on her neck.

"What you waiting for?" Simone asked.

"I gotta take your panties off." Andre caressed Simone's plump thighs and inched his hands up her legs. He gasped when his fingers reached her hips. She wasn't wearing any underwear.

• • •

The next day, a delivery guy walked into the leasing center carrying two vases. Each overflowed with a dozen long-stemmed roses.

"I'm looking for Simone Woodard," he said, glancing at the card.

"Those are for me?" Simone was stunned.

"Whoever this guy is, he really has a thing for you. I was in the shop when he came in. He specifically said two dozen, in two separate vases. He wanted me to bring them in one at a time, but I have ten other deliveries. Sign here, please."

Simone pulled the card from the flowers. It read, *Last night was unbelievable. Just like you.*

"Wow," she said. Everything about Andre was blowing her away. *I gotta do something for him.*

Simone left work a few hours early with her ideas running wild. She wanted to prepare a romantic evening for Andre at her place, but there wasn't enough time to prepare an extravagant meal.

*I can just order something from one of our spots,* she thought as she climbed into her car. *Ooh, and I can get a bunch of candles and something sexy to greet him in.*

Simone placed her key in the ignition, but her car wouldn't start.

*Ah, come on.* She tried again, but still nothing. Disgusted, she headed back inside her office and called Andre.

"Hey, what you doing?"

"I was getting ready to come see you. Why, what's up?"

"My car won't start. I was trying to run a few errands."

"Well, I'll take you to run your errands, and then we'll ride past a few car dealerships."

"Car dealerships? For who?"

"For you."

"But all my car probably needs is a battery."

"Let's just go look. You don't have to buy anything."

Andre and Simone hit nearly every car dealership in the area, in search of the so-called perfect deal. Before the week was out, Simone was driving a brand-new champagne-colored Camry off the lot, thanks to Andre and the fifteen hundred dollar check he so eagerly wrote to help cover her down payment.

"I gotta ride by and show my father. Plus, you need to meet him," she said, grinning from ear to ear.

"What about your mother? You don't wanna show her? I wanna see if she looks as crazy as she sounds."

"She's having some kind of end-of-summer cookout tomorrow. I wasn't going, but if you wanna meet her, we can swing past for a few minutes."

"When was the last time you saw your daughter?"

"A few days ago. I don't go as often as I probably should. I hate hearing her call my mother and my stepfather 'Mommy' and 'Daddy.' She has no idea I'm her mother."

"Then tell her."

"Please, and start the battle all over again? Then I'll never see her. At one point, I couldn't even set foot in their house. At least now, Jordan can spend the night with me. My stepsister has to come, too. It's like she's her bodyguard or something."

"So who does your daughter think you are?"

"I don't know." Simone shrugged. "I guess since we both call my mother 'Ma', I'm supposed to be her sister."

"Man, this is some soap-opera mess."

"I'm going to get her back soon, though. Things are almost

where I need them to be. The attorneys that I spoke with when the whole mess happened said it's hard to take custody. So, in order to win my case, I have to be squeaky clean, stable, professional…all those things."

"You're already all those things."

"Yeah, but the judge is going to compare me to the two parent home Jordan has now so I have to make sure everything on my end is perfect. I have to redo my budget and factor in a car payment now. I had money set aside to put Jordan in private school. Now I have to make sure I have money for tuition and my car payment."

"I'll help you, Simone. You know that."

"You've already proven that." Simone smiled. "But I have to show them that I can do all these things on my own. I have to get her back. I couldn't take it if I lost especially when I hadn't done anything wrong to lose her in the first place."

"Wow. So umm," Andre began, fishing for a way to change the subject. "How you like your car?"

"I love it, but not as much as I love you," Simone said as she reached over and squeezed Andre's thigh. He grabbed her hand and slid it up to his penis. "You so nasty," she said, squeezing the bulge in his pants.

He moved her hand aside and undid his zipper. Maneuvering around inside his boxers, he freed himself.

"Go somewhere and park. Let's break the car in." Just the thought made Andre good and hard, but Simone was already pulling up in front of Thomas's house.

"Too late," she said, glancing at his erection. "C'mon. Now my father will see why I really love you."

● ● ●

Simone couldn't wait to hear her father's opinion. She

called him bright and early Saturday morning. "So, Daddy, what did you think?"

"He's an a'ight guy. I like how he's willing to help you," Thomas said. "But them detectives and police officers got a lotta women. You sure you wanna deal wit' that?"

"Yeah, but he's not like that, Daddy."

"Not yet, but watch what I tell you. When he starts accusing you of stuff you know you ain't doing, that normally means he's doing something."

"Why you wishing bad luck on me?"

"I'm not wishing bad luck on you. I'm telling you 'cause I love you and want you to be ahead of the game. Is he there with you now?"

"No, he's at work."

"What your crazy-ass momma say about him?"

"She hasn't met him yet. She's having a cookout later on today, so I'm taking him over there."

"Well, I hope you don't be nothing like her."

"What you mean by that?"

"Don't get so caught up in him or any other man that you forget about your child. You got your apartment, a good job, and reliable transportation now. It's time for you to work on getting your daughter back, don't you think?"

"I'm working on it, Daddy."

Later that evening, after Andre had time to shower and change from his uniform, he and Simone headed to Angela's.

"Hi, Simone." Jordan grinned as Simone and Andre walked through the fence into the backyard.

"Hey, Jordan." Simone kneeled down and planted a kiss on Jordan's cheek. "I want you to meet somebody. This is Mr. Andre."

"Hi, Mr. Andre." Jordan said as she smiled and waved her hand.

"Hey, Jordan!" Stan yelled, strolling toward them with one of his friends. From a distance, Simone thought the guy looked familiar. "Your mother wants you."

Jordan tugged on Andre's hand. "Come meet my mommy, Mr. Andre."

"Okay," Andre replied and skipped along with her.

"Hey, Simone!" Stan hugged his sister. "What took you so long to get here?"

"Please! I wasn't in a rush to come over here. I had to wait for Andre to get off anyway. Oh my God, is this who I think it is?"

Fat Ed smiled. "What's up, girl?" he said, hugging Simone. "How you been? Wait till I tell you-know-who that I saw you. You look good, too. Shit, damn good."

"Hey, do you still talk to Ms. Kennard?" Simone asked.

"Yeah. I was telling your brother how bad she wants to see Jordan. She ain't seen her since she was a baby, and dag, look at her. I don't know who she look like, you or Kevin."

Simone looked around for Angela. She spotted Andre giving her a hug, which meant the formal introduction had been made. Digging inside her purse, she pulled Jordan's most recent picture from her wallet.

"Don't be a snitch, Stan!" Simone said as she handed the picture to Fat Ed. "Give this to Ms. Kennard."

"I'm not in it, and I don't see nothing," Stan said as Fat Ed put the picture in his back pocket.

As Angela and Andre headed in their direction, Simone noticed the slight look of irritation on Andre's face.

*Wow, she musta said something crazy,* Simone thought.

"Stan, Ed, let me introduce y'all to my boo."

Andre mingled well, laughing and joking with everybody. He became the center of attention, impressing the crowd with his heroic tales from work.

*Yeah, he's a keeper for sure,* Simone thought as she listened to the stories with a smile on her face, never once caring that she'd already heard the bulk of them.

Later, for some odd reason, Andre wasn't his normal chatty, touchy-feely self. Crashing at his apartment after the barbecue, he clung to his side of the bed and surfed through the television channels in silence.

"You okay?" Simone finally asked. "Was that too much for you?"

"Come on, Simone. Let's not pretend. You know I saw you."

"You saw me? You saw me do what?"

Andre glanced over his shoulder and shot Simone a look of disgust.

"Andre." She chuckled. "What in the world are you talking about?"

"Simone, you didn't give your brother's friend your number?"

"Huh?"

"I saw you go in your purse and pass him something. You weren't giving him your number?"

"Andre, is that why you laying here not saying anything? Ed and Jordan's dad are god-brothers or something. I gave Ed a picture of Jordan to give to Kevin's mother."

Andre wasn't buying it.

"I'm telling the truth. Look in my wallet. There's a picture missing!"

"Yeah, whatever Simone."

Just then, Simone remembered her father's words of advice. *When he starts accusing you of stuff you know you ain't doing, that normally means he's doing something.*

"Hmm," Simone said.

"Hmm, what?"

"Nothing. I was just thinking about something my father said."

# *Chapter Twenty*
## *1994*

"Simone, you have a call on line two," one of her consultants yelled through the office. Simone shook her head while scribbling a note to herself to remind the chile that she wasn't at home and that the transfer button on the phone worked well when used properly.

"Hi, this is Simone," she greeted the caller.

"Simone, this is Sandra Small from Dr. Covington's office."

"Yes," Simone said, wondering why her ob-gyn's office was calling. Her health insurance was fine, and she wasn't experiencing any known girly problems.

"I'm calling because we need to start your prenatal care."

"Excuse me? You must have the wrong number. This is Simone Woodard."

The nurse cackled. "Yes, and that's just who I'm looking for. The Simone Woodard that was here two days ago for her annual check-up which was scheduled for one o'clock. We recorded your weight at one forty-three, and if I remember correctly, you had on a cute little brown dress 'cause I asked you where you got it from," she said. "Would you happen to be that Simone Woodard?"

"Yes," Simone said hesitantly.

"Then congratulations!" the nurse said with glee. "I guess this is a surprise for you?"

"Oh, it's more than a surprise. Maybe you have my blood work mixed up with somebody else's. I mean, I haven't missed a period or anything. Plus, my boyfriend and I take precautions. We use condoms all the time." Simone whispered.

"Well, you know condoms aren't one hundred percent. Half of our expecting patients use condoms," the nurse chuckled. "And it's not uncommon to still have a cycle, especially since you're so early. But, yes, according to your blood work, you're definitely pregnant. I hope that calls for excitement."

"I'm not sure what it calls for," Simone mumbled, wondering what Andre would say. "Ms. Small, is there any way I can call you back, or better yet, can you call this other number and leave a message saying that you need me to schedule a prenatal appointment?"

"That's an unusual request, but one I can surely accommodate. What's the number?"

Lunchtime rolled around, and Simone wasn't sure if Andre had gotten the message or not. *My father's gonna have a fit*, she thought. This would be her second baby by a different man, something Thomas was sure to frown upon. Sure, Simone and Andre had been going strong for well over two years, but there was no diamond glistening from Simone's finger. And the biggest issue of them all would be Jordan. How in the world was Simone going to have another child when she still didn't have custody of her first?

"Excuse me, ma'am." Andre appeared out of nowhere and placed a vase of colorful spring flowers on Simone's desk. "And since I want a healthy baby, this is for you, too." He set a plastic grocery bag next to the bouquet and unpacked spring water, oranges, and watermelon.

"I take it you got the message," Simone said, absent of any feeling.

"Yeah, and now more than ever, I have to take care of my queen." He smiled sincerely and planted a kiss on her cheek.

"So you're happy?" she asked, somewhat concerned.

"I mean, we hadn't planned on having a baby, but," he said, shrugging away the thought, "yeah, I'm still happy."

"Well, my father's not gonna be, and Lord, I can hear my mother now. She's going to have a field day with this one."

"I don't know what's up with you and your mother, but your father will understand. Plus," he added as he pulled Simone up from her chair to shield her comfortably in his embrace, "I plan to marry you one day."

● ● ●

For the next seven months, Andre catered to Simone's every need, waiting on her hand and foot. He even tagged along for most of the doctor appointments.

"One of my partners asked me to work part-time at the club on New Year's Eve. It's a hundred dollars an hour. Are we doing anything?" Andre asked, rubbing Simone's enormous belly as they chilled in his apartment.

"Please, look at me. Do I look like I wanna do anything?"

In the midst of the so-called pregnancy glow, Simone's nose and butt had spread, her feet and hands were swollen, and the burning she felt in her chest every night had her gulping down gallons of milk against the doctor's orders. She couldn't wait to deliver her load and lose the thirty-five pounds she'd gained.

"Go 'head and make the money," she encouraged. "We gotta stock the diaper fund anyway."

"Well, I'll be outta there by three. Afterward," Andre added, "I'll just come to your place."

• • •

Eight o'clock New Year's morning, 1995, Simone awoke feeling revived and excited about the unforeseen promises of the New Year. After stretching the kinks from her restless limbs, she rolled over to kiss Andre good morning for the first time that year. But to her surprise, he wasn't there. His side of the bed hadn't been touched. Folding back the comforter, she pulled herself from the bed to check the apartment, but there was still no sign of him.

*Didn't he say he was coming here?* she thought, second-guessing their plan. She snatched the cordless from its base and called Andre's house twice, each time allowing the phone to ring off the hook in hopes of waking him, but he didn't answer.

*I must be in the wrong place,* Simone thought. She jumped in the shower, threw on her only pair of maternity jeans with one of Andre's T-shirts, and headed across town to his apartment.

The parking lot was packed. Andre's truck was parked in its usual space, but his unmarked cruiser was nowhere in sight. Double-parked in front of the building, Simone smacked on her hazards and wobbled up the three flights of stairs to check his apartment, but he wasn't there either.

Negative thoughts began to haunt Simone as she secured his locks and headed back to her place. *He gotta be at my house by now,* she thought. However, that was wishful thinking. Andre wasn't there, and as she scrolled through her caller ID box, she noticed he hadn't even returned her calls. Where the hell was he, and why hadn't he at least called back?

Simone's worry transformed into frustration as New Year's Day ticked away. Finally, early in the evening, Andre called.

"Hey, what's up?" he uttered groggily.

"Nothing. Happy New Year," she wished halfheartedly.

"Happy New Year to you, too," he yawned into the phone.

"What happened? I thought you were coming here."

"Yeah, I realized I was in the wrong place when I got here and you weren't in my bed. I was too tired to turn around."

"So why didn't you call?"

"I'm calling you now. I just woke up. I didn't get in 'til almost five. I was tired as hell."

"Five this morning?"

"Yeah," he said through another yawn.

"Five, huh?" Simone mumbled, fighting to conceal her true emotions. "I guess you been 'sleep the whole time."

"Yeah. I saw you been paging me."

"Mmm-hmm, I've been calling, paging, and I even came by."

"You came by?"

"That's what I said, but you been there 'sleep since five," Simone said more to herself. "I don't believe this," she mumbled.

"Oh, Lord," he huffed. "Don't tell me we gonna bring the New Year in arguing. You about to mess everything up."

"Andre! I came past your house this morning 'round ten o'clock, Mr. 'I was knocked out,' and your ass hadn't even been there. Your bed was still made, and you gonna tell me you been there since five, and I'm the one 'bout to mess everything up?"

"Simone—"

"Don't Simone me. I can't believe how easily that lie rolled off your tongue. So where were you?"

Andre's silence fueled Simone's anger. She had no desire to hear him breathe through the phone. She'd asked a legitimate question and wanted a legitimate answer, not the bullshit he'd tried to feed her. Irritated by his silence, she slammed the phone down. Within the hour, he was walking through her door with his face drooped to the floor.

"I'm sorry," he confessed gingerly, sitting at the foot of her bed with his shoulders slumped. He couldn't even face her. "I had no reason to lie to you."

"But you did, and now it just makes me wonder what else you've lied about."

"Simone, believe me. I've been beating myself up since you hung up on me. This girl I know was at the club with her boyfriend. Their ride left them, so I took 'em home. She ended up fixing breakfast, and I chilled with them. Before I realized it, I had fallen asleep on their couch."

Simone sat in bed, staring at the back of Andre's head, wishing like hell she had a cinder block to throw at him. But busting him in the head wasn't good enough.

"That's the best you can do?"

"What you mean?" He turned to face her.

"You stayed with them, the third wheel on New Year's Day, and fell asleep on their couch?"

"Simone, it's the truth."

Simone sucked her teeth. She wasn't buying the lame excuse.

"I know how crazy it sounds, especially after I lied, but I swear I'm telling you the truth."

"So if it were that simple, that innocent, why'd you lie?"

Andre moved closer to Simone. Dangling from the edge of the bed, he still couldn't bring himself to face her. "We've been doing so good…and here I am 'bout to fuck it all up lying over nothing. I swear," he said, tracing Simone's hand with the tips of his fingers. "I'm telling you the truth. That's why I jumped up and came right over here." He grabbed her hand and caressed it in his own. "I love you so much. Can we act like this didn't happen and start the New Year over?"

● ● ●

Kayla Marie Perkins, a ginger-colored baby with oodles of curly black hair, was the talk of the nursery. Andre, the proud father, strutted around the hospital with his chest inflated, handing out pink bubble-gum cigars.

In the grocery store, the mall, or wherever else the family ventured, Andre faithfully pushed the stroller or carried his beautiful little trophy in his arms. Yet, when there was no one to impress with his daughter's cuteness, cooing goo-goos and ga-gas in Kayla's face was the extent of his parental role. Still, Simone didn't complain, not one time. She welcomed the feedings scattered throughout the night and the shitty diapers that only she changed. She was a mommy again, and that was more important than anything.

Kicking off her brown pumps, Simone slid her coffee-colored nylons down her hips and plopped on the bed she'd neglected to make that morning. The three months she'd taken off from work had flown by. Hearing the front door close, she knew Andre was home with Kayla.

"We need to find a new sitter," Andre bellowed, absent of any greeting as he strolled into the bedroom, lugging Kayla in her seat. "I'm not feeling the one you found. It's a trillion kids over there." With a look of irritation, he sat Kayla's seat on the bed and headed into the walk-in closet to strip from his suit.

"Those kids only come in the evening. Kayla's the only baby she watches."

"Well, I don't like her. I think we should take Kayla to your mother. She's too chocolate for your mother and Ricardo to pass off as theirs." He chuckled.

"I'm glad you find that amusing."

"What?" he asked. "That old mess still bothers you? You and your mother seem cool to me. I thought you were over it."

"Over it? Andre, she stole my child! What kind of crazy shit is that?" Simone's face hardened as she unfastened the straps on Kayla's car seat.

The clicking sound startled Kayla, waking her from her catnap. Simone could tell by the way Kayla clenched her tiny fists and squinted her face that she was getting ready to light up the room with her wail.

Andre strolled from the closet in his boxers and planted himself on the bed next to Simone. "Do you know how many little girls are molested or raped at the babysitter's house every day? I'm not saying that would happened, but it was just too many kids over there for me. I know you and your mom have issues, but she's still Kayla's grandmother. Won't nothing happen to her there."

"Andre, I'm not switching," Simone shot back over Kayla's cry. "I don't have a problem with the babysitter."

Simone lifted Kayla from her car seat. Instantly, her eyes caught sight of the huge wet stain against the lining of the seat. *What the hell?* Kayla's sleeper was drenched, and the way the diaper sagged told Simone she'd been that way for hours. She knew Andre had noticed the stain, as well. There was no way he could've missed it, and although he didn't shout out in victory, it was the winning point in his defense nonetheless.

"I'll drop her off and pick her up," he said. "You won't have to do a thing until you're comfortable."

• • •

Bored out of her mind, Simone stared out the palladium window while counting down the last thirty minutes of her workday.

"Hi, Ms. Woodard." The resident stood timidly before Simone's desk in a floral-print dress and house slippers, peering over her dark-framed glasses.

Stuck in her daydream about nothing, Simone hadn't heard the door chime announce her visitor.

"I'm so sorry." Simone forced a smile and stood to give her the proper greeting. "I'm sitting here in another world."

"How's the baby?" she asked softly.

"She's fine, Mrs. Marshall. Thanks for asking. What can I do for you? Are you here to pay your rent?"

"Oh, no," Mrs. Marshall said. Gone was the timid disposition she'd bore walking into the office. Standing proud and tall, she passed Simone a white envelope. "This is my thirty-day notice. I bought a house."

"Congratulations, Mrs. Marshall!" Simone praised sincerely.

"Thanks, Simone. My accountant said I had to if I didn't want to keep paying Uncle Sam. Now I'm thinking about getting my real estate license. My agent made eleven thousand dollars off of me, and the heifer wasn't even that good."

Simone was surprised. "Eleven thousand off one house?"

"That's what I said. I wouldn't have believed it if I hadn't seen the check. I'm considering taking the class that starts in about three months. I already have the papers and everything.

212

There's a class starting in a week, but that's too soon for me, with the move and all."

*Eleven thousand dollars,* Simone repeated to herself. *Good gracious. Four checks like that and I'd pass my salary.*

Mrs. Marshall handed Simone a business card. "I can hear you thinking, girl." She chuckled. "You really should consider it, Simone. I mean, you're already getting people into apartments; why not houses?" Mrs. Marshall headed to the door and pointed up at the clock. "They don't close until seven, so you still have plenty of time to register."

"Thanks, Mrs. Marshall," she said, staring at the card. "I think I just might do that."

● ● ●

The evening real estate classes kicked Simone's butt. The final exam was a cinch, but now it was time to prep for the real deal—the state exam. However, before she could even consider picking up another book, she needed to put her feet up and relax, if only for a minute. Between Kayla, the classes three nights a week, and the long hours behind the desk, Simone was pooped, and Andre's birthday offered the perfect excuse for a getaway.

The sun hid behind the crystal-blue waters of the Bahamas. Orange metallic sparks popped from the bonfire while the steel drum sound of the Caribbean echoed down the beach. Laughter filled the evening air as the free all-you-can-drink Bahama Mama punch transformed the vacationing souls into buck-wild party animals. Hand in hand, Andre and Simone moseyed to the straw hut bar, ready to get their drink on, too. As Simone climbed on top of the wicker stool, her colorful sarong fell open, giving the bartender a glimpse of her thighs.

"Man," the bartender said in his heavy Bahamian accent.

"Your wife is beautiful."

"I'm not his wife," Simone announced, playfully fanning the fingers on her left hand. "Ain't no ring on none of these fingers."

The bartender smiled and gently grabbed her hand. "Stay here on the island with me. I'll make you my wife," he said in fun, his shoulders jiggling up and down as he chuckled. Releasing her hand, he extended his hand to Andre for the brotherly handshake known all over the world. "You two ready to partake in the festivities?"

"Oh, yeah," Andre said. "How potent is the punch?"

With a raised brow, the bartender poured the reddish concoction into two plastic cups and sat them in front of Andre and Simone. "See for yourself."

Simone eased the cup to her lips and took a sip, bracing herself for the kick. "It can't be any liquor in this." She frowned. "It taste just like fruit punch."

The bartender smiled.

"Naw, Simone," Andre said. "That thing probably loaded with extra sweet liquor. That's the kinda drink that'll creep up on you."

"Whatever. Give us three more."

"Three! Hold up, Simone," Andre protested.

"Naw, look at them." Simone glanced at the intoxicated crowd partying on the beach. "We need to catch up. So," she said to the bartender, "we'll take three a piece."

"Whoo, whoo, whoo," the bartender cackled as he began filling the additional cups. "It's gonna be however you want it tonight, my American friend."

"Yeah, if she don't throw up on me first," Andre said with his first cup in hand. "If you really wanna get drunk, we gotta drink all four cups back-to-back."

"A'ight," Simone said with a shrug of her shoulders. "Let's make it fun. Let's race."

Andre smiled, welcoming the challenge. Without warning, he yelled, "Go."

The twosome slammed the punch until all eight cups sat empty on the bar.

"Damn," Andre said. "I didn't think you could do it."

"Yeah," Simone boasted. "Now what?"

"Now," he said as he reached for her hand and eased her from the barstool, "let's go make love on the beach."

Andre wrapped his arm around Simone's waist and untied her sarong, allowing it to drift to the sand. "I told you, you don't need this. You already got these islanders going crazy; let them see that phat ass."

But Simone wasn't confident with the fifteen pounds Kayla had left behind. "Ugh, Andre. I'm all fat," she protested, reaching for the sarong.

"Simone, you don't need it." He grabbed her hands and led her out into the nippy blue ocean. "Whew!" He trembled, splashing through the waters.

"Hold up, Andre." Simone shivered as the waves rocked against her hips. "I don't wanna go out too far. I can't swim, remember?"

"I got you," he reassured, pulling her closer to him. "We gotta go out a little farther. It's dark, but I wanna make sure nobody can see us. Take your bottoms off," he instructed, "but don't let 'em go."

"Oh my God. Can you imagine?" Holding on to Andre for support, Simone slipped off her bikini bottoms and placed them around her arm. "Now what?" she asked, smiling.

215

"Now this." He freed himself from the slit in his swim trucks and guided her hand to the erection he was slowly forming. "Make me hard," he whispered, sucking on her neck.

She wrapped her hands around his shaft and stroked him until he stood at attention.

"Wrap your legs around me."

Simone surveyed her surroundings. They were out too far for her personal comfort. "Uh-uh," she mumbled. They'd been drinking, and although the alcohol hadn't caught up with them yet, she wasn't taking a chance on Andre dropping her. She turned around, splashing water until her ass rubbed up against his hardness. Looking over her shoulder, she said, "It's this way or nothing."

"You know I like it like this, too."

Andre fought against the friction of the water and worked his hardness inside Simone. "Ah, yeah," he moaned. He slid his hands underneath her hot-pink bikini top, caressing her breasts as he throbbed deeper and deeper inside of her. Finally, his body shuddered in ecstasy.

Couples in the midst of their own passion cuddled along the shore where the sand and the ocean flirted. A handful of the couples paused from their fervor long enough to applaud Andre and Simone as they strolled ashore, from the deep blue sea.

"Oh, that's embarrassing," Simone said as she shook the sand from her sarong.

"No, it's not. We don't know them." Andre grinned. "C'mon. Let's get some more of that punch."

Four punches later, Simone was tipsy and a cup away from being drunk. Andre, on the other hand, had one foot on drunk and the other on pissy. Laughing loudly, his words were nearly slurred beyond comprehension. Simone had no idea how many

Bahama Mamas he'd poured into his system. She'd stopped counting at eight.

The steel drum band broke out into a Caribbean conga, sending the intoxicated crowd into a frenzy. After clowning his way onto the makeshift stage in the middle of the beach, the MC screamed, "I need all the people who came to party over here! C'mon, y'all," he instructed as the rowdy bunch congaed their way to the dance floor, where a real party was forming. "I'm gonna teach ya' the line dances we do here on the islands. We do more than the Electric Slide and the Macarena."

The MC moved and twisted his body like a professional hip-hop dancer. He showed the crowd the basic steps to a few dances and then added his flavor to those daring enough to try.

"Some of you white people need another drink." He laughed. "But some of y'all got it goin' on." He leaped from the stage to do his thing on the floor with everybody else. Shaking his hips provocatively, he danced with a few of the women in the crowd and put a few on display by escorting them back to the stage.

"Whew, look at this sexy lady," he said as Simone danced with her back to Andre. She smiled and broke it down playfully with the MC. He grabbed her hand to lure her onstage, but Simone snatched her hand back, shaking her head no. Her partying side was ready, but the part of her uninfluenced by the alcohol reminded her of the extra weight jiggling around in her hot-pink bikini.

"Last call for alcohol," the MC roared over the mic.

The end of the party was near. Wiping the sweat from her forehead, Simone reached out and grabbed Andre by his arm.

"Come on," she said. "Let's go get another one 'fore they shut it down." He slapped her hand away. "What the fuck is wrong with you?" she asked.

"Don't even try it, Simone," he said, storming from the dance floor in a drunken fit. "Go over there wit' your boyfriend!"

"My boyfriend?" she questioned, walking quickly alongside him, trying to keep up. "Who the hell is my boyfriend?"

Andre stopped dead in the sand and shot Simone a look of disgust. She'd never seen him so upset. "Simone, you act like I wasn't fuckin' right there," he yelled, creating a scene.

Simone chuckled, shaking her head as Andre marched up the beach to the bar. *He's drunk,* she told herself over and over to keep from matching his tone.

"Get the fuck away from me, you stupid bitch!"

Simone froze, shocked as hell. "What did you call me?"

"You heard what I called you, you trifling-ass hoe. Go over there with the MC!"

Andre stormed off and left Simone standing in the sand with her mouth wide open.

● ● ●

Simone's heart pounded as she waited for her results to scroll across the computer screen.

*C'mon,* she thought. The suspense was killing her. She wanted to go back and change a few of her answers, but decided against second-guessing herself. So much was riding on her results. She wanted to quit her job and become a real estate agent full-time. The flexible schedule and the fact that she would be her own boss were both appealing. And pass or fail, Simone was hoping her results would be the tension breaker for her and Andre.

The remaining days in the Bahamas had been money flushed down the toilet. Simone had tried to strike up conversations, but Andre shattered her attempts with his one-word responses. Initially, she blamed the argument on all the alcohol he had consumed at the beach party, but when the silent treatment followed them home, she realized she was wrong. Not only was Andre feeding her one-word answers, but all of a sudden, he had a million drug cases to work on every single night. In the evening, he'd stroll through Simone's apartment simply to drop off Kayla and head back out to work. Three, sometimes four o'clock in the morning, he'd come in, climb in bed, clinging to his side the way he did when he was pissed, and doze off. He still had his apartment across town, but Simone's was more convenient. Besides, it was his idea for Kayla to go to Angela's, which made getting her back and forth his responsibility.

For two weeks, Simone relived the beach party in between cramming for her test. She remembered her simple two-step exchange with the MC, which was all in fun, just like the meaningless, innocent flirting with the bartender. Something else had to have happened, something crucial that her tipsiness wouldn't allow her to remember. There was absolutely no way Andre was walking around pissed for nothing.

The computer came to life. Seconds later, 'Congratulations' flashed across the screen. Simone leaped from her chair. "YES! YES! YES!" she rejoiced. She'd passed.

As she drove down the highway, her ideas ran rampant. Kathy, her supervisor, had already given her permission to hold a home-buying seminar.

"Having a realtor on board is just another incentive we can offer to the residents," Kathy had said. "And since the bulk of them move because they're buying a house, you may as well be their agent."

Simone reached for her cell to call Andre and share the news, but her call went straight to his voice mail.

"Hey, it's me. Call—"

*"Please enter your password."*

"What in the world?" Simone sighed. The voice mail prompt had cut her off right in the middle of her message. Hanging up, she redialed the number, and once again, his voice mail answered.

"Hey, guess what. I—"

*"Please enter your password."*

"Come the hell on!" Simone said in frustration. "I don't know the password, stupid!" Andre's password was just that— Andre's password. She never needed it or even had a desire to know it.

*"Please enter your password."*

Shrugging her shoulders, she thought, *what the hell,* and entered his date of birth. "This stupid-ass thing. Why can't I just leave my—"

*"You have one new message."*

She smiled. *Now, that was too easy. I know him too well,* she thought, realizing the one message was probably the message she just tried to leave.

"Hey, Andre," a female's voice purred into the phone. "This is Sunshine…well, Sanora. You know I'm only Sunshine onstage." She he-heed. "I just wanted to let you know that I *enjoyed* you last night. Give me a call. I'm calling to see what's up for tonight."

Simone's excitement shattered into a trillion pieces. She replayed the message again, but nothing had changed. She couldn't believe it. "Another cheatin'-ass muthafucka!"

# Chapter Twenty-One

Trash bags packed with all the mess Andre harbored at Simone's sat in the hallway outside her door. Not only had she packed his shit, but the on-call maintenance technician had changed her locks. Since the beginning of the year, Andre had been serving her bullshit on a silver platter, and she couldn't tolerate another helping. Simone was through, but Andre had no plans of letting her go.

Night after night, he tapped on Simone's door, determined to mend their relationship. He threw on the charm, wooing her the way he had in the beginning of their relationship. He explained over and over again, and his tears tugged on her heartstrings. Deep down inside, she wanted to believe his pitiful excuse—that 'Sunshine' had been nothing more than an informant who'd given him information that led to a big drug bust. Andre swore that the only thing he'd been guilty of was taking her out to dinner. Yet, the more he explained, the more Sunshine's words echoed in Simone's head. *I enjoyed you last night* was way more than surf and turf, and Andre had done more than lick his fingers.

Simone's home-buying seminar had generated a ton of business. In two months, she'd already sold three houses, and she had four sales pending. With nearly seven sales under her belt, her commission would well exceed her salary as the sales manager. She tried to hang in there with her job at the leasing center. After all, that was where six of her seven clients had come from. However, the long hours there, coupled with her clients and Kayla, were all becoming a bit too much. Though her hectic schedule kept her mind off of Andre, Simone knew she couldn't continue the pace. With Kathy's blessing, she bid farewell to her apartment and the managerial position that had ultimately revived her from the state of depression inflicted by her mother and moved in with Thomas and Mae.

Thomas greeted his daughter with open arms once again, knowing it was only for a matter of weeks. Simone was buying a house. The seventh house she sold was to herself.

Sitting on the couch in front of the television, Thomas jumped up to help Simone as she fumbled through the front door.

"There go Granddaddy's baby!" he yelled, removing Kayla from Simone's arms. "Where you been, boo-boo?" Thomas said playfully as he unzipped Kayla's jacket.

For Simone, Thomas had been more help in the last two months with Kayla than Andre had been her entire life.

"Come on over here and watch the game with Granddaddy."

"I got two surprises for you," Simone said. She plopped onto the loveseat with her attaché case.

"For who, me?"

"Yeah." Clicking open her briefcase, she tossed Thomas a

222

set of keys. "I went to settlement today!" she beamed. "That's your set of keys."

"What!" he shouted. "You really bought it?"

"Yep." Simone smiled brightly as she continued to fish through her briefcase. "And," she said, passing her father a white envelope. "That's for you, too. Open it!" she instructed, tapping her feet like a child.

Thomas eased his fingers through the seal and gasped at the five-thousand-dollar cashier's check.

Simone danced in her seat. "Daddy, say something! It's like you hit the lottery!"

"Girl," Thomas mumbled, shaking his head. "I'm so proud of you."

"Don't be proud of me because I gave you money."

"Simone, you know damn well it ain't got nothing to do with this check. My baby girl is turning out to be everything that I imagined she would. You better be the best agent out there, you hear me?"

"I'm already working on it, Daddy. And I'm ready to get Jordan back."

"Good. Now all we have to do is find you a husband."

• • •

Simone loved her house. It was everything she wanted: four bedrooms, a first-floor library that instantly became her home office, a master bath with a Jacuzzi tub, and an unfinished basement that she wasn't completing anytime soon. The house had it all, except for the cure to her loneliness. She'd exchanged numbers with a cutie or two that she'd met at the club with Lavon, but none of them wowed her the way Andre had in the beginning. Chivalry wasn't dead and she refused to kill it. With no one to date, she spent more of her free time with the girls—

Jordan, Alicia, and Kayla. While they each had their own room, they rotated camping out in either Simone's king-sized bed or snuggled up in front of the family room fireplace, watching movies.

"Hi, Simone!" Jordan grinned as she and Alicia got in the car. In the front seat, Jordan immediately began flipping through the radio stations. "Where we going?"

"Well," Simone said, backing out of Angela's driveway, "I'm going to take you to see my father."

"Ooh, good, Kayla's granddaddy. I like him. He's crazy."

"Yeah," Simone said slowly. She was tiptoeing down tender territory. When it came to Jordan, Simone walked on eggshells, obeying all of Angela's rules, spoken and unspoken. Taking Jordan to see Thomas on a regular basis was one of those things Simone knew Angela would have a problem with.

"Well, remember, he wants you to call him Granddaddy, too."

"Okay," Jordan said casually. She found a song she liked on the radio and turned the volume up.

"His girlfriend, Mae, has been dying to meet you." Simone said over the music.

"Okay," Jordan uttered, more focused on the radio than on Simone. She snapped her fingers, cleared her throat, and started singing at the top of her lungs. Her tone was beautiful, her tempo perfect. She hit every note, the highs and the lows, and hung in there with the runs and the riffs, leaving Simone in awe.

Alicia noticed Simone's expression in the mirror and said, "Yeah, Simone, she sings all the time just like you used to."

"You can sing, Simone?" Jordan asked.

"Yeah, I use to sing all the time in school. At the talent shows, the assemblies, everything. Sometimes my history teacher, Mr. Berry, would let me entertain the class. You sound pretty good, Jordan. I'm impressed. You must get that from your mother," she said more so to herself.

"Naw," Jordan shook her head, "my mother can't sing."

As they pulled in front of Thomas's house, Jordan jumped from the car and sprinted up the steps to ring the doorbell.

"Oh my goodness!" Thomas yelled. He smothered Jordan in his embrace. "Girl, look at you!"

Alicia grabbed Kayla from her car seat while Simone fished around, looking for her cell phone.

"Shoot," she said, realizing she'd left it at home. "Hey, Daddy!" she yelled out the window. "I gotta run back home real quick. I left my phone; that's my money."

"Go 'head," Thomas yelled with a fan of his hand. "I got 'em. C'mon, Alicia. Hey, Kayla-boo! Y'all come on in here."

Thomas couldn't take his eyes off of Jordan. He hadn't seen her in so long. "If you don't look like Simone...boy, I tell you!" he beamed as Mae crept up behind him.

"Is this little Miss Jordan?" Mae asked.

"Yeah, this is Jordan. I guess she's Big Miss Jordan now. Jordan, this is my sugar momma, Miss Mae," Thomas playfully introduced.

"Thomas, don't tell her no mess like that!" Mae slapped playfully at his hand.

"Granddaddy, what's a sugar momma?" Jordan asked.

"It's an old woman who takes care of handsome young men like your granddaddy."

"But, Granddaddy," Jordan protested, studying Mae, "she don't look old."

"I know." Thomas chuckled. "I'm just playing with you. You know I have your pictures all over my dresser."

"You do?"

"Yep. I got a couple of them. You just don't know how much I've missed you! How come you don't come see your granddaddy?"

"I don't know." Jordan shrugged. "You gotta tell Simone to bring me."

"Where's my camera? I need to take your picture. Who knows when I'll see you again?" Thomas headed down the hall to his room.

"Wow, you look just like your mother. I can't believe it," Mae said, smiling at Jordan. "A little light-skinned Simone."

"Huh?" Jordan said.

"Oh, umm," Alicia said, fanning her hand to get Mae's attention. She couldn't find a subtle way to let Mae know that Angela was Jordan's proclaimed mother.

Thomas's slipper–covered feet slid across the hardwood floors. "Say cheese, Jordan," he said, ready to snap.

"Granddaddy," Jordan said as the camera flashed. "Miss Mae said I look like my mother, *Simone*." Jordan laughed.

"You do. You just a vanilla version."

"Yeah, Granddaddy, but Simone's not my mother."

"That's what I was trying to tell you," Alicia chimed in. "She don't know."

Mae threw her hand to her mouth. "She don't know?"

"You got to be kidding me," Thomas mumbled in disbelief, just as surprised as Mae. "You serious? She really don't know?" He asked as he set the camera on the kitchen table.

"Mmm-hmm," Alicia confirmed.

"I don't know what? Tell me," Jordan begged.

"I want you to tell me something first," Thomas said. "What's your momma's name?"

"You serious?" Jordan frowned.

"Yeah, what's her name?"

"It's Angela," Jordan said with a silly expression to match the seemingly silly question.

"Angela?" Thomas was shocked as hell. "Then who's your father?"

"Ricardo."

"Lord have mercy." He sucked his teeth and glared at Mae. "That's a gotdamn shame."

"Yeah, this is like one of those cable movies or something."

"This ain't no damn movie. This is real life. Simone ain't never told me Jordan didn't know who the hell she was. What kinda crazy mess is that? It's bad enough Angela stole her, but then she brainwashing her, too?"

"Thomas," Mae interjected, "don't confuse her. She'll know one day."

"What?" Jordan asked anxiously. "What will I know?"

"Boy oh boy, if that ain't Simone. She was nosy, too." Thomas mumbled, smiling despite the seriousness. "Jordan, you don't think Ricardo and Angela too old and wrinkled to be your parents?"

Jordan shrugged. "Umm, I don't know. But they not wrinkled."

"So why you call me Granddaddy?"

"'Cause you told me to the last time I was over here."

"Jordan, I told you to call me Granddaddy 'cause you my *real* granddaughter and I'm your real granddaddy."

"Uh-uh?"

"Who's Simone to you?" he asked.

"Umm, my aunt. No, my sister." Confused, Jordan turned to Alicia for the correct answer. "I don't know. She's something."

"My mother calls Simone her aunt," Alicia added. "Simone says sister."

"Simone says sister? Good God almighty." Thomas couldn't believe Simone was feeding into Angela's scandal. "Listen, Jordan," Thomas said as he sat next to Jordan at the kitchen table. "I'm going to tell you this because you need to know the truth. It's one thing for Angela to raise you, but to *brainwash* you is something else. Baby Girl, Simone is your mother. Angela is Simone's mother, which makes her your grandmother and me your grandfather. Ricardo? Well, Ricardo ain't shit!"

"Thomas!" Mae yelled.

"Well, he ain't."

"Granddaddy, Simone's not my mother. Angela is."

"Alicia, tell her who her real mother is. You won't get in any trouble. If your crazy-ass momma asks you how she found out, just tell her I told her."

"Well…" Alicia sighed as Jordan waited on the edge of her seat. "Simone is your mother, but don't tell Mommy I told you."

"You serious?"

"Yeah," Alicia said. "And remember, I didn't tell you."

"When you were lying up in that hospital, a teeny-tiny little baby, Simone, *your real momma*, sat up there with you every day by herself. She used to spend her whole paycheck buying you little designer outfits and everything. You even slept in the bed with her. I used to think she was gon' roll over and flatten you like a pancake." Thomas chuckled.

"So if Simone's my mother, where's my father?"

"We'll save that for another day," Thomas said. "I can't believe *your grandmother*," he reiterated, looking at Jordan. "She shoulda been told you the truth."

"Told her the truth about what?" Simone shouted as she walked inside the house.

"That you're my mother," Jordan stood up from the kitchen table and walked toward Simone, staring at her as if she was seeing her for the first time. For the first time as her mother.

Simone froze. She hadn't expected that. "Who started this conversation?" she asked, her eyes fixed on Thomas.

"You shoulda been told her, Simone. I didn't know your momma was keeping that from her."

"Simone," Jordan said, "if you my mother, how come when we out and people ask you who I am, you never say I'm your daughter?"

The question cut deeply into Simone's heart. She grabbed her daughter's hand and led her back to the couch. "Jordan, baby, oh my goodness. Are you serious?" she said as she sat Jordan in her lap. "Who wouldn't want you for a daughter? You're the prettiest little girl in the world, you're funny, smart…oh my goodness, Jordan, believe me. I wanted to shout it to the whole entire world but you didn't know. And I was scared if I told you, Angela would start playing tricks again, and I wouldn't be able to see you. Now watch what happens when she finds out you know the truth."

"Well," Jordan said, looking down at the floor, "if I'm your daughter, how come I live with her? How come I don't live with you and Kayla?"

Simone felt herself getting upset. "Jordan, you did live with me. Your grandmother was supposedly doing me a favor by watching you. Then one day, out of nowhere, she decided she wasn't giving you back. I called the police and everything."

Thomas leaned against the archway that divided the kitchen from the living room. "Jordan, I don't want you to be mad at

229

Simone or your grandmother. Simone was young, and your grandmother's just crazy." His playful snicker caused Jordan to smile, too. "I'm just kidding, Jordan," he said as he grabbed his camera from the kitchen table.

Jordan looked up at her mother. "So, Simone, if you're my real mother, where's my real father?"

"Uh, Jordan, I think you've had enough for one day," Simone said as the unexpected flash from Thomas's camera lit up the room.

• • •

Angela could tell something was wrong with Jordan the minute she walked in the front door. She wasn't her usual happy-go-lucky self, ranting and raving about where Simone had taken her or what she had bought her. Instead, she ran straight to her room and closed her door.

"Did something happen this weekend that I need to know about?" Angela asked as she walked into Alicia's room and closed the door. The smell of fingernail polish lingered in the air as Alicia coated her toes with brick-red polish.

"Umm, something like what?" Alicia asked, more focused on the polish than her stepmother.

"Where'd y'all go?" Angela huffed, crossing her arms impatiently. She was asking the questions, not Alicia.

"To Simone's father's house."

"Did Simone's father say anything to Jordan?"

"Like what?" She blew her nails dry, not bothering to look Angela's way.

"Alicia, so help me. I'ma jump across that bed and make you eat that polish," Angela threatened through tight lips. "Don't act like you don't know what I'm talking about. Did Thomas say something to Jordan, yes or no!"

"Yes," Alicia mumbled, looking shamelessly at Angela.

"Yes, what?"

"Yes…he told Jordan the truth. That Simone's her mother."

Angela fumed. "Why didn't you say something to me?"

"'Cause she was fine all weekend. She didn't get upset until she came here. What's the big deal anyway? Simone *is* her mother."

Angela sprang across the room and slapped Alicia across her face, leaving the imprint of her hand in her flesh. "I'm her mother," she growled.

Angela stormed from the room, slamming Alicia's door. Although tempted to talk to Jordan, she decided against it. She was too upset to approach her now. If anything, she needed to make sure the pieces to her puzzle were still intact.

Tucked neatly in a secret file, hidden deep in her closet, were the papers from years ago. The papers Beatrice signed on behalf of Kevin, which allowed the judge to grant custody to Angela and Ricardo. It was all perfectly legal. Or was it?

## Chapter Twenty-Two
### Early 1996

*S*imone was a natural when it came to selling homes and catering to the needs of her clients. The top-selling agent in her office, Simone celebrated her success by trading in her Camry for a brand-spanking-new white Lincoln Navigator. Everything in life seemed to be going great. Jordan knew who she was and practically lived with Simone. Business was good, and Simone didn't have a financial worry in the world. Life would be perfect, if only she could find a faithful companion. Always ready and willing to offer his love was good ole Andre Perkins.

"So," Andre whispered as they sat on the leather couch watching a movie in the dark. Girly flicks weren't his thing, but he sat watching *Love and Basketball* with Simone anyway. Kayla was stretched out asleep between them. "You gonna tell me you don't love me anymore?"

"Of course, I love you, Andre. I just don't love us."

"What you mean by that?"

"The name calling, the lies, the strippers, you strolling in all hours of the night, the silent treatment, your attitude." Simone looked at him and asked, "Any of that sound familiar? I mean, what we're doing now is how we were in the beginning, but this ain't us. I mean, at least not the new us."

"Simone, everything you're saying is true. But please believe me when I say nothing happened between me and Sunshine."

"Whatever, Andre."

"I'm serious, Simone, and I'm sorry for everything. I know how it looked, and I can imagine how it sounded. I just wanna make it up to you."

"Make it up to me for what? Because I'm doing good?"

"Damn, how easily we forget. Did you need a down payment on your truck, or did the value in the Camry hold up like I told you it would?"

Simone was speechless. So much had happened that she'd forgotten how lovingly generous Andre used to be. In the forefront of her mind was the lying, cheating dog he'd become.

"Look, I don't know when things turned. All I know is that I love you." He draped his arm across the back of the couch and gently massaged Simone's neck with his fingers. "Why don't you let me take you away this weekend…to see if we can mend things? Let me see if I can make you fall back in love with me, or back in love with us."

"I can't, Andre. I have appointments."

"Can't you reschedule them, just this once?"

"You know the last time we went away, you—"

"Simone!" Andre huffed, cutting her off. "Stop living in the past. Let's just have a nice weekend and see if we can't start over. We have to at least try." He looked down at Kayla. "We owe that much to her. I don't want her to be like every other child out there, being raised by only one of her parents. I want her to have both of us every day."

Simone sighed. She was hesitant and it showed.

"We don't have to hop on a plane, but let me plan a little weekend for you. I'll make it one you won't forget. I promise."

The weekend came, and things didn't go according to plan.

"I'm sorry, Andre," Simone said as she pulled into the driveway of a house she was trying to sell. "I rescheduled all of my appointments, and then these clients called talking about backing out of their contract. I can't just let it fall through. It's my biggest deal, so I gotta do something to save it." She pulled the visor down and flipped open the mirror to apply a little gloss to her lips. Not enough to be glamorous, but a modest dab to accent her smile.

"Ah, man," she said as her clients pulled into the driveway behind her. "They brought their mothers."

"So how long you gon' be?" Andre asked with little patience.

"I don't know. Hopefully not long." Flipping the visor back up, she threw on her professional smile and whispered, "Wish me luck," as she climbed from the truck.

Simone's clients stayed in the house for over an hour. Every so often, she went outside to check on Andre, but the last time she checked, he'd reclined the seat and dozed off.

"I'm so sorry. I didn't know they were gonna take that long, but I saved the deal and got a referral," Simone rejoiced later. "Aren't you proud of me?" she beamed, while backing out the driveway, but Andre didn't share in the blissful moment.

"Andre?" she said again, stealing a quick peek at him as he stared out the window, ignoring her. *Now see, this is the dumb*

234

*shit I'm talking about,* she screamed inside, immediately regretting that she'd cancelled her other appointments.

The tension in the truck was suffocating. After riding in silence for nearly ten minutes, Simone was ready to yank out her hair.

"You're really killing me," she mumbled, braking for a traffic light.

"I'm killing you?" he shouted back.

"Yes, Andre. You act like I scheduled the appointment on purpose. I told you what happened."

"Simone, you could've cancelled it! You didn't have to show them the house."

"Cancel it and what, let it fall through? I had to show them damn near twenty houses before they finally agreed on that one," she raved. "And now I'm just supposed to let it fall through?"

"Man, whatever."

"No, Andre, it's not whatever. I don't get a paycheck every two weeks anymore so it can't just be whatever when I have a mortgage."

"Fuck you and your mortgage!"

"Fuck me? You know what?" The light turned green, but Simone didn't budge. Instead, she popped her locks. "Get out!"

"What?"

"Get the fuck out!" she repeated over the blaring car horns.

"You ain't said shit." Andre opened the door and hopped from the truck. He pulled something from his pocket and threw it forcefully inside before slamming the door. Whatever it was hit Simone in her thigh and fell underneath her seat.

Speeding through the light, her thigh stung from whatever it was Andre had thrown at her. She turned on the interior light and fished around under her seat until she felt the object.

*What the hell is this?* she thought with the small jewelry box in hand. She shook it but nothing rattled. She flicked off the gift box top, flipped back the velvet top of the jewelry box and gasped at the sparkling solitaire diamond ring. It wasn't a 'Lord-have-mercy, smack-ya-momma' diamond, but it was a ring nonetheless.

"Oh my God," she whimpered. "He was going to propose?"

Visions of a fairytale wedding waltzed in her head. She could picture it all—her modern-day gown that would make Cinderella jealous, her hair in a Hollywood pinup fit for the red carpet, the ice sculptures, her wedding cake—all of this and more in the midst of a white Winter December Wonderland theme.

Engulfed in the fantasy, Simone whipped an illegal U-turn and drove down the street searching for Andre. She had to find him. They had a wedding to plan for the end of the year.

## Chapter Twenty-Three

## 1997

The foamy white bubbles floating on top of the water popped, one after the other. Kevin sat on the tub's edge, tapping his foot to the familiar melody, providing the perfect serenade for a romantic evening. He recognized the catchy tune and hummed along with the melody. Yet, for the life of him, he couldn't place the song or the words.

Kevin swished his finger around in the tub. It was nice and tepid, just the way he wanted. He stood, removed the towel from his waist, and offered his hand to his date—the faceless woman swaying seductively to the music. She recognized the tune, as well. He could tell just by the way she hummed that her voice was just as pleasant as her curves. She followed Kevin's lead and untied the sash around her red silk robe. The sleek material slithered down her mouthwatering bosom and voluptuous hips and rested on the small ceramic tiles of the bathroom floor. Kevin took her soft, manicured hands into his and led her to their bath in the warm tub of sour smelling milk.

The bloody dreams that had once haunted him had gradually faded. Night after night, mysterious music played in his dreams as he romanced the same anonymous female.

Roars of chatter bounced off the pale gray walls of the recreation hall. Kevin rested his pen on the table and reclined on the back two legs of the chair, proud of the poem he'd just written in exchange for a box of Little Debbie snacks. This was by far his best composition.

As he scanned the crowded recreation hall for Dre, his newest client, Kevin absentmindedly hummed the tune that had played so vividly in his dream. All day he'd hummed the tune, unable to shake the catchy little melody. With Dre nowhere in sight, Kevin glanced at his latest masterpiece, ready to read it again.

*Shit, this is worth more than a box of Lil' Debbie's*, he thought. Tapping out the tune on the table with his fingers, he read the poem to the beat of the music.

*Damn,* he chuckled to himself. The words flowed perfectly with the melody from his dream. *This could be a song.*

The chitchat boiling over in the recreation hall settled to a simmer. Sergeant Powell's tall, lanky frame stood in the doorway, his beady eyes darting around the room looking for somebody.

*Who the hell in trouble now?* Kevin thought.

"Kennard!" Sergeant Powell gestured to Kevin with a wave of his hand.

"Get the fuck outta here," Kevin grumbled, wondering what he was being blamed for. He hadn't been in trouble in years. Not since his rendezvous with Mr. Johnson. He'd met with the parole board once, and although parole hadn't been granted, the commissioner had shared that if Kevin kept his nose clean and stayed out of trouble, parole would be an option.

Grabbing his papers, Kevin headed to the door and followed Sergeant Powell out into the hallway.

"Hey," Sergeant Powell said, "I just wanted you to know that I recommended you for a job in the lieutenant's office."

Kevin was shocked. He and Sergeant Powell had never had an altercation, but they weren't the least bit chummy. "You recommended me? Why?"

"'Cause," Sergeant Powell responded with a simple shrug. "You one of the few in here that's actually tryna get it together. Besides, half of these idiots can't even write their own fuckin' name, let alone work in an office. But hey," he threw up his hands and took a few steps back from Kevin, "if you don't want it, just let me know."

"Naw," Kevin said, knowing a job like that would surely come with special privileges. He didn't know the perks, but there had to be some. "I'll take it."

"You'd be a fool not to. You start tomorrow evening."

At six o'clock the next evening, Kevin was escorted down the forbidden corridor that not only led to the lieutenant's office, but the warden's, as well. Gold-plated frames held pictures of all the officers employed by the prison.

*So this is their lil' spot,* Kevin thought. Standing before the lieutenant's office, the guard tapped on the frosted glass door with his knuckles.

"Ah, Lieutenant!" the guard called out in a forceful voice while pushing the door open.

The dusty smell of books circled through the air of the tight, yet simple office of the lieutenant's full-time secretary. The ceramic gadgets scattered on the small oak desk and the pinkish sweater with the dainty lace collar draped across the chair told

Kevin that the full-time secretary was white, old, and country. Behind her desk were the solid double doors that led to the lieutenant's massive office.

The lieutenant swung open his door. Standing straight and tall like a decorated warrior, he looked Kevin up and down. Kevin knew not to expect a handshake or any other professional flattery. He was an inmate, the scum on the bottom of the guard's boots.

With a nod of his head, the lieutenant dismissed the escorting officer.

"Have a seat, Kennard," he ordered, pointing his nail-bitten finger toward the secretary's chair.

Kevin sat while the lieutenant disappeared into his office, reappearing seconds later with a yellow legal pad. He ripped off the top two pages and smacked them on the desk in front of Kevin.

"I need you to type this memo. The governor just passed some crazy-ass law allowing female guards to work inside the cell blocks." The lieutenant hovered over Kevin, breathing down his back. "They're no longer confined to the visiting room. Now you guys will have access to some real pussy." He chuckled sarcastically.

● ● ●

Months into the job, Kevin had gained the lieutenant's trust. It was nothing for Kevin to have the office to himself. Sergeant Powell popped his head inside the office on occasion to check on him, but even that seldom occurred.

"Hey, handsome," a female guard greeted Kevin, popping her gum as she unlocked his cell. "I've been dying to escort you. I've seen you in the visiting room a few times."

Kevin noticed the extra twist she threw into her hips as she

240

opened his cell like Vanna White or a Bob Barker beauty.

"Get that ass, Kevin!" a voice rang out from the tier above.

"If one more person calls me that..." she said through gritted teeth, slamming the cell door shut.

"That's what you are to a lot of them."

"No," she said, her eyes glued to Kevin's, "that's not what I am. That's what I have."

*Damn,* Kevin thought. His eyes roamed her body as she led the way to the lieutenant's office. She was a pork chop away from being chunky, but her plumpness was well proportioned. A beauty pageant winner she wasn't, but her brown sugar complexion and the five or so cornrows that hung to the small of her back reminded Kevin of a 'round the way' girl. Best of all, she was real pussy like the lieutenant said. He could tell by the way she swayed her hefty hips that a sample was his for the taking. He read her nametag as they stood before the office.

"Thanks for the escort, Officer Moore."

"Why we so formal?" She blew a small bubble with her gum and winked at him. "Call me Yolanda."

Yolanda became Kevin's personal escort, ushering him to and from the lieutenant's office. Day after day, Kevin matched her flirtatious comments, letting her know that he was down for whatever, whenever. Yolanda picked up on his willingness, and in no time, she began sneaking in his favorite fast food or home-cooked meals she'd prepared especially for him. He loved the attention, and the meals had him licking his fingers. But, after being locked up for damn near seven years, he wanted pussy, not Big Macs. He waited patiently, knowing that the opportunity would present itself, and finally, it did.

Yolanda followed Kevin inside the office and secured the locks.

"What you doing?" Kevin smiled, hoping and praying that today was the day he'd get some ass. The mere thought was getting him excited.

"The lieutenant's not in today," she said seductively. "And Sergeant Powell is in a meet—"

Before she could get the words out, Kevin had her pinned against the door. His hands traveled her body, groping the parts of her that had gotten his attention weeks ago. He was rock hard and knew Yolanda could feel it.

"Officer Newsome's watching out for us," she panted, pulling her lips from his as he unbuttoned her shirt. A lookout was good, but the farthest thing from his mind. A few minutes of pleasure would be worth sixty days in lockup. "But," she said, grabbing Kevin's hands to get his attention.

"But what?"

"She wanna get in here with Kong. She's hiding him in the janitor's closet."

"She can get in here," Kevin said, freeing himself from Yolanda's grip.

"A'ight, but we gotta hurry up." Yolanda undid the knot in Kevin's sweatpants and slid her hands inside his boxer briefs. "Damn, Kevin," she gasped as she pulled out his arousal.

"So what you gon' do with it?"

"You sure you cool with them coming in here, right?" she asked, her eyes fixed to Kevin's erection.

"As long as I get mine, I ain't thinkin' 'bout them."

"A'ight," Yolanda said, lowering herself to her knees. "I'ma show you what I'm 'bout to do with it then."

Kevin's liquid excitement oozed from him as Yolanda teased the head of his penis with her tongue, licking away the salty treat.

"Ah, shit," he moaned as she welcomed him inside the warmth of her mouth. Beads of sweat formed along his forehead as he fought the urge to coat her tonsils. He was loving every single lick, every suck, but that wasn't how he wanted to come.

"Come on, baby." He pulled Yolanda up from the floor.

Unbuckling her thick black belt, she knew what time it was and allowed her pants to fall to her ankles.

*Shit,* Kevin thought. *I ain't got no muthafuckin' condom.*

"Don't worry," Yolanda said as if reading his mind. There wasn't enough time to undress. With her pants around her ankles, she leaned over the small desk. "I ain't got nothing. I couldn't work here if I did."

That was all Kevin needed to hear. He guided his hardness inside of her and pounded away. Yolanda matched his rhythm and tossed her ass back. Kevin held on to her waist with one hand and watched as he eased in and out of her.

"Come on, Kevin. You know we can't be in here long." A quick tap rang across the door. "See," she huffed. "You gotta hurry up, baby."

"A'ight…a'ight."

Kevin grabbed Yolanda by her waist and plunged deeper and deeper. She cried out. He didn't know if it was joy or pain, and as his body jerked and his eyes rolled to the heavens, he didn't care.

"Shit," Kevin gasped, out of breath. "I feel like I'ma pass out."

Yolanda smiled, pulling her pants from her ankles. "I'm getting ready to let them in. I look okay?" she asked, tucking her shirt inside her pants.

"Yeah, baby. You good."

"Okay." She kissed him quickly on the lips. "You gon' be

a'ight with them in here doing their thing?"

"Yeah," he panted. "Tell 'em come on."

Minutes after Yolanda left, the smell of sex filled the office. Kevin sat behind the desk, working on nothing in particular. He tried to ignore their cries of passion, but their moans were inviting him to a party he couldn't attend. He was getting aroused all over again.

Officer Newsome held on to the arms of the high-back chair in the corner of the room as Kong worked her from behind. Not sure of how much more he could take, Kevin was thankful when Kong screamed out in pleasure, bringing the fiasco to an end.

"Shit, girl!" Kong licked his fingers and slapped Officer Newsome across her pale white ass. Pulling from her, he looked over at Kevin and said, "What's up?"

"Ain't shit, man."

"Naw, nigga, I'm saying what's up with this?" He pointed at Officer Newsome's ass. "Come over here and get you some of this. I put that shit in her ass, man. In her ass!"

"Oh yeah?" Kevin said, trying to play it off. There was no way in hell he could stand up.

"Come work whichever one of these holes you want. Shit, bustin' one nut can't make up for seven years. As tight as her ass is, you'll come in three fuckin' pumps, I promise."

Blonde strands of hair dangled over Officer Newsome's face as she tossed Kevin a welcoming glance over her shoulder. "Yeah, come on," she said, rocking her pale ass from side to side. "I can handle you, too."

*Ah, man,* Kevin thought. He'd had anal sex with Rhonda, but he'd never been with a white girl.

"Look how wet she is." Kong sucked his two fingers and

eased them back inside her anal den. Officer Newsome moaned and worked her ass against Kong's fingers. "Look at this shit, man." Kong chuckled like a crazed mental patient and held up his two wet fingers for proof.

"Hey!" Yolanda tapped on the door. "Bring that shit to an end. Sarge is on his way 'round the corner!" she whispered in a panic. "I'm gone!"

"Ah, shit!" Officer Newsome stood, struggling to pull up her pants.

Kong peeled off the semen-filled condom Officer Newsome had eagerly supplied him with and stuffed it in the pocket of his sweatpants. Fear waltzed across Officer Newsome's beet-red face. She ran her fingers roughly through her hair, knowing it was her ass if she got caught with Kevin and Kong in the lieutenant's office. She'd be fired with no questions asked.

"Oh my God," she cried. "I can't get caught in here. I'm up for a promotion!"

"Look, just calm down." Kevin tugged on the drawers of the small oak desk, but they were locked as always. "Give me something…a driver's license, credit card, anything."

"What you gon' do, Kevin?" Kong asked.

"I'ma try and get y'all in the lieutenant's office."

Officer Newsome yanked off the ID card dangling from her neck. "Will this work?" she asked, on the verge of tears. "It's like a credit card."

Kevin snatched the card from her and slid it between the door's lock and the latch. Within seconds, the lieutenant's door opened as the distant sound of footsteps grew louder.

"Go 'head. Get in there," Kevin ordered. Kong and Officer Newsome disappeared behind the door. "And lock this muthafucka!"

Kevin scanned the office. Nothing appeared out of place, but the sweaty, raunchy smell of sex lingered in the air.

*Damn, white women smell different.*

Stepping out of his beat-up, state-issued prison boots, Kevin left them in the middle of the floor. They didn't smell of sex, but they reeked of years of sweat nonetheless. Kevin plopped back behind the desk just as Sergeant Powell opened the door.

"What's up?" Kevin greeted coolly, his eyes fixed on the computer screen.

"Hey, Kennard." He walked into the office. "Everything okay?"

"Yeah," Kevin said. He glanced at Sergeant Powell and noticed his dumbfounded expression as he sniffed the air and frowned.

"What the fuck is that smell?"

"Oh, my fault, Sarge." Kevin jumped from the chair and grabbed his boots. "These things funky and they hurt. You think you can pull some strings for me so I can get another pair? I had these things for years."

"Remind me tomorrow. I'll see about getting you a new pair." Sergeant Powell headed to the door. "Shit, I feel sorry for your cell buddy."

● ● ●

Kevin came in from the yard only to find Yolanda lingering around his cell. The sight of her brought a smile to his face. He loved her, but part of him knew it had a lot to do with the loneliness behind the prison walls. Yolanda was there, supplying all the physical benefits of a girlfriend. But if he were home, she would've most definitely been a wham bam.

"Hey," Kevin said. "You okay?" he asked, noticing her sour mood.

246

"Yeah, I just left the lieutenant's office. I'm being transferred."

"Transferred?"

"Yeah, they sending me to another jail. I think your job is over, too."

"Fuck my job. I'm worried 'bout you. What happened?"

"I don't know." She shrugged. "I think they know about us."

"Damn," Kevin sighed. There were too many other guards present for him to reach out and console her the way he wanted to. "So when you leave?"

"Thirty days."

"Shit, so now what?"

"Well…I bought this for you a few days ago." Yolanda dug deep inside her pants pocket and pulled out a gold wedding band. "Kevin," she started, grinning nervously, "I don't want what we have to end. I love you, and I want to be the one you make a home with when you get out. So," she said, smiling awkwardly at him, "I want us to get married."

Kevin stood at a loss for words, staring at the ring. *Damn, she's proposing*, he thought.

"Well?" Her timid voice addressed the silence. "What do you say?"

"Yolanda, c'mon, baby. I can't let you tie yourself down wit' a nigga like me. Who knows when I'll get out?"

"Kevin, you get parole."

"Yeah, but when? Don't you want a husband you can go on a honeymoon with, one you can touch at night?"

"Yeah, Kevin, and when you get out, I'll have that."

Yolanda's eyes pleaded with him, killing him. Still, there was no way he could accept her proposal. Beyond their physical bond, they shared nothing. Without an inkling of doubt, she would be the perfect prison wife. Sexing him when the opportunity presented itself and sneaking him tasty treats from the outside. But when his freedom returned, then what? He had hopes and dreams that he'd never shared with her, and most importantly, a daughter to find. Yolanda wanted to settle for less, while Kevin wanted to reach for the moon. He had to make something of his life; he owed that to Mr. Johnson, Beatrice, Jordan, and himself.

Slumping her shoulders, Yolanda sighed and shoved the ring into Kevin's palm. "Just think about it," she mumbled. "I gotta go. I don't want them to catch me back here. I might lose my job altogether."

Months later, while sitting on his cot, Kevin twirled the wedding band around the tip of his pinky. Yolanda was long gone at a new jail, more than likely loving somebody else. Kevin hadn't heard from her since she'd left. Women had come and gone in his life, but such was the life in prison. Rhonda had written on occasion and even visited a time or two, each time acting as if there was hope for them when Kevin came home. But he knew better.

Kevin called home the weekend of Rhonda's last visit. His body tightened when Beatrice's rage pulsated through the phone. She'd found LeCount pounding Rhonda from the back like the dog he was—in Beatrice's bed, of all places. Rhonda's actions were nothing out of the norm. Yet, Kevin's own brother's betrayal had gotten to him.

Then, of course, there was old faithful Felicia, who wrote, visited, and sent money like there was nothing else for her to do but focus on Kevin. Gone were the days she spent fucking in crack houses or giving head in the apartments' laundry rooms.

With a handful of strippers, she had stepped up her game and started a so-called escort service. That wasn't the only surprise she had for Kevin, though.

"I have something I need to tell you, but I don't know how you gonna take it," she said.

Kevin was taken aback and stared at Felicia awkwardly. "Just tell me. I mean, it can't be that bad," he said.

"Okay," Felicia said, her eyes fixed to the floor. "I got married."

"You got married?" He was blown away.

"Yeah, but it's only for right now," she rushed to explain. "Your pictures are still all over my bedroom, and he knows that when you come home, it's over, because I wanna be—"

"Hold up, Felicia. Hold up," Kevin cut her off. He couldn't help but chuckle a little. "You don't owe me no explanation. It's not like that between us anyway. I just never pictured you as somebody's wife. You know, with your profession and all."

"So what the fuck you tryna say? I'ma be your muthafuckin' wife one day."

"Oh yeah?" Kevin said. He wasn't paying her any mind.

"Kevin, I'm telling you. When you get out, I'm kicking his ass to the curb, and it's gonna be me and you."

"Felicia, come on. That's your husband. How you gon' toss him away just like that?"

"I mean, don't get me wrong. I love him and everything', but not like I love you. So, look," Felicia whispered as she shifted her weight in the plastic seat of the visiting room. "When you come home, I'm divorcing his ass, and then I'ma smash you off a lil' treat."

"What kinda treat?"

"Somethin' every muthafucka want—a threesome. You, me,

and whichever one of my bitches you select. I got one that look like that green-eyed supermodel chick that was on the cover of *Sports Illustrated*, too. She was going to medical school, but she put that shit on the back burner after I turned her on to that fast money."

Kevin laughed, nearly falling over in his chair. He had no plans on humping in Felicia. He'd never been that hard up. High, maybe, but not hard up.

"Felicia, look. I told you we ain't getting down like that."

Felicia drew back and sucked her teeth. "Yeah, whatever. You keep sayin' that dumb shit, but not only am I gonna get the dick, but we gon' be together. Watch what I tell you. And," she slurred matter-of-factly, "we gon' be business partners. You gon' manage while I recruit."

Kevin didn't want any part of Felicia's upscale prostitution circus any more than he had wanted to be Fat Ed's hit man years ago. He wanted more than a job in the streets. What he wanted was for the world to hear his songs. Every poem he'd ever written had been dressed with music and transformed into a song. Poetry was no longer a service he offered to the other inmates. He still wrote their love letters, but his poetry was for a greater purpose. At least, he hoped. He just needed someone to push him, to guide him. Someone to take him seriously. To believe and share in his dreams. Yet, he hadn't met a soul that he could even share his passion with. The world outside the iron gates still saw him as the old thuggish Kevin Kennard.

Back in his cell after Felicia had left, Kevin took the gold band from his pinky and slid it down his ring finger to see if he could simply get a feel for marriage. Jordan's picture was taped to the wall. Kevin peeled it from the wall and stared at it. Jordan couldn't have been more than two or three in the photo.

*C'mon, Ed. You can get me a picture, but you can't get me a damn address?*

Kevin didn't understand how Fat Ed could feel torn between him and Simone's brother Stan, his so-called business partner. Right was right, and keeping Jordan away was wrong. Kevin hadn't signed away his rights; Beatrice had. He couldn't blame his mother; she'd done what she thought was right.

Kevin kissed the picture, wondering what his little princess looked like now. Next to chasing his songwriting dreams, Jordan was the one thing he had to look forward to.

# Chapter Twenty-Four
## 1999 – Three years after the wedding

Simone pulled her white S500 Mercedes into the driveway of their seven-thousand square-foot home. The three-car garage was still jammed with junk-filled boxes that she hadn't found the time to sort through.

As she sat in the driveway, Simone turned off the ignition and stared at the monstrosity she and Andre referred to as home. The dark reddish brick, the four massive pillars, and the manicured lawn all added to the sophisticated elegance of the house, giving it the look of old money.

Five bedrooms, each equipped with its own private bath; a two-story gigantic great room with skylights; a state-of-the-art gourmet kitchen with stainless-steel appliances and black granite counters dazzled with a hint of silvery specks; and a theater room with a booming Bose surround-sound system and plush theater seating were just a few of the home's wow factors. Decorated like a showcase, the house was impressive from the curb to the baseboards.

Simone loved the place, but for some reason, she couldn't shake the uneasiness that had settled in her gut the day she and Andre signed on the dotted line. Gone was the house she'd been so proud of, the house she'd purchased on her own. That was the place she'd hoped they'd call home after the wedding. There, Simone felt stable, safe—the way she always did with Thomas. No one could tell her she had to go, not even her own husband. But, Andre despised the house, claiming it symbolized their breakup, the breakup he'd caused.

Initially, Simone tried to drown out Andre's whining by suggesting home improvement projects. Gallons of paint in warm cappuccino shades had waited to bring the white walls to life. But Andre wasn't interested in painting or branding the mailbox with his last name. He hated the house and made sure Simone knew it each and every day. Finally, Simone gave in. She rented out her house, and together, she and Andre purchased the massive structure filled with everything—everything but love.

Simone could hear her cell phone vibrating as she grabbed her Gucci purse and briefcase from the backseat and headed up the flagstone walkway.

"Good gracious," she mumbled, ignoring the cell. Her clients called on her all hours of the night, but deep down, she didn't mind at all. Real estate had become her passion. She planted her all into the business, and in no time, the energy and creativity she'd invested flourished, and the harvest was plentiful.

Stuck in traffic, Simone's six o'clock appointment had called and requested to meet later in the evening.

*That means I probably won't get home till after ten again,* Simone had thought to herself.

The past four days, she'd only seen Kayla, her three-year-old little diva, long enough to kiss her goodnight. Seizing the opportunity, she rescheduled her client for later in the week and headed home to chill with her daughter. But her mouth dropped when she walked in the front door. The house was a complete mess.

Kayla's shoes, book bag, and jacket were thrown carelessly in the middle of the foyer. Andre's tie and suit jacket draped the chocolate leather sectional as if it belonged there as opposed to the closet or dry cleaner's bag. His shoes and the wrappings from the snacks he'd nibbled on were also scattered about.

*So much for chillin'*, Simone thought as her heels clickity-clacked along the maple wood floors to the ceramic tiles of the kitchen. Resting her purse on the table, she sighed in frustration at the array of blue and pink envelopes.

*Cut-off notices.*

Andre strolled into the room in his socks, gym shorts, and a tight-fitting T-shirt that accented his perfect physique. *What a fucking waste*, she thought. Her husband was the epitome of sexy. However, Simone needed more than a sexy body and a thick 'Peter,' and that was all Andre had offered since they'd said 'I do.' It was as if aliens had stolen the man she fell in love with and left in his place a sexy, good-for-nothing clone.

"What's up? Why you looking like that?" he asked, opening the refrigerator. Simone didn't know what pissed her off the most—the filthy house, the overdue notices, or his undaunted attitude.

"Why are these sitting here, Andre? Aren't you supposed to pay them?"

Andre twisted off the cap to the frosted bottle of water and shrugged his shoulders. "Oh. I didn't know what you wanted me to do with them so I just left them there. I'll pay them this week."

"You'll pay them this week," Simone chuckled sarcastically. "Andre, they're cut off notices. How long have they been sitting on the table?"

"I don't know. A couple of days, I guess."

Andre headed to the great room without a care in the world and settled into his favorite spot on the sectional in front of the sixty-two-inch high-definition television that he'd insisted they needed a few months ago.

Simone ripped open the gas bill, only to discover the cut-off date was two days ago. *Lord have mercy,* she thought, marching to the center cooktop. She turned the knob to ignite the gas pilot and nothing happened.

"Andre! The gas is off!"

Andre peeped over the couch with 'oops' written all over his face. "It's off?"

"Yes, it's off. I don't believe this!"

Simone ripped open the other notices. Everything was scheduled to be off by the end of the week—the lights, the cable, and even the phone.

Here she was, the six-figure making businesswoman, one of the highest-selling agents in her office, getting ready to sit in the dark. But it wasn't the first time. The utility bills were Andre's only financial responsibility. Yet, month after month, it was as if he were allergic to the bills. Something was always off or pending termination.

From the outside looking in, Simone and Andre's marriage seemed picture-perfect—flooded with material possessions and first-class travel. Their family and friends marveled over the façade, misconstruing their lavish life for happiness.

The undisputed breadwinner, Simone carried their finances without the slightest hint of hesitancy, but there was little appreciation. Andre acted like she was supposed to not only pay all the bills, but still maintain the house by cooking and cleaning while he waddled in the lap of luxury like a king. Night after night, she strolled into a filthy house that her hectic schedule didn't allot time to clean. She contemplated hiring a maid service, but she couldn't justify the cost. Not when she had an able-bodied husband who needed to get off of his ass and help. Hell, he wasn't paying anything. The least he could do was vacuum!

"I'll pay them all tomorrow," he said, strolling back into the kitchen.

Simone couldn't even respond. She was too pissed and knew it wouldn't take long before they erupted into one of their heated arguments. Arguing had become their favorite pastime. "Bitches" and "hoes" flew out of Andre's mouth with little effort. After the initial shock wore off from the first round of insults, Simone joined him. She reached into the same gutter of filth to spit back her retaliation. They argued and slung insults like road-raged strangers on a regular basis. What they had wasn't a marriage at all.

Simone's phone vibrated again, a welcomed distraction. This was why she worked so much. With real estate, she got back what she put in, unlike life with Andre.

Reaching inside her purse, she found her phone and flipped it open. Surprisingly, there were four missed calls, all from Mae. She dialed her voice mail; there was only one message.

"Simone," Mae cried brokenly, struggling to speak over her muffled sobs. "Your father's been rushed to the hospital. They found a mass on his brain. Call me, please."

• • •

The two weeks Thomas lay in the hospital nothing else mattered to Simone. Not her daughters, her husband, or even real estate. Day in and day out, Simone and Mae sat by Thomas's bedside, watching the visitors come and go. Simone knew her father was scared. He'd never been sick a day in his life. In front of company, he was his normal, jovial self, laughing his infamous hearty laugh, joking with the nurses, requesting sponge baths. He even wrote down a few lottery numbers for Stan to play for him. But when out of the blue he asked to be baptized by the hospital's chaplain, Simone knew he was nervous and his bubbliness was just an act. Knowing Thomas was serious about his request, Mae did better than the hospital chaplain. She had the pastor of her church baptize Thomas right in his hospital bed.

After finally ruling out cancer, the neurologist diagnosed Thomas with an arteriovenous malformation.

"It's what we call a baby stroke," the doctor informed. "A small amount of blood has leaked from the vessels, which caused you to feel dizzy when you moved about."

"So," Thomas said as he absentmindedly played a game of putt-putt with the few green peas on his dinner tray, "you gonna jot down a prescription and send me home, right?"

"I could possibly honor such a request, Mr. Woodard," the doctor said, "but any possible cure would only be temporary. See, if the vessels continue to leak, the mass of blood will grow and the weight will begin to add pressure to your brain, which will eventually cause a major stroke."

"Whew," Thomas huffed, blown away by the news. Dropping his fork, he said, "I didn't want to hear that."

Seated fretfully on the edge of her chair, Simone asked, "So if medication's only a temporary fix, how can we prevent a stroke from happening? How can we stop the vessels from bleeding?"

"I knew you would ask." He smiled at Simone.

The next day, Thomas was whisked into surgery. A glue-like substance was injected through his groin to the blood vessels in his head to prevent any further bleeding. Eight hours later, the procedure was declared a success, and two days later, Thomas was discharged from the hospital with a clean bill of health. There were no prescriptions to be filled or special instructions for him to follow other than the generic 'follow up with your doctor.'

Thomas's kitchen was an inferno. The sizzling July day had a 'Welcome Home' barbecue tattooed all over it. But, burgers, hotdogs, and ribs were the farthest things from Thomas's mind. After being in the hospital for two weeks, he wanted a feast fit for Thanksgiving. Thankful that her father was out of the woods and back home, Simone ignored the fact that the air conditioning had conked out and cooked the feast with joy in her heart. As far as she was concerned, it was Thanksgiving in July and she was thankful that her dad was home.

Fans were scattered throughout the house, but offered little relief to Simone as she slaved over the hot stove. Collard greens; homemade macaroni and cheese; potato salad; candied yams; a plump, juicy turkey; a pot roast covered in potatoes, carrots, onions, and green peppers—all had the house smelling good.

After the last group of people left rubbing their stomachs and picking their teeth with toothpicks, Thomas sat in his living room dressed in a brand-new pair of Nautica pajamas, staring at his daughter in awe.

"You don't know how much I love you."

"Well, if you really love me, you'll do me a favor."

"Simone," Thomas whined playfully, "I just got out the hospital. I ain't fit to be doing no favors."

"No, Daddy. I'm being serious," Simone said. "I want you to give up one of your jobs."

Thomas frowned. "Baby girl, I can't do that. Those two weeks in the hospital put us behind. Me and Mae got bills. I need my full-*and* part-time jobs."

"Thomas," Mae added. "Simone paid the mortgage for us while you were in the hospital. I told her not to, but you know how she is when it comes to you."

"Yeah, Daddy, and I'll pay it every single month if you give up one of your jobs. You being in the hospital scared me. So, I want you to take it easy. You're only fifty-eight."

Thomas stared at his daughter. "What in the world did I do to deserve you?" He smiled. "I got the best gotdamn daughter in the world."

Heading home, Simone smiled, engulfed by the warm feeling of love and peace. Finally, things were back to normal.

● ● ●

"Turn off the alarm," Simone mumbled, half-asleep. Exhausted, she couldn't even open her eyes. The irritating noise wouldn't stop, and Andre didn't budge. "Andre, please," she whined, shaking him. "Can you turn off the alarm?"

"That's not the alarm," he mumbled groggily. "It's the phone."

Simone's eyes popped open, and she sprang up in bed. The alarm clock read four-thirty in the morning.

"Oh my God!" she screamed.

Bolting from the bed, she grabbed the clothes she'd worn to

prepare Thomas's feast from the floor and jumped into the shirt and shorts riddled with the stale scents from the kitchen.

"What you doing?" Andre mumbled.

"Answer the phone!" Simone cried. Something in her gut gnawed at her. "It's about my father."

• • •

The prognosis wasn't good. Sometime during the night, Thomas had suffered a massive stroke.

"You sent him home," Simone cried to the doctor. "You performed the surgery to prevent him from having a massive stroke, and for what? He fucking had one anyway!" Half of her wanted to smack the shit out of the doctor; the other half wanted to drag his ass back to the operating room so he could undo whatever the hell he'd done and scribble out the prescription instead. What good had the surgery been?

"Unfortunately, Ms. Woodard, it appears that too much blood had already seeped from the vessels in your father's brain. The surgery was successful, but there was nothing we could do about the mass of blood that had already escaped from the vessels. The body simply absorbs that over time."

Just when Simone thought everything was back to normal, she was back at the hospital every day, holding her father's hand as she sat glued to his bedside. She was angry with herself. How come she hadn't seen it coming? She'd asked questions, but obviously they weren't the right ones.

Paralysis had set in on Thomas's right side. He couldn't walk or talk, eat or drink, and had lost control of his bodily functions. His immobile state ripped Simone apart. Each and every morning while the nurses bathed her father, she sat on the floor outside of her father's room and cried. Everyone was devastated. The nurses hadn't wanted to see their high-spirited patient leave, but they hated even more to see him back, especially in his current state.

One of Thomas's nurses squatted down on the floor and draped her arms around Simone. "We hate to see you like this," she said, squeezing Simone. But it was of little consolation. "Mrs. Perkins, your dad's going to be okay. He's too full of life to let this get the best of him. Just give it time and keep the faith."

Two weeks drifted by with little improvement. There was no magic potion or surgery that the doctors could prescribe or perform to correct the stroke. So, Thomas was transferred to a rehabilitation center.

"Visiting hours here in the center end at eight," the nurse informed as she fiddled about in Thomas's room. However, the visiting hours had never meant anything to Simone or Mae.

"The hospital let us stay all night," Simone informed.

"Well, we don't allow overnight visits here," she shared without a hint of compassion. She didn't even bother to look their way. "I'll let you stay a little while longer since it's his first day, but the hours are strictly enforced. It's best for the patient and his rehabilitation."

Mae and Simone exchanged aggravated looks.

"Simone, you go home. You need to check on Kayla anyway. I'll stay here until she puts me out." The bite in Mae's voice got the nurse's attention, causing her eyes to dart in Mae's direction.

"What time do visiting hours start?" Simone asked extra politely to make up for Mae's gnawing. She didn't want to make the nurse an enemy. Not when she was tending to her father.

"Nine o'clock."

Simone looked at Thomas lying in the bed. She reached for his hand, knelt over, and kissed him gently on the forehead.

"You're on the real road to recovery now, Daddy. Before long, you'll be teaching me how to hand dance. You know I got the basic steps." Letting Thomas's hand go, she playfully danced the basic steps to the black folks' version of swing dancing. "I got that part, right?"

Thomas smiled with his eyes.

"Now you gotta hurry up and get better so you can teach me how to turn." Simone mirrored her father's smile. "I love you, Daddy. I'll be outside casing the building at eight-thirty."

*Chapter Twenty-Five*

Simone walked in the door with a fierce headache. When she didn't spend the night at the hospital, she couldn't pull herself from Thomas's bedside until the wee hours of the morning. Before the sun tiptoed over the horizon, she was back at the hospital. Tonight, she was thankful for the early evening.

"What you doing here so early?" Andre asked from his usual spot on the sectional. Simone was surprised he was even home.

"My father got transferred to rehabilitation today," she said as she rested on the other end of the couch. "And they don't allow visits after eight. No exceptions."

She kicked off her shoes and settled into the coolness of the plush leather couch. She grabbed the faux-fur throw on the arm of the sectional and draped it across her weary body. Too exhausted to hunt for pain relievers, she closed her eyes, ready to utter goodnight.

Before Thomas's massive stroke, Simone had brought

Kayla, Jordan, and Andre to the hospital with her several times a week. Since Thomas was his usual jovial self, Kayla couldn't understand why her granddaddy was even in the hospital.

"Granddaddy, you not sick," she'd told him.

"Then tell the doctor's to let me go home so me and you can go get a Happy Meal from McDonald's."

Things were different now, though, and Simone didn't want the girls to see their grandfather in his current state.

"You already picked up Kayla?" she asked with her eyes closed.

"Naw, not yet. What's wrong with you?"

"I have a bad headache and I'm tired," she mumbled.

"Well, ride with me to go pick Kayla up."

Simone's face squinted into a knot. "Huh?" She frowned, her eyes still closed.

"Come on," he said, tapping her leg lightly. "Ride with me. We'll stop and get you something for your headache."

"Andre," Simone whined. Leaving was the last thing she wanted to do. Drained mentally and physically, she couldn't even muster enough energy to head to the bedroom, but Andre obviously didn't care. He pulled the throw off of her.

"Come on, Simone!"

Simone's eyes sprang open as she released a frustratingly deep sigh. "I guess me not feeling well don't mean nothing."

"Simone, just ride with me, and I'll get you something."

Knowing Andre wouldn't leave her alone until she was up, she pulled herself from the couch, slid halfway into her shoes, grabbed her purse, and headed outside with Andre in tow. There was no way in hell she was driving. Unlocking the doors to her car, she climbed in on the passenger side, reclined her seat, and closed her eyes.

The car bounced over a pothole, waking Simone from her catnap. She glanced out her window and realized they were nowhere near Angela's.

"Where we going?"

"I figured we'd go have a drink or something."

"Ah, Andre, I don't feel like drinking. Let's just pick up Kayla and watch a movie or something. I just wanna chill. I have to go back to the hospital early in the morning."

"Naw, Simone. You need a drink. You got a lot goin' on."

"You're right, I do, and a drink's not gonna solve it. If anything, take me to church."

"One drink might do you wonders."

"Yeah, if I wanted to go to the club. I don't want a drink, Andre. I just want to chill and pretend that life is normal."

"See, that's fucked up."

"Oh, Lord," she sighed under her breath.

"Oh, Lord, nothing. You can sit up in the hospital every day, but you can't go have one drink with your husband."

"How can you even compare the two? I'm not sitting at the hospital because I want to!"

Andre pressed the volume control on the steering wheel, turning the music up to drown out Simone as he whipped an illegal U-turn and headed to Angela's. The booming bass pouring from the radio made Simone's head pound more. She couldn't tolerate it and turned the volume down. Andre turned it back up, louder than before.

"Andre, I told you I have a headache," Simone said, turning it back down.

"Man, fuck you and your headache," he said and turned it back up. "Take your ass back up to the hospital."

The last thing Simone wanted to do was argue. Ignoring

Andre, she reached for the radio again, but this time, he grabbed her hand and squeezed it tightly.

"What the fuck is wrong with you!"

Horns blew and cars whipped around them as they tugged back and forth, sending the Mercedes across the double yellow line in the road. They tussled back and forth as Simone tried to free her hand from Andre's grip, but he maintained his hold, squeezing tighter.

Leaning forward, she bit his hand and tore open his flesh.

"Agh!" He drew back his hand in pain as blood oozed to the surface. "You dumb bitch!"

Andre turned the corner on two wheels and flew down Angela's street. Screeching to a stop in front of Angela's house, he jumped out and slammed the door.

*You lucky you picking up Kayla,* Simone thought as she climbed over the center console to the driver seat. *Or I would leave your sorry ass right here.*

• • •

The sun peeped through the blinds, giving Simone the excuse to get up after tossing and turning all night and get ready for Thomas's first day in rehab. The phone rang just as she applied the finishing touches to her makeup.

*Who in the world is this?* she thought, while snatching the cordless from its base. Kayla was resting peacefully on Andre's side of the bed. The last thing she wanted to do was wake her.

"Hello?" Simone whispered, tiptoeing into the master bathroom.

"Why in the world you whispering?" Lavon whispered back.

"'Cause I'm trying not to wake Kayla."

"Oh, me and Melanie have been calling you like crazy.

How's your dad doing?"

"Um…he's pretty much the same. They transferred him to rehab yesterday. I'm on my way there now."

"Is Andre going with you?"

"Please," Simone said, sucking her teeth. "We got into it bad last night, but that's a whole 'nother story. As soon as my father gets better, I'm not renewing my tenant's lease. I'm outta here. I'm moving back into my house."

"You serious?"

"As a heart attack. Girl, this bullshit ain't no marriage. All we do is argue all the time over stupid shit, and don't get me started on everything else. I can't take it no more. But anyway," she sighed, releasing the anger she felt building back up, "right now, it's all about my dad. I gotta focus on him."

"Well, Simone, you know I'm here if you need me. What's up with your clients?"

"I have two agents handling things for me. I'm losing a ton of business, but I don't care. Then again," Simone giggled, "I need to care. I told my father I'd pay his mortgage every month if he'd give up one of his jobs. He works like crazy."

"That's what's up, Simone. Man, I love the relationship you have with your dad. Just let me know if you need my help. I'm not doing anything today, so if you need me to, I can swing by your office and maybe return some calls and get your marketing stuff out."

"Ah, Lavon, I love you. You'd do that?"

"Simone, c'mon now! It ain't like I've never helped your butt before. Just let me know what you need me to do. Who knows?" Lavon chuckled. "Maybe one day I can leave my government job and be your assistant."

"Oh, that would be the bomb. You're an executive secretary

in human resources, too. That's just what I need."

"I'm serious, Simone."

"I'm serious, too. I can't pay you no eighty thousand dollars, but we can do something creative. You sure you can go past there today?"

"Simone, ask me something serious."

"Okay, I'll call you from the hospital and tell you what to do. I'll get the receptionist to let you in. Meanwhile, I gotta go. I'll call you later."

"Okay, Simone. Tell your father I said hello and we're all praying for him."

Simone placed the phone back in its cradle and planted a gentle kiss on Kayla's cheek. Heading down the steps, she found Andre asleep on the couch. She shook him before heading out the door.

"What!" he growled, still full of anger.

"I'm out. Kayla's still in the bed."

"How long you gone?"

Simone didn't respond. She headed to the front door and left.

• • •

Simone walked into Thomas's hospital room at nine on the nose. "Look at you!" she beamed. Freshly showered and dressed in a pair of fresh pajamas, Thomas was sitting tall in a wheelchair, working with a therapist.

"Hi." The therapist rose from her chair just a little and offered Simone her hand. "I'm Sharon Rice, the speech therapist." Her voice was sharp, yet friendly, unlike her smile. Simone could only imagine what was going through her father's head. He loved pretty teeth, and the therapist's smile came together like a jigsaw puzzle.

"Hi, Ms. Rice," Simone replied, shaking her hand. "I'm Simone, his daughter. How's he doing?"

"Well," Ms. Rice said, as she settled back in her seat, "he swallowed some water for me with no problem."

"Daddy, you had something to drink?"

"Yeah," Thomas whispered.

"Oh my God!" Simone screamed in excitement. "You're talking! He's talking!"

"He wasn't talking yesterday?" Ms. Rice asked, just as surprised.

Mae walked into the room. "What's going on in here?"

"Mae, he's talking! Oh my goodness! And, Daddy, your smile. Your smile is back! Oh my gosh!"

Mae cupped her hands together, closed her eyes and said, "Thank you, Lord!"

"Hi." Ms. Rice smiled, sharing in all the excitement as she introduced herself to Mae. "Well, as you can see, the paralysis will slowly begin to release itself, and with therapy, Mr. Woodard could be home in no time." She removed her glasses and placed them and Thomas's file inside her briefcase. "Why don't you take this celebration outside? Mr. Woodard's dressed in those nice pajamas and sitting nice and tall in the wheelchair; you ladies should take him on a stroll. There's a wonderful garden outside."

"What you say, Thomas? You wanna go?" Mae asked.

"Yeah," he whispered again.

Mae secured her and Simone's belongings in Thomas's closet. Then Simone grabbed the back of the wheelchair, released the brake, and the threesome headed to the garden.

"It's nice out here. It don't even feel like the end of July," Mae said, inhaling the gentle breeze as Simone parked the wheelchair in the shade of a mature oak tree rooted near a park bench.

"Wow, Thomas," Mae said as she plucked a speck of lint from Thomas's pants. "This is the first time you've been outside in almost a month." She reached out and took his hand. "Simone, where's Kayla? Home with Andre?"

"Mmm-hmm," Simone mumbled, nodding her head.

"What's wrong? You and Andre arguing again?"

*Don't we always,* Simone thought to herself. She caught her father's eyes. The last thing Simone wanted was for him to worry about her and her pitiful marriage.

"No," she lied, "we're cool. They were knocked out when I left."

The threesome sat in silence, enjoying the cool summer breeze and the marvelous views of the landscaped grounds. Simone tapped Mae on her leg and pointed at Thomas, now sleeping in the wheelchair.

"You think we should take him back upstairs?"

"Yeah, we may as well." Mae released the brakes and grabbed the handles of the wheelchair. "That way, he can get some real sleep."

The nurse from the prior night strolled in to help Thomas back in the bed.

"I'm sorry, ma'am, but we didn't get your name last night," Simone said in her professional voice.

"I'm Nurse Elaine."

"Nurse Elaine, I'm Simone, Mr. Woodard's daughter, and this is Mae, his wife," Simone lied. Thomas and Mae weren't a bit more married than the man to the moon. "You'll be seeing a lot of us. Do you need some help?"

"No. His left side is perfectly fine. I'm just going to assist on the right. Hopefully, your father will regain full use of his right side, but in the event there's some impairment, he needs to know how to cope. So," she said as she tucked her body under Thomas's armpit, "remember," she panted, "you can't do everything for him."

With Thomas tucked in bed, Nurse Elaine dimmed the overhead lighting and passed Simone the remote to the television secured to the wall. Before the nurse's foot could grace the threshold of the room, Thomas's eyes popped open, and he started gasping for air.

"Daddy, what's wrong?" Simone jumped from the chair.

Panic reigned over Thomas's face.

"Oh my God!" Mae cried.

Turning on her heels, Nurse Elaine took one look at Thomas and said, "He's having a seizure." She pressed the call button to summon the nurses' station and yelled, "We need a doctor in 2C."

Simone grabbed Thomas's hand. "Calm down, Daddy. Calm down," she encouraged. "You're having a seizure."

The doctor barged through the door. "Okay, I need this room cleared, now!"

"Okay, ladies," Nurse Elaine said, ushering Simone and Mae to the door, "we need you to wait outside the room."

Simone tried to peep over Nurse Elaine's shoulder. "Why, if he's just having a seizure?"

"Nurse Elaine!" the doctor yelled. "He's not having a seizure. Call a Code Blue!"

"Oh God," she cried out, and then screamed down the hallway, "CODE BLUE! CODE BLUE! Stay out here," she ordered before rushing back in Thomas's room.

Seconds later, "Code Blue in 2C" was announced

throughout the hospital.

*What the hell is a Code Blue?* Simone wondered as the hospital turned into a madhouse. Doctors and nurses scrambled about in a frenzy, all heading to Thomas's room.

Mae burst into tears as Simone tried to decipher the reasoning behind the chaos unfolding before her eyes. Nurses and doctors were scrambling all over the place.

"What's going on? What's wrong?" Simone wondered aloud, but her question fell on deaf ears.

"Umm, excuse me." A tender, relaxed voice stood out in the midst of the confusion. "Hi. I'm the hospital chaplain responding to the Code Blue. Can we gather your family? I came to pray with you."

Simone stared at the blonde-haired white man dressed in a simple pair of khakis and a burgundy button-up shirt. *What the hell?* She backed away from him. What was really happening? Why was a chaplain sent to pray with them? As Mae fell into the chaplain's forced embrace and released a flood of tears, Simone reached out for one of the doctors.

*Somebody's going to tell me what the hell is going on.*

"Excuse me!" she hollered out. "Excuse me, please," she pleaded. "What's wrong? What's going on?"

"You need to clear this area," he said without anything further.

"Excuse me," Simone called out again to one of the nurses, rolling a huge piece of machinery into the room.

"Ma'am, you can't be in the hallway. Somebody call security," she yelled toward the nurses' station.

Nurse Elaine rushed from Thomas's room. Simone grabbed her by the arm. "Nurse Elaine, please," she pleaded. "What's going on? You said he was having a seizure. What's a Code

272

Blue?"

Nurse Elaine stopped and looked intently into Simone's eyes. "Sweetheart," she said softly as she grabbed Simone's hands and squeezed. "You need to go somewhere and pray."

"Oh my God," Simone whispered as Nurse Elaine released her hands and hurried down the hall. "I gotta pray," she mumbled. Looking around in a daze, she saw that Mae and the chaplain had disappeared.

"Excuse me, ma'am." A security officer stormed down the corridor dressed in a black and gold uniform that sagged from her small frame. Simone sized her up, knowing the small, unarmed officer wouldn't be a challenge if she really wanted to stay in the hallway. But, she wasn't looking for a battle; she needed to pray. She needed to find the hospital chapel. "You gotta clear the hallway."

"Okay, but can you tell me where the chapel is? The nurse said I need to pray."

"It's in the basement. C'mon, I'll show you where it is."

Simone followed the security officer to the elevators.

"Okay, this is my first week here," the officer shared as the doors closed. "I don't know exactly where the chapel, is, but we'll find it."

A thin, cool breeze greeted them the moment the elevator doors slid apart, exposing the creepy-looking basement. Furniture covered in white sheets crowded the hallway. Spider webs drooped from the ceiling.

"What is this?" Simone said, hesitant to step from the elevator.

"It flooded down here a while ago," the guard said as she exited the elevator. Rubbing away the chill, she looked around, apparently having no idea where to go. "They're still remodeling. I don't think any of the offices have even moved back."

"Yeah, but is the chapel down here?" Simone asked impatiently.

"Yeah. C'mon, we'll find it."

Simone followed the guard all around the ghostly basement. The click-clacking of their hurried footsteps bounced off the walls as they searched office after office for the chapel.

"Oh my God. Where is it?" Simone panicked. She had to get to her knees in God's holy place and beg God to please, please help her father.

"We've only checked half the basement. C'mon, let's check down here," the guard said.

"No!" Simone cried, angry with the stupid guard. They were back at the elevators. "We already checked down there. We just went in a big-ass circle."

"Well, let's just look one more time."

Simone stood frozen. Her eyes pooled tears as a weird, yet peaceful feeling engulfed her in a seemingly ghostly embrace.

"Do you feel that?" she whispered.

"Feel what?" The guard stared at Simone from the corner of her eye. "You're scaring me."

The doors to the elevator slowly squeaked opened. "Oh my God," Simone said. Waking from her daze, she jumped onto the elevator that no one had summoned and frantically pressed the CLOSE button over and over again. "Close! Close!" she screamed as her train of tears fell.

"Hold up!" the guard yelled, jumping through the closing doors. "Where you going? We didn't find the chapel."

"I gotta get upstairs. Something's wrong," she cried. "And I didn't get to pray," she mumbled. "I didn't get to pray."

The elevator doors opened on Thomas's floor. Mae was standing in the lobby, screaming at the doctors. Simone shot past the small crowd and ran to her father's room, ignoring the yells from the nurses and doctors.

Running into the room, she screamed, "Daddy! Daddy, you okay?"

Once in the room, she snatched back the curtain. Thomas was stretched out on his back with his hands at his sides. His eyes were wide open in a blank, ghostly stare.

"We're sorry, ma'am," the doctor said, entering the room. "Your father had a blood clot in his leg."

# Chapter Twenty-Six

A light drizzle splattered from the sky as Simone sat on the pile of dirt that had become her father's resting place. She'd come to the gravesite every day since the funeral a week ago.

*God, why'd you take him?* Simone cried.

"Excuse me, miss," the elderly groundskeeper called out to her. "Are you okay? I don't have an umbrella, but I can get you a bag or something."

"No," Simone cried, wiping her face with the back of her hand. "I'm okay."

"Well, I'll be in this general area if you need anything. Hey, umm…is that your Mercedes? I think that's one of them unmarked police cars. I hope he ain't getting ready to give you no ticket. I'll go talk to him."

"No, no," she said, recognizing Andre's cruiser as he slowly drove off. "That's my husband. I guess he's just coming to check on me."

"Oh, okay," the groundskeeper said as he pulled the few

weeds sprouting from a grave a few sites away.

Simone pulled her cell phone from her pocket and called Andre. *Where's he going?* she wondered as he whipped a U-turn, heading back towards the entrance.

"Yeah," he answered.

"Where you going?"

"I was coming to make sure you were a'ight, but I see your boyfriend's taking care of you."

"My boyfriend? Andre, he's an old man."

"Yeah, whatever. I'll talk to you later."

"Where'd your husband go?" the groundskeeper asked as Andre's car disappeared.

Engulfed in her emotions, Simone couldn't even respond. Instead, she looked to the heavens and cried, "You see what you left me here with?"

The groundskeeper gingerly strolled to Thomas's gravesite. Standing before Simone, he studied her as she sat in the midst of the dying flowers.

"Sweetheart," he said in a raspy voice, grunting as he knelt down next to her. "I've seen you out here crying by your lonesome the last few days, and God wanted me to tell you that your father is *fine*. He's in a place far better than what we have here on earth. A place so marvelous that the entire city is made of gold and jewels." The groundskeeper's eyes slowly closed as he recited the wonders of the spiritual place. "A place where pain and suffering no longer exist and people live in the everlasting arms of peace and love. Umm...man, oh man," he said, snickering just a bit as he opened his eyes. "I get excited just thinking about it."

"You act like you've been there," Simone mumbled.

He looked at her with a raised brow. "Yeah, I guess it does

sound that way, huh?" He smiled as a blast of thunder tore through the sky. "Come on, Miss Simone. Your daddy wouldn't want you sitting out here in no storm." He pulled his aging limbs from Thomas's resting place and extended his hand to her. "Remember, weeping may endure for a moment, but joy will surely come in the morning."

"How'd you know my name?" Simone asked, standing.

"Excuse me?"

"You called me Simone. How'd you know that was my name?"

"Oh." He chuckled, dismissing the question with a wave of his hand. He then pulled a folded trash bag from his pocket and passed it to her. "Put this bag over your seat. I'll look after your father. I mean, his site of course."

Simone accepted the bag and said, "Thank you, Mister..."

"Johnson." He smiled. "Curtis Johnson." Another blast of thunder tore though the sky. "I know. I know I've said too much," he mumbled as the rain came down in buckets.

With the bag in hand, Simone headed to her car, unhurried.

*He never told me how he knew my name,* she said to herself. "Mr. Johnson!" she yelled, looking over her shoulder. But Mr. Johnson was gone.

That night, Andre flooded Simone with apologies. While lying in bed, Simone listened as the bullshit explanations spilled from his mouth. She couldn't comprehend his words as she lay there thinking about her life, her future. She was tired of him, tired of the lopsided union they referred to as a marriage. But how could she leave now? She needed the scraps of love Andre tossed to her now more than ever. There was no other love available.

Andre positioned himself on top of Simone for yet another

round of makeup sex—the only kind of sex present in their marriage. Simone didn't protest. She simply lay there and allowed him to pound away until he was finished.

A week later, Andre surprised Simone with a family trip to Orlando, Florida. "You need to get away for a while," he convinced her.

"When are we coming back?" she asked halfheartedly, tossing her things into the suitcase. "I have to get Jordan on Friday. Angela and Ricardo are going away."

"You need a getaway more than your mother. She didn't just lose her father," Andre said, while tossing his bag of toiletries into the suitcase. "Man, had I been thinking, I would've included Jordan, too. It was so last-minute. I wanted us to stay for a week, but we can stay a few days and fly back Friday morning. I'll have the tickets changed."

"That's fine." Simone sighed as she closed the suitcase. "Just call Angela and let her know. The last thing I need is to hear her mouth."

● ● ●

Simone tried to fight the grief hovering over her like a cloud as they bounced from park to park. Kayla was in awe at the sight of Cinderella, Snow White, Sleeping Beauty, and all the other characters. Simone tried to share in her daughter's excitement, but in the midst of all the fairytale princesses were elderly men holding the hands of their grandchildren while they stood in line for ice cream and autographs. The images were daggers to Simone's heart. Her girls would never have such a luxury.

In the midst of all the grandfathers, Simone spotted men and women wobbling around with their impairments. Their stiff limbs or the limps in their walks told Simone they, too, had possibly suffered from a stroke. Unlike Thomas, they'd made it through.

"I gotta go back to the hotel," Simone said as she let Kayla's hand go. "It's one of those days."

"Just fight it," Andre replied. "Don't let it get the best of you."

"I've been fighting it all day. I can't take it. Y'all stay here and have fun."

"Simone, just fight it. Cry if you have to."

"I don't wanna walk around the park crying, Andre." She stood, fanning her face in hopes of drying the tears before they fell. "Y'all go 'head."

Sucking his teeth, Andre mumbled, "That's what I get for trying."

Back at the hotel, Simone lay across one of the freshly-made double beds. *I should call and check on Mae*, she thought as she grabbed her cell from the nightstand. Simone had two messages.

"Simone, where are you at?" Angela huffed in the first voicemail. "We want to leave today. Give me a call back."

*Andre never called you.* Simone sighed as she dialed Angela's number, knowing she had probably left the second message, too.

"Hey," Simone said plainly. "Andre didn't call you?"

"Call me for what? Did you get my message?"

"Yeah, I got your message, but we're in Orlando. We fly back tomorrow—"

"Orlando?" Angela cut her off. "Simone, I told you that I needed you to keep Jordan so Ricardo and I—"

"AND!" Simone yelled over her mother. "I just told you we fly back in the morning. Andre was supposed to call you."

"Thanks a lot, Simone," Angela said, slamming the phone

down.

"You're welcome," Simone said as she tossed the phone on her bed. She had a surprise for Angela. It was time—past time.

• • •

Back in town, Simone pulled into Stan's driveway and tooted her horn. Months before Thomas had passed, she had not only helped her brother buy a house, but she'd signed over her commission check to cover his down payment.

"He wouldn't have done it for you," Thomas had told her. "That boy just like your momma. I'm glad you got my heart."

Simone tooted her horn again. She knew Jordan was there. Stan was Angela's only other option. Finally, Stan opened his front door in a wife-beater, jeans, and slippers. He looked at Simone and shook his head questioningly.

"What?" Simone yelled from her window. "I know you not getting ready to say she can't come."

"I'm not gon' tell you nothing," Stan said as Jordan brushed past him with her bag, smiling like always. "If Ma gets upset, that's on you."

"Yeah, whatever. She ain't seen upset yet."

Simone wasn't sharing Jordan anymore, and she was more than ready for Angela's wrath.

"Hey Simone," Jordan greeted, jumping in the car. "Y'all went to Disney World?"

Simone backed out of the driveway as Jordan fastened her safety belt.

"Yeah, Andre planned the trip. He figured I needed a get-away. If I had known, I would have taken you, too."

"Ugh...I don't wanna see Mickey Mouse and Cinderella."

"It's other stuff to do. We could've hung out in downtown Disney. They have a superstar studio where you sing and make

CD's."

"Oh, now that's different. I was just telling Ma I wanna take vocal lessons. She ignored me, though."

"That's so funny, Jordan," Simone smiled. "I've always wanted to take lessons, too."

"For real?"

"Yeah, I'm serious. Matter of fact, that's something we can do together. I'ma find us a vocal coach."

"For real, Simone!"

"Yeah, why not?"

"Yes!" Jordan beamed. "So now where we going?"

"Well, I'm taking you shopping." Jordan's face beamed even brighter. "But there's something we need to discuss first."

"Okay, what is it?"

"How would you feel if I told you that I'm not taking you back to Angela's? I'm keeping you with me."

"But I kinda already live with you."

"I know, but I'm talking about all your stuff being at my house and I'm taking you to school every day, not here and there."

"Mmm," Jordan moaned as her excitement seemed to dwindle. "Would I have to change schools?"

"No. I could still drop you off the way I do now. After school, you can go to Angela's and I'll pick you up from there."

Jordan smiled. "And I'll still get to see Ma' because I'm going there after school," she said more so to herself.

"Yep. So…you're cool with the idea?"

"Yeah, I'm fine, but…"

"But what?"

"You and Andre argue a lot."

"I know. We'll work on that. But right now, my focus is

you, Kayla, and real estate. Now let's go shopping."

A week later when Jordan was due to return to Angela's, Simone called her mother, ready for battle. She wasn't the naïve little girl who'd trusted her mother and clung to her every word. She was a successful businesswoman with savvy connections a phone call away. If Angela wanted a legal battle, Simone was ready, willing, and able to serve her one on a silver platter.

"Jordan's not coming back."

"Umm," Angela groaned into the phone, unfazed. To Simone's surprise, her mother didn't challenge her decision. "She shoulda been with you. I'm getting old, and I could mess around and have a stroke just like your daddy. Besides," she added, "the hard work is already done."

# Part Three

"If it comes back to you, it was meant to be"

# *Chapter Twenty-Seven*
## *2004*

Fifteen-year-old Jordan climbed on the barstool and slumped over the countertop, still dressed in her flannel pajamas late in the afternoon.

"What's for dinner?" she mumbled, tapping her fingers along the granite counter.

"Lasagna. Something quick and easy."

Jordan didn't respond, and Simone knew from her bleak demeanor that dinner was the farthest thing from her mind.

Simone turned off the pot of boiling pasta, crossed her arms, and gave Jordan her undivided attention. "So, you wanna tell me what's wrong, or do I have to guess?"

"You promise you won't get mad?"

Simone looked at Jordan cockeyed, wondering what could possibly be so serious.

"It's about my father…my real father," she said, sitting up. "Why'd y'all break up?"

"Why'd we break up?" Simone repeated more so to herself.

"Was it because he went to jail?"

"No," Simone said as she dumped the pasta in the colander to drain. "We broke up because he cheated."

"He cheated? While you were pregnant with me?"

"Yes, ma'am."

"How'd you find out?"

"I called his house and the tramp answered the phone," she said playfully. "I'm just kidding, but some chick did answer the phone, claiming to be his girlfriend. We exchanged pleasantries, and blah, blah, blah," Simone said, dismissing the ordeal with a wave of her hand.

"Simone! Don't blah, blah the good stuff. Did y'all fight?"

"No, I went over there, but we didn't fight. The bad part is after it was all said and done, I never heard from your father again. Well, let me take that back. Your granddaddy was complaining about somebody calling from prison. So," Simone added with a shrug of her shoulders, "I guess he may have tried to call once or twice."

"How come he didn't want me with you?" Jordan asked.

"What?" Simone frowned, taken aback by the question. "Where'd you hear that nonsense?"

"Remember when Granddaddy told me you were my mother?"

"Yes," Simone said, wiping her hands on a terrycloth dishtowel.

"Well, when I went home, Ma showed me a piece of paper that my father signed."

"What kind of paper?"

"Um, I don't know. I guess custody papers. It was signed by Kevin Kennard."

"That doesn't make any sense," Simone said. "I don't know

what Angela showed you, Jordan, but it's probably some mess she forged. Your father wouldn't have signed anything. He didn't have a reason to."

"I just wish I could meet him. I'm the only girl in the world who's been fooled all her life. I don't even know what he looks like."

"Jordan," Simone sighed, knowing her point was valid, "I don't have a problem with you meeting him. I just don't know how to get in contact with him or his mother. Your father could be out of prison, married, and living with the elves in the North Pole, for all I know."

"Well…can you help me find him?"

"And where do we start looking?"

Sucking her teeth, Jordan slid from the barstool in defeat and headed upstairs to her room, leaving Simone to ponder the idea. In the still darkness of her room, Jordan lay stretched across her bed with the earphones of her iPod stuffed in her ears. All evening she sulked in her room. She didn't even bother to eat dinner. Before turning in for the night, Simone opened Jordan's door and flicked on her light.

"Simone!" Jordan whined, throwing her pillow over her face to block the bright light.

"Oh, well. I guess you don't wanna know that I've decided to help you find your father," Simone said, switching off the light and closing the door.

Jordan sprang up in bed, yelling, "No, Simone! Come back!"

Simone chuckled. "I thought you would get up then," she said through the crack in the door. "Now listen. Don't go getting your hopes all up, because I don't even know if this is going to work."

"What?" Jordan asked.

"I'll send a note or something to their old address, and we'll just have to see what happens. I doubt if they still live there."

"Can we just go check?"

"Don't push your luck. I think you should be happy with the note. Now goodnight."

● ● ●

"Simone! Simone! Simone!" Jordan screamed like a maniac through the phone. "I talked to her! I talked to her!"

"My goodness, calm down," Simone said, adjusting the volume of her cell. "You talked to who?"

"My grandmother! She just called me. Can I go over there tonight, please?"

"What! Jordan, she called you already? I just mailed the note a few days ago."

"Yeah, she got it today. She was crying on the phone and everything. Can I go over there, please, Simone? Can I go?"

"She was crying?"

"Yeah. I was on the phone talking to my friend Alexis, and the line beeped. I started not to answer it, but I clicked over, and she said, 'Is this Jordan?' and I said 'Yeah, who's this?' And she was like, 'Oh my God,' and I could hear her crying."

Simone couldn't help but chuckle as Jordan ranted on and on.

"Then she was like, 'I can't believe this. I can't believe this. Baby, it's your grandmother.' She was crying and everything, Simone. Oh my goodness, she wants me to come over there tonight. Please, can I go? Please! It's Friday, and she said my father calls her every Friday evening."

Simone couldn't believe how fast everything was happening. She had known with all certainty that the card would be returned to her stamped 'Addressee Unknown.' However, Ms. Kennard was still there after all these years.

"Simone, can I, please? I wanna talk to him."

"I just can't believe she lives in the same place," Simone said, more to herself.

"Please, Simone? Can I go?"

"I need to talk to your grandmother first," she said. "I'll be home in an hour or so, and I'll call her then."

"Oh my gosh. Thank you, Simone, for mailing the card. I love you. I'm going to pack my stuff!"

• • •

The overwhelming smell of cleaning products stung Simone's nose the minute she walked into the house. Jordan knew Simone dreaded coming home to filth and disorder.

"Hey, Simone," Jordan hollered from the kitchen as she loaded the dishes into the dishwasher. Simone couldn't tell what sparkled the most, her daughter's smile or the kitchen.

"The house looks good, Jordan, but you need to open the windows. Smells like you used a gallon of bleach."

"You want the phone so you can call my grandma now?"

"Sure, Jordan," Simone said, knowing there would be no peace until she finished what she'd started. Jordan wanted to meet her father. "Dial the number," Simone told her while opening a few windows herself.

Jordan grabbed the cordless and dialed the number she'd already committed to memory. "Hey, Grandma!" She giggled into the receiver. "Simone's here now. You wanna talk to her? …Okay, here she go."

"Hey, Ms. Kennard!" Simone greeted, plopping down at the kitchen table. "How you doing?"

"Simone, Simone, Simone. I'm going to say this, and I'm

going to say it without crying, 'cause Lord knows I've been crying *all* day." She paused as if she were trying to get herself together. "Kevin's supposed to call here tonight. I know he's gonna have a heart attack when I tell him." Simone heard her sniff and realized the tears had won. "Simone, thank you from the bottom of my heart and from the bottom of Kevin's heart. That boy has been though a helluva lot, and all he talks about is finding his baby once he gets out."

"Well, I just want you to know that I wasn't the one who kept Jordan from you or Kevin. I was lucky to see her myself."

"You know, Simone. That's the past, and I'm not trying to dwell in it. I just wanna see my grandbaby. Are you going to let her come over tonight? You know she'll be in excellent hands."

"Sure," Simone said, her eyes fixed on Jordan. "I'll bring her in a little while."

"Okay, sweetie. You see I'm still in the same place. I vowed not to move until Kevin came home. The parole board finally agreed to give him a chance. He should be home in two years as long as he keeps his nose clean. Thanks again, Simone. I can't wait to tell him what you did."

Leaping up and down like a contestant on *The Price is Right* Jordan sprinted down the hallway just as Andre walked in. "I'm going to see my grandmother!"

"That makes you that happy?"

"Not Angela," she informed, running up the steps. "My father's mother."

• • •

Simone's cell rattled like crazy against the metal cup holder in her car as Andre blew up her phone calling back-to-back. A smidgen of her was tickled that for once he had something to worry about. It was payback for all the nights he had strolled in whenever he so desired, leaving Simone to draw her own conclusion. The other part of her simply didn't care about him or his feelings. Before Thomas's untimely death, she'd been mentally prepared to walk away from her piece-of-shit marriage. But now, leaving Andre and having absolutely nobody was a scary and foreign land that Simone didn't care to travel. So, she stayed, and instead of focusing on Andre's bullshit, her focus was her father's wishes. She'd gotten Jordan back and even opened up her own real estate company.

Simone snatched Lavon from her high-paying government job in human resources and paid her handsomely to run the rapidly growing office. Melanie had fallen in love and married some geek she met in college. Though she lived miles and miles away, she hopped on a plane and put her marketing degree to work.

The threesome had brainstormed into the wee hours of the morning on how to make the company a huge success. Once the wheels were in motion, Simone had her attorney draw up papers making both Lavon and Melanie silent partners. Career-wise, Simone and her company were at the top of their game.

When the vibrating stopped, Simone powered off her cell and sat it back in the cup holder.

"So Andre's mad?" Jordan asked sheepishly, feeling she was to blame.

"I don't know." Simone shrugged. "I guess I should've told him about the note card, but I really forgot, and I definitely didn't think things would happen this fast. As far as Andre knows, your daddy's home and I'm going to see him. Speaking of which," Simone said as she pulled in front of Beatrice's building. "We're here."

Simone wrapped her arm around Jordan, leading her to

Beatrice's apartment on the terrene level. "This is the day you've been waiting for," Simone said as they stood before Beatrice's door. "Knock."

Jordan beamed from ear to ear. She took a deep breath. "Okay, okay," she uttered and tapped on the door. "I hear somebody coming," she whispered, listening intently to the squeaky floor on the opposite side.

Beatrice swung the door open and gasped at the sight of the granddaughter she hadn't seen in years. "Oh my God," she mumbled as tears of joys dropped from her eyes. She grabbed Jordan, smothering her in her embrace as she rocked from side to side. "You look just like I imagined."

Simone watched the reunion and cleared her throat when it felt like Beatrice had rocked Jordan dizzy. "Umm," she said playfully. "You're getting snot on my child."

"Come here, girl." Beatrice chuckled. "Let me put some snot on you," she said, nearly squeezing the life out of Simone. "Y'all get on in here and have a seat."

Closing the door, she couldn't take her eyes off of Jordan.

"Boy, oh, boy. If you don't look just like your daddy."

"You think so?" Simone questioned as she sat on the couch. For fifteen years, she'd heard Jordan was the vanilla version of her.

"I see both of you. But Kevin's image steals the show, mostly because she has his complexion."

"Grandma, can I see a picture of him?"

"Yeah. I already pulled some out. They right here on the table."

Beatrice sat on the end of the couch next to Jordan and passed her a handful of snapshots and an eight-by-ten picture in a frame. Jordan took the photos and studied them one by one.

294

"Grandma," she said, in awe of the eight-by-ten photograph of Kevin standing with a basketball at his side, absent of any expression, "can I have this one?"

"Yeah, baby. That one's yours. Can you see the resemblance?"

"Yeah, I can," Jordan mumbled.

"Let me see." Simone couldn't help but smile as she stared at her old love from back in the day. She caught Beatrice watching her as she passed the picture back to Jordan.

"What?" Simone said, feeling a little guilty. *Was I not supposed to look at the picture?*

"Simone, you look good, girl," Beatrice complimented, nodding her head in approval. "I mean really good. I wish a certain fellow was here to see you for himself. His eyes would pop out his head. And to think you were supposed to be his wife."

"She was?" Jordan asked.

"Mm-hmm. Your daddy put a ring on layaway for your mother and everything. I wonder what happened to his money," Beatrice mumbled more to herself.

"I didn't know anything about a ring," Simone said, surprised. "Too bad he cheated." *And went to jail*, she thought.

"Grandma, what time is my daddy supposed to call?"

*Daddy?* Simone was shocked by Kevin's instant title. *I'm Simone and he's Daddy?* She'd automatically assumed Kevin would be Kevin, just like she'd been Simone.

"It's Friday, baby," Beatrice said, patting Jordan's knee. "He should be calling in a little bit."

"How's Daddy doing?" Simone asked somewhat scornfully, but neither caught on to her disapproval.

Beatrice's expression turned a little somber. Kevin's

incarceration had obviously taken an emotional toll on her.

"You gotta remember he's been in there a long time. Damn near sixteen years. He did manage to get his GED, which is good, and he's become quite the poet."

"Really?" Simone chuckled. "Kevin Kennard, a poet?"

"Yeah, I'm just worried about when he comes out. Society's not gonna give a hoot about the shooting being an accident or that he went as the peacemaker. All they're going to see is a murderer or convicted felon."

"Yeah, but it's not gonna be tattooed on his head."

"No, but he'll have to disclose it on his job applications. And heaven forbid he get caught up with a chickenhead. You know, one that if he so much as sneezes wrong, she's threatening to call his parole officer."

"He's too old to even consider messing with a chickenhead anyway."

"Yeah, but these are all the things that I have to look forward to. Anyway, I wanna take Jordan to see him this weekend. Felicia's taking us tomorrow, but I gotta find a ride for Sunday. I may have to break down and drive those two hours myself."

"Grandma, is Felicia his girlfriend?"

"No, no, no, sweetheart," Beatrice said, shaking her head. "She's like his best friend. So, Simone, it's okay if Jordan goes?"

"Of course," Simone replied. "Remember, I'm not the one who kept her away."

"Yeah, we're gonna have to have a heart-to-heart real soon, too."

"Most definitely." Simone glanced down at her watch. It was late, and she had appointments starting first thing in the morning. "Well, I wish I could hang around and tell Mr. Kevin hello. I have a million questions for him, too."

"Well, what are you doing on Sunday?" Beatrice asked.

"She's not doing anything!" Jordan jumped in as if on cue. "Sundays are her off days. Simone, you can go with us to see my father!"

"No, Jordan." Simone frowned in protest as she stood to leave. "I don't need to see your father. I just wanna talk to him."

"Actually, that's not a bad idea, Simone. I'm sure he'd love to see you, and then we can all have our heart-to-heart, face to face."

Simone pondered the idea. *I should go so I can ask him about those so-called custody papers.*

"Simone, please!" Jordan begged as she anxiously tapped her feet.

"And it would prevent me from having to drive those two hours. Them highways scare me to death. That's how I know I'm getting old."

"Okay," Simone said with a simple shrug. "What time should I pick y'all up?"

● ● ●

Simone's appointments had gone successfully, just as her mind told her they would. Though she was exhausted, her jittery nerves wouldn't allow her to rest as she second-guessed going to see Kevin.

*Why in the world did I agree to go?* she thought. Jordan was back where she should've been all along. The papers, if any, didn't matter now.

Close to midnight, Simone headed downstairs to grab a few cookies. The alarm chimed as Andre walked in. His shift had ended at four.

"Hey," he said, strolling past the kitchen and heading up the steps. He hadn't even looked Simone's way.

"I need to talk to you," she said, following behind him with a napkin full of Oreos.

"Oh God, Simone," he whined, "don't even start."

"What are you talking about? Don't even start what?"

"What do you want to talk about?" he said impatiently. Inside their bedroom, Andre flopped on the bed and bent over to untie his shoes.

"You have a lot of nerve," Simone said as she climbed into bed.

Out of respect for the pieces left of her marriage, she had explained the note card she wrote to Beatrice when she came home and found Andre pacing the floor. Yet, Andre seldom shared the reasons behind his questionable behavior. She'd left her plans to see Kevin out of her explanation because she doubted she'd even take the trip. Now, as she sat listening to the irritation in her husband's voice, she figured, *why not go?* If for nothing more than a simple outing.

Licking the creamy vanilla icing off of one of the cookies, Simone said, "Kayla's with Mae, and in the morning, I'm taking Jordan and her grandmother to see Kevin."

"What?" Andre spun around to face her. She ignored his glare. "I know I must be hearing things," he said. "'Cause I could've sworn you said you were going to see your jailbird baby daddy."

"I did," she added nonchalantly. "Those were my exact words."

Andre chuckled sarcastically. "Yeah, well, I tell you what. You can go if you want, but I promise you won't have to worry 'bout me no more, that's for sure. I'll be good as gone."

298

## Chapter Twenty-Eight

*K*evin lay in bed and allowed his tears to flow at their will as he relived the visit with Jordan over and over into the wee hours of the morning. Finally, he'd looked into her eyes and held her hands. He saw himself in his little beauty, but Simone's image was just as present, knocking on his mental door. It had been by far the best day of his life, and in a matter of hours, he'd be able to hold her hands and take inventory of her again. This time, she'd be there with Simone.

After tossing and turning all night, Kevin was thankful when the morning rays from the sun glared through the dusty blinds of his cell, granting him permission to get up. He showered, dressed, and checked himself in the mirror over and over, ignoring the butterflies churning away in his stomach. He knew Simone had a million questions for him. However, before they launched their powwow, he had to take her hand and guide her back into time to. To the day their relationship fell apart over his stupidity. Simone was married now, and, according to Jordan, a big-time professional real estate agent with her own company. Kevin figured his apology and explanation wouldn't mean squat now. Still, he had to let her know that nothing had happened between him and Rhonda, if for no other reason than to cut the tension and ease the flow of their conversation. They had bigger fish to fry, but Kevin wanted to fry them all.

"Kennard," the guard yelled over the intercom a little shy of eleven, "you have a visit."

● ● ●

After picking them up, Simone navigated down the thoroughfare, listening halfheartedly to Jordan and Beatrice's conversation. For the past two hours, her mind had been somewhere else, wondering if Andre would actually cash in on his threat to leave. It amazed her that he would leave over something as meaningless as her trip to see Kevin. Had he taken an interest into why she was taking the trip in the first place, Simone would've shared the alleged custody papers. Yet, Andre hadn't asked, and Simone had called his bluff when she peeled from their bed at seven that morning. Deep down, she wished that Andre and all of his things would be gone when she got back. He was dust in the air that lacked purpose. With the expiration of her tenant's lease thirty days away, Simone could move back into the home she'd bought years ago, slap a 'For Sale' sign in the lavish green yard of the monstrosity she shared with Andre, and tell her husband to kiss her ass, like she should've done a long time ago.

*Yeah, be gone.* She smiled, liking the idea more and more. Her house had taken a beating after enduring three sets of tenants, but fixing it up would be fun. In no time, she could have it up to par.

"Man, I can't wait to see his face when he sees you," Beatrice said as they headed down the walkway that connected the visiting center to the main building where Kevin and the other inmates waited.

Metal fencing nearly fifteen feet tall enclosed the seemingly never-ending compound. Tiny razors protruded along the circular barbed wire that topped the fence and dared the inmates to even think about climbing it.

"So, is he behind a glass or something?" Simone asked.

"Nope," Jordan said as they entered the sweaty-smelling building. "He sits right in front of us. We can hug him and everything."

Standing at the entrance of the visiting room, Beatrice said, "Go ahead, Jordan. Lead the way."

Jordan stood on the tips of her toes, scanning the crowded room. "I don't see him," she said, until Kevin stood and waved his hands in the air. "Oh, there he go!" she said, marching over to her father.

"Hey, beautiful." He smiled, embracing Jordan. "I love you," he said as he planted a kiss on her cheek.

"I love you, too, Daddy." Simone watched Jordan turn into a pile of mush.

"Hey, boy!" Beatrice yelled, taking her turn. "I haven't seen you two days in a row since your trial."

"Yeah, I know," Kevin said, chuckling nervously. He embraced his mother, but his eyes were glued to Simone, checking her out after sixteen years.

Simone could feel his glare. Refusing to acknowledge it, she carelessly glanced around the room.

"There's your girl," Beatrice introduced, taking her seat on the opposite side of Jordan.

"Hey," Simone said awkwardly. She had no choice but to look at him then. His hazel eyes, his million-dollar smile, nothing had changed.

"Damn, girl," he mumbled as if intoxicated. Slowly, he wrapped his arms around Simone's waist, embracing her as if they had all day. "You look good," he said as Simone peeled from him and took a seat next to Jordan.

"Don't she look good?" Beatrice said.

Kevin couldn't stop smiling, and shaking his head in disbelief. The pounds Simone had collected over the years had thankfully fallen in the right places. Her breasts were fuller and her ass was rounder. She wasn't the pretty little freshly-developed teenager Kevin had fallen in love with years ago. She was a gorgeous woman—grown and sexy.

"Mmm, mmm, mmm," he mumbled. Kissing his two fingers, he placed them on Simone's thigh and made a playful sizzling noise. "You hot, baby," he said, before redirecting his attention to Jordan and taking her hands. "So how you doing, baby?"

"I'm fine, Daddy." Jordan chuckled, entertained by her mother's nervousness and her father's bewilderment. "How you doing?"

"I'm fine, baby. Marvelous," he said, winking at her.

Jordan filled the next several minutes with tales from her childhood, all the things that Beatrice, Kevin, and even Simone had missed. Her school plays that Angela had kept a secret, her report cards, and playground brawls. Listening halfheartedly, Simone took in the massive room filled with yellow and blue plastic chairs and inmates dressed in casual clothes.

"Dang," she mumbled when her eyes fell upon another couple who were openly displaying their passion in front of the entire visiting room.

"What's wrong with that?" Kevin asked, following

Simone's eyes to the couple. "That's how I used to kiss you."

Beatrice and Jordan laughed, causing Simone to smile, too.

"Naw, but that's all we're allowed, so we gotta make it worthwhile. Ain't no conjugal visits up in here. If anybody's caught doing more than that, they get sent straight to solitary confinement."

"How can you do more than that in here anyway?" Simone questioned.

Kevin raised his brow. "Oh, they get creative."

"What's the most you've..." Simone followed Kevin's eyes to Beatrice and Jordan sitting on the edge of their seats. "Oops," she said, as they shared their first real laugh in years.

"Uh-uh," Beatrice said. "You lucky Jordan here. 'Cause I would wanna know the answer to that question, too. Then I'd want to know who else was present."

"It was nothing like that," Kevin said. Simone could tell from his facial expression that oh, yes, he had some stories.

Smiling at Simone, he grabbed one of her hands. He felt her tense up, wanting to pull her hand back, but Kevin maintained his hold. He rubbed her hand gently with his thumb, stumbling across her wedding bands. He studied Simone's simple gold-plated band and diamond ring. Though they weren't impressive, he envied Andre, for he was the lucky man who'd slipped them on her finger.

"I didn't cheat on you, either."

"What?" Simone said, sucking her teeth.

"I mean, I know it doesn't make a difference now, but I didn't cheat on you. Nothing happened between me and Rhonda. She was an old flame. I let her come over because I wanted to tell her about you and Jordan," Kevin explained, smiling shyly at his daughter. "Me and her had always been so on-again, off-again and I wanted her to know that we were done. But things got outta control because I forgot she was coming over. Before I knew it, y'all were going at it, a bunch of niggas was outside, and you were swinging a bat."

"Simone," Jordan said, "you had a bat?"

"Simone?" Kevin repeated. "What, you one of those new-age mothers? You let your kids call you by your name?"

"No, my mother stole my child and my title, but you still have yours," Simone said. She tried to ease her hand from Kevin's, but he held it even tighter, staring at her.

"What you mean, your mother stole your child?"

"Yeah," Beatrice added, "what do you mean?"

"Should I even be here for this?" Jordan asked.

"It's up to you, baby," Kevin said.

Simone traveled back to when her heart was freshly broken and Jordan was teeny-tiny. She shared it all—Big Bob selling the drugs Lavon found and the crack-filled baggie that had fallen from her pocket in front of Alicia; the scent in her clothes from an innocent trip to the movies. Most importantly, she shared how Angela had volunteered to watch Jordan while Thomas's van was being repaired. Simone tap-danced all over her old wounds, bringing the pain back to life. Her father had helped her through those rough times, and just the thought that he was no longer around made the pain even worse.

"She wouldn't give her back, so my father told me to call the police."

"Wait a minute," Beatrice said, nearly dangling from the edge of her seat. "Your mother called and told me she had to call the police on you."

"Naw," Simone said, "I called the police on her. My girlfriend Lavon can tell you that. The police met us over there.

I had to show them all kinds of ID and everything. Then when I got there, they told her she had to give Jordan back the next day. But I go the next day and she all of a sudden had custody."

"And," Jordan chimed in, "I didn't even know Simone was my mother until my grandfather told me when I was like eight. That's when my mother…well, my grandmother told me that she was raising me because y'all didn't want me with Simone, and she showed me a piece of paper that you signed, Daddy."

Beatrice sighed deeply. She looked at Kevin and uttered, "And you told me to call her. You knew something wasn't right."

"What?" Simone asked, looking at Kevin. "So you did sign papers?"

"Simone," Kevin said, grabbing Simone's other hand. He didn't want to point the finger at his mother and would take the blame if he had to.

"Simone," Beatrice said, knowing her son would protect her at all costs, "your mother was calling me left and right. One minute, you were on drugs. The next minute, you were leaving Jordan there with her for days and a bunch of other mess. Then when my neighbor said you were high and Alicia said crack fell out of your pocket, I believed it all. I kept telling Kevin about it, and he never believed it. But that night when she called me ranting and raving 'cause she had to call the police on you, that was it. So it was me. I signed the papers on his behalf that night after the police left. That's how she got custody the very next day."

"You signed papers?" Simone asked, surprised at the news.

"Yeah, Simone, and I'm so sorry." Beatrice's words seemed genuine. "I believed everything your mother said. I mean…" She chuckled. "She was your mother. What mother would do something like that to her own child? Like you said, she stole your baby."

"I can't believe she did all that to get me," Jordan said.

"Well, we got you back now. I'm your father, and this is your mother. And after hearing everything that she went through, we gotta find a way to drop that Simone stuff, baby. I mean, I've loved you your whole life, but we just met yesterday, and instantly you call me Daddy. I love hearing those words. It's music to my heart, but I think you need to be singing the same song to your mother. Don't you think?"

Jordan looked at Simone and mumbled, "Yeah, I guess."

"Simone, you okay?"

"I mean..." She sighed. "What can I do? What can I say? Saying I'm shocked as hell would be an understatement. It's so ironic the papers were signed, giving Jordan to my mother and Ricardo, and Ricardo was the one on drugs. But," she said, "it's done and over with now."

"You know, my mother was only—"

"I'm not mad at you." Simone cut Kevin off and spoke directly to Beatrice. "I mean, I wish you would've called me, but, like I said, it's over."

"Yeah, I wish I would've called you, too. Look what happened once the papers were signed. Baby Girl was taken away from everybody." Beatrice grabbed Jordan by the hand. "C'mon," she said, pulling Jordan's hand as she stood. "Let's go get a soda."

With Beatrice and Jordan gone, Kevin asked, "So you really not upset with her?"

"I can't be upset with her and not be upset with my own mother."

"So how are we gonna handle your mother?"

"What you mean?"

"I mean, she just flat-out stole Jordan like you said. I'm sure there's something we can do."

"Well, whatever we do to my mother, we have to do to yours, too. My mother orchestrated the whole fiasco, but your mother was a mighty powerful player, as well. A simple little phone call would've ended it all."

"So, you really don't wanna do anything?"

"Nope. It's like two tears in a bucket."

"So fuck it? Just like that?"

"I mean," Simone said with a shrug of her shoulders, "if you want to do something, I guess you can take my mother and Ricardo out to dinner."

"Out to dinner?" Kevin was taken aback. "How you figure?"

"Think about it. You didn't have to provide any financial support and neither did I. I mean, I did for Jordan, but only what I wanted to do, when I wanted to do it. My mother and Ricardo did it all."

"But, Simone, we didn't ask them to. Your mother lied to get Jordan and raised her as her daughter."

"Yeah, all that's true, and I actually thought about everything this morning while I was getting dressed. My mother's my mother, and I love her. The last thing I want to do is start up a war. Despite everything we've been through, she and I are finally like mother and daughter. We go shopping; we talk; we laugh, and I don't want any of that to change. Plus, I can't harbor ill will towards people. You know how much energy it takes to remain in that space? Just think if I did that, you wouldn't have met Jordan. Besides," Simone added, "all my mother wanted was a family, and I know how that feels. I mean, I wouldn't steal a baby, but I kinda understand the void."

"But you have a family. You have a husband and two daughters."

"Sounds good, huh? But my husband will probably be gone by the time I get home."

"Gone?"

"Yeah, long story. Just make sure when you get married, you and your wife focus on life after the wedding, not just the actual wedding day. I was so focused on the reception, my dress, my cake, that I didn't realize who or what I was marrying. Anyway, that's enough about me. What's going on with you?"

"Hell, nothing compared to what's been happening with you." Kevin smiled. "I can't believe how good you look. You look like a supermodel."

"Of course I do to you. Look what you have to compare me to," Simone said, surveying the room.

"Females work all through the prison, Simone, but you're top-shelf, baby, for real. Your husband's a fool."

"Hey, I heard you're Mr. Poetry now. What brought that on?" she asked, changing the subject.

"Oh, yeah." Kevin smiled bashfully. "I started writing poetry for some of the guys years ago. They tell me their little situation, their feelings, and I compose either a love letter or a poem for them to mail to their girls."

"Really? You should try to do something with your poetic talents."

"Well," Kevin said, preparing to unleash his real passion for the first time. "I don't write poems anymore. I mean, I do," he said, shrugging his shoulders. "But I've turned them into songs. I probably have about two hundred now."

"Two hundred? That's impressive. Sing one."

"Huh?" Kevin choked. "I can write 'em, but I damn sure can't sing 'em. I've written a couple of letters, trying to sell some of my compositions, and I got a few responses—"

"Hold up!" Simone interrupted. "Are they copyrighted?"

"Naw, not yet. I was just testing the waters a little."

"Kevin, its sharks in the water. Somebody will steal your compositions, produce them, and take all your credit. If you want, mail them to me, and I'll get them copyrighted for you. I'll see if I can find some books on the music industry and send them to you, too. Who knows? Maybe Jordan and I can sing some of them."

"Y'all sing?"

"Yeah. I'm surprised Jordan didn't share that with you. We took vocal lessons a while back and everything."

"You serious?" he said, laughing in disbelief. "This is so wild. You know, Jordan told me yesterday that you out there doing your thing with real estate. She said you opened up your own company and everything."

"Yeah, I love it, too. Lavon and Melanie are my partners."

"Get outta here. Y'all still tight?"

"Yeah. Lavon manages the office, I oversee the agents, and Melanie, even though she lives a million miles away, handles the marketing."

"Damn, that's all right."

"You need to think about what it is you really enjoy doing, and see if you can make a career out of it. Real estate doesn't even feel like work."

"Yeah, that's how I feel when I write my songs."

"Then make being a songwriter your goal. Matter of fact, I'll send you a journal so you can write down all the things you plan to accomplish when you get out. If you keep your ideas trapped inside your head, they're just dreams. Think about when you have a dream at night. You know how hard it is to remember the entire dream the next day, let alone months from now. Well, it's kinda the same thing, which is why you have to have goals and write them down. Then," Simone raved, "once you mail me your songs, maybe Jordan can make a demo. I can take her to Stan and Fat Ed's studio. I'm not moving too fast, am I?"

"No! I'm loving your speed and your zest. You can be my partner."

"Okay, we'll talk about that later. But now, I need to ask you something serious," Simone said, shifting gears.

"Ask me whatever you want. Is it about Rhonda?"

"No." Simone frowned. "It's about the victim. The one who died."

"Oh," Kevin said. His body slumped as he shifted uneasily in the plastic chair.

"How often do you think about him?"

"Every day. Literally every single day. It's the first thing on my mind when I wake up and the last thing at night. That's one of the reasons I'm so determined to be successful. I owe it to him, my mother, Jordan, and hell, probably you, too."

"You don't owe it to me."

"Yes, I do. Had I been mature enough—hell, even man enough to handle the situation with Rhonda back then—things would've been different. Who knows? Maybe I wouldn't even be in here. I could've been your husband. And," Kevin added, "you damn sure wouldn't have these cheap-ass rings."

Simone snatched her hands away. "No, you not talkin' 'bout my rings!" She laughed.

"Yes, I am, too. See, if I was your husband, we'd be planning a cookout for tomorrow, or we'd be somewhere out of town."

"For Labor Day?"

"Yeah…Damn, it is Labor Day," Kevin said more so to himself. "Didn't we break up on a holiday?"

"Kevin, I don't know. That was a million years ago."

"Naw, but think about it for a minute, seriously. It was during a holiday, because that's the only time Rhonda came home. Just think about it for a second."

"Okay," Simone said. "My father moved me on a weekend, I guess. Hold up. All this happened the weekend Melanie went away to school. Damn, it may have been Labor Day."

"Damn," Kevin said, nodding his head. "It had to be Labor Day, which means we last talked sixteen years ago today."

"You mean we broke up sixteen years ago today."

"No, I mean we had a huge misunderstanding sixteen years ago today. I never broke up with you, and I didn't cheat. You did," Kevin said, looking at her rings.

"Here you go, Kennard." The guard approached and handed Kevin and Simone a piece of paper.

"What's this?" she asked, looking at the paper.

"It's your hall pass. It's time to go."

"Dang…already?" Her disappointment was obvious. She was just starting to relax.

Kevin kissed Simone's hands and pulled her to her feet. "You can stay with me if you want. We can celebrate our anniversary."

"The anniversary of our breakup?"

"What I just tell you?" Kevin asked playfully. "You're still mine."

"That's not what my driver's license says." Simone smiled. "Sorry. Too bad I can't stay."

He mirrored her smile and raised a brow. "It's for the best. I'd have to fight a million dudes off of you."

"Kevin, you'll be forty years old in a few years. Hopefully, you've outgrown your fighting days."

"Oh, yeah, baby. I haven't been in any trouble in over twelve years. I gotta keep my nose clean. Hey, listen. You gotta promise you won't tell anybody what I'm about to tell you."

"Okay…"

"There's a chance I could be home by this time next year."

"But your mother said two years."

"I know. That's what I told everybody. I'm just trying to surprise her, that's all. You're the only one who knows the truth. Damn," Kevin said, "you're the only one who knows a bunch of stuff. No one knows about my songs either." Kevin smiled. "Hey, but remember, you can't tell anyone. Not even Jordan."

"Speaking of Jordan," Simone said as she looked around the room. "Her and your mother never came back."

"I guess she figured we had some things to discuss. Jordan gave me the number to the house. It'll take a few days before I can call. You don't mind that, do you?"

"Please. Jordan will probably be waiting by the phone."

"I may want to talk to you, too, you know." He shrugged. "Since you're going to be my partner."

"We'll see," she said, initiating the hug. "But don't forget to mail me your songs."

"I won't. I hope things at home work out the way you want. Be careful," he said as he watched Simone walk out of the visiting room and back into his heart.

312

• • •

Simone was in no rush to combat the rage she knew waited for her at home. Despite the hurtful things she'd discovered during her visit with Kevin, she'd really enjoyed herself. For the life of her, she couldn't explain the peace she felt. Maybe it was their easy conversation. Other than Lavon, Simone didn't have anybody to really talk to. Or could it be the excitement she felt for his music. Or maybe it was that her old wounds had been addressed. Whatever it was, she didn't want the feeling to slip away.

Instead of rushing home, she scooped up Mae and Kayla. She even swung past Angela's and made her hop in the truck, too.

Beatrice felt extremely guilty and expressed it over and over again during the two-hour ride back from the prison. Simone agreed to forgive her only if Beatrice could find it in her heart to forgive Angela. Though Beatrice wasn't eager to accept the compromise, she agreed. She and Angela greeted each other like old girlfriends at a twenty-year class reunion. With the truck loaded, Simone treated everybody to dinner.

Andre's cruiser wasn't in the driveway when Simone and the girls finally made it home. Still, that didn't mean squat. Andre and his cruiser were seldom there. Inside, everything appeared the same, but something about the air felt different to Simone, almost lighter.

*Maybe it's because I want it to feel this way,* she thought as she headed to the bedroom, not knowing what to expect. Flicking on the light, she saw everything was still in its usual place. The bed was unmade and the plasma television was still on, entertaining itself. She held her breath as she strolled over to Andre's closet and pulled open the double doors.

"He did it," she whispered in shock as the empty closet stared back at her. "He did it. He moved."

# Chapter Twenty-Nine
## Early 2006

"What's up, sexy?" Andre licked his lips, admiring Sanora as she strutted into the post office, tossing her hips and slinging her long, blonde, bone-straight weave. Her skintight jeans, four-inch boots, and the skin tight leather jacket made more for style than warmth had every man, old and young, catching whiplash. Strolling in behind her was her manager, or Ms. Fe-Fe, as she was known in her world.

"Hey, Officer Friendly!" Sanora smiled and sashayed in Andre's direction, batting her green eyes. Easing her hand across his back, she whispered, "You ready to handcuff me again?"

"You liked that, huh?" Andre smiled.

"Mmm-hmm. I thought you did, too. Let me find out I was too much for you."

"Please. The last few times, you did more moaning than I did. Hell, you should pay me."

Sanora sucked her teeth. "Oh, there you go. But who did all

the moaning that New Year's Eve?"

"You always bring that up but it don't count. It was too many years ago, I was drunk as hell, and I haven't moaned like that since."

"Yeah, whatever. It's been a minute, though. My feelings are kinda hurt. How come you haven't called me?"

"I thought you were turning in all your G-strings to practice medicine."

"I got my master's in nursing. I can start a small practice with that one day. But right now, I'm making too much money off of all these horny-ass men."

"Agent Perkins, you look like you need to call my office and schedule your appointment." Felicia finally spoke.

"I ain't been scheduling no appointment."

"Yeah, Fe, he's one of my special clients."

"So what's been up? I'm surprise y'all have time to come to the post office." Andre said as he waited in line to turn in his change-of-address card.

"I'm in here with her," Sanora said. "She getting a money order to mail to her boo-boo."

"Damn, girl," Felicia mumbled as she laid her envelopes on the counter and fished inside her purse. "Just tell all my muthafuckin' business."

Andre glanced at the envelope and did a double take. "Get the fuck outta here."

"What?" Felicia asked as she searched inside her purse.

"Kevin Kennard?" he read out loud. "You know Kevin Kennard?"

"Do she know Kevin Kennard? *Please*," Sanora said. "That's her future husband. She's waiting for his ass to get outta jail so she can divorce her husband and marry him."

Andre chuckled.

"What the fuck is so funny?" Felicia asked with a hint of an attitude.

"Don't bet money on it."

"Don't bet money on what?"

"My ex-wife gon' get him before you do."

"What the fuck you talkin' 'bout, Perkins?"

"You heard me. Kevin Kennard. Hazel-eyed, light skin, been locked up for 'bout fifteen, sixteen years for murder?"

"Yep," Sanora confirmed, "that's him."

"He destroyed my marriage."

"What you mean, he destroyed your marriage?"

"You see I'm getting ready to turn in this change-of-address card."

"And?"

"He and my ex-wife got a daughter together. A few months ago, they all recently reunited like one big happy family."

"What! Your wife is Jordan's mother?" Sanora questioned. "Damn, Felicia was the one who took Jordan to see Kevin for the first time a few months ago."

"What?" Andre chuckled. "Well, Simone took Jordan and his mother again the very next day. But keep your money. He's in good hands. My ex owns Woodard Realty. She'll take real good care of him."

"Next," the postal clerk called.

"Good thing I saw that envelope, huh?" Andre said as he proceeded to the counter.

"Hey, hold up, Perkins," Sanora said. "What's your new address? Maybe I'll stop by and give you a lil' housewarming gift."

• • •

The minute the weekend rolled around, Felicia was in her car heading to the prison. *That's why his ass hasn't been calling me,* Felicia thought as she walked inside the visiting center. *You back with your baby mama? The bitch that kept your daughter away all these years...*

"Kennard, six-seven-two-nine-nine-two," Felicia recited before the guard had a chance to ask.

*This bitch magically pops up after I've been coming to this muthafucka on a regular for umpteen years. Driving your mother up and down the fuckin' road,* she thought as she took a seat, waiting for the guards to yell Kevin's name.

The minutes ticked away. Felicia glanced at the clock. She'd been waiting for over an hour. *What the fuck is taking him so long?*

"Excuse me," she said, approaching the guard's desk. "Y'all don' called everybody but Kennard. Is he coming down? I ain't waited this long since he first got locked up."

"Oh, yeah," the guard said, scribbling in the logbook. He didn't even bother to look up. "Someone just called down for Kennard. He has another visit coming, so he can't accept yours. He said he'll call you."

"He'll call me?" Felicia frowned.

"That's what he said." The guard finally looked up, but the glare he offered Felicia wasn't friendly. He held his hand out for her badge. She slid it across the counter the same way he'd given it to her and marched from the prison, allowing her anger to erupt into a ball of tears.

"I don't believe this muthafucka," she cried, slamming her car door shut. She searched her purse for her cell phone. *I've been coming up to this bitch forever,* she thought as she dialed Beatrice's number.

"Hello," Beatrice greeted.

"Can you believe…?" Felicia paused to catch her breath.

"Hello," Beatrice said again. "Who is this?"

"Kevin just denied my fucking visit so he can see that bitch!" she screamed into the phone.

"What?"

"I know what's going on!"

"Felicia? Girl, I didn't know who the hell you were at first."

"Ms. Kennard, I've had your son's back for sixteen years! Sixteen muthafuckin' years, and he gon' turn my visit away for some bitch who wouldn't let him see his child!"

Beatrice sighed. "Felicia, where are you?"

"I'm sitting in the jail parking lot waiting for that bitch. I'ma fuck her up when I see her, too. Andre already told me what kinda car she drive and everything."

"Andre? Andre who?"

"That bitch's husband, that's who! I ran into his ass a week ago on a fuckin' humble. He told it all. Wait till that bitch pull up."

"And then what?"

"I told you," Felicia cried. "I'ma fuck her up! What, you think I'm playin'?"

"Okay, well, I don't know what's going on. And if something were up, why would you care? I thought you were doing for Kevin because he was your friend and you felt guilty 'cause he got locked up over mess that happened at *your* house. Mess that *you* invited him to. Or is there something me and *your husband* need to know?"

"What!" Felicia screamed. "You thought I was driving up and down this highway, sending him money 'cause he was my friend? I love him, and Kevin knows that," Felicia cried hysterically into the phone. "Shit, my muthafuckin' husband know it, too. That shit ain't no secret. I'm divorcing my husband when Kevin gets out."

"Lord have mercy," Beatrice mumbled into the phone. "Listen, Felicia. Get yourself together and leave. Kevin turned your visit away so he can see his daughter. And if you touch her mother, not only will the guards lock your ass up, but Kevin will really cut you off then. Is that what you want? This girl ain't done a thing to you. And why the hell her husband's starting mess is beyond me. That's some fishy shit, too."

"But I've been here for him. Me! Writing letters, sending money, coming to see him—me! Not that bitch!"

"Then take your ass home and write another letter," Beatrice said, chuckling just a bit. "Look, girl. Did Kevin ever once express an interest in you while he was home?"

"I mean, we weren't—"

"Felicia, the answer is 'hell no.' You knew what the hell you were doing. Now you thinking Simone's out to do the same thing when all she did was allow Kevin and Jordan to meet." Beatrice paused, waiting for Felicia to speak, but she said nothing.

"Listen, don't get me wrong, Felicia. I appreciate you being there for my son. You my girl and you know that. But you had motives, honey, and even beyond that, you have a husband. So does Simone, for that matter. He may've left, but legally, they're still married."

Felicia's sobs spoke on her behalf.

"All Kevin wants to do is see his daughter," Beatrice said.

"But I could bring Jordan when I come."

"Felicia, Kevin don't want Jordan traveling in your circles."

"But I wouldn't—"

320

"Look," Beatrice said sternly, "I don't wanna hear no more. Now, I think you need to start your car up, take your tail home, and wait for Kevin to call you."

# Chapter Thirty

*A*ndre was in rare form, gossiping like a bitch on her period, all in an attempt to taint Simone's image. Her agents and people she hadn't talked to in months all knew that Andre had left her. And if that weren't enough, they all knew about her jailbird baby daddy.

Not only was Andre acting like a true bitch, but a true bitch with big-ass balls. Rumors created by his lips manifested like the plague. Yet, every morning since their split a few months ago, he woke up from wherever he was staying and seemingly forgot about the shit he was starting. The only thing that appeared to be on his mind was what he'd left behind. He called Simone at the crack of dawn every day hinting at counseling, which was the farthest thing from her mind. She'd tasted life without Andre and savored the joyous flavor it offered. There was no way in hell she was going back.

Simone's phone began ringing all hours of the night. She ignored the calls, assuming it was Andre. Then she noticed a private number on her cell and on her caller ID box in her office.

*If you have to block your number, we don't need to talk,* Simone thought to herself, but the private caller became annoying and determined to speak with Simone.

"Yes!" she snapped, irritated by the interruption in the middle of the night. The phone had rung every hour on the hour.

"Hi, I'm so sorry, Miss Perkins. I really am," the delicate voice said. "But I needed to speak with you."

"Who is this?" Simone asked.

"I'm so sorry, Mrs. Perkins. My name is Tina, and I've been, well, I've been dating Andre for a while."

"What?" Simone snapped.

"I know, I know, and I'm not trying to be disrespectful, but I just needed to know if you two are getting back together."

Rubbing her eyes, Simone couldn't help but chuckle. She and Andre had only been separated for a month. "What do you mean you've been dating him for a while?"

"I met him coming out of a club the earlier part of this year. We've been talking ever since."

"Just talking?"

"I mean, no. We've been intimate. I mean, we're a couple."

"You're a couple." Simone repeated sarcastically as she sat up in bed. "So, you're telling me that you've been fucking my husband for almost a year and now you're wondering if we're together or not? How'd you get my number?"

"Who can't find you, Mrs. Perkins? Your advertisements are all over the place."

"You're right, Ms. Tina. They are. And unless you're looking to buy or sell a house, please don't call me again."

Boxes were scattered all over the house. In a few more days, the contractors would finally be finished. The entire house had been painted, and the carpeting and all the appliances had been replaced. Any inch of doubt that Simone may have felt was dismissed the minute she ended her call with Tina. Soon, and very soon, Simone and her girls would be wiping their feet on a new welcome mat and Simone would be filing for her divorce.

Andre realized that Simone was dead-serious when he pulled up in front of the house and saw the Woodard Realty 'For Sale' sign. Though he hadn't agreed to sell, Simone knew there was no way in hell he could cough up the $4,000 mortgage payment and maintain the utilities. Besides, with the upgrades they'd made, they each stood to walk away with nearly $150,000.

Engulfed in the peace of her own house, the highlight of Simone's day seemed to come when Kevin called. She and Jordan shared the phone, and before long, after Jordan laughed and joked with her father for a few minutes, she retreated to her room to chat on her cell, leaving Simone the phone. Their conversation flowed so effortlessly, just like their laughter. They each shared their hurts over the years and their dreams for the future.

Cradling the phone with her shoulder, Simone swiveled back and forth in her high-back office chair, engulfed in her conversation with Kevin. She reached for the remote to her CD player and clicked on her music. The O'Jays' greatest hits purred through her speakers.

"Did you write any goals today?"

"Yeah, I added a few more. Hey, what's that you listening to?"

"Oh, you can hear it?"

"A little, but I can't make it out. I hear you humming. I can tell you can sing," he said with a smile in his voice. "What you listening to?"

"Don't laugh, but it's the O'Jays' greatest hits. Oldies remind me of my father. Especially Bobby Womack, Barry White, and Marvin Gaye. Those would have me boo-hooing, though."

"Is that all you listen to?"

"No, I like everything. My all-time favorite entertainer is Michael Jackson."

"I know. I remember you telling me how your jacket used to be covered with buttons when you were in high school."

"Wow, you remember that?" Simone said more so to herself. "Hey, can you hear this?" Simone turned up the volume. "This should be our song!"

"I can't hear it. Turn it up a little more."

Simone started the track over and increased the volume to the max.

"Can you hear it now?" she yelled into the mouthpiece. "It's 'Back Stabbers.' I know you know it. What black person don't?"

"Oh my God," Kevin mumbled.

"What's wrong?" Simone asked, turning the volume down.

"Naw, the guard is waving me off the phone. Let me go. I should be able to call you back later."

• • •

Kevin held on to the receiver, twisting the cord around his finger. He thought his feelings for Simone were gone. Yet, the minute he laid eyes on her after so many years, his heart skipped a beat. And after talking to her for months on the phone, it seemed as if the love he had for her so long ago was back as if it had never left. It wasn't simply her looks that had wowed him. It was the constant encouragement, support, and positive energy that she offered over and over again. No one had ever reached out to him the way Simone had. No one had ever inquired about his goals or his interests. And unlike Yolanda and Felicia, her help came without conditions or motives. She offered her hand simply because.

But, Simone was in a different league now, rubbing elbows with society's upper tier. What could Kevin possibly offer her? But as the introduction to the O'Jays classic hit rang through the phone, Kevin froze. He'd heard that melody in his dreams with the faceless woman more times than he'd cared to remember. He'd even written a love song to the melody, knowing he would have to get permission to sample the tune. Now he realized who the faceless woman had been—it was Simone. The funny smelling milk had been baby formula.

Kevin headed to his cell and stretched his body across his worn mattress. *Simone, Simone, Simone,* he thought. The springs squeaked and poked him in his side as he leaned over and grabbed the journal she had sent him. Following the instructions of his heart, he flipped the book open to the first page. His dreams were huge, but his feelings for Simone were enormous. His brain took the instructions from his heart and sent the signal directly to his hands. In the top margin of the page, above all his other goals, he wrote in all capital letters 'SIMONE WILL BE MY WIFE.' That was now Kevin's ultimate goal.

## Chapter Thirty- One

Four guards rushed past Simone and Jordan as they headed inside the building to see Kevin.

"Stand back! Stand back!" an officer ordered in a panic to Simone, Jordan, and the other visitors. "You don't want to see this."

But, the warning was a little too late. A blood-drenched inmate was coming through on a stretcher with a stab wound to his neck.

"Oh my God," Jordan gasped at the bloody sight.

"Hey," the guard said with a simple shrug of her shoulders, "this is what you get when you put all the bad guys in a room together. Watch where you're stepping," she said, tossing a handful of napkins on the floor to wipe up the blood with her foot. "We need a janitor over here," she said into her walkie-talkie. "You can go 'head in."

Shaken by the blood incident, Simone and Jordan scanned the room of inmates for Kevin. They spotted him sitting near the back with a huge grin on his face.

"Hey," Kevin beamed, squeezing them and kissing them both on the cheeks. "Did y'all get caught up in that mess?"

"Yeah, Daddy. Were you out there?"

"Naw, I've been in here for 'bout two hours. They called me for a visit early this morning."

"So you had two visits today?" Jordan asked.

"Naw. This is the only visit I have left for the week, and I knew y'all wouldn't be here at no nine o'clock. So, I had one of the guards call and see who it was."

"So who was it?" Simone asked.

"Felicia. I had to turn her away."

"Dang, you should've told me she was coming," Simone said. "I could've just brought Jordan another day. She drove all the way down here for nothing."

"I didn't know she was coming. I'll call and explain it to her later."

"She's probably pissed," Jordan said.

Kevin took Simone and Jordan's hands. "She'll be okay. I've turned her away before."

"Really?" Simone asked.

"Oh, it wasn't like you're probably thinking."

"What am I thinking?"

"You're thinking that because I'm in here with all these men, I would jump at Felicia's visits, right?"

"Yeah," Simone said, "pretty much."

"That's what I thought you were saying, and it wasn't like that," Kevin said with a raised brow.

"Oh, really. Then how was it?"

"I mean…" He shrugged.

"What?" Jordan said, curious as well.

"I mean, I've had a few pen pals, and I was dating this guard for a little over a year."

"You were dating a guard?" Simone was shocked.

"Yeah." Kevin chuckled. "She proposed to me and everything."

"Shut the fuck up!" Simone said. Kevin raised his eyes, shocked that she would cuss in front of Jordan. "Kevin, please. I'm sure she says worse at school, don't you?"

"She proposed to you for real, Daddy?" Jordan asked, quickly changing the subject.

"So we know the answer to that question," Kevin said with his eyes glued to Simone. "But, yeah, she proposed. I still have the ring."

"How come you didn't marry her?" Simone asked.

"Because," he said to Simone, "she wasn't the one."

"So how do you know when the person is the one?" Jordan asked.

"You should feel it, and then you shouldn't be able to imagine your days without them. They should be your friend, your partner for life, your lover, your—"

"Please, Kevin. You've been reading too many fairy-tales. I don't think all that's possible," Simone interrupted.

"Oh, yes, it is. When you're married, you should be virtually inseparable. Absolutely nothing should be able to come in between you."

"Well, I've been married before and—"

"That wasn't a marriage, Simone. Not based on what you've told me. That was just an experience."

"An experience, huh?" Simone chuckled.

"Daddy, Simone said you were mailing your songs, but we still haven't gotten them."

"Can we address something real quick?" Kevin said, changing the subject.

"What's that, Daddy?"

"It's that same old thing, baby. I'm Daddy and your mother's Simone. I can't take it. I don't understand how it's not killing you."

"I guess I'm immune to it," Simone replied, shrugging her shoulders. "I mean, she's been doing it since she's been able to talk."

"Jordan, we gotta do something, and we gotta do it today. You still call your grandmother Ma?"

Jordan nodded.

"Ugh." Kevin moaned. "I was never with your grandma, baby. C'mon, can't you call your real mother Mommy, Ma, Momma, something. Just not Simone. That bothers me."

"I'm not saying Mommy." Jordan pouted. "That's too babyish. Kayla don't even say that."

"What about Ma?" Kevin asked. "Can we try that instead of Simone?"

"Would you even answer me if I called you Ma?"

"I might look around the room at first, wondering who the hell you talking to," Simone said jokingly. "No, I'm just playing," she said, squeezing Jordan's thigh. "Of course, I'd answer you."

"Then it's Ma from this day forth?" Kevin questioned with uncertainty, waiting for Jordan's answer.

"I guess," Jordan replied, somewhat hesitate. "I might slip up here and there, but…okay."

"That's all I'm asking you," he said, smiling at his daughter. "And I mailed the songs a few days ago. Y'all should have them within the next couple of days."

"You finally mailed them. Wow, I'm proud of you," Simone said.

"Yeah. It's time to start cracking down on my goals. I'll be home in a few months, and I need to have some things in motion. I might need help with my ultimate goal, Jordan."

"What kinda help, Daddy?"

"He probably wants you to record some of his songs."

"No, not just that, but we'll talk." With a sly smirk, he winked his eye at Jordan.

• • •

Kevin tried calling Felicia a couple of times, but she didn't answer. *I wonder if Ma talked to her*, he thought as he dialed Beatrice.

"Hey, Ma. How you doing?" he said when Beatrice answered.

"Wow! I've been waiting for you to call me."

"Why, everything okay?" he asked.

"Have you talked to Felicia?"

"I guess she called you, huh?"

"Yeah, she called me. The girl was having a fit. It seems that Simone's husband is starting some shit."

"What you mean?"

"He ran into Felicia somewhere and filled her head with some crazy mess. That's why she came to see you today, but then you turned her visit away. The chile was in the parking lot going crazy, talkin' 'bout she was waiting for Simone."

"WHAT?"

"Yeah, but I calmed her down, so obviously nothing happened. What the hell is going on between you and Felicia anyway?"

"Nothing like what she thinks. I mean, we've talked smack

back and forth to each other over the years, but it was just fun and games. I mean, I'm not tryna sound shallow, but I'da stuck with Yolanda before I messed with Felicia. We cool, but we just friends. Every single time she started hinting at something else, I told her wasn't nothing happening. Hell, she got a husband."

"Hmm, well, her feathers were truly ruffled."

"Yeah, I'ma call her. I can't believe Simone's husband. I mean, she told me some stories, but I thought she was exaggerating."

"Yeah, Jordan's told me a story or two, too," Beatrice added. "That girl's had it rough."

"Yeah, I know," Kevin said softly.

"I'm sure Simone can handle her husband. What are you gonna do about Felicia?"

"I guess I'll keep trying to call her. It's not that she can't come up here. Just right now, all my visits belong to Jordan."

"Yeah, okay." Beatrice chuckled. "I saw the way your face lit up when Simone walked in the room. I know it's not just Jordan that you wanna see. Just make sure you talk to Felicia."

• • •

Felicia's husband, Mark, lay across the bed butterball naked, snoring loudly. His part-time bisexual lover, Jay, lay next to him with the wrinkled linen covering his now-limp private. Felicia had worked her frustrations out on both of them. Sucking one, jerking off the other, until finally they ended up tangled inside each other.

"What you over there doing, girl?" Jay asked in his feminine, high-pitched voice. Propped up on his elbow, he lay cuddled up next to Mark, playing with the few hairs on his chest.

"I'm thinking about buying a house."

"Good for you, honey," Jay cooed through his yawn as he eased under the covers on Felicia's side of the bed. "Just make sure I have a room."

*Look at this bitch,* Felicia thought as she stared at Simone's image on her website. With a simple click of the mouse, she enlarged one of the photos and studied Simone's image—her curves, her shoulder-length hair worn in loose, fluffy curls, and her smile. Never had Felicia felt threatened by any of Kevin's prison flings. She'd waited out Yolanda and the numerous pen pals. But Simone wasn't like any of them. She was in a league of her own. Beautiful and successful, she wasn't looking for a prison fling, and that alone would spark Kevin's interest. Jordan made Simone's package sparkle even brighter.

The phone rang, just as it had done several times when Felicia was tangled in the sheets with Mark and Jay. She glanced at the caller ID, though she didn't have to. She knew it was Kevin—very few called on that line.

*I don't wanna hear about your baby mama or your daughter, for real,* Felicia thought. Deep down inside, though, she craved the cool, subtle rasp of Kevin's voice.

"Hello," she snapped.

"What's going on?" Kevin greeted nonchalantly, oblivious to the bite in Felicia's tone.

"I don't know. You the big man, screening your visits and shit. You tell me what's going on."

"I'm not screening my visits. I told the guard to let you know that I couldn't accept your visit because my daughter was coming. So who should I have turned away, my daughter or you?"

Felicia peeped over her shoulder. Jay and Mark were both knocked out.

"What's this shit about you and your daughter's momma?"

"Naw, I got an even better question," Kevin said. "What's this shit about you waiting in the parking lot for her? If she'da pulled up, then what?"

"Then what you think! You know how I feel. I love you," Felicia said, quickly glancing over her shoulder again.

Mark knew Kevin was Felicia's hero for saving her and her daughter so many years ago from being killed. That justified Kevin's pictures being scattered all over their house and the trips she took to the prison. But, Mark didn't know that the minute Kevin was released, Felicia was sending him and his gay tendencies packing.

"Look, Felicia," Kevin huffed into the phone. "From day one, I told you that me and you ain't never ever gon' be like that. Yeah, we write letters, talk shit, and toss sexual innuendos back and forth, but ain't nothin' up with us. I can't even offer you nothing. So what is it that you want? What, you wanna fuck when I get out? Is that what you want, some dick?"

"For starters."

Kevin sighed. "Listen, Felicia. We cool, and as far as I'm concerned, we gon' always be cool. But right now—"

"Cool?" Felicia interrupted. "I don't want us just to be cool, Kevin. I want—"

"Felicia!" Kevin shouted, cutting her off. His sudden outburst caught the guard's attention. He had to regain his composure or his phone privileges would be over for the night.

"Look," he whispered into the phone. "For once in your life, will you shut the fuck up and listen for a change?" Felicia said nothing. "You of all people know how long I've been looking for my daughter. *My daughter*, Felicia. She's fifteen-years-old, and I never got to hold her, talk to her, or even fucking see her because I been stuck in here. I had no way to call her. No way to write to her. I missed out on her entire life, but now that I have her, I don't plan to miss out on nothing else. All I can offer her right now is my undivided attention, which means all my visits, calls, letters, everything belongs to her."

"I understand, Kevin, but hell, you act like I can't bring her to see you. Shit, it was cool for me to bring her up there the first time, so why can't I do it again? Besides, her and Mercedes need to get to know one another anyway. That could be their lil' bonding time," Felicia suggested, referring to her sixteen-year-old daughter.

"Felicia, thank you but no thank you. I don't want her traveling in your circles. Shit, you mess around and have her strippin' some damn where." Kevin chuckled, entertained by his comment.

"Fuck you, Kevin. And shit, her lil' ass got the curves to do it, too." It was Felicia's turn to he-he.

"Now, that shit wasn't funny. Deep down inside, your ass probably for real," Kevin said.

"Whatever, man." Felicia sucked her teeth. "You know I was playing."

"Seriously, though, you know I've been waiting for this moment just as much as my release. So, don't fuck it up. I'll still write and call when I can, but chill on the visits and on the threats. Jordan's mother ain't don' nothing to you or anybody else. The last thing I need is for you to start some shit and fuck everything up. If you scare them away, then I'll be back at square one. You feel me?"

"Naw," Felicia whispered seductively into the phone. She'd talked dirty to Kevin on many occasions, arousing him over the phone. She even welcomed him into her private sessions with her vibrator. "But I'ma feel your ass when you get out, though. I remember that muthafucka, too. The way he taste and everything. You remember when I sucked him, don't you? I can't wait to taste him again. Mmm…" She moaned into the phone.

"Yeah, look. The guard been jive watching me since we started talking. You have me all worked up."

"Oh no, baby. I haven't worked your ass yet. You can't come for me real quick?"

"Naw, he looking right at me. I'll try and call you later."

Hanging up the phone, Felicia felt horny, but Mark and Jay were knocked out. *Shit, where them videos we saved on the computer?* She shook her mouse, bringing the computer back to life with Simone's image, killing her sexual urge.

*Simone Woodard-Perkins, the big-shot real estate agent.*

"Don't get it twisted," Felicia said. "You not getting my Kevin, baby. Fuck that shit."

In the search bar, she typed the words 'plastic surgeons.'

*Yeah. I got two years to get myself together and be ready for you, Kevin. Mmm. Maybe I really should buy a house. But your baby momma won't get my business, that's for fuckin' sure.*

# Chapter Thirty-Two

*J* ordan stepped from the school bus with a huge grin on her face, clutching the flyer she'd gotten at school like the Olympic torch. She couldn't wait to show her mother as she rushed down the street.

"So you're really going to audition?" one of Jordan's friends asked.

"Yeah, I'ma do it."

Turning the corner, Jordan rejoiced at the sight of both her mother's truck and the car parked in the driveway.

*Yes, she's home*, Jordan thought, checking the mailbox. Since they'd moved back into Simone's first house three months ago, more and more Simone found herself working from home.

"See you tomorrow, Jordan," her friends chanted as they headed home.

"Okay," Jordan yelled as she pulled a large brown package from the mailbox. *What's this?* she questioned, reading the return address. *It's from my dad,* she said to herself as she hurried up the walkway.

"Ma!" Jordan screamed, tossing her book bag to the floor. "Ma!" she yelled again, rushing down the hallway to Simone's office. Jordan read the look on Simone's face through the glass of the French doors as she talked on the phone.

*Oops.* Jordan giggled. "Sorry, Ma," she mouthed as she paced outside the office, waiting for her mother to get off the phone.

Simone had warned her and Kayla about yelling through the house. "You never know who I'm on the phone talking to," she'd said a million times.

"I'm sorry," Jordan said, bursting through the doors the minute Simone hung up.

"Jordan, I've told you about that a million times."

"I'm sorry, I'm sorry. Here," Jordan said, placing the package on Simone's desk. "I guess these are some more of my father's songs, but it feels like something else is in there, too."

Simone grabbed a pair of scissors from her desk. She cut through the clear tape and pulled the papers out. "Yeah, it's a few more," she said, flipping through the papers. She'd already sent the first collection off to the Library of Congress.

Jordan pulled out the cassette tape. "Look, Ma," she said, "I'ma go get my boom box."

*Hey Gorgeous,*

*I stumbled across this guy who had a tape recorder, the kind from back in the day. He gave me a tape and let me do my thing. Don't laugh, but I'm sending you five songs. Four for Jordan, and there's one I'd love to hear you sing. I recorded all five.*

*Love, Kevin*

"One for me?" Simone smiled.

"What, Ma?" Jordan asked as she plugged her boom box into the wall.

"Four of these songs are for you, and ones for me."

"So he's singing on the tape?"

"That's what he says. What was that piece of paper in your hand?"

"Oh, yeah," Jordan said, passing Simone the flyer. "They were passing them around in school. It's for the Xtreme Teen Talent Competition, and auditions are two weeks away."

Simone smiled, reading the flyer just as the office phone rang. She glanced at the caller ID box and saw it was Kevin.

"Answer it, Jordan. It's your father."

"Hi, Daddy, guess what? We just got your songs and this tape. It was perfect timing, too."

"Oh, yeah? Perfect timing for what?" he asked, glad to hear his daughter's voice.

Jordan pressed the speakerphone button and said, "You on speaker, Daddy. Say hi to my mother."

"Hey, beautiful. How you doing?"

"Fine, how are you?"

"I'm good. So why's the tape perfect timing?"

"I got a flyer today in school for the Xtreme Teen Talent Competition. Auditions are in two weeks. I wanna audition, and now I can sing one of your songs."

"That is perfect timing. Have y'all listened to the tape yet?"

"No, not yet. So you're singing?" Simone asked.

"If that's what you wanna call it." Kevin chuckled. "I just wanted y'all to know how the songs went. Four are for you, Jordan, and one is for you, Simone."

"They're all for Jordan," Simone said.

"Why?"

"Hey, Daddy," Jordan interrupted. "I'ma let y'all talk while I go listen to the tape. Ma, can you call and schedule the audition? They said our parents have to call."

"I'm on it. Maybe we'll call Uncle Stan and see if he can put these songs to some music."

"Hey, and like I said, I want all of us to be a team," Kevin said. "Y'all hook 'em up however you see fit."

"So you're cool with my brother putting them to music? He's good. He won't set you up. I can actually see you partnering up with him and Ed when you get out."

"I trust your opinion, but the partner position is filled."

"By who?"

"You. I told you that before. Look how you're already helping me."

"Yeah, but I don't know anything about the music business."

"Then we can learn together. Where's Jordan?" Kevin asked.

"I'm right here," Jordan said, heading to the door with the boom box and her father's package.

"What you think about that, baby?"

"Sounds good to me."

"Are y'all coming to see me this weekend? I miss y'all."

"Yeah. Sorry about the last few weekends. I had appointments, but I don't have any this weekend, so we'll be there."

"Uh-oh," Jordan said. "I can't. Remember, it's Shanna's birthday this weekend, and then next weekend are the auditions. Ma, why don't you just go?"

"That's an excellent idea, Jordan. You come, Simone. That

way we can talk in person."

"I gotta, umm…" Simone said, looking for a reason to cancel.

"Stop looking for an excuse. Besides, I'm closer now, so you wouldn't be driving two hours by yourself. It's like what, thirty minutes maybe?"

"Go 'head, Ma," Jordan added on her way out the door. "Stop being scared."

"So what's up, Simone? What you think? Well, actually, before you answer, I have a surprise for you."

"Really, what is it?"

"Something I wrote just for you."

"A song?"

"I guess it could be, but not just anybody can sing it. Maybe I'll take lessons and sing it to you."

"Outside my window with a guitar?"

"Naw, I was hoping to serenade you in person. All of these things were running through my mind. I couldn't even sleep last night. I had to get it on paper. It's like a letter of promise."

"A letter of promise to me? Wow, read it to me," she said curiously. "I want to hear what you're promising me."

"Okay." Kevin cleared his throat as he began to recite his letter.

"I opened my Bible and referred to the first book of Moses called Genesis, verses three and four. 'And God said, 'Let there be light.' And there was light. And God saw the light, that it was good. And God divided the light from the darkness.' You are my light, the darkness, my past. I love you. So, to you, I promise to love without limits or conditions. I promise to give you the life you so deserve; a queen would be jealous of the way I'm going to cater to your every need. I promise never to cheat on you, not even with a roaming eye. I promise never to lie to you or hide things from you. I promise to hold no secrets, for my darkest you will know. I promise to love you in sickness and in health. I promise to display my affection and love for you to the world. I promise to protect you the best I can; I promise to protect you even when you're not around. I promise to love you more every day. I promise to help fulfill your dreams and fantasies, both the wild and mild. I promise always to say I love you. I promise you happiness if you ever grow sad, for I will move those clouds and shine for you even if you don't want me to. If there are earthquakes of any kind, I promise to calm them. I promise to satisfy you in any way possible. I promise to lead you the days you want to follow and follow you the days you want to lead. I promise to be your strength when you're weak, and I promise never to let you go. And if I forgot to promise anything else, I promise that, too."

"I love you," he confessed.

"Kevin." Simone was speechless. "That was…I mean, wow. You truly have a gift *and* an imagination if you think you love me. We're not in 1987 anymore. You don't know me to love me. You think you do because you're lonely. Once you get out, you'll find your real love."

"Are you crazy?" Kevin asked. "I'm not gonna lie. I do get lonely as hell. But lonely and desperate are two different things. If I were lonely the way you're talking, I would've married Yolanda, the prison guard. Simone, it's not the walls, baby. When I came in here, I loved you. I thought it was gone. But when you walked back up in here, you stirred it back up. And underneath all your sexiness and maturity, deep down inside you're still the same Simone."

"But are you the same, Kevin?"

"Parts of me are."

"You're so nasty." Simone chuckled.

"See, that's you. I wasn't being nasty," he said. "My heart is the same, but my thinking is different. Being in here and going through what I've gone through made me grow up. I can't wait to get out. You know, once my music jumps off, I want to open up some type of facility for the youth. Something to keep them off the streets. I really want to get my program started, my music jumping. And before you ask me," he added. "Yes, I've written this all down in my journal. But my ultimate goal is you. I'm going to make you my wife. I wrote that in my journal, too. So, it's not just a dream."

"Suppose I don't wanna get married again? Remember, I've done that."

"Like I told you, baby, that was just an experience. No one can love you like I can."

"Oh, really?" she asked sarcastically.

"Simone, will you come see me by yourself?"

"Kevin, Kevin, Kevin," she whispered more so to herself.

"C'mon, baby. You don't have any appointments, so why not?"

"A'ight…I guess I can." She sighed into the phone.

"Well, I think I better apologize now."

"Apologize for what?"

"Because I'm going to try and kiss you. So, if you don't want me to, maybe you shouldn't come."

Kevin had really surprised Simone. They shared so many things of interest, so many things in common that they'd overlooked when they were teenagers in love. He was gentle with his words, and his touches sent tingles through Simone that she tried to deny. Still, he was a convicted felon and couldn't offer anything more than his heart. Would that be enough? Simone had had the short end of the stick for years, and she didn't want to venture into another pitiful relationship. However, even with those thoughts, Simone couldn't shake him. Kevin's calls and letters were the highlights of her days. She felt his love and questioned the feelings stirring around inside her. But how could somebody so successful be in love with a reformed bad boy who'd been incarcerated most of his life?

Lying in bed that night, Simone closed her eyes and allowed her thoughts to take her away. Away to Kevin. It had been years since they'd been together, experiencing each other's fervor. Yet, it wasn't the fervor to tussle in the sheets that she wanted— just simply to look into his eyes, to see his warm smile. She wanted him to take her hands in his and kiss them the way he did during their visits. If only he could be sharing the warmth of her bed. She'd rub her hands down his entire being to confirm it wasn't a dream. Not for anything sexual, but just to feel the love that escaped his pores, helplessly jumping into her own. She welcomed his love and allowed it to fill her insides with much-desired warmth. She felt something, too, but wouldn't dare allow the words to flee her mouth. Closing her eyes, she drifted off to a peaceful sleep and welcomed Kevin into her dreams with open arms.

● ● ●

"Oh my God, Kevin!" Simone ignored Kevin's open arms. "What the hell happened to your eye?"

"It's nothing," he smiled, flattered by her concern. "Where's my kiss at?"

Simone turned her head, dodging his puckered lips. "It is something, Kevin. I thought your fighting days were supposedly

344

over."

Kevin grabbed her by her arms, but she still refused to look his way. "Simone, if I was fighting, I'd be on lockdown." He placed his hands on her face to keep her from turning away. "Can I have my kiss?" he whispered, allowing his lips to graze hers.

Pecking him lightly, Simone pulled Kevin's hands from her face and sat in one of the plastic chairs. She stole a quick glimpse and noticed the bruise was larger than the two Band-Aids he'd tried to cover it with.

"Simone," he said as she sat fidgeting with her visitor's pass. "Baby, I was playing basketball. This guy ran into me with his head, and before I knew it…what?"

Simone crossed her arms and stared off into space, impatiently swinging her crossed leg. She had no patience or tolerance for the old Kevin.

"You don't believe me? Simone, it's not just a black eye. Look at my nose," he said.

From the corner of her eyes, Simone studied Kevin's nose and noticed the slight slant. "It's fractured," he added. "It happened right after I talked to you yesterday. I couldn't even sleep last night. That's how bad it hurt."

"Did you have it checked out?"

"Yeah, but they can't do anything unless it's broke. Matter of fact, the dude sitting down there on the end was playing, too. He saw the whole thing." Kevin pointed to another inmate sitting a few seats away. "And," he said, taking Simone's hands, "if I were fighting, I'd be on my way back to the other jail. They'd kick me out of work release."

"Yeah, well, you need to retire your jersey. Just imagine if Jordan was here. She'd have a fit."

"I'm all banged up, too. I couldn't see out my damn eye last night and got my 'man' caught up in my zipper."

"Did the doctor look at that, too?"

"Naw," Kevin said, "but she 'bout to."

Leaning back in the plastic chair, Kevin studied the positions of the guards. As always, they were too engulfed in their own conversations to worry about the goings-on of the visiting room.

With his chair resting back on the floor, Kevin lifted his shirt and toyed with the drawstring of his sweatpants. "I wore boxers today, too."

"Kevin, what are you doing?"

"Hold up," he said as he scanned the room again for the guards. "See, look."

Simone laughed and turned her head away.

"Simone, seriously, look," he said, tapping her leg. "Look at the head," he whispered.

Realizing he wasn't going to fix his clothes, she looked. "I don't see no scratch," she said, looking at the head of his penis.

Kevin took her hand and ran her finger along the cut on the head of his penis.

"Oh, I do see it," she said, while rubbing her finger along his head. "It's getting swollen, too. You want me to kiss it for you?" she asked playfully.

"Good God, girl," Kevin said as his excitement oozed to the surface. "I wish you could kiss it."

"You really wanted me to see it, huh?"

"Yeah," Kevin said, lowering his shirt, unable to rid his smile. "I really wanted you to see the scratch."

"It's a very nice scratch. One of the nicest I've seen. Now fix your pants, 'cause it's getting hot in here." Simone fanned herself and undid the top few buttons of her suit jacket.

"Damn," Kevin said. The tank top she wore underneath her suit jacket advertised her cleavage. "I like that top."

"Kevin, fix your pants."

"I can't." He smiled. "He won't fit back inside the opening of my boxers."

"Uh oh." She giggled, nodding her head toward Kevin's shirt. "I think you sprung a leak." He glanced at the small stain forming on his shirt from the excitement oozing from his penis. "What would happen if the guards caught you like this?"

"I don't know," Kevin said, shrugging his shoulders.

He shifted his attention back to the guards. No one was watching. He pulled Simone forward and kissed her the way he'd wanted to when she first entered the room. Simone was hesitant at first, but she followed Kevin's lead and allowed his tongue to part her lips.

"Wow," she mumbled, feeling a little awkward.

"I love you, baby."

To avoid Kevin's eyes, she glanced down at the floor.

"Damn, look," Kevin said, lifting his shirt. He was fully aroused.

"Ah, shit."

"What?" Kevin asked as Simone's facial expression changed.

"One of the guards is coming," she said, quickly glancing down at Kevin's pants.

The guard walked past the first row of chairs, heading straight toward Kevin and Simone. There was no time for Kevin to adjust his clothes.

"Come with me," the guard said, tapping Kevin on his shoulder.

"Shit," he grunted under his breath.

Simone's heart stopped, as did the chatter in the crowded visiting room. Every head fell silent, bouncing from her to Kevin.

At the front of the room, Simone watched Kevin extend his arms out to his sides. The guard's eyes fell to the crotch of his pants and Kevin yelled, "Man, you serious?"

Simone's nerves rattled out of control as Kevin was escorted out the room.

"That's messed up," another inmate yelled. "Y'all weren't even doing nothing." His comment drew too much attention to Simone as she sat in the back of the visiting room in her professional attire under the jailhouse spotlight.

*Everything's going to be fine,* she told herself over and over again. It had to be. An ounce of trouble would kill everything and possibly add on to his time.

A female in uniform walked into the visiting room. Simone knew from the stripes on her white shirt that she was an officer of some sort. She looked over in Simone's direction and summoned her with a wave of her hand.

"Come with me," she said with all seriousness.

Simone followed her out of the visiting center and down the hallway.

"Listen," she said when the coast was clear, "you don't have to worry. I'm Lieutenant Newsome. Kevin and I go way back. He's in trouble, but it's nothing I can't fix. Next time," she smiled, "y'all better watch that kinky stuff."

"Oh my God," Simone gasped, clutching her chest. "I was scared to death. Where's Kevin?"

"They sent him back to his cell. He's probably thinking he's in trouble, but he's okay," Lieutenant Newsome assured her, patting Simone on her shoulder. "I'm going to let him know that I saved his ass. Hell," she whispered, "he saved mine years ago."

"Well, can you do me a favor since you're going to see him?" Simone asked.

"Sure, what's that?"

"Tell him I said I love him."

# Chapter Thirty-Three

*J*ordan was calm and cool the day of the Xtreme Teen audition, but Simone was a nervous wreck.

"Your audition's at two, right?" Simone asked as she bore off the highway.

"Yes, Ma. It's one-thirty, and the navigation system says we're only ten minutes away. Calm down 'fore you make me nervous."

"No, I'm cool. You're not nervous? Not even a tiny bit?"

"Not one little bit. I'm excited, but not nervous. Why are you? You quick to get up and sing karaoke and everything."

"This is different. It's you, not me."

Simone and Jordan could hear another vocalist performing as they entered the theater.

"You here for the audition?" a young lady asked, sitting behind a long folding table.

"Yes. I have a two o'clock appointment," Jordan said confidently.

"Jordan Woodard?"

"Yes."

"So where do we go?" Simone asked.

"Well, it's a closed audition. Jordan, you can go inside the auditorium. Mom, you can wait out here with us."

"Ah," Simone said. "I can't go in?"

"No." The young lady smiled. "You have to wait out here. Do you have your music? A lot of people have been using karaoke CDs, so if you brought one that's fine."

"No, I'm singing an original song, and I have my CD."

"Oh, good for you." She smiled, obviously impressed. "Just go on inside. Good luck."

"Good luck," Simone said as she gave Jordan a quick hug.

Pacing the floor, Simone heard the introduction to Kevin's song. Within a few minutes, Jordan's voice filled the auditorium.

"Wow," the lady behind the desk said. "She's the best we've heard all day."

With a huge grin on her face, Simone listened closely. Jordan hit each note of Kevin's upbeat song perfectly. Simone was so proud, she didn't even realize she was crying.

Ten minutes later, Jordan burst through the auditorium with a huge grin. A burly white guy hurried out the door behind her, wearing a smile, also.

"Ma, I made it!" Jordan boasted as she tap-danced her excitement.

"Yes, ma'am, your daughter was magnificent. Hi," he said, extending his hand to Simone. "I'm David Thornagon, the person," he said, making quotations in the air, "in charge of this event."

Simone shook his hand.

"The competition's a month away, but your daughter could

easily perform today. Here's the information on the dress rehearsals, and we need a copy of her music within ten days." He glanced down at his clipboard and asked, "Is my next audition here?"

• • •

Kevin paced back and forth in front of the pre-release center with his first furlough pass tucked in his pocket, waiting for Simone. He tried to imagine every second of the six-hour pass, but his anxiousness couldn't get past the initial shock. This was his first time outside of confinement without handcuffs, shackles, or supervision in years. Finally, he was getting a taste of the world he'd left behind.

The glistening white Cadillac Escalade pulled into the parking lot. Kevin's heart pounded, knowing Simone had arrived barely five minutes late. After moving back into her old house, Simone had sold her Mercedes and traded her Navigator for the Escalade. She also wanted to ensure her home had the proper balance of peace and harmony. After skimming through a feng shui article in a magazine, she'd decided that anything polluted by the union she shared with Andre had to go, starting with their old bedroom furniture, which she donated to the Salvation Army.

"Kevin!" she beamed, jumping from the truck.

"Good God," Kevin mumbled as Simone rushed to him dressed like he'd never seen.

Her sophisticated brown dress flirted with the gentle spring breeze and sat nicely on her every curve. The slight plunge in the neckline gave Kevin a glimpse of her cleavage. Click-clacking against the asphalt, her strappy high-heel sandals gave her shapely legs an extra dose of seasoning. Her hair, her makeup— everything about her was flawless.

*Mmm, mmm*, Kevin thought. Her husband had been crazy to walk away from something like that. But Andre's mistake was Kevin's future, his key to life. The Simone he thought was breathtaking during their visits stood before him even more beautiful. The thing that attracted Kevin the most was that Simone's inner-being matched her outer exquisiteness.

"Hey," she greeted, nearly knocking him down.

He matched her excitement and welcomed her into his arms.

"You are so damn gorgeous. I love you," he said.

"I love you, too." Simone could barely get the words out before Kevin greeted her with his passion. They kissed outside of the building like they hadn't before.

"Hey," she said, peeling her lips from his. "Is this where you wanna spend the next five hours and fifty minutes?"

"Hell, naw." Kevin smiled.

"Then come with me." Smiling seductively, Simone grabbed Kevin's hand and led him to the truck.

"Damn," he said, amazed by all the digital gadgets. "This truck is crazy."

"Yeah, on your next furlough, we have to go to Motor Vehicles and get your driver's license. Then you need to open up a bank account and probably get a cell phone. We have to get you some credit, too. I would add you to my cell phone account, but that wouldn't help you," she said as he fidgeted with the truck's gizmos.

"The manual's inside the glove compartment if you want to figure out some of this stuff. I don't even know how to work half of them."

Kevin reached over the center console, grabbed Simone's hand, and brought it to his lips. "I love you so much, Simone," he said as his lips grazed her hand. "I can't even believe I'm here with you," he uttered from his heart, barely above a whisper.

She eased her hand from Kevin's and rubbed the side of his face, touched by the way he closed his eyes and inhaled her scent.

"You need me to pinch you?"

"No," he said, then kissed her hand again. "I just need you to love me forever."

Simone smiled at such an easy request. "So how do you wanna spend your day? I mean, you don't want anyone to know you're out for a few hours, so what do you want to do? Want to go to the movies or…"

He squeezed Simone's hand. "As long as every second is with you, it doesn't even matter." His answer was filled with so much love.

Barely half a mile away, Simone noticed the hotel sign. She eased her hand from Kevin's and prepared to turn into the parking lot.

"Well, we wouldn't be alone at my house because the kids are there. And—"

"Simone," he interrupted, "how you unlock these damn doors?"

The minute the elevator door closed, Kevin was all over Simone. His hands traveled up her dress, caressing the plumpness of her ass that the thong didn't shelter. He detoured from her sweet lips and nibbled gently on her neck, sending her wild.

"Mmm, Kevin," she moaned. He knew for certain that she could feel his rock-hard erection.

The elevator stopped on their floor. Without any words, Kevin grabbed Simone by the hand and led her down the hall to their room.

"Boy, things have changed," he said, watching as she opened the door with the key card.

Before her foot could grace the threshold, he lifted her and carried her inside the dark room.

"I'm glad I lost those twenty pounds." She giggled.

Kevin placed her gently on the bed and stood before her. "I wish you hadn't. It would've been more of you to love."

With his eyes fixed on Simone, Kevin peeled his shirt off. The time he'd spent behind bars had done wonders for his physique. His chest, abs, and arms had never been more defined. He stepped from his shoes, unbuckled his belt, and stripped from his jeans and boxers. Shy and ashamed he'd never been. His manhood stood at attention, stiff as steel. As he coasted down to the bed, he ran his fingers up Simone's legs to the hem of her dress and eased it up. Simone grabbed his hand.

"No, Kevin." She kicked off her sandals and rose from the bed. With her eyes fixed to his, she inched the dress over her head and allowed it to join the pile of clothes already on the floor. There she stood, in her brown satin bra and thong, allowing him to take her all in.

"You are so sexy," he breathed.

She undid her bra, exposing her perfect cantaloupe-sized breasts. Kevin's manhood grew a mind of its own, leaking the early stages of his pleasure and jerking in anticipation. While watching her slip from her thong, he could only imagine what was in store. Gone was the bashful teen who once hid under the covers to undress.

• • •

Simone sat on the edge of her seat, anxiously awaiting the announcement of the winner. Seated one row ahead, Melanie turned around and smiled at her. "You sweating bullets."

"She gotta win," Lavon said, seated next to Melanie. "She was the best one."

"You think so?" Simone asked.

Everyone had come out to support Jordan—Angela, Ricardo, Stan, LeCount, Beatrice, Mae, Kayla, Fat Ed, Melanie, and Lavon were all there, to name a few.

The judges led the contestants across the stage. Jordan walked out as confident as ever, wearing her signature smile.

"She looks like a superstar already," Simone heard Fat Ed say to Stan from the row behind her.

*Yes, she does*, Simone said to herself. She was so proud of her daughter.

The first envelope was opened, containing the third-place winner. Simone braced herself and breathed a sigh of relief when Jordan's name wasn't called. The second envelope was opened. Simone closed her eyes, and yet again, Jordan's name wasn't called.

"I told you she won," Lavon grunted underneath her breath.

"Yeah, she got this," Stan agreed.

"And the first-place winner of the 2006 Xtreme Teen Talent Competition is…"

"C'mon," Simone said, tapping her feet as the judges stalled. She caught Jordan's eyes and read her lips as she mouthed the words 'I love you, Ma' to Simone.

"I love you, too," Simone mouthed back from the edge of her seat, ready to scream her heart out, knowing with all certainty that Jordan had won.

"Latisha Stanford!" the judges screamed.

"What?" Simone said. She had to be hearing things.

All week Jordan had rehearsed the song and her routine over

and over again. Every night she gave Simone and Kayla a performance. She'd practiced so much that Kayla and Simone had the routine down, too. Simone pumped Jordan up all week, knowing without a shadow of a doubt that she was going to win the competition hands down. But now, as Jordan cried on her shoulder, Simone didn't know what to do. Angela had tried to console Jordan, as did Beatrice, but Jordan wanted her mother—she wanted Simone.

"It's okay, Jordan," Simone said. "You know how many celebrities lost their first few talent competitions? It's the record producers that you have to impress, baby," she said as someone tapped her on the shoulder.

"Yes?" she said as politely as she could. Too many people had already walked by expressing their surprise at the outcome.

"She has a right to be upset," he said, extending his card to Simone. "How you doing? I'm Don Brandon, owner of DB Records. I'm also a talent scout for a few of the major record companies. Do you think we can step outside and talk? It's a bit noisy in here."

## Chapter Thirty-Four
## 2006

The hostess cradled the menus in her arm as she sashayed down the paisley-printed carpet, leading Kevin and Don to a booth in the back of the upscale restaurant.

"How's this, gentlemen?" The question rolled off her tongue in her Latino accent. Slinging her silky tresses over her shoulder, she raised her brow and smiled seductively. The high-back booth was tucked in a corner away from the Friday night hustle and bustle, just as Don had requested.

Don quickly surveyed the restaurant as if looking for other options. "This should work fine. Thank you."

The minute they'd entered the establishment, Kevin noticed Don gawking at the hostess. Yes, she was attractive, with her bronze skin and youthful hourglass figure. *She can't be that much older than Jordan,* Kevin thought, thankful he was only there to discuss his music and not his child.

Don eased across the smooth chocolate leather. Kevin followed suit, sitting directly across from him. The hostess passed the menus, sending with them a faint whiff of her fragrance. Don brought the menu to his nose and sniffed.

"You smell wonderful. What's that you're wearing?"

"Umm..." She placed her hand on her hip and shifted her weight as she glanced up at the ceiling in thought. "I can't remember, but," she shrugged, "thank you."

"You're quite welcome. If you think of it before I leave, let me know. Maybe I'll buy you a bottle or two."

"Well, if you promise to bring handsome back with you, I'll make up something." The hostess winked at Kevin and strutted away with Don's eyes glued to her ass.

"I guess I'm too old for her, but she sure was ready for you," Don said.

"Yeah, I like mine potty-trained and weaned from the bottle, though," Kevin joked sarcastically as he opened the menu.

"Yeah, well, let me hear you say that when you become a big-time songwriter. Women of all ages be at the video shoots ready to drop their drawers in a heartbeat. Tell Simone to get a bat or something ready, because she's gonna be beating women off of you."

"Been there, done that. Bat and all."

"Really?" Don peered over his open menu.

"Yeah, and believe me, we're never ever traveling down that road again. That I promise you."

The waiter approached, decked out in his black suit and bowtie. "Hello, gentlemen," he greeted with a courtesy bow. "May I offer you tap or bottled water?"

"Bottled water, please," Don said without hesitation.

"I'll be right back."

Kevin studied the stylish décor. He smiled as he glanced down at the formal setting before him.

"What?" Don asked, noticing Kevin's sly grin.

"Oh, nothing. You know, being away for so many years, places like this only existed in magazines."

"Oh, wow, Kevin. I wasn't even thinking. Don't worry, if it's too intimidating, I can help—"

"Don, I'm cool," Kevin interrupted, quickly putting Don at ease. "Simone saw to all that. She sent me a million books, even ones on etiquette that I left behind for the prison library. I'm good. We've actually been here. The glazed stuffed chicken's pretty good."

Don smiled approvingly. "Yes, that's one of my favorites, too."

"Yeah." Kevin chuckled. "I've only been home a few weeks, and Simone's already taken me to a million places. She wants to show me the world, and I'm dying to see it, just not at her expense. She's been through a lot."

"Then there's no better time like the present to discuss my proposal." Don placed his leather attaché case on the seat next to him and popped it open. "You know," Don said as he shuffled through his papers, "Simone is something special. I would love to make her and Jordan stars, but they're not interested, huh?"

*Hell no*, Kevin said to himself. To Kevin's surprise, Simone had had her basement finished and equipped with a modern, state-of-the-art recording studio just for him. She'd sung a few of Kevin's tracks that Don had listened to and even fiddle-faddled behind the scenes with Kevin. But, she had no interest in the limelight. Jordan, on the other hand, was a different story and Kevin's personal project.

"Naw, we don't know what we're going to do," Kevin lied, but his plans were already in order. With Stan and Fat Ed's expertise, Jordan was going to record a few of Kevin's personal

360

favorites, the ones his gut had labeled hits years ago.

"Okay, well, for now, we'll discuss the songs I'm interested in. The songs that Simone sang. Speaking of Simone, where is the gorgeous lady? I'm surprised she's not here with you."

"No, I want to surprise her. I'm not going to tell her about this until after I propose to her. Besides, she's in court getting her divorce finalized."

"Propose, divorce, hold up…hold up." Don frowned, shaking his head in disbelief. "I thought you two were already married. Who the hell is she divorcing?"

"No, we're not married yet. I was supposed to marry her a million years ago."

"Okay, I'm confused."

Kevin dumped the soap-opera-filled years in Don's lap. He didn't hold back a thing. The young love he and Simone had shared, his troubled youth, his fake friends, killing Mr. Johnson, Angela's web, Thomas, Andre…everything.

"So," Kevin sighed with a simple shrug of his shoulder, nearly out of breath. "Say something."

Don sat speechless. "Man," he finally gasped, "please tell me you just sat here and made all that up."

"Naw, it's all true. She walked back into my life eight months ago, and I'm never letting her go. Simone's my baby. My partner for life. I have to propose, and I have to do it right."

"And, Kevin, you will. I'm going to make sure of it. Tell me what you had in mind."

● ● ●

The seamstress Don referred Kevin to did a wonderful job embroidering Jordan's name along the front of her jacket and the seat of her pants. The red stitching across the winter-white velour suit was drawing a lot of attention.

"Gotdamn, Jordan," a young patron said in passing.

"A'ight, you ain't wearing those pants no more," Kevin said as they entered the arena, ready to watch the Wizards take on the Miami Heat.

Simone had done a lot of things, but she'd never been to a NBA game. This was their first of firsts together.

Kevin, Simone, Jordan, and Kayla headed to their seats, just three rows behind the Washington Wizards players.

The first two quarters of the game overflowed with excitement and Simone's questions. "Kevin, what's a technical foul?" Or "Kevin, what's goaltending?"

"Ma," Kayla said, seated in between Kevin and Simone, "just watch the game."

Minutes to halftime, Jordan stood and said, "Come on, Kayla. I'm going to the bathroom, so you may as well come with me."

"Good idea," Simone said as she unconsciously blew a bubble with her gum.

Kevin grinned, admiring Simone in his Wizards jersey and cap. "You look like a little girl."

"Thanks, R. Kelly." She smiled.

Scooting over to Kayla's seat, Simone planted a kiss on Kevin's cheek. No words were spoken as the two simply smiled, while staring at each other. The halftime buzzer sounded, and the players headed off the court. Kevin had no idea who was winning as his insides scrambled about. He grabbed Simone's hand.

"Why your hands so sweaty?"

"I don't know. I guess it was your kiss," Kevin said, squeezing her hand. "It made me hot."

The lights went dim.

"Dang," Simone said, looking over her shoulder. "I hope Jordan and Kayla don't miss the halftime show." She glanced at Kevin and noticed the beads of sweat forming on his forehead.

"Kevin, you're sweating up a storm, and it's not that hot in here. If you're not feeling well, we can leave if you want. We just have to find the girls."

"Naw, baby," he sighed. "I'm cool."

"You don't look cool."

A spotlight shone in the center of the court. The jumbo monitors came to life throughout the arena as a sweet, soft voice sang. "Take her hand; Hold it tight; You belong to her; For the rest of your life. Hold him close; Show him love; You're the only one he's thinking of."

Simone's mouth dropped open as Jordan appeared center court and beautiful.

"Oh my gosh, Kevin. That's Jordan…and she's singing your song. Oh my God, Kevin!" She tried to leap from her seat, but Kevin held her hand, preventing her from doing so. "Kevin, Jordan's singing—"

"Simone, baby," Kevin said as he eased from his seat and took a knee on the bleachers. Another spotlight appeared, beaming on Kevin and Simone. Their faces appeared on the monitors. Simone gasped as Kevin reached for her hand and from behind his back came the most precious five-carat diamond ring imaginable.

Kevin signed a contract with Don, selling ten of his lyrical compositions that he and Ed had laid to tracks for twenty-five thousand. Kevin knew he was being robbed, but he needed the money. So, in addition to selling ten of his tracks, he negotiated another five songs and got Don to advance him another twenty thousand. Although the contract required Kevin to sign over all of his rights to any future royalties, he was excited about the deal nonetheless. Once one song made it to the Top Ten, artists would be pursuing him, and his negotiating powers would be higher. For now, the initial goal had been accomplished. He'd secured a handsome lump sum. Two weeks later, the check had cleared, and with Don's help, the arrangements for the proposal and the wedding had been secured.

Jordan continued in her broken voice, shedding tears as the spotlight beamed on her parents. "I'm sorry," she said over the microphone, "but those are my parents." The arena filled with screams and chants.

"I love you, Simone." Kevin stood and pulled her up with him. The lights shone brightly throughout the arena just in time to catch him saluting his wife-to-be. "Now, I'm ready to go."

The super-stretch limousine ushered them from the arena to Thomas's resting place. Kevin wanted Thomas to be a part of his proposal. Kneeling in front of the marble headstone, Kevin said, "I love your daughter with everything in me. I promise to take care of her forever."

Simone looked over at the hazel-eyed thug she'd fallen in love with so long ago. Never in a million years could she have fathomed that her appetite for love would be as satisfied as it was. And by Kevin of all people.

Kevin strolled off, allowing Simone some time alone with her father. "Oh my God," he uttered as he fell to his knees.

"What's wrong?" Simone asked as she strolled to the gravesite a few resting places from her father's. Her eyes scanned the headstone. "Curtis Johnson. Curtis Johnson?" The name seemed familiar.

"This is Curtis Johnson," Kevin said. "My Curtis Johnson."

"Oh, wow," Simone said as she knelt next to Kevin to pay

her respects. "I met a Curtis Johnson out here a few years ago. Did he have a son?" she asked, rubbing Kevin's back for support.

"Naw," he muttered, "he didn't have any kids."

"Wow." She frowned. Her eyes darted from her father's site to Mr. Johnson's. "But he was picking weeds from this very site."

• • •

Simone was sexy, yet angelic as she stood on the immaculately landscaped grounds of the resort, mesmerized by the emerald waters of the Rodney Bay.

"I can do this," she said to herself, waiting for her cue as she prepared to walk down the aisle alone. "You ready, Daddy?" She sighed, wiping a lone tear as her emotions toyed with both joy and sadness.

The steel drum St. Lucia band began to play softly. Simone followed her cue and proceeded to the runner stretched out just for her. The handful of guests stood, directing their attention to the bride. Oohs and aahs rang out across the resort.

"My God," Kevin whispered as his eyes fell upon his wife-to-be. Simone was more beautiful than anything he'd ever imagined.

A tropical breeze swayed the palm trees from side to side. Kevin inhaled the scent of the land and allowed it to relax him. As the winds began to settle, he found himself draped in a loving embrace.

Mesmerized by the perfect harmony, Kevin closed his eyes and inhaled the love floating through the air. He didn't realize that someone or something was leading him down the aisle to his bride. Simone took two steps and stopped in her tracks to watch her groom come to escort her ever so gracefully. She loved Kevin and knew that he'd been heaven-sent. A special delivery in a tattered package. A package most would've merely pushed to the side. Yet, Simone blew the dust from the package and looked beyond the torn wrapping. And there, she found the man of her dreams. A man who knew how to love her mentally and physically. The loneliness that once haunted her had been filled beyond her imagination.

"You okay, baby?" he asked. He ran his long fingers down the smoothness of Simone's face, stopping at her chin. Gently, he eased forward and kissed her tenderly on the lips. They hadn't been pronounced husband and wife, but as far as he was concerned, her lips belonged to him, and he didn't need permission from anybody to salute her.

"Now I am," she whispered.

"I love you so much, baby," Kevin said as he took Simone's hand into his own. "I've waited forever to do this. You ready to be my wife?"

"Of course, I am," Simone said as they headed down the aisle, ready for the priest to officially declare them one before God's tropical glory.

Halfway down the aisle, Kevin felt the loving warmth again. He glanced at his bride and noticed the puzzled expression on her face. Her eyes filled with tears as they darted from side to side as if she were looking for someone.

"It's okay, baby," Kevin whispered to her. "It's your father."

"Oh my God, Kevin. You feel him, too?" she whispered.

He smiled. "Yeah, so let's hurry. We can't hold him up. I'm sure God has other things for him to do."

# Epilogue

eads of sweat formed along Simone's forehead. Grasping for air, she fell back on the bed, thankful that the ordeal was over. Off to the side, Kevin stood in complete awe as the doctor wrapped a warm receiving blanket around their son.

"Who wants the little prince?"

Kevin chuckled nervously. "My wife can hold him first. I mean, she did all the work."

"No, Kevin," Simone responded, "you hold him first."

Kevin stood there, lost and confused, his eyes darting between Simone and his son. He'd never held a newborn before.

"I don't know how to hold a baby. Plus, he's so tiny. I don't...."

"Here, Mr. Kennard." The doctor forced the cushioned glider from the corner with her foot. "Just sit here."

Kevin lowered himself into the chair with uncertainty scribbled all over his face. Ignoring his uneasiness, the doctor placed the baby in his stiff arms.

"Now, just relax and cuddle him in your arms like a football. A football you cherish with all your heart. Let him feel your love and your strength. You're his daddy."

Squirming in Kevin's arms, the baby's eyes slowly blinked open.

"Ah," the doctor said barely above a whisper. "Look at his little gray eyes."

"Gray? Uh, oh," Simone said through chattering teeth. "I meant to tell you about my fling with the cable guy."

Kevin's lips curled into a slight smile as he began to relax. Gently, he glided back and forth in the chair. "My eyes were gray when I was first born, too."

"Mrs. Kennard, other than the apparent chills, how are you feeling?" the doctor asked. A faint cloud of powdery dust flew about the air as the doctor snatched off the latex gloves.

"I'm glad it's over." Simone shivered. "Now I just need something for these cramps and another blanket. Man, I'm freezing."

"Not to worry," she told her while patting Simone's leg. "The chills are a common side effect. I'll have one of the nurses bring you something for pain, and I'll have them grab a nice warm blanket from the warmer," she said as she headed to the door. "Other than that, you guys did great. Congratulations."

Cradling the baby in his arms, Kevin eased from the rocking chair and planted himself along the edge of the bed, facing his wife.

"Thank you so much, baby."

"Umm, Kevin, I think you helped a little." Simone smiled.

"Hey, little man. Can you see your beautiful mommy?" Kevin cooed to his son. He held the baby up and pulled the receiving blanket back just a little. "Me and you are the two luckiest men in the world, do you know that?"

Simone shivered. "Man, I wish they'd hurry up. I'm freezing."

"Baby, you want to hold him while I go check on the blanket? Or I can throw our coats over you."

"Knock, knock," a female's voice interrupted as she strolled inside the room, pushing a bassinet across the floor. "Hi." The nurse smiled. "I'm from the nursery. I'm here to take the baby."

Confused, Kevin held the baby closer to his chest and looked down at Simone for confirmation.

"It's okay, daddy," Simone said through a yawn. "They have to clean him up, weigh him, count his toes, and all that other stuff."

"But you didn't get to look at him, hold him, or nothing."

"We can go and get him once I'm in the room, right?" Simone asked, directing her question to the nurse.

"Oh, yeah," the nurse replied as she reached for the baby, ignoring Kevin's subtle resistance. "In a few hours, he'll be all yours," she said as she pried the baby from Kevin's arms and laid him in the bassinet. "Can I see your bracelets, please? It's for security purposes." Kevin and Simone extended their arms. "Great," she said, then snapped on the baby's ankle bracelet. "Three Kennards. That's what I need."

"Can you do me a favor and see if someone's bringing me something for these cramps? I feel like I'm still having contractions, and I'm freezing."

Kevin frowned. "Is that really normal? You sure you okay?"

"Yeah, but I'll be doing better when I'm completely outta labor."

"I work in the nursery, but I'll see what I can do. It's been crazy busy today. Your son is the ninth baby born tonight."

Kevin chuckled as he stood to reposition himself next to Simone. "I guess everybody was doing the booty nine months ago."

The nurse chuckled. "Yeah, I guess so."

Kevin's lengthy body hung off the side of Simone's bed as he snuggled up next to her, trying to keep her warm.

Glancing up at her husband, Simone asked, "So was your stomach in knots after watching all that?"

"Naw, not like I thought it would be. I was more amazed than anything. I mean, that was us, baby. We created a little life. Then, to watch him come into the world like that…Man, it was amazing."

"You know you can go down and watch them examine him if you want."

"I can?"

"Yeah. It might not be such a bad idea considering they're so busy. We don't wanna take a lil' Korean baby home."

"Yeah, but then who's going to stay here with you? You still haven't gotten your pain medicine and you're shivering."

"I'm a big girl, baby."

"Not no more. You just lost 'bout twelve pounds," he joked as he peeled from the bed. "You sure you're okay, though? I feel strange leaving you."

The door crept open. Another nurse strolled inside the room toting two small Dixie cups in hand. "I guess you've been waiting for these." She smiled. "I just got here, and one of the nurses asked me to bring these to you."

"Thank the Lord. You got my drugs. Go 'head, Kevin," Simone said. "I'm really good now. I'll probably be out cold by the time you get back. Plus, you need to call everybody."

"Damn, baby. You right. Should I call them, though? It's almost four in the morning."

"Yeah, still call, but check on the baby first."

"Yes, mommy, I will," he said, heading toward the door. "Damn, where do I go?"

"You're looking for the nursery?" the nurse asked.

"Yeah," Kevin replied.

"Just go down the corridor and make a right. You can't miss it," she said as she set the two cups of pills on Simone's bedside tray. "You'll walk right into it."

"Okay. That's precious cargo right there. Take care of my queen."

"Awww…" The nurse smiled as she poured Simone a cup of water from the pitcher on the tray. Resting the cup on the tray, she picked up the first cup of pills and said, "Here's some codeine for the pain." Picking up the next cup, she said, "And these two are for bleeding and gas."

"Oh my gosh. My youngest daughter is twelve, but I remember the gas pains after having her like it was yesterday."

"Your nurse was working on discharging a patient, so I'll get you a warm blanket. Someone will be coming to take you to your room shortly. If your nurse doesn't come back soon, then I'll come back and check on you."

"I didn't know the hospital did discharges in the wee hours of the morning."

"Not a lot, but it does happen."

"Hmm," Simone said with a simple nod.

"Can I get you anything else?"

"Uh, uh," Simone mumbled as she swallowed the last pill. "Just the blanket and I'm good."

"Okay. I'll run and get that now."

While the nurse ran off to grab the long-awaited blanket, Simone closed her eyes and eased further under the sheets.

"Excuse me?"

Simone's eyes popped open. "Yes?" she replied, startled by the nurse's presence.

"Are you Mrs. Kennard?" the nurse asked.

"Yes."

When the nurse pulled a needle from the pocket of her lab jacket, Simone caught a glimpse of her plain clothes. All the other nurses wore scrubs.

"Who are you?"

She flashed the badge around her neck. "Oh, I'm a nurse. I'm getting ready to get off. I told them I would handle this before I left."

"Well, I'm straight now, I guess. I just took some pain killers."

"This is a little cocktail that'll help fight off infections. It'll help you relax, bitch." She mumbled the insult under her breath as she poked the needle inside the intravenous tube, injecting the fluid.

"What did you call..."

• • •

Kevin followed the nurse's instructions and headed towards the nursery. "Here it is." He smiled and tapped lightly on the door glass.

"Hi, can I help you with something?" the elderly nurse asked.

"Yes, the nurse just brought my son down," Kevin said as he tiptoed inside the room.

"Do you have a bracelet?"

Kevin extended his arm.

"Hmm…Kennard," the nurse read more so to herself.

Kevin followed her eyes to the dry erase board on the wall and scrolled down the long list of names.

*Jacobs, DeChavez, Ford, Lincoln, Hampton, Byrd, Brown…. Hmm, she probably hasn't had a chance to write his name down,* he thought to himself.

"Um…we don't have a Kennard yet, sir."

"They should be here by now. Maybe I'm in the wrong nursery."

"Oh, your baby was premature?"

"Naw. Well, I mean, he wasn't due for two more weeks, but…"

"No, so he was full-term. The other nursery is for our preemie babies."

"Well, the nurse took him from us like fifteen minutes ago. He should be here by now," Kevin said as he strolled through the rows of bassinets, scanning the name tags taped to each one.

"What's the mother's last name? Maybe he's registered under her…"

"Miss," Kevin sighed.

The nurse read Kevin's uneasiness. "Sir, it's possible that it's under the mother's name."

"She's my wife. Her last name is Kennard, too."

"Well, who's your doctor? I can page them to…"

"I don't remember the doctor's name. It's whoever's on call for Doctor Covington. And what do you need her for? The nurse came and got the baby."

"Well, let me page the doctor anyway," she said as she picked up the phone. "I'm sure everything's okay. The nurse may have stopped for supplies or maybe she went back to your room. I'm sure they'll be…"

"I'll go check my room."

Something wasn't right. *Why am I feeling like this?* Kevin thought as he pushed through the nursery doors and headed back to Simone's room. His walk turned anxious. *Okay, calm down, Kevin. Calm down. You trippin' for nothing.*

Before he crossed the threshold of Simone's room, Kevin said, "Hey, baby, did the nurse…" His eyes fell upon his wife, who was out cold with her head cocked to the side in a way he'd never seen. No, something wasn't right. He hurried to her bedside and grabbed her cold, limp hand.

"What the fuck," he mumbled. "SIMONE!"

He scooped her up in his arms and patted her face lightly with his hand, but she was unresponsive. "Oh my God, baby." He checked her pulse only to find a faint throbbing.

Kevin laid Simone back in the bed and frantically pressed the call button over and over again. He ran to the door, screaming at the top of his lungs.

"Hey!" he yelled down the corridor. "I need a doctor in here! I need a doctor now!"

Hearing his frantic pleas, the nurse rushed from the patient's room next door.

"What's wrong?"

Kevin recognized her immediately. She'd given Simone the pain pills. Without a second thought, he snatched her from the rubbery soles of her feet and pressed her into the wall of Simone's room.

"What the fuck did you give my wife?" he yelled as he wrapped his hands around her neck. "What did you give her?"

The nurse clawed at Kevin's hands while gagging. "You're choking me!"

"Bitch, I'ma do more than fuckin' choke you," Kevin threatened as he tightened his grip. "WHAT THE FUCK DID YOU GIVE MY WIFE?"

"Pain killers," she struggled. "Her nurse asked me to bring them to her."

Kevin loosened his grip and allowed the nurse to fall to her knees as two nurses hurried into the room. Seeing the chaotic scene, one yelled into the hallway, "Call security," before rushing to the aid of her co-worker.

"Oh my God!" the other cried as she stood at Simone's bedside. "Code Blue! She's going into cardiac arrest!"

# Book Club Discussion Questions

1. Parent/child relationships are critical. Discuss the relationships the characters had with their parents and the impact, positive or negative, that they had on their life.

2. If you were Simone, could you forgive your mother?

3. Simone's feelings for Kevin re-emerge during a point in his life when he has nothing to offer her other than his heart. Could you love someone who had nothing but love to offer you?

4. Why is *Two Tears in a Bucket* a hip-hop novel? What makes it hip-hop: its themes or issues raised, characters, scenes, language?

5. Why are good girls attracted to bad boys? Why do men let good women slip through their fingers? Women, discuss a love or interest you may have had with a bad boy and the outcome. Men, discuss the wifey material you let slip through your fingers.

6. Do the characters seem real and believable? To what extent do they remind you of yourself or someone you know?

7. How do characters change or evolve throughout the course of the story? What events trigger such changes?

# About the Author

Traci Bee is an author and the CEO of King George Publishing, LLC, named in honor of her angel, her father George. A native of Prince George's County, Maryland, Traci Bee enjoys creating soulful works of fiction, karaoke, and entertaining family and friends. She's currently putting the finishing touches on two novels scheduled for release in 2011. To learn more about Traci, visit her at www.tracibee.com.